ANNALS OF THE PURPLE CITY

ANNALS OF THE
Purple City

Frederick Lees

Orchid Press

Frederick Lees
ANNALS OF THE PURPLE CITY

First published 1995; Crane Books, Hong Kong and London
Second edition © Orchid Press 2010

ORCHID PRESS
PO Box 1046,
Silom Post Office,
Bangkok 10504, Thailand

www.orchidbooks.com

ISBN: 978-974-524-129-9

For Jeremy and Matthew

AUTHOR'S PREFACE

The Annals of the Purple City was inspired by Macao where I lived for some years in the early nineteen fifties. Despite that I must assert that neither the real Macao, nor any of its inhabitants past or present, are depicted in the book.

My emphasis is on the word 'inspired' for Macao, as it was in those days, was certainly a place to inspire. Then, it was not a city of huge buildings and jostling traffic but a beautiful place which, over the centuries, had become a backwater most gracefully.

Of course, I am speaking of the town of elegant buildings, tree lined boulevards and stately colonial houses gazing over an indented coastline towards low islands and distant mountains. It was far from being so beautiful for everyone. The place teemed with refugees and poverty was widespread. The offices and factories and all the modernity of present day Macao would have seemed to the ordinary people of those days far more paradisial than the old churches, palaces and temples whose destruction we would so deplore today.

Many of the old buildings in Macao have indeed been lost but the best of them are well preserved. The visitor will not, however, find them grouped together in an 'Intra Muros' as in the Purple City. Rather, they are spread about the colony, sometimes on prominent heights but sometimes, too, quite hidden so that when you come across them you are pleasantly surprised. The Intra Muros of the novel has grouped the ancient buildings of the city into a single location so that they may be invested with symbolism as the gateway to that mystical Purple City to which all the characters of the book relate in one way or another.

Nevertheless, certain aspects of the novel have some basis in fact. The extraordinary imagined invasion of the city by the Chinese authorities and its ransoming by a local bigwig really occurred. Celebrations like the great Banquet described in Part Two, were features of the Macao Club. The Military Club, the Casino, the brothels and the opium dens were all similar to those described. The largest opium house, the 'Old Pawnshop' did stand unashamedly along the Rua do Felicidade though it does so no more. Above all the anachronistic formal society of old Macao (Salazar was still the right wing dictator of Portugal) has passed away bearing with it those chaperoned young ladies, those proud military and naval officers, those sad political exiles from Lisbon, and those distinguished ecclesiastics who were such a feature of great occasions in the Governor's palace. Few would want all that back, but it is right that its existence should be recorded.

The novel is concerned with the interplay of a diverse group of local and expatriate characters living in something of an emotional goldfish bowl. Their relationships, at different levels, sensual political and inward, are sometimes moved forward by the use of dreams, poetry and heightened reality, as in the Chinese classical novel. The title is related to the Taoist concept of the mystical inner city, which, if we are of the right mind, may grow in all of us.

Frederick Lees
April 2010

CONTENTS

We have lived our lives in different worlds
But tonight we come together
To talk—while the lamplight lasts...

Tomorrow mountains and valleys
Will divide us again
And each of us will return
To his own affairs

Tu Fu
From lines written to the scholar Wei

PART I

Felicidade

PART I

Felicidade

On the south coast of China stands an ancient Portuguese town, a colonial relic tolerated until quite recently by the People's Republic. Once remote, it is easy to visit now on the hydrofoils that skim across from Hong Kong; and it is this historic place, this point of contact between two worlds, that forms our stage. But it is not the Purple City, for She is an enigma. She is as that mysterious Planet whose rays draw all mankind. What is more, She is capricious, keeping her inner ways secret, yet sending different visions of herself both to women and to men. Should such a vision ever come your way, take care. Some She sends to deceive.

In that town, back in the early nineteen fifties when the Korean War was at its height, the best opium house you could find was the Old Pawnshop, and that was what it had been built as; an impregnable tower, its five storeys stood well above the sing-song girl houses, eating places and gambling joints, lining the narrow Rua da Felicidade. Amidst the confusion of Chinese signs and bright banners, loud voices and shrill music, the ceaseless carnival of the narrow Street of Happiness, its leaden bricks and slit windows seemed alien and forbidding. But what were appearances to opium addicts? Or what did they care that their way of life was under threat by communist China whose territory all but surrounded the colony? Endlessly they came and went; the house was never empty and never closed its door, a black aperture fortuitously within the range of a pair of powerful binoculars, which Diana Sheraton was holding to her eyes some half a mile away.

An exasperated "No" escaped from her lips. The figure of a slightly built young man had come into view. Unlike the black haired throng milling about him, this man had long fair hair though he was dressed in black Chinese trousers and jacket. "Peter, don't go in. Don't go in." She repeated the words several times deliberately, willing him to obey. But her efforts at telepathic control were useless. True he seemed to hover for a moment in the doorway but then he vanished through it. "Dearest Peter. Please. Come out," she gasped, now urgently. "Think of me and come here." With one last stare, hoping that the impossible had happened, she gave up her vigil and went slowly along the corridor, past the studio where her husband Robert was quietly working away, to the balcony at the front of the apartment. There she slumped down listlessly in a long wicker chair.

Only an hour ago she'd felt quite happy—as happy, that is to say as was possible in this forgotten dump. Peter's voice over the phone had been confident and cheerful. "Don't worry Diana. I'm working I promise you. I've translated two poems already. And I'm pleased with them. See you in the Cabaret tonight." Then, ten minutes later when she'd phoned him again, just to say she loved him, his servant Ping had huffed, "Master gone out. That devil boy came for him."

The balcony which was deep and cool, with a black and white marble floor, was really a protruding room, open on three sides save for a balustrade of ceramic and plaster running between the columns that supported the roof. Its broad front gave on to a superb view: shimmering in insubstantial haze and strewn with rocky islets, the meeting place of the Pearl River estuary and the South China Sea. The guide books said that the colony, so happily placed, was a jewel but Diana thought of it with hostility, which was the opposite of her feelings towards another colony, Hong Kong, only a few hours away but seemingly as remote as the moon. That was her idea of a jewel, bright and desirable, even though it too was vulnerable, a carbuncle that the communists could lance at a moment's notice if they chose. But no. There was no comparison. This place was a mere pimple; she was sure they wouldn't even deign to scratch it—despite everyone's constant apprehension. No release for her through a cataclysm of that kind. At length, "What a beautiful view," she said aloud, her voice full of mockery and decidedly stagey. "How terribly, terribly beautiful. How too thrill creating to be here." Abruptly her mood changed. Why act? There was no audience. Only that mute expansive seascape with nothing moving but slow, brown winged junks. What was the point of wings if you couldn't fly? What was the point of anything here? The tedium was absolute. Even the beauty was absolute. Nothing could be added to it. Of course, every damned Chinese scroll painting she set eyes on seemed to have contented sages perched beside waterfalls smugly accepting the transcendent beauty of nature. But nature made her feel superfluous. Oh God, I wish I was back in Sydney, walking along Pitt Street, somewhere ordinary, somewhere with not a blade of grass in sight, she thought. Then the humid heat overcame her and she sank back in the wide chair letting her legs flop either side of its built on leg rest. Not at all elegant but she didn't care. She closed her eyes to the scene, now broken by the green balusters and wondered why she accepted the fact that it was beautiful. Define beauty, she admonished herself. Go on you lazy bitch. Define exactly what you mean by it when everything in sight fills you with gloom. The stern inner voice fell away into silence, as though the half conscious creature that had prompted the words had found something better to do down in the depths. Anyway, who was it to order her about? Why should she discipline her thoughts? Why subject herself to any form of discipline? Peter didn't and he was happier than she was. Or at least I think he's happier than I am, she thought. If he took you with him to the Old Pawnshop, or rather if Robert let you go there with him, you wouldn't prate to him about the

5

awful dangers he's running. Yes. To take up Peter's vices might be more purposeful than her present existence. Her mood of futility deepened. It wasn't as if she'd deliberately decided to come here. She had just drifted, following her husband, who maybe knew where he was going in his way, into an alien world, like a little boat lost in a swamp. She was going to rot away here without any doubt. The mould and the decay that were everywhere in this oppressive summer would insidiously spread like a cancer in her brain and in her soul. Define what you mean by soul, herself or that irritating creature inside her said derisively, but again the command that had begun so stridently ended in a whisper. Everything here began and ended like that, in nothingness. She remembered Robert only the other day saying rudely to a Portuguese acquaintance, "This town's the arse-hole of the world." And she nearly giggled at the nonchalant reply that had made Robert's face flush: "Yes Signor Sheraton, and as you're passing through, you should know."

Almost at once she felt guilty to have been amused at Robert's discomfiture—though he had deserved it. He was devoted to her, he must be—everything considered, and the way of life he provided her with was hardly to be disparaged even if it wasn't on the scale enjoyed by those rich Chinese wives who were forever off on shopping sprees to Hong Kong or Manila. Their apartment was old and beautiful with all modcons—there weren't many places where you could live so elegantly at such a price—and they had servants which gave her leisure to do what she wanted. The question was: what did she want? All she felt sure of was that something fearful was about to happen to herself or to the world—madness, natural disaster, revolution, she couldn't say what but she knew it was waiting for her and would be a thousand times worse than anything to which she could put a name. Despite the heat she experienced a coldness that came not from the atmosphere but from somewhere in her mind.

Since she was constantly being lectured by Robert, and for that matter by Peter, that work was the best defence against such terrors, she snatched up the Cantonese Primer she'd told Robert she was going to study while he painted. But before long Father O'Melia's thick volume with its sentences such as: 'Those several Fathers are not wearing their long gowns,' or, 'God the Father, God the Son, and God the Holy Spirit are the Three Persons of the Trinity,' seemed wildly irrelevant to her present situation or to the situation of anyone she really knew. She put the book down and watched its pages being flipped over by the eddies of the overhead fan, wondering the while why religious institutions always seemed to print their books on such thin paper. Absurdly she felt sorry for the defenseless volume and picked it up again, realising as she looked at it that she'd have to switch the lights on, for the sun was sinking to the horizon between two silhouetted islands far away. Why bother? The lights would only attract a swarm of insects and she'd have to move.

Numbly she stared at the silent red disk hanging vast and distorted, eight minutes away as light travels, she told herself, fleetingly considering the incomprehensible nature of the universe. Sometimes it grew oval, then like an hour glass. The watery atmosphere even made it split horizontally like a celestial amoeba reproducing itself. Everything was suffused with its fiery light as though the earth was approaching its final hour. At last it quivered for a while on a glowing pedestal through which it was sucked down slowly into the sea. But Diana refused to be dwarfed by such sublimity. It was no more significant than she was. And it was a bloody cheat. It had really gone eight minutes ago; it couldn't put it over on her. This odd thought tended to reassure her. If she could be so dispassionate about it, she could afford to be cool about her own dilemma. In due course that would disappear too. Who could say? Perhaps her discontent had really vanished eight minutes ago and what she was experiencing now was nothing but an echo.

Or was it? She put her hand to her throat as though to ward off invisible fingers trying to throttle her. Here she was four thousand miles from home—she still thought of that dark stoned Tasmanian presbytery, staring with small eyed windows over the ocean, as home—yet she remained as much a prisoner as she'd ever been with her father, still suffocating in overbearing care. "But it's what you want really Diana," she remembered Peter telling her in his mocking, know-all way. "The beautiful dicky bird, safe in its cage, flapping its wings when it sees the wild birds outside, but glad when they come a cropper. That's how it'll be with me. But in the meantime it won't stop you being envious." Peter's words could be so bloody intrusive. Yet his brittle manner was nothing but a protective shell; it couldn't wound her but it could irritate her—very much indeed. Sometimes it seemed that he went out of his way to live up to an unpleasant stereotype, especially when she thought she was on the point of getting really close to him. Let him go to hell then in the Old Pawnshop. Let him smoke himself to death in the arms of his bloody Ah Tung. Yes, Ping was right. That boy was a devil; he was manipulating Peter and just now she hated the very thought of him.

Robert's voice suddenly burst out of the studio, singing, or rather growling, "Life in the tropics is seldom dull, seldom dull, seldom dull," to the tune of 'here we go round the mulberry bush'. At once her anger and her will were dissipated; she felt the sound dissipating her personality as well. His idiosyncrasy no longer amused her. He could afford to sing all right. He had his work—the centrepoint of his existence. And he had his women. She was peripheral to his way of living. Did he even see her as existing except as an ornament of his own, she wondered. But there had been a time when she'd hoped to penetrate his self-containment. Now, impossible, impossible. Tears welled up in her eyes. I don't envy you Peter. Because you're in a cage too. But with you I exist. With you I feel free, whether there's a cage or not.

Once through the vestibule of the Old Pawnshop, Peter entered an atmosphere that was murky, heavy and sweet. The stone flagged pit was covered with half naked bodies, the poorest addicts who craved the quick action of heroin, not the subtler, more expensive pleasure of opium. As he picked his way amongst the sprawling limbs, voices cried, *"Nei ho mah?*—How are you?" and, *"Sik jor faan mei ah?*— Have you eaten rice yet?"—the common Chinese greeting, or his name, *"Moh Shin Saang*—Mr. Moh." The nearest they got to rendering Morgan.

Though he was dressed much as everyone there his European features made him stand out. But no one found his presence odd, for this unaccountable western devil (despite which misfortune they considered him quite handsome) who always seemed to be in a dream until he spoke, was an habitué of the place. However, he was not accepted as one of them just because he could talk away in Cantonese and was familiar with their way of life, just as they knew he'd been well born in Hong Kong and misspent his youth there; no, addiction to a common vice, not familiarity, was what had broken down the barriers irreparably.

The greetings cheered him. He urged himself yet again to accept the place for what it was, just a *t'aam wa sat*—a chatting house, no more harmful than a country pub. But it wasn't true. Some of the heroin addicts lying about told a different story. A few, little more than animated skeletons, would soon be dead. Others, less fortunate, would be flung into the street the moment their last cent had gone. The policy of the ruthless manager, fat Lim, was cash or out. Peter knew that most of the people there had started smoking to escape the wretchedness of their lives, but the very absence of relief, once they were hooked, added to the misery of existence. The doses had to be increased. They were embarked on a geometric progression to hell. A residual puritanical part of him believed that the house should be closed down, destroyed, together with the people that ran it. That was what had happened to such places over the border when the communists took over. Remorse that he went on coming here at all made him hesitate before climbing the rickety stairs. Yet again he had to admit the ambivalence of his attitude: it didn't matter if he came here but others should be stopped. Which was worse, he wondered, his paternalism or his arrogance?

The low ceilinged wooden galleries above provided some comforts—mat covered beds with porcelain pillows, and privacy in open ended cubicles ranged round the central well like theatre boxes. On the fifth floor, Ah Tung, his guide in the lower regions, merely raised a quizzical eyebrow as Peter took off his jacket and sandals, stepped carefully over the smoking paraphernalia, and lay down. Drawing deeply on his opium pipe, Ah Tung was content as a child at its mother's breast. There was no point in speaking to him.

Peter turned away disconsolately, propped himself on an elbow and gazed over the bed rail into the pit below. Appalling it might be, but the human carpet, heightened here and there by the glow of tiny lamps, had an ambiguous beauty, as unlikely as an illustration to the Inferno. Indeed the whole building had a dream-like quality. A Chinese sage had written that only fools thought they were awake and understood the world. Perhaps the Old Pawnshop and everything in it, himself included, were in the imagination of someone else—written down in a book maybe. And whose dream was the writer of that book in?

The drone of conversation that floated up was constant but seldom loud, though occasional words stood out—work, food, women and money being the commonest. Yet in the midst of his abstract speculations, such basics were unreal to Peter. Suddenly, from nearby, diaphanous music arose, plectrums fluttered like butterflies over lute strings and time entirely slipped away. But could it be that within its vanished confines he'd already been tried and condemned to this grotesque dream world, never be told what act he was to expiate?

Adjusting the cool pillow beneath his head, he lay on his back glaring up at the massive roof beams that seemed intent on crushing his spirit. Perhaps it was already too late to stop coming here. One day maybe, he'd never be able to leave at all. His mind grew agitated at the thought and he had to calm it down by lying completely still and concentrating his consciousness at a point between his eyes. The trick worked and after a while his thoughts began to flow again: how could he ever change his life when all his efforts failed, and when, maybe, the deepest part of him didn't want any change? This morning had been typical: he'd risen early, taken a long cold shower, eaten a huge breakfast and got down to work translating a Han Dynasty classic, *The Nineteen Pieces of Ancient Poetry*. Ah Ping, who looked after him as she would her own son, had beamed with pleasure to see him at his desk and went off to make him a jug of fresh lime juice which she said was excellent for the brain. "Very good work, very good work," she commented squinting at the pages and moving her lips silently, though she couldn't read a word. In the middle of the afternoon, no doubt to encourage him in the heat, she carried in a bowl of flowers which unfortunately made the room sickly sweet. But Peter couldn't bring himself to move them. By the time he'd finished Poem Thirteen—

Some seek immortality in elixirs
many take to drugs
But it is better to drink good wine
and wear simple clothes

...he was convinced that he could live the scholarly life on his own. He'd said as much to Diana when she'd phoned him, being careful to add, just to keep her happy, "Provided I could go on seeing you each day, sweetest." But a few minutes after getting back to work the door had burst open and he saw Ah Tung's spare body before him, clad only in yellow shorts and glistening with sweat like an oiled athlete. Cynical eyes became angry slits as they took in what Peter was doing. "Oh you're working. I'll go then."

"Stay a while," Peter begged. "Stay with me." But the contemptuous face said, 'No' in silence. "Ah Tung, where are you going?"

"The Old Pawnshop. You don't have to come." Ah Tung picked up the book of poetry, glanced at it, threw it aside and made off. Peter stared down at the open pages from which line one of Poem Fourteen mocked back in terse classical style, "*Ch'u che jih i shu.*—What has gone gets further day by day." Willy nilly he followed in his master's footsteps.

It was Ah Tung, not opium, that kept him here. If Ah Tung had been interested in sport or gambling or kite flying, those would have been Peter's interests. When they were apart, a deeper layer of his mind knew that his surface actions were a mere filling in of time. Only in Ah Tung's presence did anything seem to matter. When he was in those masterful arms, he thought he had some inkling of what people meant when they used that enigmatic word `love'. His need for Ah Tung was absolute. Without Ah Tung he had no being; but with Ah Tung there was no content.

Waiting edgily for Robert to come out of the bedroom for dinner, Diana reflected that she hadn't always felt apprehensive at the mere thought of his presence. She remembered the quick pleasure of that rainy evening when she'd found him drinking in the one hundred percent tatty Kings Cross bar he'd often told her about and informed him she'd left home for good. "I can't stand it a day longer even if my brother can," she'd panted, shaking her soggy hair and drying it as best she could with his scarf. "Anyway let him do the damned work for a change. I'm making a complete break." On and on she'd gabbled whilst the tarts stared stonily and Robert nodded sagely as though he knew everything there was to know about her. And in fact he did know a lot for he'd once paid a strained, mistaken visit to her home at St. Mawes, a half forgotten port a few hours from Hobart. Under other circumstances he might have been inspired to paint by what he'd seen there, once the bungalows were left behind: the sublimity of the coast, its vertiginous capes swathed in mist, the towering rainclouds sweeping in from the turbulent sea, not to mention the most redeeming feature of the presbytery: a large unkempt garden on one side of which an ivy-grown ruin straddled a river with a pointed arch. But even his sketch book stayed unopened. He was too mortified by the infinitely more gothic spectacle of the Reverend Stanley Trevorrow stubbornly coercing Diana to perform the domestic duties of his allegedly saintly wife who had died (Robert was told at least three times) "giving birth to my only son and heir James." His daughter, it seemed, didn't get a look-in.

Naturally Robert had needed little persuading to put her up for a while. But it hadn't been for a while nor had she ever intended it to be; she'd set out at once to make their living together a comfortable habit in which getting married had seemed nothing more than a logical step for social convenience. Friends had warned them that she was too young for him, that she would be marrying a man willfully eaten up with himself, in short that they were courting disaster, but they went ahead, though almost for certain he never would have married her if she hadn't, with fulsome promises, at last convinced him that she wouldn't interfere with his work or the habits formed by years of bachelor life. "The mystery is," Peter said when told the story, "Why, if you wanted to be free, didn't you get a job—any sort of a job—and stand on your own feet?" Oh yes, he'd gone to the heart of the matter at once. She fought back the anger that rose against him; anger that by now he so thoroughly understood her fear of being alone yet failed to do enough to help her.

In fact, she had kept to the first part of her promise. No matter how bored she got, Robert's work came first. But as to the second part of the undertaking, which, come to think of it, was as mad as Peter said it was, it seemed to her that ever since the third week of their marriage, when Robert took to seeing some woman he'd known for ages again, the sincerity of her words had been ruthlessly and constantly put to the test, as though he resented what had happened to him. Was she, then, to spend the rest of her days facing up to his resentment?

She stood up abruptly and walked across to the balustrade. Spread out before her the sea, calm and black, glistened in the moonlight. The sky was free of clouds now and brilliant with stars. Everything out there was invested with a marvellous clarity and everything in her world was crystal clear to her; above all she could see that she wasn't necessary to Robert. He must long to escape from her but couldn't bring himself to be unkind to her. That must have been why he'd started to rove all over the place, first in Europe and then around the East, trailing her like a piece of unwanted luggage. It made her think of a dog rolling this way and that to shake a can off its tail. That's what you are, she told herself, a rusty old tin can. Well tonight when Robert's asleep, I'll put an end to it. I'll get a trishaw and take the early morning ferry to Hong Kong. Peter will see whether or not I have to cling on to someone. She looked defiantly out at the darkly brilliant world. There's nothing to be afraid of out there. I'll be alright.

Her resolution, which had been gradually developing ever since she'd lived with Robert, and which had, in fact, reached this point before, was interrupted by the sound of angry voices. She could hear him shouting angrily at Group (their servant Kwan always liked to be called by the English version of her name). But he seemed to be getting as good as he gave. Diana went into the sitting room to find him red faced and sprawled on the sofa. Dutifully she poured him his usual brandy dry and put it beside him. She recalled that Group had been poker faced all day but hadn't thought much of it since the weird girl currently had some theory about not going to the lavatory more than once a week in order to save her vitality. The discomfort must be enough to make a saint bad tempered.

"That girl's a nut case," Robert stated. "She'd argue with the devil to get her own way."

Diana spoke gently. "She's all bunged up. She's preserving her vital heat." A slight edge had entered into her voice as she added quite unnecessarily, "We all need to do that, don't we dear."

Robert averted his eyes and said in a matter of fact way, "Odd she doesn't want to put red candles in those candlesticks you bought. I thought red was a lucky colour."

Oh my God, thought Diana; why doesn't he learn the bloody language? "What did you say for candles Robert?"

"*Laap ch'eung*, what else?"

"*Laap ch'eung*. Oh marvellous. Really marvellous." She roared with laughter. Quite abruptly the whole world had changed from total depression into sheer hilarity. "That means dried snags. A candle's *laap ch'uk*." She took to mimicking the altercation between Robert and Group over whether candles or sausages should be stuck in the candlesticks, becoming each protagonist in turn, Group's obstinacy alternating with Robert's, though his was depicted with greater malevolence. Suddenly conscious of this she confined herself to laughing, wondering the while how many human efforts from marriages to empires must have foundered on the rock of some linguistic balls-up. Then, inexplicably, a vision of Robert with his growing pot belly making passionate love to a girl called Fiona Ch'ong who had rather bandy legs sprang into her mind, and her mirth redoubled. Even Robert started to join in, though he wouldn't have done if he'd known the second source of her amusement. When she'd recovered she got Group to put two sausages in the ornate Portuguese candlesticks she'd just bought. Group's guffaws must have set up considerable internal pressures for she rushed out of the room shouting, "*Oi daai bin.*—I want to shit. *Oi daai bin.*"

Dinner completed Robert's recovery; Group had excelled herself with stewed chestnut chicken and he made away with most of the deep fried honeyed apples. Having expressed his gratitude with a resounding belch, he asked Diana to come to the studio to see the picture he'd finished. Since she'd determined that whatever other falsehoods were proliferating between them, the honesty of her criticism of his work must stand firm, she went with misgivings. The canvas was the latest mutation, now abstract and brooding, of a scene originally showing fishing nets drying on a frame. In her view the atmospheric grace of the first version had been progressively disappearing as the series continued. It was as though his stuffy English fear of exuberance was gripping him again. No doubt the galleries in Sydney and London would like it; it was in the current vogue, but if he was going to paint like this, well, he might as well have stayed at home instead of coming here where everything was radiant with colour and light. When she stated firmly, "It lacks vitality," she knew she might as well have said, 'You lack vitality,' to judge by his peeved silence as they went onto the balcony. There, Group had already brought the coffee and brandy and, as another special service to kind Mr. Sheraton, his pipe tobacco.

Sitting beside Robert, Diana did her best to relax; but it wasn't easy. She shouldn't be plaguing him with her existence at all. Her voice sounded peculiar and her speech stilted. "Wouldn't it be to some extent preferable to abandon your present subject—for a while that is to say?"

"That is to say what?" he replied which didn't seem to mean much so she held her tongue. Obviously miles away, his eyes were gazing into his brandy glass as into a crystal ball, his finger ever circling the rim. She glanced at him in profile; what did those doll-like cabaret girls see in this middle aged man? Money of course, but what else? To her, those broad features which she'd once thought manly now seemed heavy and dull. Yet the wiry grey hair flecked with white at the sides was as distinguished as on the day he'd first smiled at her in a Hobart café. But why, despite the care she took of him did he go on wearing those baggy pommy trousers? Soon he'd look just like those tweedy parents of his who, to judge by their letters, thought their only son a new Constable, and who didn't approve of her because, she suspected, she wasn't the sort of girl whose photo had ever appeared in Country Life as theirs and several of their house had.

Yet with each criticism she made of him her own sense of guilt became sharper. The peculiar notion came into her mind that anyone coming onto the balcony now would see a hideous black toad sitting right next to Robert. Yet people said she was beautiful. How strange it was that though she knew they weren't lying, she still retained her childhood conviction that she was plain, skinny, too tall, her mouth too big. Knowing things rationally didn't help to exorcise old fears; look how she went on dressing so carefully to mask her imagined defects—and running the risk of being thought vain.

Robert put his glass down quite suddenly, flung his arm around her and gave her a kiss—fatherly perhaps but nevertheless a kiss, "Sausages, candles," he said throwing his head back with a laugh. Then he looked shy. "You're right about the painting. You always are. God knows why, considering you're such a bloody ass. I'll just keep the first version. It's the best one."

Before his eyes Diana came to life again. Her eyes widened and sparkled. Her face took on that adoring look he hadn't seen for some time. He was reluctant to lose it, though more because it suggested the possibility of harmony between them than out of any desire to respond amorously to her. Yes, they must spend the evening on their own for once instead of joining that mob in the Cabaret; and who could say, perhaps a walk along the sea shore in the moonlight, then a drink and an early night would do the trick? Sea and sand and rocks always made him feel younger, or at least remember more clearly what it felt like to be young. Full of enthusiasm he made his suggestion, but before she could reply a little frown puckered his face as he remembered the date he'd now have to break and Diana, who responded to his moods as rapidly as a well lubricated weather vane to a fleeting breeze, said off-handedly, "It doesn't matter Robert. In fact I've promised to see Peter."

"Oh screw Peter," he butted in. "You saw him last night and the night before and the night before that. As far as I can see you do nothing but see him. Can't you give him a break?"

Back flooded her resentment. "So you're beginning to see how bloody monotonous my life is, are you? Good. It's about time." But simultaneously tears came into her eyes at the thought of how briefly the recent moments of happiness had been.

Robert took refuge in his pipe and soon the tangy tobacco smoke competed victoriously with the sea air. Neither of them dared to look at the other and Diana leant over the balustrade to stare down at the trishaw boys lolling in their vehicles drawn up against the sea wall waiting for customers. Was she expected to sit waiting, go nowhere, do nothing all day and now, it seemed, all night as well—like one of those local housewives whose husbands did what they felt like in the brothels of the Rua da Felicidade? Ah, but that was different—or so those idiotic Portuguese matrons seemed prepared to believe: 'men are like that, Senhora Sheraton. Just like little boys. It is very difficult for them to control that thing they have, senhora—even for priests. But it doesn't mean anything.' What a load of crap. It meant a lot to her.

It was too late now for Robert to say, "Oh come on. I didn't mean anything nasty. Let's go for a walk together. It's a beautiful night." She used both hands to sweep back some imaginary strands of hair from her forehead and then swung round on him. "How very pleasant. How very, very pleasant. Thank you so much. No. You go on your own, darling." She hated the last word and only used it heavily underlined when she was angry. (Robert braced himself for the rising storm.) "And I'll go on my own too. I don't need a keeper. But I will do something for you. Don't bother to go to the Cabaret. I'll ask Peter to call a girl here for you. Who would you like? Spring Plum, Golden Oriole, Vibrating Fanny?

A girl with one of those 'near perfect Chinese shapes' (her words were etched in the air in tones of acid) you so like to talk about. Or shall we ask your wonderful Red friend Mrs. Kwok Soolan to come and discuss the dialectics of shagging with you. You phoned her today, didn't you? Oh I know about your real plans for tonight. I'm not stupid you know. You really think I'm a bloody fool, don't you? Don't worry. I've got the message. I can stay at Peter's. If you have her here on her own, something's bound to happen. That's what you want, isn't it?"

Robert couldn't resist, when she finished her tirade with a reiterated, "Isn't it? Isn't it?", saying in the driest of tones, "Have you ever thought of going on the stage Diana?" She glared at him for an instant, said bitterly, "You shit." and went off to her bedroom pausing before slamming the door to call out, "You mightn't have noticed it, lover boy, but your precious Soolan's got duck's disease."

Robert lay down on the sofa and closed his eyes. Why is your mind in such a mess he asked himself, not sure whether he was addressing himself or Diana. Then he let his inner eye dwell on the visions that came bubbling up from deep below; he was far down in clear green water and below him at different depths there glided obscure purplish shapes that moved rapidly or slowly, scattered or exploded in response to some mysterious force. It was so fascinating that Diana's outburst was as though it had never been and he would have gone on drifting down and down if he hadn't heard Group's heavy tread about the room. Opening his eyes he saw her grinning at him, malice in her eyes. She must have been listening to the whole scene from behind the kitchen door. He patted his stomach and said in English, "No pudding tomorrow. Get too fat." Group giggled, so to add to her amusement he stood one of the sausages between two peaches on the table saying in his best Cantonese, "*T'aai ch'eung, t'aai pok*—too long, too thin." Since Group's mirth was set to become so great that Diana might think they were both laughing at her, he made off to his bathroom singing, again to his favourite mulberry bush theme, "Long and thin goes too far in, too far in, too far in, long and thin goes too far in, at any time in the morning."

Peter laid down his opium pipe and turned to look at Ah Tung who was stretched out flat on his back, whether asleep or awake it was impossible to tell from his eyes. Were they open? Were they closed? Was he watching? But his obstinate mouth was open, just a little and his arms and legs were spread out widely in an attitude of supreme content. With a feeling of loss Peter remembered the days when those powerful thighs used to pedal him home in a trishaw from the Cabaret and their conversations as they went along by the sea in the early hours of the morning. It was then he'd learned, several times over, how Ah Tung's family had been ruined by his father's heroin addiction and early death, of the days of starvation leading to Ah Tung becoming a thief to keep his mother and brothers alive. How true it all was, Peter wasn't sure but the story was always told with great conviction even if there were inconsistencies with retelling. Nor was he so sure that Ah Tung had later made his living just by working as a trishaw boy. The Triad tattoo marks on his arm, his knuckle dusters and that iron bar tightly bound with cloth, not infrequently concealed under his clothing, suggested other forms of employment. Peter had never intended his friendship with such a character to become close. It was Ah Tung who made the first move.

Peter remembered that night vividly. It was raining heavily but, as was his custom, he was going to get out of the trishaw at the foot of the hill road that led up to his house. Ah Tung didn't stop pedalling but called out, "I'm driving you up."

"You can't. It's too steep."

"I can."

"I won't let you." Knowing the weight of the trishaw, Peter started to get out from behind the plastic rain cover. Ah Tung slammed on the brakes, jumped from the saddle and pushed him back roughly. His face was menacing, his fists clenched. "Stay inside. Do what I say. Do you hear? Do what I say." That moment of submission had set the pattern of their life together, the pattern that had ended up here, in the Old Pawnshop.

He stretched out his arm and touched Ah Tung's foot. It was at once pulled away. Of course he knew it would be. Ah Tung always had to say no; everything must be done in his time. Even when they lay together, if Peter asked, "Turn to me," he was sure to be faced with the too familiar knots of that long spine and the words, "I'm more comfortable lying this way," whichever side of the bed he lay on. What makes me put the pressure on him like that, Peter wondered. He knew that if he stayed silent, his difficult lover would sooner or later turn towards him. It was like some ritual courtship he had to go through, the pain of refusal more necessary to him maybe than fulfilment. Diana had put her finger on the flaw in his character when she'd told him, "There's no reason at all for you to stand this nonsense, except that you enjoy being tortured. And the more you enjoy it, the deeper you'll get into the rut."

Such wisdom did not prevent him from staring angrily at Ah Tung's still body and wondering what sort of love, of friendship even, was this? He might as well be on his own at home. Whatever it was, the contrast with the easy happiness he enjoyed with Diana was obvious. A resolution formed in his mind: tonight in the Cabaret he'd tell her he was going to spend more time with her from now on. Ah Tung would be reduced to the level of a mere sexual outlet, then an acquaintance, and before long, phased out. What was more he'd make a determined effort to stop smoking opium. Make an effort indeed. What nonsense. His need for opium would disappear with his need for Ah Tung. At last when he'd got used to living a more orderly life, he'd return to the outside world and get a job again. Soothed into unreality by opium, his mind encompassed the whole situation serenely and dispassionately, together with the reasonable solution.

In the midst of all this hopeless scheming he felt Ah Tung's foot touching his head, not at all by chance but most deliberately, stroking his long hair, grasping strands of it between his toes and tugging it playfully. "*Hung mo gwai, hung mo gwai*—red haired devil, red haired devil," the throaty voice teased. Peter replied, "It isn't red, it's gold, beautiful gold—the stuff you love." The foot had to be withdrawn quickly as a waiter came in with some tea. But the brief action had been enough to change Peter's mood. He had to mean something to Ah Tung besides money and, since he wanted that something to be what he himself desired, he was always ready to see in his captor's slightest hint of affection the proof of an enormous hidden love.

The opium bowls on the tray were already empty, used up mainly by Ah Tung. "Bring some more," Peter ordered the waiter. They would share it together—after all, what harm could opium do, taken in moderation? His euphoria grew. He'd smoke until he drifted into that timeless wakefulness in which thought and action were extended and then he'd call for the bone thin masseur whose fee was always converted at once into heroin, and let those caressing fingers hovering over his body produce a drawn out sensual ecstasy. Later maybe he'd ask the blind lute player, who knew many stories about ancient emperors and heroes, to play for them. Who could say? In that music he and Ah Tung might together chance upon some single note that contained the mystery of all music and all things and it would weld them together forever.

At last, when the opium had given birth to a chimera that completely ruled his brain, Peter lay quite still gazing into the flame in the lamp glass before him, sometimes commanding it to approach like a burning furnace and sometimes to recede so that a galaxy, now become a speck of light, it beckoned to him, its lord and creator, from outer darkness. Was reality, even the reality of Ah Tung, any less of an illusion than the experiences the drug could bring? The foot touched him again. This time he took it in his hands greedily, kissing the sole, sucking the toes, licking between them, paying homage, acknowledging his own servitude. Ah Tung watched him curiously, wondering how far his pathetic lover would go and why those heavy lidded blue eyes brimmed with tears.

For the first time that day Peter was full of joy, though there was no substantial reason for it. All thought of Diana banished from his mind, he was only thinking of going home with Ah Tung and of the sweetness of lying close to him. "Rest. Rest. You look very tired," Ah Tung said with unaccustomed kindness. "Lie back and rest." Peter did as the god ordered and very soon his body relaxed and he sank into a deep sleep.

Full of remorse, Diana sat alone in her bedroom staring in the mirror at her strained face. "Serves you right you jealous swine," she said aloud. "You'll get no sympathy from me. Then she put off the lights and went to stand at the open window. The fragrance of blossom filled the warm air; the voices of the gardener's family rose up from their little house beneath the canopy of trees. A full moon was low in the sky and she could see the ancient buildings on the hilltops standing out with black severity; but over the town centre its cold beams were held at bay by the yellow glow of street lamps. At the top of the Casino's great bulk, neons flashed on and off signalling all lost craft like herself to make for the haven of its Cabaret. And where else could she go? In this trap, hemmed in by the sea and communist territory, it was the only place to meet people who behaved as stupidly as herself. The thought of seeing Peter cheered her up. They could play the fool together and she'd forget her misery. She flattered herself also that she'd be doing him some good as well, keeping him from his vicious lover and drug taking. Tonight she would hold on to him and make him see her back home.

After her bath she sat at the dressing table and gazed at her nakedness as though at the body of someone else. The young woman who stared back at her was far from plain. Her black hair falling down over her shoulders was lustrous and wavy, her pale skin flawless, at least in the artificial light; her face oval with rather haughty features that frightened some people but often excited men with their challenge. Some passionate Celtic strain, Diana liked to think, must be flowing there for two of her grandparents for certain, and maybe three, had emigrated from Cornwall. How else had that stick of a girl become so voluptuous.

Then her viewpoint changed again and she felt outside herself looking at the mixed up creature staring at the woman in the mirror. The woman in the mirror was a mere shade to be romanticised about in that foolish way but the woman looking at her must be going off it. She had lost all integrity and could do nothing but act parts and pretty rotten parts at that, parts made up of unrelated, scattered emotions and whims that possessed her at random like devils.

And now something sensual about the sight of those two women gazing at each other drew her back into the scene though she was unsure whether she was the woman who watched or who was watching. Both women turned sideward, looked critically at each other aslant and touched their lips with gentle fingers. Wasn't one of their mouths too wide? Didn't the other possess a hint of more than ordinary sensuality? What did they see in each other? Their hands were passing slowly down to their breasts, cupping them pleasurably, then straying over their bellies to rub subtly between their thighs. And while the fingers played, thoughts of Peter drifted back to her mind: his kindness, his fun, his penchant for languages, his own poetry, always about men; his versions of Greek poetry, always about boys. But it was a line from a coy Victorian rendering of a Norse poem he'd read that had stuck in her head: `Not

in war alone are men the greatest joy of men.' What was
it like this passion that could bind warriors, or mates in
the outback? Was it simpler yet sharper than their desire
for women? It must involve something deeper than mere
youth and beauty. Or was there nothing to Peter's love but
that? Her eyes closed on the two women before her and she
lost herself in a fantasy of strong men in fierce embraces.
A gasp escaped her lips. Where was she in the orgy? Why
let it excite her when she had no part in it? She opened
her eyes suddenly and saw a strange woman staring back
with wild eyes, terrified at the passage of time. Then the
wildness faded and the face took on the enigmatic look of
a blind statue.

When she'd finished dressing she sat down again at
the mirror to put on some earrings. Robert's hands rested
lightly on her shoulders; she started, turned towards him
and pressed her face against his chest, grasping his arms.
It was a few moments before she noticed he was unusually
well dressed in his new suit. "How smart you look. How
smart." She sat back to admire him, then clasped her hands
and shook her head. "Forgive me. Forgive me." He kissed
her brow like a parent proving there was really nothing to
forgive. "It's just this foul climate. You'll feel better in the
air-conditioning."

"Yes. Yes. I will." She did her best to accept the fact
that the complexity of her problems could be reduced to a
question of degrees Fahrenheit. "I'll be alright there. But
we won't stay too late if you don't want to." She followed
him meekly downstairs, then down the steep garden path
and into a waiting trishaw to ride to the Casino, for their
customary meaningless night out.

The first sight that met Peter's eyes when he awoke was
the nakedness of Carlos Nolasco whose hand lovingly
caressed his hungry god that rose up like dark Proteus from

among curly black waves, a thick-headed specimen perfect in shape for love making, according to Chinese experts in such matters. Carlos lay quite absorbed in a Hong Kong pin-up magazine in which girls with gargantuan breasts posed brazenly between borders of bilingual script, scrutinizing each one with the consideration a connoisseur might lavish on a newly discovered masterpiece.

Peter glanced at his watch—nearly midnight. He should be at the Cabaret but was reluctant to quit his artificial paradise. Ah Tung held the jade mouthpiece of an opium pipe against his lips, at the same time stroking back the hair which had fallen over his cheek during sleep. "Take some *hak mai*—black rice," he said and Peter started to inhale as the solicitous voice went on, "And it's time you had your hair cut. I don't want you looking like a woman." Peter decided to put the Cabaret off for a while, emptied his lungs and started a second inhalation, enjoying Ah Tung's combing fingers and the sight of Carlos' body, as more morphine invaded his brain.

He wasn't sure whether it was the opium or the subaqueous light but it seemed to him that, whereas Ah Tung's skin was burned and hardened by the heat from above, some particle of the sun had found a home inside Carlos, making him glow from within, keeping him warm and alive, powerful yet at the same time sensual. It was beauty to be appreciated but not desired. Yet he knew that the splendour of the young man's body—a palimpsest of Lusitanian history—was the result of endless mingling of Portuguese, Chinese, African, Malay and much other blood, and the relaxed appearance a reflection of consummate laziness and a life of ease—Carlos was a policeman. It was probably some nefarious protection racket, made possible by his work, that had caused him to become a crony of Ah Tung.

Carlos put down the magazine and caught Peter's eyes. An innocent smile made his face even more handsome. Then, since he loved admiration he raised his hips a little—Peter noted the inguinal line precise as on an archaic torso—and squeezed the base of his greatest pride and joy to display it in full majesty. This harmless action irritated Ah Tung who rasped, "Aren't you ever on duty, you lazy wanker?"

Carlos gestured languidly at Peter and said, "Chinese are weird. They used to get randy over women's feet. Now they're going for men's hair."

"There are stinking black dogs and stinking white dogs," Ah Tung commented, with a thoughtful look at the roof. "But the filthiest dogs are the mongrels. You can't tell the shit from the fur." He gave a final tug at Peter's hair, lay down and took to cleaning his opium pipe with meticulous care.

His adversary, equally nonchalant, picked up a magazine. "Ah Tung's got a good job you know, smoking opium all day. He wants to join his father."

"Better than yours—sucking Portuguese arse holes."

Carlos raised a leg and let fly three farts of diminishing force, the last with an expression of pained concentration. "I have to live. And the shit tastes good."

"Aiyaah. And how you love it. *Ch'au hang hang*—what a foul stench. It's a wonder we haven't all passed out. Go on then. Call for a woman. We don't want to watch you playing with yourself all night like a half wit. Get it over with."

"Get it over with. Get it over with." Carlos' voice quivered with contempt. "Haven't you heard the news? Some people like fucking women, as much as you like," there was a malicious pause, "fucking up Peter."

Ah Tung's face set. Things were going too far. Peter propped himself up, with some effort, and glared at them. No wonder they enjoyed cock fighting, razor blades fixed to tiny claws, flying feathers and spurting blood. More than once their bickering had led to blows. Peter always found the peace making operation tedious; each of them hated to be thought in the wrong. Preventive action was called for. "Cool it," he warned. "Call for a woman. Carlos. Give us a show."

"Don't mind us Peter." Carlos' voice was now oily. "It's just the heat." He leaned over to pat Ah Tung's arm. "I won't harm my little brother. He loves me too much." He tried to drag Ah Tung's hand towards his groin but Ah Tung whipped it back and began to twirl a viscous bolus of opium on a bodkin above the lamp glass. Carlos chuckled. "Leave him to his opium. You'll get nothing from him tonight. Let's have a couple of girls. We'll both be tiger men Peter. Call for little girls—the smaller the better. See who can make them squeal loudest, like piglets. Ah Tung, is it true that trishaw boys screw pigs?"

The poised bodkin looked dangerous to Peter and so, as a way of restraining Ah Tung, he leaned over him to press the call bell but, as his finger touched the grimy plastic button, something quite extraordinary happened, so extraordinary indeed that later he often had a fantasy that the pressure he exerted had set off the whole trail of events that followed. For in that instant the Old Pawnshop reverberated from roof to foundations in response to a great explosion from somewhere outside. The three of them froze and stared at each other in amazement. After a moment of total silence a barrage of heavy gunfire opened up and pandemonium broke out. People shouted, jumped up and pushed their way about, most making for the narrow stairway, the wooden soles of their sandals adding to the racket. Carlos' cockstand drooped pathetically but Ah Tung coolly worked the ball of opium into his pipe bowl as though nothing out of the way was happening; the gleam in his eyes suggested that he was enjoying the disbelief on the faces of Carlos and Peter more than the opium.

"They're coming. They're taking over. God. What's happening?" Peter sprang to his feet, his eyes darting from Ah Tung to Carlos. "Yes. They're coming. That's it." Everyone in the place must have shared his view that at this very moment Chinese troops were on their way in. Carlos was already half dressed. "Stay here," he ordered. "I'd better report for duty. (No one believed him.) You two wait here— the walls are thick. It's pretty safe. I'll see you later."

"Carlos." Ah Tung's voice was full of concern. "Get a change of clothes. You might have to ditch that uniform." Carlos gave him a friendly nod and left the cubicle. A moment later he was back for his pin up magazine, then he was gone again.

As the building emptied the barrage sounded heavier. Peter was afraid; for an instant he thought it was physical fear alone. Then he knew there was more to it than that. Something was happening that everyone there had often imagined, often discussed and often feared which made it possible for him to recognize at once that everything was going to change. The whole of his life would be upset. He'd have to leave. All foreigners would be pushed out. But what of Ah Tung? Could he get away? It was most unlikely. "I'm sure it's nothing. Everything will be alright," he faltered guiltily as he put his arm around Ah Tung's shoulders. They went taut under his touch.

"Of course it will—for you." Ah Tung's tone was cold. "Foreigners will just be sent packing. On those nice ferry boats. I'll give you no more trouble. You'll be in Hong Kong, and a well paid job. You'll forget me in a week."

"Don't talk like that. How could I leave you?" Peter sounded vehement.

"If we'd gone to Hong Kong—like I said—we'd be alright. How many times did I ask you to take me. A hundred at least." Ah Tung's voice rose resentfully. "But no. You have to stick here. Now we're washed up. It's your fault. Do you hear—your fault. Ah well, it's what you want. I hope you're happy now." He affected to smoke nonchalantly, but Peter snatched the pipe and brandished it in his face. "Lay off it. It isn't my fault at all. I can't help it if the Reds take over. But you'll seize any excuse to have a go at me, won't you? Why can't you..." His lecture was interrupted by the sudden clatter of the bamboo curtain roughly snatched aside. The next instant none other than the normally aloof and generally surly manager of the Old Pawnshop pushed his way in. He was clearly terrified. "I'm finished. What shall

I do? I'm finished." His voice trailed away in a long moan. They stared at him in disgust; his puffy face streaming with sweat and his short fleshy body were repulsive. Ah Tung clapped his hands and hooted gleefully. "Yes Lim. You are finished. It's all up. People's Trials next week. You're dead already." He seized the pipe and sprayed Lim with bullets. "Gak. Gak. Gak. Gak. Gak."

Lim collapsed on the bed and with shaking fingers took the cigarette Peter offered. His brain reeled with the screams of victims burned, sliced, torn to pieces. He remembered the Trials broadcast a couple of years ago from the Sun Yat Sen Memorial Hall in Canton and the noise of the vengeful mob calling for death. "They won't go for small fry like me, will they Ah Tung?"

"Small fry. Hah. Come off it Lim. In the old days you were high up in the Canton police. What about those Party men you tricked. They were executed by the K.M.T.— slowly, weren't they? Hah. Small fry. Everyone's heard the story. You're a wanted man and you know it. They'll have something special ready for you; a lingering death that'll make you scream for hours, thrashing around in agony. Yaaah." Ah Tung's bloodcurdling yell was accompanied by a clawing movement between Lim's fat thighs. The terrified man curled up on the bed crying, "I had to do it. It was my job. They were outlaws then." But Ah Tung had told the truth; it would be the end for him if the Reds came. Looking round desperately he begged, "You know the boat people Ah Tung. Help me get away. I've got money. We could all get away."

"Take no notice of Ah Tung." The once pitiless Lim was now cringing but all the same Peter felt some pity for him. "Pull yourself together. How do we know they're coming? Ah Tung doesn't really believe it. He wouldn't be so happy if he did. Look at the tattoo marks on his arm. The Reds come down on Triad members too."

"And on red haired devils," Ah Tung spat back, furious to be undermined. But Peter's re-assurance lost its effect a moment later as the old timbers of the building creaked under the impact of a more powerful explosion. Even Ah Tung looked alarmed and Lim renewed his wails. "They're coming alright. I'm finished. I should have got out long ago."

"The roof." Ah Tung said, jumping to his feet. "Let's get up on the roof and see what's going on." He made off for the stairs with Peter and fat Lim, supporting one another like a couple of drunkards, following behind.

In the open air the firing seemed less violent and, they could now see, was only to the north, probably along the border. The Old Pawnshop had been like an echo chamber magnifying the sound. Out here the guns still sounded threatening but at least nothing was exploding in the town. Peter's anxiety began to ebb and, as he gazed at the peaks across the estuary over which the moon drew a glistening line, the feeling of detachment that the opium induced took him over once more; he was hovering like a god looking down on this human pandemonium as indifferently as a man might glance at a broken ants' nest. In a moment, weary of it all, he would fly off to the mountains leaving everything below to dissolution. But as he surveyed the City, with its cupolas, pinnacles and towers, the ruin of St. Paul's on its low hill, so serene in the silver light, his mood changed again to a selfish certainty that it was pointless to have shared in anyone's fears when there was nothing to fear at all. This City, his hidden refuge far away from that baneful world of family, fortune and convention, could never fall.

Yet, ever vacillating, he began to be doubtful again when Ah Tung drew him aside and whispered, "The Reds are about to take over, for certain. Whatever's happening it will be an excuse to blame the Portuguese and take over. But they'll make demands first. So we have time. We could still get away—in a small boat." The voice was urgent. "Are you listening to me? It's too risky to stay. Nothing's going on along the water front yet. Let's go to Hong Kong. With that racket going on along the frontier we could easily slip away. Lim's got the money—a boat would be a snip."

"Yes, yes," Peter replied vaguely for the very idea was preposterous though not, quite evidently, to Ah Tung who persisted, "We'll be happy there. You'll see. We can both work. No one need know about us."

"Yes Ah Tung. Yes. Speak to Lim about it." Peter gestured wearily towards the manager who was cowering against the wall at the corner of the roof, then he beat a retreat in the other direction and looked across at the towering Casino. On its twelfth floor a band of light marked the Cabaret where Diana would be expecting him. He was surprised that, despite the gunfire, the strains of distant music should still suggest that business up there was as usual. Maybe it was the last time their frenetic meeting place would ever be open and everyone was making the best of it. He wanted to be there too if that was so.

Across the roof Ah Tung had taken to playing cat and mouse with his victim. "Well, I suppose it could be done," he conceded. "I know someone who'd let us have a boat. You'd have to pay though. A lot. Five or six thousand—maybe more. No, you couldn't afford it. Forget it." Lim weighed his purse against his terror and then whispered, "Does Morgan want to get away?"

"Ask him yourself." Ah Tung's bitterness was misconstrued by Lim who insisted, "No. He wouldn't listen to me. You make him come. He'll do anything for you. And he can manage a boat. I've seen him sailing."

"Alright, I'll ask him." Ah Tung yielded reluctantly. "But not for money. That's your side of the bargain. We'll need it in cash you know."

Lim gasped with relief; as though he'd trust himself alone with the likes of Ah Tung! "Yes, yes. Don't worry. I'll pay for the lot. I can't chance staying. I must go."

Ah Tung screwed his eyes up looking still doubtful, then nodded. "It's a deal then. Go and get the money. Now. And no tricks. We'll meet in an hour at Old Chong's hotel," Lim patted his saviour's back gratefully and made off. A smile played over Ah Tung's face as he cocked his head to listen to the gunfire, now as little threatening he felt, as distant thunder. Then he stole up behind Peter and put his arms around his waist. "Dreaming still, foreign devil. What are you dreaming of this time?"

"Are you still mad with me?" Peter asked, despite his misgivings hungry for those imprisoning arms and kneading fingers.

"You know me. I wanted to make you mad at me. It doesn't mean anything." Ah Tung's hands pressed over Peter's body harshly. "Oh, you like this, don't you? Nicer than dreams, eh?"

Peter felt his resistance weakening. He knew what was coming next and tried to forestall it. "If we left, what about your family?"

Ah Tung dismissed Peter's concern. "I can send them money. That's more use to them than me. Jobs are easier to get over there." His voice became gentle, almost crooning and he made his breath come and go quickly like someone in the grip of passion as he spoke. "What do they matter. You're the only person for me, Peter. You're number one." The last words were in English. Peter turned his head and murmured Ah Tung's name as the longed for lips touched his cheek. Grasping the probing hands he pushed them downwards saying, "It's up as soon as you touch me. See. As soon as you touch me."

"I know you love me. I want to stay with you. Don't spoil it for both of us. Listen to me Peter. Listen." Ah Tung's fondling and kisses were intensified. "Fat Lim's getting money for a boat. He's desperate to get away. We can go with him tonight. Oh Peter, I don't want to lose you."

Peter kissed the upturned mouth—"*ngoh oi nei*—I love you," he sighed—and the calculating eyes. "But don't you think we should wait a bit?" he pleaded. "It might be risky. Let's see how things turn out." Ah Tung's exasperation boiled over. "*Ngoh oi nei, ngoh oi nei.*" He mimicked the sweet talk. "Always talking about love, love—*oi ts'ing, oi ts'ing,* when all you mean is this." He rubbed his thumb up and down and pushed Peter away. "Go. Go to your rich friends up there. What do I matter. I'm just a trishaw boy you pay to screw you." He ended with another phrase in English, picked up from visiting British servicemen come over from Hong Kong, "Fuck off yellow bastard."

Anger made Peter's Cantonese supremely fluent. "Why should I always do as you want. For weeks you've turned away from me. 'I'm tired', 'It's too hot', 'You need a good sleep Peter', (now it was Ah Tung's turn to be mimicked). You're never too tired to come here. Yes, and fuck women I suppose. You're only nice to me when you want something. Don't think I can't see through you." He stopped abruptly; had he gone over the line that divided what might only be a charade of love from economic reality? This could be the row to end it all.

But instead, Ah Tung's head bowed and his arms hung limply at his sides. After a deep sigh he said, "I've been with no one. Do you hear, with no one. But what about you and Sheraton *taai taai*. You can do what you want with her. It's different for me though. I depend on you don't I? On you and your money. It supports my family doesn't it? Aiyaah, you don't know what it's like to be poor. Huh, you and your money. I only keep a bit for opium." Then he squatted down on his haunches, his hands over his eyes. "Yes Moh *Shin Saang*. You can afford love can't you. You can afford to sit around with your books or go to the Cabaret. But what about me? Thousands are out of work here. The only thing I can do is ride a trishaw but I'll never do that again. Never. Never. I'm not a beast. I'm a man. A man." His words were spoken in a matter of fact way, without a hint of passion, and because of that, though he'd heard it all before, Peter was more than unusually moved. He knelt beside Ah Tung and held him. "Forgive me. I've not helped you as I should." Then his own unexpected capitulation burst out. "We'll go with Lim. I'll get you a job in Hong Kong; send you to school. Anything you want. Just love me a little."

Ah Tung looked into Peter's eyes in silence. When his voice came it was musical in a way Peter had never heard. "You're blind Peter. Love me a little! Can't you see I love you? But I'm not a girl. I love you as a man." For a few seconds he was lost in thought until, grasping Peter's hands, he implored, "Never mind about Hong Kong. Listen. There's less firing. Perhaps it's nothing after all. Let's go home now. Let's go. Now." A mirror voice in Peter's mind echoed. 'Go with him. Go. Now.' But well trained to keep appointments, or was Diana more important than Ah Tung, he replied like a fool, "What about my friends? I promised to meet them." Torn between love and obligation he hesitated but at length ignoring the inner voice's warning, he said, "We'll meet here later. I won't be long." The fleeting moment of choice had gone.

They hugged each other and walked to the stairway, but on an impulse Ah Tung turned to Peter and held him close once more. Then they left to go their separate ways.

As soon as Carlos set foot in the Rua da Felicidade he found himself in a panic stricken crowd. Seizing an old man by the arm he shouted, "What's going on?"

"In that uniform and you don't know? They've crossed the Barrier-Gate. They're coming. Half an hour and they'll be here. The Portuguese are finished—and their running dogs!" The old man was borne away by the throng. Unnerved, Carlos took off his cap and jacket and rolled them up. The police had many enemies over there; old scores would be settled.

Everyone was making for the Hong Kong ferry wharf and cars were starting to turn up as well. This worried him; if the rich were getting out, things must be serious. Approaching the quay where the ferry boat, brightly lit, lay alongside, he hid behind a pillar to watch.

The cars and the mob were congested near the quay entrance. Men and women, some with babies or dragging tired children, pushed forward yelling and jostling to get on the boat which could only be boarded by two narrow gangways; raised arms waved bank notes—proof of a right to escape. The continuing barrage would have passed unnoticed but for flashes in the sky. No one was in control; it looked certain that fighting would break out.

There was a roar of engines and a convoy of military vehicles drove up and halted at the edge of the melée. Soldiers jumped down and forced their way through the crowd; for a moment Carlos thought it was the start of a Portuguese pull-out. He was about to throw his uniform away, when he saw people being forced from the ship. The poorer folk ran off quickly, frightened by the soldiers; the car owners went on answering back as they were ordered away. Before long the mob dispersed and the soldiers mounted guard on the wharf. They looked nervous and trigger happy which discouraged even the most determined of the would-be escapees from hanging around.

Carlos made his way stealthily to Old Chong's hotel. As he reached the doorway a black Rolls Royce swept up to the ferry and a young man jumped out to argue with an army Captain. After a while he got back into the rear compartment, gave some order into a microphone and the driver reversed to leave the way he had come. Carlos caught a glimpse next to the young man of the wizened but unperturbed face of Lung Yeung, the richest man in the Colony. If Lung Yeung couldn't escape, no one could. The Portuguese were still in control. An inordinate capacity for looking after number one told Carlos to hang on to his uniform, lie low at Old Chong's and see how things went.

Lung Yeung didn't drive back home as the Captain had suggested. Sooner or later his intervention in whatever situation had arisen would be required. To save the Governor the embarrassment of having to ask for his help, he'd call on him at once to ask what was happening.

Clad in a black Chinese gown, Lung Yeung's frail body, huddled diminutively in the corner of the seat, was practically invisible against the dark upholstery. Only his pale face with its wispy beard showed up beneath a black skull cap. Next to him his vizier Ming Yuk, his short powerful body immaculate in a cream western suit, exuded confidence. He wasn't in the least perturbed that their planned visit to Hong Kong had been stopped; on the contrary it was with pleasure that he anticipated watching the role his master would play in the new circumstances. Lung Yeung was irritated by the gold-tipped holder through which Ming Yuk smoked with affected ease. He himself was nowhere near so sure of his capacities; the Communists were not like the Nationalists, the Portuguese, the British or for that matter the Japanese. With them it was possible to weigh the factors and calculate. With the Communists there was an unpredictable element his shrewdness found disconcerting. His survival depended on his usefulness to them but even this might be ignored if their weird ideology so dictated. When he remembered his past journeys to Canton for those bleak discussions, a chill descended on his spirit; he knew he'd at last encountered the power which one day might destroy what he'd created. That day could be at hand.

The stillness of the Communist shore convinced him that for the time being no general attack was under way; as the car drove on, the gunfire was hardly audible. Beyond the last warehouse he glanced at the temple of Kuan Yin, the Goddess of Mercy, half hidden amongst stunted trees and boulders. Behind the doors the Goddess was gesturing towards the granite floor; the thought of the emptiness within, redolent of incense, filled him with desire for its silence. He envied the monks their intoned prayers and the harmony of their temple clinging beneath its carved beams and yellow tiles to the earth by incorporating rocks into its structure; but the car bore him on to actions devoid of such reality.

The headlights sweeping the water caught the swift upward movement of a fish trap as its frame, tautened downwards to dip a great net beneath the waves, was released. Water and a few fishes glistened in the meshes; the swell seemed whip-lashed. Then the lights probed the curved shore of another bay, picking out the steps up to the cliff-top villa where Diana and Robert had their apartment. As the car approached the gateway below the house, the driver slowed down, expecting an order to stop and rightly, for Lung Yeung was indeed wondering how the Sheratons were faring though guessing the bombardment had caught them in town.

Ming Yuk disapproved of his master's friendship with such foreigners; they weren't rich and had no influence, even in Hong Kong. He thought the time Lung Yeung spent with Mrs. Sheraton who came to talk and look at his porcelain and scrolls, wasted. Worse, it was a friendship from which he was excluded. Nevertheless, having glanced at Lung Yeung's face, he asked if he should find out whether they were in. "The Sheratons?" Lung Yeung repeated absently. "No, I don't think we should disturb them so late. But if you want, go up and tell them to keep calm." After his steep climb, one hundred and five steps, to the apartment, Ming Yuk was informed by Group that her master and mistress were indeed at the Cabaret. "Then there's no need for you to worry," Lung Yeung said gently on his return. "They'll not be afraid in company." Ming Yung didn't care if they received a direct hit but he nodded his head gravely and banked his anger against the western couple for some day when it might be used to punish their innocence.

At length they drove up the wooded approach to the Governor's residence, a graceful building with salmon hued walls enlivened by brilliant white window frames, shutters and pilasters. Renewed gunfire could be heard as the car stopped. Lung Yeung smiled; for once the Governor might have some information before he did about events in Portugal's domain. The ADC greeted him at the porticoed entrance as though he had been long expected. "Ah, Senhor Lung. His Excellency is with the Head of Security. Pray come up."

In the study, the Governor stood behind his desk with Colonel Lobato literally on the Chinese carpet before him. Nodding deferentially at Lung Yeung and beckoning him to sit, the Governor said, "Well Senhor Colonel, continue if it's not too much trouble."

The Colonel, an imposing figure with proud features, gray hair and grand moustache, looked like a school boy accounting for a breach of discipline. His fury at having to do so before an outsider—and a Chinese outsider at that—was greater than his embarrassment. Firmly he stated, "It wasn't our fault Excellency. The Communist guards were very provocative. If one of our soldiers so much as put a foot across the line, a Red would try to pull him over. For the last few nights they've been spoiling for a fight. They've just seen service in Korea."

The Governor puckered his lips, which hardly improved his appearance. "Senhor, this is childish." He turned to Lung Yeung for acquiescence but received an impassive stare. "The answer was simple. Orders should have been given for our men to keep well back."

Lobato glared at the porcelain blue ceiling whence cloud-borne putti derisively presented pink dimpled buttocks. His voice, louder than intended, retorted, "Such, Excellency, were their orders. Your officers are not totally lacking in intelligence. Unfortunately no one foresaw how the Angolese would react."

"Really Colonel. Really now. And you say my officers aren't lacking in intelligence. Yet some of them have served in Angola." His voice fell. "You for instance. I've heard you speak of your four years there. But please continue Senhor. We'd all like to hear what this not total lack of intelligence gave rise to."

The Colonel wished he could resign on the spot; the Governor was outrageous. His opinion was shared by Lung Yeung. "Your Excellency, I'd like to withdraw while the Colonel has his audience." The Governor slumped in his chair and passed his hand over his forehead. "I'm overwrought;

forgive me gentlemen." He gestured them to join him at the conference table. There the Colonel, his dignity somewhat restored, proceeded. "The Angolese thought it was all a game. Some walked up to the frontier, stuck a foot across and ran back laughing when the Communists rushed up. Unfortunately, as we all know," Lobato looked first at his Excellency and then at Lung Yeung, "over there they don't know what a joke is. Tonight when the flag was lowered a Red came up to the barrier and lobbed a grenade over. Two of our men were killed outright. Another died later. Several were wounded."

"So, we were definitely not the first to attack." The Governor emphasised the words for the benefit of Lung Yeung who sat expressionless but wondering why clever men should even affect to be surprised at the idiocy of underlings.

"Definitely not Excellency, I can assure you." Lung Yeung nodded that he'd taken the point, but the matter of first or last to fire would pass unmentioned in the bargaining.

"Naturally," Lobato continued, "the Angolese got wild. One of them—he'd been struck by shrapnel—hurled a grenade at the Red guard house. It went through a window; there must have been casualties. The frontier came to life— then came the first rifle shots. Again Excellency, they were the first to open up. Of course we replied and they came back with machine guns."

"What about the mortars?"

"They were the first. But the shells fell in the rice fields. There was little damage. I'm sure the same can be said for our fire."

The Governor cupped his hand over his chin. "Well Senhor Lung. You've heard the lot. What are we to do?"

"There's nothing we can do Excellency until hostilities cease. The longer they continue, the more Canton will demand. And as long as firing goes on the unpredictable can happen."

They'd been reminded of the one humiliating course open to them. The Governor leaned back in his gilded chair, his bald head eclipsing the arms of the House of Braganza. "You want me to order a cease fire unilaterally, don't you?" Lobato began to protest. "Your Excellency, they were the first...," but the Governor silenced him with an airy gesture. "That is so, isn't it, Senhor Lung?" To which the serene arbiter said, "I'm sure your Excellency will do what's best."

"Your Excellency, we must consider the morale of our men." Lobato was no longer to be silenced. "And our honour is at stake."

"Honour!" the Governor's voice was shrill. "Honour indeed. Our only tactic is to swallow our pride; that's how we've kept this place so long. If we go on being careful, maybe we'll be here in four hundred years' time (but even Lobato didn't believe that). Honour's for those who can afford it, Senhor Colonel. Of course," he concluded in the tone of the Salazar régime's most ardent supporter, "if they really tried to come in, I'd order resistance. In the meantime Colonel, to avoid such a contingency, you'd better tell our men to hold their fire." But before the Colonel could leave, Fate made a snap decision to test the Governor's sincerity; the A.D.C. came into the room, followed by a flustered Captain. "Well Captain what is it?" His Excellency was irritated by the lack of protocol.

"There's been a landing Excellency. We've just received a report from a Police Post west of the Barrier Gate. Our men are resisting stubbornly." Lobato rose and looked challengingly at the Governor at the back of whose head a little donkey engine began to spurt blood in quick jets up to his brain. He turned to Lung Yeung as though addressing the United Nations. "I cannot order a cease-fire whilst foreign troops are on Portuguese soil. Does the news of the landing mean anything to you Senhor?" An oddly phrased remark, Lung Yeung thought; the Governor must suspect him of being party to some plan of the Communist authorities to take the Colony over. Yet if the news was true, the only meaning it had for him was that he should get away at once—his value as a middle man, and his business, were finished. "Your Excellency, have the report checked; I find it difficult to believe." The Governor looked dubious but ordered Lobato to investigate. "And if it's false, I want a cease fire without delay."

Lung Yeung asked permission to leave. "I'll be at home and at your disposal Excellency."

"I very much hope so, Senhor Lung."

As he left the residency and climbed unsteadily into the car, assisted by his ever-attentive henchman, Lung Yeung felt peculiarly relieved. Why try to pacify the Communists just to maintain his empire a bit longer? He possessed wealth enough to last ten full lives abroad and enjoy his remaining years in peace. Why not follow the example of his wife and younger son, who lived in Hong Kong, Paris or wherever they chose. Now he'd be forced to do what hitherto had been merely a temptation. He glanced sideways at the ambitious young man who worshipped power and wondered how he'd take the decision. Badly, for he'd find no scope in the retreat his master proposed for himself. "Ming Yuk, this time it's too difficult. Things are out of hand. See the launch is made ready. We're leaving tonight. Tell the driver to move quickly."

Ming Yuk's voice seemed unnaturally shrill as he gave the order. Then he drew in his breath deeply in what sounded like the opposite of a sigh. Had he lavished his devotion on a powerless idol? He hated those words, 'out of hand' from the lips of the man who controlled his entire existence. Nor could he accept them. Just then, approaching the greatest house in the colony, Lung Yeung's rambling Pearl River Mansion, brilliant with security lighting above its wharf, they saw that the Governor had foreseen Lung Yeung's move; troops occupied the boathouse. A smile flickered about Ming Yuk's mouth; at least the Governor knew how to assess his master's capabilities. Of course Lung Yeung could settle everything.

A dense crowd seethed on the Cabaret dance floor, clustered round tables and besieged the long bar. Yellow jacketed waiters rushed about tirelessly but it was still difficult to get served. When Diana's glass was empty Robert produced a bottle of cognac from under his seat. "I bought it just after the guns started," he shouted. She laughed casting her eyes up and replied, "Typical of you." But it was far too noisy to talk across the table and Robert was glad Doctor Luiz Figueiredo, as ever both mournful and elegant, was sitting beside her. It left him free to observe how people behaved when their way of life was threatened—a modern Holbein preparing a new Dance of Death. What a pity he hadn't brought his sketch book with him.

By now the din all but drowned the music of the Filipino band though the percussion, battered by a delirious drummer high on hemp, underscored everything with a mindless beat. Not that it influenced the dancers jammed into a globular mass that rotated like gruel stirred slowly by an invisible spoon. Couples clung to each other, some hysterically cheerful, others gazing soulfully into each other's eyes as though their brief affairs were grand passions now moving inevitably to a tragic doom. The sybaritic life, half Chinese, half European was, it seemed, sinking irrevocably like the Titanic. But when the people at the next table linked arms to sing Auld Lang Syne in Chinese, Robert couldn't make up his mind whether the whole business was sad or merely ludicrous.

How quickly the place had filled up, as though people had been waiting outside to come in on cue like an opera chorus. From every part of the great Casino they'd flocked in: from its bars, gambling rooms, restaurants, massage parlours, from the brothel and from the private rooms. In the heart of their temple of pleasure, surely they'd find out what was happening? They were disappointed. But the underlying anxiety engendered by several years of living on the brink of the uneasy Communist volcano boiled up in a mood of apocalyptic frenzy. The hour was not at hand; it had come.

From time to time people in the crowd called out to Diana and Robert and they shouted back or waved. Robert felt the need for a ready-made phrase like 'Happy New Year'. Sometimes a Portuguese officer came up to the table, greeted them, but especially Robert, with effusive politeness and asked Diana to dance. When this happened Luiz' body quivered nervously like a spaniel about to lose a bone. Robert half expected to hear a whimper or see a paw on Diana's lap. It struck him as odd that these young blades should be there at all. If there was a threat why weren't they on duty? And how about Luiz? A doctor should be near the front to staunch the flow of blood. But lacking sympathy for the right-wing Portuguese régime, Robert didn't pursue such lines of thought. It was no business of his what happened to a colonial relic. "Yes Diana. Go on. Dance. Enjoy yourself," he'd urge, exuding unpossessiveness, at the same time directing a bland smile at the officer which really meant, 'Dance with her till kingdom come, my man but you'll never get her'. In places like the Club Militar, where the officers' attitudes were as antique as its architecture, Diana was the subject of much bragging rivalry and Robert knew it. Presumably she suggested pleasures more voluptuous than the ones they bought so easily from the trim Chinese taxi dancers.

Diana hadn't the slightest intention of leaving her observation post. From it she could see in the pinkish wall mirrors every little glance that passed between Robert and various girls dancing behind her and this whilst still contriving to listen, or appear to listen, to Luiz' flattery. Why she took such an obsessive interest she herself wasn't sure; knowing who Robert went with wasn't going to stop him. Gazing at whoever had asked her to dance with a melancholy smile as though pitying their never to be gratified longing, she'd invent an excuse. At the same time some little gesture would be made to Luiz, a sideward glance, a knowing smile, a hand placed lightly on his arm (he'll come in his pants if she does that once more, thought Robert), which pleased the dapper little man mightily.

Robert changed his position with deliberate movements; one foot was placed on the couch so his arm could rest on his raised knee, the other foot stayed on the floor—the position in Chinese sculpture of 'royal ease'. But he felt neither majestic nor easy. He really wanted to drift around the room on his own, chatting up some of the girls, or better still to disappear with one of them for a time. Shining eyes, mouths open in animated chatter, skin made lustrous by the heat and above all their doll-like movements as though they were string puppets, had charged the air with sensuality. He was lured by unspoken opportunities. Inevitably he found himself hoping Soolan wouldn't turn up; this wasn't the night for conversation. Why the hell, he asked himself, couldn't the Portuguese officers be more persistent. For once he regretted the absence of Colonel Lobato. That middle aged Romeo would never be put off so easily by Diana, if only to demonstrate to his juniors that he could succeed where they failed. Despite the serene expression Robert maintained on his face, his eyes stared stonily across at Diana only to receive in return the gentlest of looks. Once she leaned over towards him, took his hand, stroked it a little and spoke his name, tenderly. It caught him off guard. When he felt like it, he was as adept as anyone at those intimate little glances lovers exchange to indicate their real residence on another planet. But as far as the eyes being windows of the soul, he knew that was nonsense; they were just highly differentiated tissues. The trick lay in how one used the muscles surrounding them. Yet irrationally Diana's glance, so lacking in stratagem, mortified him. Foolish, temperamental, uncontrolled she might be, but if there was such a thing as love of the romantic sort, she must understand it. He remembered her words in one of their many arguments. "You've never been in love, so you don't know how much people in love can be hurt." Had he caused so much suffering to her, then? A fleeting desire to be different passed through his brain to be followed by the certainty that he couldn't change. "You're the most beautiful woman here," he said, putting his face as close to hers as the table would allow, unable to think of anything more original—but after all the statement was defensible. A dark look came into her eyes; she at once looked over his shoulder to ask the mirror if he was telling the truth, or, for all he knew, to make sure she was there at all. He marvelled at her lack of self assurance. Sometimes he had to fight hard to stop her self disparagement affecting his own opinion of her. It was making him over-protective as though he was her father. Was that why he'd become so cold towards her— some hidden incest fear? Ridiculous, he thought; that came of reading too much Freud when he should have been doing something better.

The rhythm stopped, the jogging mass paused. But the neon lights above the band that gave the results of the latest throw in the adjacent gaming room went on flashing, drawing cheers and groans from the revellers, some of whom were by now sending out waiters to place big stakes. The babel of voices rose in waves, broken occasionally by shrill peals of laughter. A small Chinese man, grinning and tipsy, a well known big spender, was pulled towards Diana by a slender Eurasian girl with olive skin, heavily outlined eyes and platinum blonde hair. "Diana sweetest. It's an age since I saw you." Diana blinked with surprise; she'd only met the girl once and said almost nothing whilst listening to her life story, or rather to the saga of her lovers, all of whom, it seemed, were rats. Robert couldn't make out everything she was saying now but snippets stood out: "I'll never forget how good you've been to me, Diana," and, "Think of me in a labour camp." Then there was something about her real lover trying to get a divorce from a clinging wife. "Oh Christ, I'd give my life for him", the girl stated passionately. At this, rather curiously, a dictum of Mao Tse-Tung came into Robert's mind—Soolan had quoted it a few days ago: "Sex is as materialistic a need as food and water." That was more to his own way of thinking than this girl's romantic twaddle.

The music started again. Big Spender was dragging the Eurasian girl, who was now tearful, away from Diana and Luiz. She disappeared into the throng calling, "So long Diana. So long. For ever. I'm going down wearing my make up." Luiz looked cross, said something about the girl being a disgrace and received a withering stare from Diana. "I can't remember her name at all," she said to Robert who replied rather absently but quite certainly, "Patsy de Souza. You met her at a party in the Bela Vista." This made her snap, "Of course, you would remember," after which she turned away to look at the dancers.

Soolan's appearance was abrupt. One moment she wasn't there, the next she'd taken up her position beside Robert as though it was her rightful place. Diana and Luiz turned to see her looking at them, self possessed and assertive. On the table was deposited her large square handbag, or was it a small brief case? As usual she wore European clothes—a well cut two-piece suit—and upswept hair that added to an impression of authority. Diana felt herself contracting inside and, as the star of her confidence collapsed, from a black point at its centre, waves of animosity began to radiate in all directions. Naturally an obsequious waiter descended on them to ask what Soolan wanted and naturally she ordered Scotch and soda as though speaking to a robot. As was to be expected, the swirl of dancers retreated a little from their table like an ebbing tide. And for sure, from now on, not a single officer would come up to ask Diana to dance. Soolan's slight figure seemed to represent the might of the People's Republic in the midst of all this decadence. Like everyone else, Diana had heard the rumour that some years ago this handsome woman, with her long Japanese looking face, was the mistress of some one very high indeed in the Communist hierarchy, first in Yenan and later in Peking, and that her husband had just disappeared from the scene. No one dare mention any names. It was also common knowledge that whenever she went to Canton to see her two children who were at school there, she stayed at the house of a member of the South China Bureau, well known for the number of attractive women, former actresses and the like, on his staff.

47

Clearly only someone with friends in extremely high places could live as freely as Mrs. Kwok Soolan.

Diana saw how Robert's manner had changed. He didn't look at Soolan the way he looked at other women; there was no obvious suggestion of desire. Instead of lolling on the couch he sat up properly, attentive to her words. His eyes rested on her frequently, full of admiration. "Come on Soo," he said. "If anyone knows what's going on, you do. Let us in on it." Diana wasn't interested in any reply that might be forthcoming. The word 'Soo' suggested too great an intimacy by far. Let Soolan dare call him 'Bob'. Of course Diana could understand Robert being impressed by the woman and her connections and by that mysterious job of hers—keeping tabs on everything and everybody, no doubt. But any one of the Cabaret girls was more attractive, which was frightening: Soolan didn't want money, she wanted something more serious.

"It's some sort of misunderstanding, an accident probably." Soolan's reply was offhand. "Such things happen." She leaned forward and looked steadily at Diana, for the first time paying any attention to her. "I'm so glad you're wearing the ear rings I got for you in Shanghai. They're charming on you." She doesn't know what's going on at all, Diana surmised, she doesn't know a bloody thing. But she replied in an excessively polite tone, calculated to irritate, "How very nice of you to say so, Mrs. Kwok; nevertheless are you not, as usual, praising your own good taste rather than mine?" Robert's bushy eyebrows for an instant looked like a water plant rippled by a current. A voice in the crowd behind her shouted, "Diana," and she wheeled round hoping it was Peter but it was only some acquaintance who was already being borne away. She longed for Peter's support. None would be forthcoming from Luiz who was busy ingratiating himself with Soolan.

As Diana had suspected, Soolan was quite ignorant about the position on the frontier. She'd already contacted the Chinese Chamber of Commerce, paradoxically the nerve centre of Communist power in the Colony, but her suggestion that their executive committee should meet had been resisted by the man she spoke to. No instructions had been received from Canton and it was clear the committee members didn't want to take action until they knew what the action should be. Despite her outward confidence Soolan was ill at ease. Could the radicals in the unions, who had no appreciation of the need to preserve the status quo, have cooked something up without letting her know? And had they been hand in glove with their counterparts in Canton? A flicker of anger passed through her mind at the thought. The people that mattered in Peking would vent their ire if the role of the Colony as a channel for the passage of war materials, for use in the struggle against the American imperialists in Korea, was now jeopardised. Abruptly she decided that tonight she'd ignore the complexities of politics as much as she had just ignored the hostility of Diana, and since there was nothing she could do for the moment about either she might as well give some attention to her personal life. She lit a cigarette, blew a jet of smoke at the black ceiling studded with starry points of light and abandoned herself to the mood around her. It was especially seductive because in her mind the Cabaret was associated with Robert, the first person to bring her here. And there was something else further back. The excitement reminded her of a night when she was still a student in Shanghai and an undoubtedly decadent uncle had taken her into the French Concession to a luxurious night club in the Rue Giraud. Although the ardent young Marxist she'd later married taught her to see the iniquities of such places, the experience remained a siren song in her memory and the cause of occasional regrets. Why shouldn't she enjoy the easier luxurious sort of life? Suppose she'd married one of the rich young men more typical of her parent's cosmopolitan set. She stifled the idea sternly; in another age, yes, but not now. Yet in Robert she couldn't help glimpsing, if not another age, the gilded life of the T'ang or the Sung dynasties, then at least the sophistication of another society altogether. He was the sort of man she'd have looked for, if she'd not been born into a time of ferment. For an instant, as she put down her glass, her hand touched his warm arm and she was surprised by the intensity of her sudden longing for him. Then she saw Diana looking at her coldly and leaned forward to say something to Luiz.

Diana felt a pang of guilt. It was rude to have spoken as she did. After all the ear rings were no ordinary present; they were of white jade and once belonged to Soolan's mother. She made herself listen to what Soolan was saying to Luiz, something about equipment for the Chinese Hospital, hoping to put in an intelligent comment when possible. Two hands suddenly rested over her eyes; she guessed at once who it was and turned to Peter. They looked at each other without speaking and she knew he saw the strain she was under. "Come on love. Let's dance." He drew her on to the floor without more ado and they were carried away in the stream.

Luiz glanced at his watch and said abruptly, "Oh God. I must be off. We'll have to talk about the hospital some other time, Soolan." To Robert he added, "Please give my apologies to Diana. Duty you know. I'm on duty." Robert felt sorry for him and was fulsome in his farewells, assuring him, though without reason, that there was nothing to worry about; the Colony was safe. He had the appearance of being Soolan's lieutenant as he spoke, turning to her slightly for confirmation which she gave with a puckering of her lips. When they were alone, she immediately stated with a forthrightness that took him aback, "In my opinion Diana should give Luiz a bit of encouragement. The poor man's crazy for her."

"And do you expect me to tell her that? She is my wife, you know." Robert gave an enigmatic little grin as he spoke. Soolan replied sardonically, "I'm married, you're married, he, she or it is married. Most people are married. Married shouldn't mean chained."

"There speaks the good Communist. You wouldn't suggest that to a peasant in your own country."

She surveyed him with a disarming smile, "But dear Bob, haven't you noticed: a) you're not a peasant—well you can't be, can you; there aren't any peasants in the U.K.; b) this isn't Communist China; and c) how do you know what I'm suggesting?"

"I don't. Tell me."

"In so many words?"

"In as many as you want."

She put her elbows on the table and rested her cheek on her fist. Robert found the gesture somehow masculine; it was like being interviewed for a job, he thought, as her searching eyes examined his face and his clothes. Perhaps he should open his mouth so she could inspect his teeth. "I'm suggesting…" She paused. "I'm suggesting we both get together, close together (she closed her eyes in mock rapture), with our arms around one another, our bodies pulsating together—on the dance floor." When Robert suggested that dancing might lose them the table, she said firmly, "No one, but no one will dare take this table."

On the dance floor they were indeed pressed together. "Is this close enough for you?" said Robert and Soolan's laughter was as gay as any sing song girl's. But her attentions went further than he wanted, considering the circumstances. It didn't matter about her pressing her leg between his thighs, a hostess' trick really and unnoticeable in that crowd, but why did she have to put her head so close to his. Soon, the law of cussedness inevitably impelled them right next to Diana and Peter who, sniffing the danger at once, decided to be facetious. "Me surplised you come Cabalet comlade. Position on flontir velly, velly bad." Soolan, who was adept at shooting back, hunched her shoulders Italian style and said, "Me no speaka da English. But me get you nice boy, Signor." Peter replied, "Yes, please," and then asked, "Have you left the Fig on his own? He won't like that. How cruel you are." Robert shouted above the din, "Oh, he's just gone off. He suddenly remembered he had to do a brain transplant." As everyone giggled and the danger seemed to have receded, then why the hell, Robert wondered, did Soolan have to come out with, "I hope you don't mind me borrowing Bob?"

Diana's smile, false to begin with, vanished entirely; she stood still for an instant watching Soolan's face turning green, red, orange and back to green again as a coloured light above whirled around. Then she said contemptuously and deliberately, "Bob's your old uncle." A moment later the subtle ebb and flow of the dance floor had borne the two couples apart but none of them had missed the hurt expression on Robert's face. Diana started to cry convulsively and Peter held her head close to him, kissing her and telling her to be calm. "Take me away from here," she implored. "I can't go back to that table. I can't."

People nearby were staring. Peter didn't care at all what anyone said about him in this place where everyone knew everybody's business, but Diana, so he felt, needed protection. "He's only dancing with her. Be reasonable. Look how we're dancing. Anyone would think we're in love."

She threw her head back so he had to look at her full in the face. "I do love you", she said. "I do love you. You're the only friend I have here." She took his face between her hands and kissed him. When his lips were free he gave an embarrassed little laugh and asked, "Now what d'you think everyone will say about that?"

"But it's different. I love you deeply. Not all that going to bed rubbish. Real love." She was vehement and obviously believed her own words.

"'Reel luv. Not all that going to bed rubbish.' Next you'll be telling me you're going to be a nun and love God. Come on. Forget about Soolan. It's nothing."

"Alright. But I'm not going back to them. I can't face Robert just now. Leave her with him. She wants him. It's not like you and me. You don't want to separate Robert and me. Give her a chance and you'll see what happens." Her own command made her determined. "Alright, I will give her a chance." She seized his hand. "Let's go now."

He let her lead him through the crowd; it was no use arguing. As they passed between the many-splendoured door dragons with hideous protruding electric light eyes, the music trailed away and they heard excited voices shouting things such as, "Broken through", and "Here in half an hour." Peter wanted to listen, but as far as Diana was concerned what was happening didn't matter. "I can't stay. Not an instant. I'll go on my own if you won't come."

They had barely left the Cabaret when a deep heavily accented voice came over the loudspeaker; it belonged to the 'Duchess', a decayed White Russian woman who hung about cadging drinks from Hong Kong visitors, a woman who had spent a lifetime fleeing from revolutions. "Everything finished. My friend Konstantin the chef, 'phone me from the Palace. We speak in Russian. Lung Yeung go to the Governor to ask him surrender. Portugal finished." She threw up her hands in a gesture of abandon.

Dismissive shouts were heard like, 'Ballocks' and 'Chuck her out,' but the majority of people were impressed. Cassandra-like, she stood before them, her skinny arms outstretched. "Everything quiet. Listen." In the hush that followed, her point seemed proved; the heavy thud of the mortars had stopped. "You see. No more firing. Who say Glasha lie."

"The woman's drunk," Soolan said in the hubbub that followed but her voice was thinner than usual. Robert looked about anxiously for Diana, but in vain. "I must find out what's happened. Let's go," Soolan whispered urgently, making for the door. The crowd let them through as easily as the Israelites passing between the waters. Soolan's face was so serious that not a few bystanders saw in it the harbinger of less gay times ahead. Though inwardly she was fearful that the unpredictable had happened, she found it difficult to believe Lung Yeung had made any arrangement with the Governor. What could he gain by the Colony's surrender? As they reached the door there was a sudden incomprehensible burst of laughter from the Filipino band and almost at once the music started again. The dancing was resumed with even greater zest. If the Reds were coming they'd find a party in full swing.

Outside the Cabaret the foyer was quiet. A little knot of people was at an open window listening. Soolan went over to them, spoke to a man she knew and was told, "There's still some firing, but only machine guns." A sporadic tat-tat-tat in the distance confirmed his words. She turned abruptly and bumped into Robert. He steadied her in his arms. "It's just mass hysteria in there," she began. His grip on her tightened and he pressed her to him. "Just hysteria. It's all crazy." She faltered a moment and then said, "Let's leave here; we could go to my place. Peter will look after Diana."

Almost at once Robert's desire for Soolan began to recede. Better to slake his need for sex with one of the Cabaret girls with no prospect of trouble, then afterwards a quiet ride home. Of course Peter would look after Diana. So he said, "Let's keep things as they are Soo. We're both alright as we are. I don't want you to get hurt." He also tried to give her a consolation prize kiss but she drew away, stooped to adjust a strap on her shoe and left him at a higher altitude to stare purse-mouthed at a Coca-Cola advertisement. To hide his embarrassment he strode into the fantan room and saw the Duchess watching a lone customer guess wrongly how many buttons were left from a pile reduced four at a time by the dealer. "I told you, two not three," she said as though the man was a fool. Then she saw Robert and sidled up to him, demanding a dollar when he asked if her announcement inside was true. "True? What is true? They want to hear everything finished, so Glasha tell them everything finished. I make everybody happy." She cackled. "What is true?" The floor captain who didn't like her pestering customers came up to Robert and asked, "Can I help you?" while the crone vanished into thin air.

"My wife. Have you seen her?"

"Ah yes sir. She left with Moh *Shin Saang*. They went off together—very good friends." The captain grinned maliciously, revealing his life-savings encompassing rotten teeth. Robert nodded indifferently and followed Soolan to the stairs.

On the next floor down a door burst open and a naked girl tried to escape the embraces of a priapic satyr; other satyr voices inside bellowed. A waiter stopped to watch the sport and as she was dragged back, mimicked, "*Pei ngoh hui*—Let me go." Robert jeered at Soolan, at himself, at the world in general. "That's all we are, animals with a bit of extra brain struck on." His desire for any of the girls evaporated and Soolan shouted, "Male pigs."

The barn-like restaurants on the mezzanine with names like, 'Ten Thousand Springs Pavilion,' and 'Palace of Delightful Visions,' were all empty and, therefore, far more ominous than the crowded Cabaret above. Without breaking her silence Soolan drew Robert into a small dining room marked, 'Northern Quietness.' Seated opposite her in a high backed mother of pearl studded chair he appeared shrunken and bereft of his usual serenity and she felt herself pitying him. "I'm sorry. I shouldn't have asked you to come back with me. It was wrong."

"Wrong. Nonsense. I didn't mind at all. But I don't want to get involved again. I want nothing complex. I've got that already."

Soolan was inclined to answer. 'Diana's an emotional leech.' but thought better of it. "She'll grow out of it by and by. I won't come between you, I promise. I won't demand anything." She noticed the look of doubt that passed over his face. Well, true or false, it was at least a statement of intent. "Jasmine tea," she ordered to a waiter who appeared bearing fragrant hot towels.

Why should this woman, older and less beautiful than Diana, be able to touch the capricious spring of desire in him at all? And why did he doubt her? She was old enough to know her limitations. His confidence began to return as he looked at her sitting so calmly before him. How sensible she was; with her there'd never be those black nights, awakened in the early hours to talk uselessly, to solace someone whose pleasure lay in not finding comfort. The warm towels made by the Eternally Happy Clothing Factory wiped a number of years away. He sipped the flowery tea and shuddered. "It's very cooling," she remonstrated using that weird word that had nothing to do with temperature. "Come," he said on an impulse. "Let's get away from here."

In front of the Casino, the Avenida Carlos de Silva was quiet. But the row of trishaw boys and Charlie the pimp, lurking to cater to anyone with more bizarre sexual proclivities that couldn't be satisfied in the Casino, were evidence that the world was as it should be. Robert's mood of despondency began to return; he wondered where Diana had got to and felt like a parent pining for a lost child. Something like a sigh that was not a sigh began to rise in him, originating it seemed near his heart and mounting into his brain. Why was he standing there like a zombie letting Soolan take control by ordering a trishaw? "Come on Robert," she said the moment she was ensconced on the green plastic seat. "We'll ride by the sea." Obediently he climbed in and sat beside her in silence, trying to get his brain going by deciphering some of the Chinese characters in the forest of vertical signboards bordering the street.

As they turned onto the Praia Grande they saw the Club Militar brightly lit and alive with people. The courtyard before its squat Doric columns was filled with cars disgorging members of the Colony's upper crust. Seizing the unexpected opportunity for further procrastination, Robert said he would like to go in to find out whether the military knew anything definite about the situation. Irritated, yet also amused, Soolan followed him into the entrance hall, the beauty of which was somewhat muted by a long formal portrait of a gloomy-faced Dr. Salazar, where she tactfully made off in a different direction.

The hurriedly put on elegance of the women present gave the Club the air of a festive occasion. Even rooms normally closed had been thrown open so that an impromptu party could be accommodated. Glancing into the dining room, Robert saw glittering lights reflecting the gold of the window curtains onto the deep green walls and over faces whose animated chatter had grown to a crescendo. The bar was doing a roaring trade and the quantities of liquor consumed were adding to the second atmosphere of improbable gaiety that they had experienced within the hour.

Before long an officer acquaintance had given him a garbled version of what had happened at the Barrier Gate. Now, he learned, all was well; a cease-fire was being negotiated but the firing wouldn't stop altogether until there was agreement. He was also told 'our gallant troops' had driven off a landing, killing a number of Reds with no loss to themselves. More exaggerated versions of this were being retailed about the Club and people who earlier were expecting a real invasion were now treating them as reports of a famous victory. "Are the stories true?" Robert at one point asked Colonel Lobato who was strutting about with the air of an eighteenth century General returned to an adulating court after a victory of manoevres. "Indeed so," he replied, then slipping into more confidential mood, hand on Robert's arm, adding, "But if we'd followed Lung Yeung's advice and stopped firing at once, we might have left them with a toehold in the Colony. Robert replied, "Ah," wondering what the reality behind such a tale could be.

Soolan got the true story out of Luiz Figueiredo who had been at the Club bar since arriving from the Cabaret. "There was no invasion at all. What lies. A handful of Chinese fisherfolk up river made a bolt for it in the confusion. They'd been wanting to come here for months. It seems they felt sure they'd be safe landing on the northwest side of the colony; everything was quiet up there. But there's a moon and just as the women and children were wading ashore, some of our guards spotted them and…" Soolan looked piercingly at Luiz who felt himself shrivelling up before her. "It was an easy mistake to make," he burst out. "Everyone was nervous, what with the firing further along the frontier. Imagine it: black figures coming up the shore. No wonder our men fired."

"Was anyone hurt?"

"Ten or so killed and fourteen wounded, perhaps more. The casualties are in the Chinese Hospital. Yes, I know it's terrible but it was a mistake." Soolan, busy thinking how the incident could be used to embarrass the Portuguese, replied coolly, "Oh, I realise mistakes can be made. It wasn't your fault in any case." Luiz, not too successfully pushed the guilt he felt to the back of his mind, smothering it with mental cushions marked, 'All a mistake' and, 'They're being well cared for', and even, but that was too ludicrous, 'Free funerals at state expense.'

Everyone there knew the provincial government in Canton would put the screw on the Colony, or rather its businessmen, for a large indemnity; this would be negotiated by Lung Yeung and paid for later by the ordinary people when prices went up. "But that's Lung Yeung's business," Lobato said airily. "We're not concerned with what he negotiates, so long as the Province (as though it was half an hour's drive from Lisbon) and our cultural mission in the East is unaffected."

"Thank you Senhor Colonel. I'm sure that on Lung Yeung's broad shoulders your cultural mission has the strongest foundations."

Lobato's wince extended slightly beyond the extremities of his moustache but he replied, "And where is Senhora Sheraton? I haven't seen her, I regret to say. She's such a light in our dull little society." Used to the Colonel's fulsome compliments about Diana, Robert responded with an air of boredom, "Oh she's around somewhere," and lost himself in the crowd.

Drifting from group to group he listened to the rumours and retailed a few himself with facetious embroidery. At the same time he felt sympathy for these pygmies bolstering their own morale with drink and talk of victory: how unreal their position yet how audacious—real opera buffa. The crush bore him near Soolan again and he heard Luiz pontificating, "... and I'm not saying that a great deal has been achieved here in the way of cultural synthesis, or that we Portuguese weren't interested in profit, but I do think we approached China somewhat differently from our European neighbours." The high, precious voice was obscured by the gabble, through which it nevertheless sounded like a thin woodwind in a difficult passage for full orchestra. In one of those pauses which can occur in the most crowded place, Soolan's "Rot" was a subtly scored burst from the tympani, after which more voices and Luiz' "...hardly an ardent Catholic but I deeply admire the way the seventeenth century Jesuits tried to relate Catholic civilisation to Chinese cultural values." A spot of Marxist rebuttal followed from Soolan who the next moment disappeared from view. Robert felt a twinge of regret, for brandy had revived the desire for her which gossip had deadened. A gloom, unaccountably deep for such a temporary setback, took hold of him. Disconsolately he made his way through the crowd, nodding, greeting, smiling—empty gestures to hide his emptiness—towards the door and down the steps where chauffeurs were carrying out a shadow version of the radiant internal party in the tobacco flavoured darkness. He thought of returning to the Cabaret. Then he heard a short burst of fire. Best to go home; Diana would surely be there. But by the sea a trishaw was waiting. "Sai-Lei-Tong *Shin Saang*," Soolan said in a cabaret girl voice and looked at him shyly such that the image of herself as a young girl for a moment shone through. He was glad to be so called and sitting beside her, kissed her tenderly while the trishaw boy, now soft-winged Eros bearing a cargo of love, sped them swiftly into the fleecy night.

Carlos had no intention of reporting for duty until all the guns had stopped. He gave a coded tap on the door of Old Chong's seedy hotel and after a minute or so, Mr. Chong himself unbarred the heavy door. "Come in. I suppose you want a room?" Carlos nodded. Old Chong was always willing to help policemen who knew too much about his dope smuggling activities. "Go up to room four. Is there anything you want?" After a moment's thought Carlos asked indifferently, "That plain girl Mei Ling. Is she in? I'd like her to play for me?" Old Chong nodded and rubbed his hands together. "Yes, of course. She'll come in a few minutes."

Carlos went upstairs. The moment he'd gone Mrs. Chong who'd overheard the conversation, let her shrill tongue fly at her husband. "Why d'you pander to that lazy sod. He never pays. What about the couple in room two? They've asked for Mei Ling." Mr. Chong took silent refuge behind a newspaper and his buxom wife, who fortunately for him never resorted to physical violence, stalked off into the kitchen. There her fourteen-year old niece Siu Ching was hard at work salaciously terrifying two servant girls no older than herself with lurid prophecies of their fate when the Red soldiers came. Leaning towards her audience, now well conditioned to the wickedness of men in uniform, she added, "I've just heard Carlos come in. He's going to rape Mei Ling. He's got a hold on Uncle Chong. He can get anything he wants out of him. Later, he'll do you too. No one can stop him." The two girls exploded into 'Aiyaahs' of fear and delight whilst their mentor, ever happy to talk of Carlos, went on. "And you wait. I saw him naked the other night—when he was with Jade Flute. It'll make you scream. Just like a cucumber." The girls gasped at the boldness of Siu Ching's espionage and went into hysterical giggles. It was too much for Mrs. Chong, who shouted, "No wonder this place is such a mess; look at it, mess everywhere. And all you do is talk about men. Men. Huh." They smothered their laughter but weren't perturbed. Mrs. Chong's moods were so erratic, one moment joking, the next scolding; no one took her too seriously. At that moment Mei Ling came in from the yard. Mrs. Chong nagged, "You, Mei Ling. Get up to room four. Your admirer's here again. And don't be up there too long." Mei Ling went reluctantly to a cupboard and took out her lute case. The very sight of it set the girls off again and this time Mrs. Chong joined in. Siu Ching shouted, "If he pulls it out, call for me," and rubbed one of her fingers in and out of her closed hand. Mei Ling tossed her head and said, "You can have him any time you want." She left the kitchen quickly but not to escape the coarse talk—she was used to that. She didn't want anyone to see her embarrassment.

As she passed through the dingy hall she saw Mr. Chong in urgent conversation with the manager of the Old Pawnshop. For once fat Lim didn't leer at her or ask her why she wouldn't come to work in his place. His face looked pastier than usual and his eyes were staring. Mr. Chong was obviously trying to calm him down with words like 'Be careful', 'Wait and see', 'It mightn't be so serious', but his advice seemed to be falling on deaf ears. Mei Ling hovered on the staircase, curious to listen. "Room Four," Mr. Chong shouted at her. "Be off, nosey."

Languorous on the bed, Carlos was staring at the ceiling and indulging in a sensual fantasy about Mei Ling. She wasn't beautiful and when she got older her open face might become like a dumpling. But for the moment she was fresh and innocent, her eyes large and brilliant, her nimble grace a walking advertisement for Old Chong's good treatment. She reminded him of a Tan, the warrior maiden in Chinese operas, capable of vanquishing all evil forces with the swift movements of the art of self defence. He saw her as a challenge and he wanted to be the first. However, all he got now was a distant nod as she took out the lute, drew the plectrums across it in a cascade of sound and began to sing:

> *Alone in a mountain hut staring at the wintry sky*
> *What shame when the imperial banners fell.*

Snow sweeps over the ruins and the dead
Yet still the cold wind bears the cries, the grief.

In sorrow recalling the Chiu Yeung T'in palace
Wine shops, shrines that stand no more.
Where should I flee to, where make my home?
Fluttering sleeves and silk robes, nowhere to be found.

Gone are the courtiers, gone the high officials
Imperial concubines vying before the throne.
Gone the music of the Pear Tree Garden
Silent the voice...

Mei Ling broke off. Carlos saw her tears; the song must have some personal meaning for her. "You sang well. I've not heard that before."

"My mother taught it to me. She was a clever woman—well educated too." She paused. "Do you want me to go on?"

Carlos revealed his superb teeth in a film star smile and went over to her. Gently but firmly she removed his hand from her shoulder. "Why are you so cold to me, Mei Ling? I want to talk and be friendly." But the lute was already back in its case. "I'm not a flower house girl. Just a lute player with a few songs. I'm not clever at conversation."

Carlos planted himself before the door. "Don't be so stuck up. Those girls earn an honest living. They don't take something for nothing. Old Chong picked you out of the gutter. Who do you think you are?"

Mei Ling glared at him. "I may be poor now. But my family was a good family, respected in the district too." There was pride in her voice. "I won't give myself to anyone. Huh. And who do you think you are? Get out of my way. Let me go."

"If you want to stay a virgin that's your loss. I don't want it if you don't." He sat down dejected, expecting Mei Ling to leave. Instead she looked down at him thoughtfully, then asked, "Shall I call another girl—Jade Flute perhaps?"

"No. Don't play for me again. Stick to Ah Tung; I've seen you both together."

But Mei Ling enjoyed playing for someone as attentive as Carlos, and he'd liked her mother's song. "It's lonely here." She looked round the drab room. "I'll stay and talk a while." She ran her fingers over the table to test for dust. "You're so vain. You think you're so handsome every girl must want you. So vain. Ah Tung's good looking, too, almost as nice as you—but that's not it, not it at all. I like talking with him. He's kind to me. He helped me when I was down; before I came here, when I was a refugee. But there's nothing between us."

"What do you talk about?"

"Oh, all sorts. About Hong Kong and how to get work there, about Moh *Shin Saang*. Ah Tung likes him doesn't he?" She gave Carlos a funny look but he said nothing. She prattled on. "Have you ever seen that beautiful red haired devil Moh *Shin Saang* goes about with? I'd like clothes like hers."

"Everyone in town's seen her, and her clothes. She must think a lot of herself," Carlos said carelessly. "I'm more interested in what Ah Tung talks about."

"Well, sometimes he asked what it was like in my village when the Reds came. He knows a lot about politics. I think he's very clever."

"Oh very clever." Carlos thought he saw through Ah Tung's methods.

Mei Ling shook her head. "Not everyone has that on his mind all the time. Ah Tung's interested in other things anyway."

"Like opium?"

"Clever people often smoke opium. They say it makes you think better." But Mei Ling doubted it.

"Clever people like girls."

"Then you be clever. Make me like you. You expect girls to go out like a candle when you've finished with them." She picked up the lute case with a show of indifference. "I've got to go. Do you want a girl?"

"I've had enough of this hole. Tell Old Chong I'm leaving."

"He's talking to fat Lim." Carlos pricked up his ears, wondering what the two old devils were up to. But Mei Ling was already on her way. At the door she hesitated, turned and said shyly, "I'm sorry you were disappointed. If you... Perhaps..." Blushing she went off to the kitchen where Siu Ching and her friends were still in plenary session.

Carlos went downstairs slowly, humming the song he'd just heard. In the hall he was surprised to find Lim talking rapidly with Ah Tung who had an open bag stuffed with clothes. Ah Tung was muttering something about boats and sails and nodded his head when Lim said he'd got the money. "How about Morgan?" Lim went on. He looked at Carlos suspiciously, then decided there was no harm in him listening. "Is he ready?"

"He's on the boat checking the gear. There was something wrong with the tiller." Ah Tung was very matter of fact. "It's time to go. Bring down that stuff of yours. I'll be waiting outside. He gave a signal to Carlos to follow him as Lim went upstairs for whatever it was he was bringing.

"What's the game?" Carlos asked as soon as they were through the door. If money was involved, he was going to get a cut. It was hardly the first time the two of them would be partners in crime. Ah Tung cracked his knuckles and looked thoughtful before saying, "Alright, I'll let you in on it. There's big money. But I wouldn't mind some help." Carlos grinned and suggested a fifty-fifty split which Ah Tung accepted with an air of irritation. "That's over two thousand," he said half to himself. Carlos' interest began to outweigh his doubts. "What was that about Peter going too?" he asked.

"He's not crazy. But Lim's going to run whatever happens. He's shit scared of the Reds, for good reason. He's hated by the people. No, Peter knows nothing about it. Once on the boat I'm getting my hands on most of the money before he clears off. He's an evil devil," Ah Tung added to weaken any scruples Carlos might have. "Anyway there's no risk. Lim will be so glad to get away, he'll forget his losses. "The trouble is, he's a big man. I'll need help. The boatman's reliable; he's my cousin. But he'll have to look to the boat. Now, if you were there…"

"You're sure he's got so much?" Carlos demanded, his suspicions still trying, though vainly, to keep at bay the prospect of all the fun, especially in its sexual form, that so much money would bring.

"Sure. He's cleaning out. He'll take every cent he can lay his filthy hands on. Now listen; when he comes out, say you're going to the boat to say good-bye to Peter."

A look of consternation suddenly appeared on Carlos' face. "What's up?" Ah Tung asked.

"Listen. There isn't much firing. He'll never leave if he thinks it's safe. Keep the fat devil on the grill. Stretch his nerves." The last words Carlos had picked up on his police training course. Ah Tung grinned. He knew Carlos was with him.

The door opened and Lim came out carrying a suitcase. He peered up and down the road apprehensively. Ah Tung said, "Carlos has heard the Portuguese are giving up. Let him come with us. He's got the same problem as you, Lim. Police will be in for it with the Reds here." Carlos caught on and begged for help, adding he knew enough about boats to help Morgan.

"Yes, yes, anything, anything. Let's go." In his mind's eye Lim could see the Reds pouring through the Barrier Gate.

As they started to make their way along the arcaded footway of the quayside godowns, there was sporadic rifle fire. After one particularly long burst Carlos cried, "Did you hear that? It came from the town. From indoors—that's why its muffled. They've started liquidating people already." He clutched Lim's arm. "Mother of God. Don't leave me behind."

Lim seemed glad to have a partner in terror. "I've friends in Hong Kong," he said breathlessly. "I can get the two of you fixed up." And remembering Carlos' tastes he added, "and with girls too! There's a much better choice there."

"You're a real friend," Carlos replied. "I'll not forget you. But shut up and keep in the shadows." Still holding onto Lim, Carlos saw that they kept up a good pace but sometimes he whispered, "O God," or "Jesus, Mary and Joseph," as though he was desperately fighting his own inner fears with prayer.

Before long they were opposite a decrepit jetty which probed like an emaciated finger into the deep water. On the down current side a solitary boat with a stern cabin was moored. "Look." Ah Tung squinted his eyes as though penetrating the darkness. "Someone's going into the cabin. It's Peter. Or the boatman. Why don't the idiots keep out of sight?"

"I can't see anyone," said Lim. In fact the entire scene was one of moonlit tranquillity but just then an army lorry sped by and they pressed themselves against the wall. "Officers going to the dockyard," whispered Carlos. "Those rats are sure to get away."

"Come on. Run," Ah Tung commanded. They followed him across the road onto the jetty and along it to the boat. Their footsteps on the old planks started up a loud rumbling sound. The structure quivered eerily. It was definitely unsafe.

"Where's Morgan? And the boatman?" Lim asked plaintively. Doubts were stirring in his mind as he stared down at the small craft, tethered by a single straining rope, bobbing about on the rushing water. Could they really get to Hong Kong in such a shell? Why hadn't he taken more notice of Old Chong? "There's no one down there," he complained. "Perhaps we..."

"Quiet. I've told you already. They're in the cabin. Carlos, take the luggage and get Lim in with them." Ah

Tung's manner was coldly efficient as he grasped the case and handed it to Carlos who was already on the ladder.

The fat man groaned; the case held a fortune in heroin. "Are you sure?" he whined.

"Don't be afraid; we're all in this together." Though Ah Tung's voice was firm it did nothing to reassure Lim. Moreover it persisted fiercely, "Let's go. Look. The tide's with us. That's good. Climb down. After Carlos. I'm right behind you." Reluctantly Lim went down the rickety ladder and stumbled into the boat which rocked dangerously low in the black tide.

"Follow Carlos into the cabin, quick." Ah Tung hissed angrily. "You don't want to be seen." Fearing even to glance at the water, Lim crawled towards the black aperture. But once through it, within that confined space, he knew he was trapped; there was no Morgan, no boatman, only the gentle voice of Carlos greeting him with, "Got you, Lim." Horror stricken, he turned to be seized by Ah Tung's steely hands which grasped his throat and forced him down until he lay with a knee grinding his fat stomach. One of the hands released him briefly but the next moment it was back jabbing a knife below his ear.

"Make a sound and you're dead. Carlos, get his money belt and open the case." Deft hands removed Lim's belt; then wallet and keys were taken from his pocket. His watch was torn from his wrist. The match Carlos struck momentarily lit up Ah Tung's hard face above him and Lim knew he could expect no mercy.

"Where's the heroin?" Carlos said rooting in the case. Ah Tung pressed the blade against Lim's flesh. "Inside the crabs," he croaked. "Ah Tung, have mercy. You're hurting. I've always been good to you."

"Liar, you've never been good to anyone except for cash."

"I've people on my back too. Mercy."

"What are you going to do?" Carlos' voice sounded thin but Ah Tung only asked how much money there was.

"Several thousand I guess. I can't see." Carlos found himself trembling as he replied. How could he have been so easily led? How could he have let his greed blind him to the inevitable?

"Get outside; I'll be with you in a minute." Carlos felt Lim's terror filling the cabin. He hesitated at the door and again asked, "What are you going to do?"

"Don't you want the money?"

"Yes. But I thought that was all we…" He broke off, appalled now at his own stupidity, as Lim implored, "Let me go. You can keep everything. I'll tell no one."

"You know what I'm going to do, don't you mother fucker." As he spoke Ah Tung gashed Lim's neck and the cabin was filled with a porcine squeal. Carlos pushed his way out. "Give the money back. Let him go. I don't want any of this. What about his clansmen? If they find out, we're dead. Let him go." His steps sounded rapidly across the boat and up the ladder, then died along the groaning jetty. For a few seconds both men listened intently until there was no sound but the creaking of the timbers and the sobbing of the water. Then Lim took to beseeching in a thin dry voice. "We'll forget everything. I'll give you money—as much as you want. Ah, the blade's hurting. I'm bleeding. Get off me. Do as Carlos says."

Ah Tung hesitated and heard Lim gasp with relief. But suddenly there came the sound of his own voice as the voice of someone else calling hoarsely from afar. "Yes, let him go. Let him ruin more men." The voice rose in force like a breaking storm. "Like he ruined your father. Yes, let him starve other families. Like your family starved." The voice was hysterical. Lim whimpered, "What are you saying? I've never seen your father."

"My father and ten thousand fathers," Ah Tung screamed. In rage he smashed and clawed the fat face and crushed the struggling body between his thighs; its agony raised a savage lust in him. Pressing his left hand over that bawling mouth and gouging the eyes with his nails, he drove the knife under Lim's ribs to his heart. The manager of the Old Pawnshop lay dead.

Peter still clasped Diana's hand as he led her into the maze of cobbled streets behind the Casino. The whole area was deserted and sepulchral in the clear moonlight, each louvred window and jalousie shut, each door barred so that the quaint houses with their painted stucco walls, low tiled roofs and wrought iron balconies looked like stage façades. On any other night, even in the small hours, the place would be teeming with life but tonight the nervous population cowered inside, waiting. "We're the last humans on the planet," said Peter still anxious to divert Diana by some flight of fancy. "You and I have got to repeople the world." She threw him a winsome smile; they linked arms and went on, careless of the noise of distant guns.

He could see that just being alone with him had made her recover her spirits more quickly than he'd thought possible. But after all, scenes with Robert had taken place in the Cabaret before; probably this one would soon be forgotten like the rest. Before long she was peering through narrow arches that led to intriguing passageways or at some strange bit of architecture that took her eye, just as though Robert and Soolan didn't exist. Her way of dealing with problems was, it seemed, simply to ignore them, as a child does by going out to play. Perhaps that was the natural way of dealing with sorrow; maybe, Peter reflected, he had so widened his own consciousness that any transient difficulty he faced became a source of perpetual anxiety. Certainly the desire to possess and be possessed that was at the heart of his love for Ah Tung never left his awareness completely. A twinge of jealousy made him play her up. "Before you came I hardly ever went to that dump," he said resentfully.

"Poor thing," she replied throwing him a condescending glance. "And how did you pass your precious evenings? Translating Confucius into archaic Greek verse I bet. I have dragged you down haven't I?" Her mockery ended in an irresponsible giggle,

"The likes of you would find it impossible to imagine; I went to bed early, got up early, lived quietly—glad to be on my own after that tedious job in Hong Kong (Diana began to play an imaginary violin). Probably I'd have left here if you'd not come. There'd have been no Cabaret night after night. Therefore no Ah Tung. Yes, it all comes of meeting you. Bloodsucker."

"You? Leave here? What a joke!" She pointed at him gravely. "So. You're not grateful to me for Ah Tung, the love of your life. Now that's really interesting, isn't it? You're not so glad you met him after all. You know he's really your evil genius. Good. You've still got a bit of sense left." She opened her eyes wide as though something had just dawned on her. "Yes. I get it at last. The penny's dropped. You don't really like men in the least. You just like danger. Taking risks. That's what thrills you." She walked in front of him swaying her hips Mae West like and leering over her shoulder. "Come on then honey. Take another risk. Give me a try. You can have yer small change back if you can't get upstairs."

"You can't fool me with that shit. You don't like men either. Just leading them on. Prick teasing—like you do with Luiz the Figleaf."

"I suppose you're right. You must be. You're the expert on pricks." She walked backwards before him, her face all repentance "Oh, Father, St. Bridget and the Blessed Virgin herself both know oi'm nuttin but a depraved woman so oi hope y'll be givin' me a real heavy penance." She began to sing a diddly daddly sort of Irish tune and to jig, arms at her sides, feet a-springing. Peter joined in, ever more absurdly, outclassing her of course, until she exploded with laughter at which he said, "Yer beyond redemption dahtar. But in future when the demon Lust gets inter yer, come straight to the presbytery an oi'll show you a good old fashioned way of gettin rid of 'im." She genuflected and he blessed her gravely. Why, he wondered, couldn't she forget Robert and always be like this? At once a contemptuous hidden voice demanded why he didn't apply such common sense to his own vortex with Ah Tung and that made him angry. Seizing Diana's hands he stared her in the eyes. "You know what? You're a bitch. The way you bugger up Robert's life. You're jealous, self centred, a real horror. You deserve everything you get." But his rough tone didn't intimidate her one jot. She replied, "Oh really Mr. Justice Morgan. Talking about ourself, are we? Well you might as well know: I'm even worse than you think; and your life I'm going to bugger up good and proper. I'm a Celtic witch. With terrible powers. Just see."

"I know what happens to witches. They get burned. Especially phoney Aussie witches. In bushfires I dare say"

"Oh dare you, old bean," she jeered. Then, like a name-calling school girl yelling, "Pommy queen, you couldn't burn a bit of crumpet," she pulled away from him and bounded off. "Come on Father Peter. I'll lead you a real witches' dance."

He was game for a run after being cooped up all night in the Old Pawnshop and the Cabaret, places where life and its problems were compressed like the iron core at the earth's centre, the pressure intolerable. When there was no room to manoevre, small worries became monsters but out here, where the streets ramified in all directions and the towers and hills soared upward, and far beyond them was the sky, at least proportion returned. He could almost believe that he was free to choose. And now, how good it was to run, to laugh, to shout, playmates together in a happy revival of childhood.

Suddenly she turned around, her arms outstretched towards him as he caught up. "Peter. Let's live together. I'll leave Robert. You could still see Ah Tung—any man you fancied. I'd bring you both things in bed; tea, toast, bottles of gin, anything you wanted. We'd shelter behind our own little Celtic fringe. Let's try it—like brother and sister. We'd be content."

He knew she meant it alright so he hedged with, "Content's not enough, for Celts." But he did respond to her embraces by kissing her which made her say, "Maybe you'd even get to like me as a woman." Something inside him immediately recoiled. No, it wouldn't work. It could never work because, lurking in the background, there'd always be the hope she'd just expressed. Life with Ah Tung might be hell but it must be what he wanted. Perhaps the misery of it kept him going. Diana pressed against him again insisting, "Let's try it. It's worth trying." Touched by her persistence he put his arm about her waist as they walked on again. "I wish it was possible," he said. "Really I do." His regret became something akin to sadness that it could never be so and, that being the case, he saw no point in pursuing the matter. "Let's do something crazy," he cried. "Up on St. Paul's hill. Don't ask me what. We'll see when we get there. But don't try to be serious about anything. If you make me take the world seriously I'll go crazy."

They began the ascent to St. Paul's walking slowly between rising terraces of majestic houses that might have been in some old Mediterranean town. Over doorways an occasion coat of arms or ancient lettering recalled the residence of a family from Algarve or Estremadura, though now the houses were taken over by Chinese who lived packed in the many cubicles into which the great rooms were divided. But outwardly few signs of Chinese occupation could be seen, for the Government did its best to preserve the buildings' external appearance. How bizarre, Peter thought, that these classical hunks of Europe should teem with people who must find such buildings dull indeed compared with the fantasy of Chinese architecture—if ever they gave a thought to such matters. Halfway up the hill he sat on the parapet of a little fountain while Diana examined a relief of some saint being martyred rather nastily. "Who's the human pin cushion?" he asked.

"Quite a nice young man. St. Sebastian I'd say. He's your patron saint I suppose."

"Wrong. I don't practice acupuncture." Having chortled at his own wit he went on, "God, the way you examine things. Like an earnest German tourist. You know, you should have been one of those poor frumps that no one wants. You'd have been much happier. You should have been some sort of academic—in a girl's school. Yes, I know—a geography teacher taking parties of girls on field expeditions, with little black note books. You'd deal with that quite well. An academic spinster who never had a bit of dicky." Putting his fingers in his mouth he gave a piercing whistle. "Rally girls. Form a crocodile." Diana threw a shoe at him; it fell into the basin. A chase around the fountain and some water splashing followed. Then they resumed their walk.

"Maybe you're right. At least Robert would be better off."

"Poor Diana. He married you for your beauty and now all he wants is your brain. I've never heard of such a thing. I can't think how you'll ever escape from him. You're quite unemployable and unlovable now. What will become of you?"

"I've let him down you know. I'm no help to him at all. He sees me as a self centred child. He finds me boring."

"I can understand that. Robert's so intensely wise. He exhausts me after five minutes—no three. Jesus. Can't you see who's self centred, who's really boring? Can't you see that you could do anything you want? That you have a good brain?"

But Diana wasn't listening. Her voice rose angrily. "If he's fed up with me why doesn't he tell me to clear off. It's like being back home—obey the conventions but never your feelings. He likes other women but hasn't the guts to tell me I make him sick." She noticed Peter giving her an odd look. "What's up? What is it?" she asked.

"I hope you won't mind me saying something."

"Go on you fool."

"Well." His voice fell.

"Perhaps…"

"Yes?"

"Perhaps you've got a stinky you-know-what."

"Oh you silly bastard!" She pummelled his back and ran after him laughing and fooling to the top of the zig zag street where he clambered onto a terrace wall above her reach and recited:

> Diana a hag from St. Mawes
> Suffered from piles and foul sores
> Even dogs in the street
> Wouldn't lick the green meat
> That drooled in festoons from her drawers.

We're just kids playing silly pranks, Diana thought as she climbed up to sit with him. Or are we playing with fire? "What would I do without you, Peter?"

"Grow up I suppose."

"You take me out of myself." She stroked his neck and kissed him.

"Into what?"

"Into—into not carrying a damn for anything."

"Pity you can't be like that with Robert. Why don't you try? It doesn't matter if he screws Soolan—a screw's only a screw—or cabaret girls, or boys, old men, dogs, cats, ducks. By the way do you know some people here really do screw ducks. You sit with it on your lap, insert your membrum virile and quack like mad when you come. It's wild. At least the duck is."

"Lor fucka duck. I don't think I could do that."

"I hope not. Ask Robert to try. What was I saying? Yes. Just leave him alone for a while."

"Yes Peter. Clever Peter. And tell me what else should I do?"

"Find a lover. Of course it might be difficult. You're so vile. Never mind. I'll find you a nice young man."

"That rules out Ah Tung then."

Peter immediately glanced at his watch. "Hey, listen. The firing's stopped."

"So what?"

"Come on. Last one up's a lemon."

They started up the magnificent steps that led to the baroque facade, all that remained of the ancient church of St. Paul. They were familiar with the three sculptured tiers: on the lowest, statues of Jesuit Saints, some like Francis Xavier and Loyola placed there before they were canonised; in the middle, the Virgin Mary flanked by angels, a fountain and the Tree of Life, a ship and a gorgon, a monster from the Apocalypse and a skeleton awaiting the day of resurrection; and above them all the risen Christ and the dove. The building wasn't really dedicated to St. Paul but to the Mother of God, as was proved by the Mater Dei above the doorway. The ruin seemed vaster and more beautiful than ever in the moonlight; the details they knew by day were obscured but the well ordered columns caught the gentle light as they rose towards the slender obelisks and the massive scrolls that crowned the pediment.

They no longer seemed to be walking up the steps but rather floating on a gentle breeze that bore them inexorably up to the space in front of the great temple. There, Peter made Diana wait whilst he disappeared behind the facade. All was silent save for the murmuring of the wind through the apertures and pinnacles. When he reappeared he was naked but carrying some white flowers which he scattered about her. Raising his arms towards the moon he declaimed:

> *Come Diana*
> *mistress of the night*
> *come from your mountains*
> *quit your sacred groves.*
> *Maiden Huntress*
> *with the red-eared hounds*
> *now I invoke thee:*
> *Dreadful Queen*
> *appear, appear, appear.*

Diana pulled off her clothes and walked with her arms before her towards Peter who backed in obeisance through the doorway. Beyond him everything was in darkness and Diana knew she had descended from the sky to a nether world. As she stood in the square of light falling through the doorway Peter again addressed her, now in a ham Shakespearian voice. "Speak Goddess. Speak. Reveal your fearsome doom." Combing her fingers through her hair, distorting her jaw, and rolling her eyes, she cackled like a witch and, from her lips, quite unpremeditated, came the words:

Hear me now
disdainful boy.
The Dreadful Queen
reveals your fate.
Another's knife,
another's life,
yet thou
art in the balance.

Peter drooped a limp hand saying, "Get you Delia," and she shouted, "There's only one dreadful queen around here and it ain't me."

He lay on the grass with Diana beside him. She stroked his skin which was soft and flawless. Her lips sought his lips and he gave her a peck of a kiss; her hands caressed his thighs, fondled him to stand. So masculine, so well-knit his body seemed to her now. Yet all the while he lay passive, not so much as a single touch, so that though she wanted him she was not aroused. Only his quickened breath as she rubbed his cock betrayed his excitement; his thigh thrashed against her as he came. She kissed him again and they were still. Now, she expected to feel flat but unexpectedly she was filled with the keenest anticipation. No sad memories of Tasmania, no gloom over Robert, no fears for the future troubled her. Just for a while she was sure that in this small, not at all satisfying moment of love with Peter, for it was indeed love, she had taken a necessary step. It was her first act of infidelity to, no of freedom from, Robert. She looked up at the moon and said to herself with all the sincerity of a devotee, "Free me. Help me. Guide me." Then she rested her head on Peter's stomach, took his no longer responsive cock in her hand and pressed it against her cheek. And since nothing further could be expected of him, Peter stroked her head and spread her long hair like a mantle over his chest. She thought she heard him whispering something but wasn't sure. Later, as they went slowly down the steps, they paused to gaze up at the tall facade moving proudly against the clouds. "I prayed to the Goddess," Diana said offhandedly. "I hope she doesn't give me a nasty shock."

"Who knows? Gods answer in their own way. Mine did."

"By sending you Ah Tung? What a divinely warped sense of humour."

The frolic was over. "Come. I"ll take you to the Old Pawnshop," Peter stated firmly. "Ah, you look pleased. Well, it'll do you good to see what it's like. I'll ask Ah Tung to teach you to smoke—just to annoy Robert." They walked on in silence until he remarked casually, "You weren't the only one to pray."

Diana uttered a protracted yawn. "Oh, here we go; another of your Ah Tung poems, I suppose." Her voice sounded bored and dispirited. The poems Peter wrote, always now for that contumacious Ah Tung, irritated her, not out of dislike for them but because the person to whom they were addressed was so unworthy (so she believed) of them. Yet the softness of Peter's voice, not to mention her curiosity, obliged her to turn towards him to hear:

> I prayed to Herakles
> lover of Hylas
> and my prayer was granted
> for the god has given me
> a perfumed rose
> surpassing in beauty

all the flowers
in the garland of Meleager
even soft-haired Myiskos
or Ouliades
a delicate sprig of thyme.
Tyrian God
bestower of favours
let the honey of my soul
be burned to ashes
if I neglect you offerings
for the blossom of Kypris.

What a world he lives in thought Diana. Boys two thousand years dead mean more to him than I do. I'm not even a twig in his blasted garland. Everything had gone stale again.

Lung Yeung put down the telephone as though it was something unclean and lay back wearily. A few years ago he would have felt gratified that his advice was being followed. Now, all he experienced was bored indifference, though at the back of his mind lurked regret that the collapse of the whole set-up was not imminent. The Governor had said, "You were right about the cease-fire. Everything's quiet. The Chamber of Commerce will have to send some-one to Canton to get things back to normal without delay."

"I fully understand Your Excellency. I'll ask the President of the Chamber to call a meeting quickly."

Of course there was no need to consult the Chamber of Commerce. He would have to conduct matters because his interests were the most vitally affected; yet the preservation of his empire brought him no comfort—merely the taking up of new positions from which further expansion would be necessary. In the hills of Burma, Thailand and Laos, more white poppies would be grown and more pack-animals bought to smuggle opium down from that 'Golden Triangle' along jungle-fringed roads and over frontiers to the sea. More officials would be sucked into the pool of corruption; the drug would be smuggled in steamers, junks and sampans into the town or to Hong Kong for re-export to other parts of Asia or away to Europe and America where more people would fall into its trap. The dollars from its sale would flow back in increasing volume. With them gold would be purchased for resale to the people of Asia who trusted in it more than bank accounts. His network was securely established and yearly his imperium grew, its boundaries limitless as the stupidity of mankind. Yet now he was merely an indispensable middle-man, a glorified functionary who couldn't step out of office because, if he did, too many people and organisations—not to mention governments—would be inconvenienced. If only some machine could be devised to perform his functions, to save him from becoming a machine himself.

He watched Ming Yuk moving noiselessly about the room, attending to small jobs and his lassitude increased. Ming Yuk saw to his needs as an acolyte might serve a deity but he didn't resent this jealous care for he could no longer stand a lot of people, especially servants, around him. He envied the youth that made such faith possible, even though he himself was for the younger man the ideal embodiment of power, wealth and wisdom for which youth itself was the most inadequate substitute.

There was a time when he had enjoyed testing the extent of Ming Yuk's obedience; it was fascinating to observe how, if a henchman needed punishment, Ming Yuk would take appropriately stern action or, if someone betrayed a confidence, Ming Yuk would ensure that pain, nicely calculated to prevent any repetition, was inflicted, all without pity or compunction. One day it was discovered that an employee whose duty it was to bribe the police, had been selling information about the organisation to the Hong Kong Special Branch. When the man was dragged into his office, Lung Yeung remembered he was a relative of Ming Yuk. Here at least family sentiment should provoke a plea for mercy.

"Strip him, bind him," Lung Yeung ordered the guards. "Now Ming Yuk, this man has betrayed my trust and yours too. You know the punishment." Ming Yuk hesitated; he was the one on trial. Lung Yeung continued. "If you want I'll pardon him because of your past services; but if you believe our organisation can allow no one, no one at all, to get away with treachery, then you must carry out the punishment— with this." And Lung Yeung held out a whip sparkling with steel teeth.

For what seemed an age Ming Yuk's hand hovered in the air, held back maybe by the pleas for mercy from the man on the floor. Then he seized the whip handle and brought the long tapering coil down and down again around the shrieking body which writhed about in vain to protect itself.

Lung Yeung recoiled from the submission to his will rather than the suffering. Ming Yuk's shouts of, "Die, die," each time the whip descended mingled horribly with the screams that filled the room. At length the victim was still and Ming Yuk's arm trailed the whip. His eyes glazed, his mouth loose and wet, he kneeled before Lung Yeung repeating, *"Chue yan, chue yan*—master, master." After that, testing the extent of Ming Yuk's devotion had become meaningless, for its limit, like the edge of the universe, must be beyond reach.

Tonight thoughts of his own limitations preoccupied Lung Yeung's mind; what was the use of power when his body was beset by frailty? Why did the habit of exercising power live on in him, despite his wish to be rid of it? He longed for sufficient strength to face up to the journey and the endless conferences in Canton. The rejuvenating injections of tissue sliced from still living lamb foetuses he'd been given in a Swiss clinic had done no more for him than they had for the Pope. But perhaps there were other ways—ancient charms and spells, which the rational part of his mind rejected. Not too long ago he'd tried the teachings of Yin Taoism which claimed long life could be achieved through sex. But if the Yellow Emperor had achieved immortality through making love to one thousand two hundred women, no such results had come Lung Yeung's way; he was glad to give up the effort. Yet what of the legends of immortal beings like fox-fairies who could suck the vitality from the young. Mightn't some antique truth be contained in such tales or in the Taoist doctrine of the Golden Elixir of Life.

Amidst the silken hangings of his ornate bed he reflected that it was not just youth he desired but the hope that stirred in youth. Even Ming Yuk's faith in him was a form of hope such as he himself would never experience again. Yet that capricious seer on the island in the estuary, a man much older than him, was in no way preoccupied by such problems as the absence or presence of youth and hope; beyond the Jade Pass there were no such considerations. Lung Yeung shook his head despairingly. No. How could he, burdened as he was with iniquity, follow in the Way? The ancient master had spent a lifetime in its discipline; wasn't it too late for an old businessman to study the esoteric teaching? He must go to the island again and seek the master's advice. His drowsy thoughts began to stray along cool corridors; he could smell incense, see carp pools in a courtyard and hear the boom of deep lunged gongs and the droning sutras of holy men.

"Your bath master." He felt Ming Yuk touching him gently, urging him towards the great bathroom. As he lay on the marble slab, his mind's eye roamed about that sea-girt monastery as though he were a visiting Bodhisattva while Ming Yuk's soapy hands gently massaged his parchment skin. Then warm water sluiced him and Ming Yuk asked him to enter the pool to swim.

"No, you go alone tonight; I'm too tired." He pulled a robe over his shoulders and shivered at the door leading into his air-conditioned bedroom. But for a little while, before he returned to his bed, he watched Ming Yuk's naked body thrusting, strong and muscular, through the distorting green water of the pool and the desire for youth came back with a harsh stab. There must be some way of regaining his lost strength; he'd leave no stone unturned to find it. Later on could come the act of renunciation and the Way.

The lights were dimmed and Ming Yuk approached the bed. "Is there anything else for me to do master? Any orders for tomorrow?" There was a brief silence, then Lung Yeung said, "Thank you for helping me so much." Ming Yuk was startled but gratified; such recognition of his services had never been made. He wanted to do more to show his worth and so he repeated his question. "No, there's nothing else. Oh yes. Mrs. Sheraton is due at four. I can't see her with all this trouble. Tell her I'm very sorry."

"Of course," Ming Yuk replied, glad to receive this order. He was about to go but felt he should say something else. "You can always depend on me," he stammered. "I can be like you own arm." He put out his right arm and Lung Yeung felt its warmth near him and touched it. "Your arm is strong. The days ahead will be tiring. I'll need your strength beside me."

Ming Yuk's cup was running over; he was recognised as Lung Yeung's sustainer. The grasp on him grew tighter. "Yes, I need your strength, I need your youth. I feel power coming into me from you. Don't begrudge it to me."

A shudder passed through Ming Yuk's body as though he were the victim of a vampire; he didn't know whether he was afraid or joyful, nor what was expected of him as he leaned over the bed whispering, "You can have whatever you want from me." His master was touching him softly, caressing him with a withered hand; a toothless mouth sucked on him and, wonderful to relate, aroused him. He remembered talk of prisoners of war surviving by doing this to Japanese soldiers. Yes, if this could help Lung Yeung to be strong, it was good. He'd give his strength to Lung Yeung like this, as much as Lung Yeung wanted. Yes. Everyday he'd let Lung Yeung drink his strength. He was coming; yes, his strength was becoming the strength of Lung Yeung.

His lips drew in the jet surging up the stem of the opium pipe to suffuse his tired body with pleasure and well-being, but Ah Tung couldn't banish the memory of Lim's death, those pleas for mercy, the peculiar feel of the dagger going into the body. He shuddered to think of that last scream. Where could the body, pushed into the water, have got to, and the boat which he'd shoved out into the current without bothering to pick up the money. His own safety now depended on the outgoing tide; it would get around that Lim had planned to leave, but if the body or the boat was found, he'd be dead.

He felt he'd done well to hole up in the Red Pleasure Pavilion where, despite everything, a packed crowd was smoking and gambling; in fact, through the round opening in the floor of the room where he lay, people were letting down bets in little baskets to the gaming table on the ground floor with more abandon than usual. No one would think of looking for him in such a public place. Before long he'd get a message to Peter; now the two of them would have to go away, to Hong Kong. No, somewhere less risky. What about Sheraton *taai taai*'s country, Australia? She must have a kind family who would put them up for a while. But they could decide all that later, when he had recovered his balance.

Doing his best to forget his problems he listened to the crippled masseur Pai Chai rambling on about the difficulty of making money. Despite his repulsiveness, the malformed legs that gave him a staggering gait and the shaking head completely devoid of hair, Pai Chai had the reputation of possessing a magic touch; many men would have been surprised to know their mistresses submitted their bored bodies to those soft white hands with their long fingernails for the pleasure their lovers failed to bring. Ah Tung always pitied Pai Chai for he knew that the sorrow of his life lay in the fact that whilst women's charms often lay open to his gaze and touch, his loathsome appearance put their real possession out of the question.

Pai Chai played the servant well. When a refill was wanted he was ready with it, squatting on his haunches and holding the pipe for Ah Tung to inhale. He watched the lips pressed to the mouthpiece with a tender expression, vicariously enjoying the calm he himself knew so well. Pai Chai's imperfections made him take an abnormal interest in other people's bodily pleasures. His long experience of soothing people told him Ah Tung needed everything the drug could give and more, to move upward to the harmony that still lay far above.

On the black screen of Ah Tung's mind, images began to appear from far back in his childhood when his mother had enough money to take him to the opera. There was a wide stage with two contending figures: his father and fat Lim dressed in glorious costumes brilliant against the darkness. Whirling in patterned armour, gaudy with silver and gold and studded with flashing mirrors, the fearsome figures circled round, flags and banners protruding from their backs and long pheasant tail-plumes flailing as they tossed their heads in angry gestures. Each carried a horse whip and a tasselled spear with which they lunged and parried. Lim was white-faced and evil, his father in the good black-faced style. As they performed their steps of battle, raising their knees majestically and thrashing out their arms, their awesome faces became confused, the black and the white interchanged. Their anger began to flow away from one another towards Ah Tung and he no longer dared to look. He opened his eyes and saw Pai Chai squatting near him.

"You need more." Pai Chai prepared another pipe. Ah Tung stared at his translucent skin suggestive of leprosy then turned away and looked beyond the dim lamp at two addicts who were sharing a pipe between them. They lay one behind the other and he saw the nearest figure was a haggard woman who'd once been a famous opera star in Shanghai. When she finished inhaling, her thin fingers put the pipe down slowly and she peered through the lamp flame and beyond it through his own gaze to some far away place where once more she was the cynosure of ten thousand eyes.

He thought of Peter and longed for the only love he'd been given in his life. Why hadn't Peter gone home with him when he'd asked? He was Peter's lover, not Sheraton *taai taai*. A yearning to get away began to rend his mind and body; he sat up gasping for breath. Pai Chai said, "Your mouth's dry. Here, have some tea."

Delicate fingers opened a packet of heroin and sprinkled it into an opened cigarette; Pai Chai's long gasp of pleasure as he exhaled reminded Ah Tung of his father long ago. The cigarette was held out to him; he took it but hesitated. Closing his eyes an instant he saw white-face exulting over black-face and staring at him in triumph; when he opened them again he was already drawing on the cigarette. Pai Chai was nodding. "*Ho lah, ho lah*—very good, very good," and putting more heroin in another cigarette. Ah Tung tried to say, "Peter. Come for me. Take me away," but he was already experiencing a wave of pleasure. The second cigarette was put between his lips and he was going up higher. He was in a white world, white the colour of death, white hands, white fingers, the white face of dead Lim, a dazzling expanse of soft white heroin, a white breath of pleasure drifting forever and ever among cold white clouds.

The horror of the jetty drove Carlos straight to Mei Ling. They went into the backyard of the hotel where he told her everything that had happened. It gave her a shock but all the same she was flattered that he'd come to her for advice. Then she noticed the fear in his eyes and put her arms around him even though she herself was frightened lest anyone in the hotel should come along and suspect anything. "You've told me the truth haven't you?" she whispered.

"Yes. Yes."

"Did anyone see you along the road?"

"I don't think so. No. I'm sure."

She thought it over; why bother about Lim? Everyone knew he was a foul exploiter. Her loyalty lay with Ah Tung who'd befriended her and now, it seemed, with Carlos. "Old Chong knows Lim and Ah Tung went to the boat. He doesn't know you were with them. If anyone asks, I'll say you came round to the back door to see me again. The girls were asleep so they can't deny it. Do you understand?" Do you understand me, Carlos?" He looked so frightened she thought he wasn't listening.

"Yes, Mei Ling. Thank you. Thank you."

"Did you hear any noises from the boat after you left?"

"No. I ran. Like bullet."

"Then you don't know for sure what Ah Tung did."

"No. I'm afraid he must have..." He didn't complete the sentence. As they looked at each other both feared the worst.

"If you find him, tell him to lie low. I think it's best if you go to the Old Pawnshop now."

"Why?" He looked alarmed.

"Say you've come to see Mr. Lim. Then no one will suspect you later. Obviously you knew nothing. And if he is there, you'll be sure everything's safe."

Carlos was impressed by Mei Ling's cool handling of the problem. He clung to her and then felt surprised that she'd let him touch her at all. "There, there," she said patting his cheek. "I won't let you down." She gave a demure look. "I like you—very much." Even though you are a bit stupid, she thought to herself. "I'm sorry I was rude earlier."

The promise of her affection was the best tonic for his troubles. He insisted that he'd come and see her soon, "and talk", he added. "I'll not trouble you that way again."

"Oh. How do you know I won't want you to—one day. Anyway, go now." She peeped into the alley to see the coast was clear and let him out.

When he got to the Old Pawnshop he found Lim's assistant and said, "I've come from the barracks. Everything's quiet now; there's no need to worry. I told Mr. Lim I'd come and see him. I hope he isn't asleep."

"So, he's expecting you?"

"Of course he is. Didn't I just say so?"

The assistant rubbed his hands together. "I knew he couldn't have gone away. I'm sure he'll be back soon. Go right up to his room." On the way up the stairs Carlos put his head into the cubicle where he and his friends usually met to see if Peter was there but it was empty.

He had never been in Lim's room before and was surprised to find it very comfortable. On the floor was a thick sulphur coloured carpet with a blue pattern. Before an altar, burning joss sticks filled the air with incense. Hidden away somewhere an air-conditioner quietly hummed away. There were four black chairs and a low table studded with mother-of-pearl while on the walls, glowing yellow in the light of a magnificently ornate lantern, were hung a number of antique scrolls. At the back of the canopied bed a low mirror was set in an elaborate frame above which was a row of pictures which, Carlos soon noted, illustrated libidinous episodes in the life of Ch'ing Hsi Men, hero of the novel, *Chin P'ing Mei*. Carlos had never associated Lim with such interests; for one thing his obesity had always suggested age. But on the shelves he discovered that the pictures of Hsi Men's activities were but a hint of Lim's collection; there were volumes such as Chao Tzu Ang's *Spring Palace* showing the thirty-six positions of vernal dalliance, pornographic figurines, photographs and magazines and a variety of erotic toys and gadgets, some of most peculiar shape.

He walked about the room looking at the scroll paintings: the first four, each depicting several events simultaneously, told how the tyrannical Chou Hsin, last Sovereign of Shang, to please his consort Ta Chi, decreed in the forest a lake of wine beside which he gave a banquet; from the trees hunks of raw meat were hung so that Ta Chi might watch naked warriors and girls gnawing and clawing at them with the lustful consequences depicted in the other scrolls on which the same revellers were shown, amidst gravely indifferent leopards and tigers, making every possible contact with one another's bodies, without the coy expressions of the ladies ever showing a hint of passion as their bodies yielded to the muscular soldiery. Against each section of the scroll, a line of verse in flowing characters superfluously described its content—'they enjoy the delightful spasms of flying brush and dancing ink', assigned definitions as in a catalogue—'a greedy steed galloping to the manger', 'the rabbit nibbles the hair' or recorded Ta Chi's less poetic cries of delight such as 'Shove it right up, you rutting dog.' A fifth scroll in a different style, a single picture of great delicacy, a misty expanse with figures merely hinted at, showed the intemperate Duke Ling of Wei demeaning himself, in the eyes of his courtiers, by sharing a peach with an almond-eyed page. The two protagonists' gestures suggested depth of feeling but the lines beside the picture said, unambiguously enough, `condescending prelude to the exquisite intimacies of the rear vermillion portal.' At length, sated with it all, Carlos undressed and sprawled on the bed looking at his own body, innocent beside the rioting forms about the walls, dreamily reflected within the confines of the mirror. Within a few minutes the turmoil of the day brought its reward and Mei Ling's pride, Lim's terror and his own anxiety were all lost in sleep.

And so he lay when Diana and Peter arrived at the Old Pawnshop looking for their friends. Diana was astonished at the contrast between the room and the squalor through which they'd climbed. Peter gazed with admiration at Carlos whose body, it seemed, had turned into gold. He was also relieved; if Carlos was here, Ah Tung couldn't be far away.

"There, just as I promised." He had to make the claim. "Your Endymion." Diana, however, was reluctant to go too near this sumptuous idol of which one half-sleeping member was clearly not of clay, even if the feet hidden beneath the crimson folds of the coverlet were, and even though Peter gushed "Isn't it marvellous?" in her ear. He seems to think he's giving a present to a child, Diana thought. Does he expect me to say, 'Oh thank you Uncle Peter, thank you for such a beautiful toy.' But she replied, "I'll leave you to play with `it'. Women don't think in that way, my dear Peter."

"Oh really. How fascinating. Well, I believe you're frightened. But never mind. It's only a viewing—you don't have to buy if the price is too high." Then he complained, "You never seem to know when I'm joking." Yet did he know that himself? "Good," he rattled on. "There's some opium. Be like Alice; try it—maybe you'll grow up (or shrink, she thought). We won't wake Endymion; we won't even risk covering him. In no way shall he be disturbed."

To prove her indifference to all this nonsense she sat on Endymion's bed and took some of the cold tea left on the table while Peter, now perched elf-like on a stool, watched her impatiently but waited her Titanian observations in vain since she merely gazed at the design on her cup as though it was something of great significance rather than a common pattern of stylised ducks. Soon he tired of his Puckish role and got up to look at Lim's pictures; only then did she turn and allow herself a furtive glance at Carlos like someone contemplating theft. That was when she noticed the artwork above the mirror—of course it was entirely appropriate to the place; its absence would have been more remarkable—and when she was suddenly taken by the notion that the entire room was unreal—a cube of golden light suspended in a black sky in which the stars were silvery boys poised to dive into the sea at the approach of dawn. Did it really matter what she did in here? This hidden place wasn't the ordinary world of marriage and money and living. Here she was nothing but an image in the dream of a beautiful youth who'd preferred everlasting sleep to the sorrow of death.

"Very well. I'll try some of your wonderful drug. Will it give me visions?" (but Xanadu itself couldn't have much over this place). As she spoke, Carlos made a purring sound and turned on his side toward her. She glanced at her watch without taking in the time. "Never mind. I think we'd better go." But it was too late; her bedfellow began to murmur and somehow or other rolled forward as it were in sleep, so that his leg pressed against her. She said loudly, "Yes, I'm going." Carlos opened his eyes, gave a startled cry (Peter knew it was all fake.) and wrapped the coverlet around him like a sarong in a superfluous show of modesty. "Where's Ah Tung got to?" Peter asked. "Oh sorry. This is Diana." Carlos gave her an intent look, dead in the eyes, said, "Hello. I'm Carlos," and then went on vaguely, "Ah Tung. Ah yes, I did see him." He sat up and gazed at the coverlet. "At Old Chong's Hotel—that's where it was. There was some talk of getting away to Hong Kong. I didn't really listen. I had to go back to the barracks." He looked quickly round the room. "Fat Lim isn't back, is he?"

Peter was uneasy. Could Ah Tung have been mad enough to try to get away by sea, perhaps tempted by Lim's money? No, impossible; Ah Tung would never leave him like that. But Carlos suddenly remembered. "Yes. He said he was going back to your place." (Carlos did think that would be Ah Tung's best hideout.) Peter sighed with relief.

Diana was finding Carlos awake less intimidating than asleep. "Stop bothering about Ah Tung," she said. "He'll never leave you. He knows which side his bread's buttered." Carlos gave her a radiant beam as though she'd said something brilliant and the ice between them began to melt in large lumps when she returned it fulsomely.

"We'll stay if you want to then," Peter replied, intrigued by Diana's swift change of mood. `Women don't think in that way,' she had just said. Then how did they think? Hypocritically? He began to thumb through Lim's photographs. The badly taken pictures reminded him of the days when sex had been like that for him—crude and loveless, but undeniably pleasurable. It was different with Ah Tung; beneath the harshness there was affection, even, dare he believe it, love, though not so much pleasure. Diana didn't know about that—or about many other things. "Look." He thrust a photograph under her nose. "What about this, milady?" Carlos pushed it away. "Don't look," he ordered. You shouldn't see such things." Diana laughed and said in a blasé voice, "Why should it bother me?" Carlos drew back his hand. She blushed. Peter crowed, "Told you so. Not 'pure' like you and me playing together naked in the moonlight."

"What's this? What have I been missing?" Carlos looked from one to the other. No one enlightened him and Peter began to finger the opium pipe like a piccolo (he's going into one of his crazy moods, Diana thought). "Go on you two," he cried, "Dance naked for me. That's what I'd like to see." "Give her some opium," Carlos said firmly. Peter bowed like a well-trained houseboy, repeating "Yes *shin saang*," as he went obediently about his task. Carlos chuckled. "I want to see Diana smoking. Who'd have thought of it? An Englishwoman smoking in here. I wonder if you'll enjoy it." Twirling the opium over the lamp, Peter said, "Of course she'll like it. But not if you accuse her of being English; she's Australian. Which means she'll enjoy doing anything offbeat, won't you darling?"

Dance for me, smoke for me; I wonder what the next order will be, Diana thought but she replied, "Offbeat? He must be talking about himself," to an unlistening Carlos who'd started to draw her attention to the seamy pictures above the mirror. "For instance, these would definitely interest Peter more than me," she insisted. "But I don't remember Hsi Men doing that in the version I read." Carlos pressed against her and whispered, "Hsi Men could do anything. He's my hero, you know." The pressure of his body against her tended to prove his statement. Diana moved to the edge of the bed; she must be cracked to carry on like this. It wasn't what she wanted in the least. Yet instead of deciding there and then to leave, she started a conversation. "So you've read the *Chin P'ing Mei*. I thought you were educated in Portuguese." Her words sounded like an opening gambit at a drinks party and Dr. Carlos Nolasco, adjusting his sarong, replied airily, "I was. My father saw to that. But my mother made sure I learned Chinese—in fact I read it better than Portuguese. And of course I learned English; you miss too much," jettisoning his doctorate with a leer, "if you can't speak English."

"But what do you think in?" She was now an anthropologist posing the sort of silly question that elicits a fabricated answer. Ignoring Peter's, "He doesn't think, he feels," she continued, "And how do you think—like a Chinese or a European?"

"I think like myself of course. And I don't divide people up—like different kinds of rice. Yes I do—into men and women; that's the best division—and people like Peter." From amidst a cloud of fumes Peter said, "People like me, indeed. But we are different I suppose. Sky born, that's it." He flourished the opium pipe, "Akin to the gods." Diana felt rather foolish—Carlos wasn't just another of Peter's beautiful oafs. There was something else about him. Already inclined to invest him with laudable attributes, she persuaded herself that it must be self-assurance without the slightest hint of arrogance.

Peter handed her the prepared opium pipe and Carlos, settling down behind her, said, "You can't smoke sitting up. Here, lie down. I'll help you." The Chinese bed was hard against her hip so with much fuss he put one of Lim's dainty pillows beneath her.

"We must get Robert to paint you like this," Peter murmured. "An odalisque with Carlos as a eunuch." He steadied the end of the pipe over the lamp while Carlos held the mouthpiece to her lips. She took a long deep inhalation and then lay back gazing at the canopy, all gold and red, phoenixes and flowers, above her. "I don't feel a thing. It's all a hoax."

"Wait a bit and have some more." Carlos stroked back some strands of hair that had strayed over her face. His hand remained against her neck and he leaned over her eclipsing the canopy; how voluptuous his half opened lips, his dreamy mentally undressing her eyes with those long upcurling eyelashes. His hand stroking her cheek, her shoulder, caressing her breast, was soothing, sensuous warmth after a long chill journey; why bother to stop him? This was what she should have done earlier. She was surprised to realise she didn't care at all what Robert was up to; Soolan or cabaret girls, what did it matter. It was his business. And this was hers. In this magic box, life could start afresh.

She closed her eyes and sighed; everything was so peaceful. She was floating gently amidst clouds of incense, yet vividly aware of herself and, without opening her eyes, of the whole room about her. Lips moved lightly over hers, fingers explored, clothes slipped away, resistance was ended. "Come," she whispered. "Come and lie with us, Peter." She stretched out her arm and as he got on the bed she turned towards him. Taking his hand she drew it across her so he could hold that part he would surely most appreciate of Carlos whose embraces of her had also become more intimate. Then she shuddered and said, "It's cold. It must be the air-conditioning." Carlos threw the coverlet over them like a fisherman netting fish. Trapped, she thought, but that was nonsense; what was happening now was inevitable the moment they'd entered the room. Had Peter engineered the situation or had she still been stalking him—but who cared? Hidden up here where everything was a mirror reflecting her need for love, she was able to do as she chose. Gradually she abandoned herself entirely, her heart, so she thought, to Peter, her body to Carlos whose practised lips and flickering tongue strayed everywhere but most wonderfully over her breasts or between her legs, arousing her, leading her to freedom. Then let it be as in the scroll paintings—the oblivion of indifference in a sea of desire; let Peter love her with the strength he drew from Carlos. The three of them were soon playing at Twin Dragons teasing the Phoenix, though it took a little while to master the subtle rhythms of the game; sometimes her lips met those of Carlos and sometimes Peter's, or her eyes would open to see her two lovers kissing like passionate boys in an ancient myth. In the golden light she caught a glimpse in the mirror of an idyll to stimulate a jaded Empress; they'd become a mere addition to Lim's collection. Carlos led them on but it was not only their images that were moving in the gentle light; above the mirror Hsi Men turned towards Golden Lotus and all the skilled concubines and cherry-lipped singing boys who'd ever delighted him. Their master's frolics were observed by gleeful girls hidden behind screens, until lascivious yearning made them run to the banks of a willow-fringed river to play with lusty fisher-boys in the lecherous sport of Mandarin Ducks. The excited cries of Chou Hsin's spintriae could be heard bringing their regenerative rites from among the meat-laden trees into the golden room; sophisticated ladies with demure eyes let muscular arms and legs entwine them like vines as they were impaled on jerking warriors; photographs disgorged coupling figures happy to escape from shabby Siamese hotel rooms and the prurient eyes of photographers to revel wherever they chose; the *Chin P'ing Mei* opened up and from its pages trooped beautiful women and ardent youths, throwing aside their embroidered clothes, their tasselled hats and painted fans to join in the frenzy. The air was filled with the sound of gamelans and gongs, shrill *t'i tsi* flutes and subtle rhythmed drums. Erotic instruments were used in a thousand different ways; men were loving women loving women loving men loving men loving women; there was no longer the love of any single person or the love of self but only a cascade of golden fire pouring down to dance within and about them, illuminating their bodies and their hearts with delight. At last the quivering light receded and the lantern glowed softly in the corner of the room; the tangled lovers returned to their frozen positions in the scrolls and Hsi Men and his companions were behind glass frames or vanished into the pages of an ancient volume. The music ceased and awakening from their joyful frenzy, the three lovers lay still in each other's arms on the carpet of sulphurous gold.

The dawn bathed Soolan's apartment in its paradoxical light; it would be another of those damp hot days calculated to fray the spirit. Robert was irritated already. The antique air-conditioner that wheezed and spluttered in response to the enigmatic electricity supply, chilled him one moment but the next encouraged his sweat with a blast of warm air. It was like lying in a swamp. But there was another paradox; if his night of love making had been so satisfying, why had he woken up full of anxiety about Diana instead of thinking of pleasures to be repeated.

From the bathroom came a duet of water and song, gay sounds that yet tended to depress his spirit. How pointless was pleasure when it brought nothing but regrets. He should have worked things out more carefully. Trouble lay ahead. Soolan loved him, no doubt about it, and a relationship with her couldn't be ephemeral. The cause of his disquiet was only too clear; he might be expected to make a choice. The idea annoyed him so much he put it out of his mind and tried to remember what he'd been dreaming of. There was a vague memory of Diana working to support him. "Ha," he exclaimed aloud at such an unlikely inversion of reality. Then Soolan's voice chimed from amidst cosmetic activity now too painstaking, it seemed, to let her sing. "What did you say dah-ling?" "Just coughing," he replied; but a second later he had to repeat the phrase in a bawl, in reply to a, "What?" distorted by lips holding hair pins. Her "I won't be long dahling," that followed, suggested a further misinterpretation; she must be fixing her face or making some other disposition for renewed dalliance. Such activity summoned various mildly erotic pictures of the Boucher type to his mind: la toilette de Vénus, la toilette d'Arethuse, la toilette de Mlle de bewigged-and-powdered this, that or the other between times with Louis XV, all amidst silken hangings with little grinning black boys in turbans—I wonder what happened to them sometimes when Louis was off hunting—and fat cheeked Cupids holding up mirrors.

How different that perfumed world was from Soolan's. What choices might be forced on her. Or would she be allowed to make a choice at all. He covered his head with the bed sheet and thought hard of solutions but how could he come up with any when he didn't know all the questions. Yet after all, it wasn't too late; even if his body hadn't behaved with much restraint, he could still detach himself without more ado. Nothing must come between him and his work, only to that should he give absolute enthusiasm, only in that exercise any capacity for decision. Before he could even decide to get up, the watery music next door ended with a cadenza on the WC, and the naked body of Soolan appeared and at once exerted its fascination. Why resist a woman who wanted him so much and did everything to gratify. He 'had his way with her' again or was she 'having her way' with him? When he'd come, she persisted in caresses that suggested her love was of an enduring nature. Robert responded with a mechanical practice adequate to dispel suspicions of indifference whilst all the time wondering how much longer he should stay there before withdrawing his firmly held tool. At length by, as it were, accidentally benumbing her leg with the weight of his body he caused her to shift and took her little grimace as a hint that their amorous conflict was over. "You're not getting up yet Bob?" She enticed him down once more but he gave a sad little smile of regret, shaking his head the while, as though in the movement of her leg he'd suddenly glimpsed the invisible worm secretly destroying the sick rose. "Oh you've had enough of me. You need a little rest. I'm selfish keeping you awake so long."

"How could anyone ever call you selfish dah-ling?" You've given me so much love. It's never been like this before..." (Why do lovers always use that phrase, he thought.) She continued in like vein all the while fondling him so he began to feel schizophrenic as his hide began to rise again. But good Dr. Jekyll regretted, "Saying that only makes me feel worse. I shouldn't give you any sort of love, upsetting you, making us want to see each other again." He must be seen to be making an act of renunciation. "We belong to different worlds. Do you think they'll let you carry on with me—a decadent artist at that?" To which there was nothing for her to say but, "I don't care a damn. We could leave here tomorrow. I'd give up everything for you. I love you so much. It didn't just start last night."

If he replied, 'And I love you too,' it would need to be qualified with, 'but not completely, not without limitations.' The facts were all against her; above all there was the nagging uncertainty of what he felt for Diana, that connection without the tidal rise and fall of his fleshly self to which his feelings for Soolan were subject. "I can't," he said quite simply. "I can't bring myself to leave Diana."

Soolan somehow mutated the nature of her warmth from passion to compassion. "I know you still love her. Or rather you imagine you love her. Things will work themselves out." Later over coffee she said, "Don't think I'd be giving up nothing. As long as I live here, I can still go to Canton to see my children. And I love my country. I feel I'm part of what's happening there. Do you understand that? You wouldn't be the only one making a sacrifice."

"Sacrifice, love," Robert repeated uncertainly for the words echoed thus in his mind without much meaning yet producing the suspicion that they were falsehoods however used. He slipped into one of those nihilistic moods which generally occurred when he awoke alone in the night and the contemplation of vacuity was preferable to that of the problems of living. At such moments it seemed that the observing 'I' within himself was as illusory as a mirror image and what he chose to call 'himself' was capable of neither truth nor falsehood, because being nothing it could know nothing. Those parts of himself that thought and acted were outside the hollowness; eyes saw, brain assessed, fingers painted, all programmed by genes and external stimuli creating an illusion of being; but the 'I' within had no reality, receding like quicksilver if a grasp was made towards it, even beyond the sphere of conscience and will, away into the darkness. "I'm nothing," he said. "Believe me there's nothing to love in me. When I say, 'I love', I haven't the slightest idea what love means. I don't even know what `I' means. It's like talking about someone else. Everything concerned with me is an illusion near the surface. How can anyone really say, 'I love you?'"

"If love's just on the surface, it's there all the same. Think of light on the surface of water—perhaps that's not there at all but it's still beautiful." As she tried to reassure him, Soolan was struck by the look of doubt in his eyes. "Don't believe anything I say to you," he replied but the words suggested, 'I don't believe anything you say either.' "Even if I say, 'I love you', just remember I can let you down."

"Don't reproach yourself where I'm concerned. At least you won't let Diana down." The touch of envy made him avert his eyes but he subtly converted the movement into a negative shake of the head, simultaneously hinting at disparagement of himself and despondency. He said, "Ah, she's so immature. How could I?" Soolan thought, 'How indeed,' but since she was close to tears the words remained unvoiced; she rested her head against him so he shouldn't see her. Her closeness almost made him decide to stay but he compromised and said, "I shouldn't come here again but I will; I promise I will—if you want me?"

Recollection of his amorous prowess made him glad to have given the promise. As he walked home along the sea front even the Communist gun boat that hovered offshore looked less hostile than usual. He repressed a silly desire to wave to it in a symbolic if futile gesture of friendship. He must be casual about the world, about Diana, about Soolan, letting things be and enjoying what came along. The initiation of action wasn't his role; above all he must observe the phenomena about him. That huge white bird out there for instance hovering above the seaweed covered rocks jutting from the waves; how serenely it poised for an instant, snatched something up—a fish maybe—and made off into the air. He left the road and walked over the rough shore to take a closer look, recalling, with a touch of envy as he did so, how superbly Chinese artists had once caught such moments, expressing the birdiness, the rockiness, the fishiness as if they themselves were birds, rocks or fish. An exquisite picture by Hsu Hsi came to his mind, an arctic heron momentarily alighting on a jagged branch, its great white wings entirely mastering the secret of stillness. The sea bird dived again but at what; he shaded his eyes against the sun and suddenly recoiled. Between the brown rocks to which the bird was ever returning, where the water surged up and down with forceful thumps, there was a rising and falling shape in the water, a human body, its face disfigured.

He remembered the massacre of the would-be refugees—it could be one of them—and turned quickly away, going as fast as he could back to the road. The white bird swooped by again and he knew it must be poised gracefully above the water whilst its hard beak tore—at what? Lips, throat, eyes? Wings beat above him and he yelled at the bird; something glistening dropped ahead of him and he gasped out, "I don't want to see. I don't want to see." But although he didn't look, his mind's eye saw a gaping socket in a dead face. Stumbling over the rocks he tried to forget the white wings, the inert body and the vision of the eyeless head, concentrating as hard as possible on other things, anything but the objects near those indifferent rocks. At length as he walked along the road his mind took refuge in the thought of Diana.

Soolan too attempted to divert her thoughts as she sat alone in her apartment; for a while she concentrated on the minutes of the last meeting of the Chamber of Commerce but the insincere 'left wing' speeches of the Colony's businessmen, playing safe to hold on to every cent they possessed, disgusted her. She opened the windows and gazed over the jumbled rooftops of the town towards the mountains of China. Across there a new world was being made, one in which women would one day be able to live and to love as freely as she wished to do now. But all that was far off in the future; the present China was a hard place, very different from the comfort of the family life of her childhood. In her youth she too had made a mistake in marrying hastily. 'I've only one life,' she thought bitterly. 'Damn it. I've only one life.' Soon afterwards she left the building.

Outside, a trishaw boy asked where she wanted to go and she gave the address of the Communist Party Headquarters. The boy drove her along slowly in disapproving silence. Through the branches of the banyan trees she could see the sun over the eastern sea. The thought that its redness should so often be used by the Party as a revolutionary symbol suddenly struck her as presumptuous. What right had they to claim the redness of the sun as their own; it would go on rising, red or gold or obscured by grey clouds in the east and setting in the west for centuries and aeons to come, long after Communism was forgotten, until there were no longer Chinese and Europeans, no longer men and for all she knew, no longer life at all; it would rise vast and furious on some ultimate day when the whole globe would shrivel up; a day with no more meaning than the one on which she must turn to dust. A sense of futility oppressed her, the futility of working for a cause in as primitive a way as dancing round a tribal totem. Only in love could there be any significance;

her love for Robert had such meaning. But would he throw it lightly away?

"Why are you going to the house of the Communist toads?" the trishaw boy asked sullenly. At any other time she'd have lectured him on the correctness of the cause but she replied, "I don't know. I just have to go there." The boy pedalled on vigorously surprised to have received a reply which gave him no chance for raillery. For a while her mind went blank as she listened to the reiterated squeak of the driven bicycle chain until, all at once, as though the monotonous sound had been toting up a power to open a door in her mind, she entered upon a ground of certainty that she could find as much significance in love for the Communist cause—whether it was worthless or not didn't matter—as she could find in love for Robert—whether he loved her or not being just as immaterial. Under different circumstances she might hate Robert and love someone else, or hate the Communists and find purpose in struggling against them; in those acts and feelings too she could find meaning. It didn't matter whether she hated or loved, built or destroyed. The significance lay in the moment or rather in the commitment of self during the moment; this alone would sparkle for a brief time in the darkness like a firefly before it fell down, to be borne away in a black river which never knew any other light. Deliberately she forced her troubles from her mind and began to sing softly, but loud enough for the pleased trishaw boy to hear:

> On the road to Sze Chwan
> I pause for a while where the steep road hangs
> high on a cliff above the pine-clad gorge.
> Far far below the white winged heron flies
> circling for prey above the thundering waves
> roaring in cataracts between the boulders.
> Faintly from the opposite shore
> the wind bears the tolling of a monastery bell
> bidding me cease my journey and forget
> the hazardous way that twists and bends ahead.

On the road to Sze Chwan
it is better not to stop,
trying to ease your troubles.
Only think as you labour upwards
how the paved road and the wild river
following their different courses
both lead to the red pavilions
and the pleasures of Chang-tu."

PART II

Intramuros

Intramuros

'City of God, Light of the Eastern Seas, None Exceedeth Thee in Loyalty to our Crown, None in Faith to the Creator of the World.' The Latin title of the city encircled a coat of arms borne by two angels kneeling uncomfortably on an array of antique swords and spears. Above the heraldic carving, the crown of Braganza rested serene if slightly lop-sided.

Now a museum piece at the end of the Club committee room, the device extended the military expression of the Chairman, Colonel Lobato, all about him like a gigantic nimbus. The Colonel, if not conscious of this theatrical effect, was certainly aware of the majesty of his surroundings; long ago the Club had been the Palace of the Intramuros, the ancient City within the walls, and from it the Captains-General had directed Portugal's eastern policies. But the matter the Committee was discussing, rather than history, was the more likely reason for Lobato's defensive hauteur.

It was universally accepted that Lung Yeung's success in arranging the City's ransom at so low a price had to be recognised. The contradictory 'agreed' communiqués, each politely assigning blame to the other side, issued by the Chinese and Portuguese authorities had been entirely lacking in rancour. Even before the Chamber of Commerce had handed over the million patacas privately demanded by the Communist Party big-wigs in Canton, trade had begun to revive. But whereas the commercial groups wanted a big demonstration of gratitude, the Government of the Colony was not so sure. Lung Yeung was, ostensibly at least, a supporter of the People's Republic; anything in the nature of a public display of praise for him might easily be interpreted as a Portuguese humiliation. So after much confabulation it had been agreed that an officially private banquet in his honour should be held in the Club, or rather to use its ancient style for such an august occasion, the Palace of the Intramuros. In this way the public wouldn't be much involved.

But the meeting to discuss the arrangements wasn't going to be so easy; to conservatives, and this included Lobato, a celebration for an unbeliever, a comprador of vice and narcotics, in the Intramuros, was desecration. "Behold unto what patrons the Romans were pleased to commit their City's safety. O piteous error," the Bishop, quoting St. Augustine, had already fulminated from his pulpit. Father Antonio, the Church's much milder representative, said to Luiz Figueiredo before the meeting, "I wish that old fool had kept his mouth shut. We should be grateful to keep this toe-hold in China." Luiz had nodded and, proceeding to an item of gossip which interested him more, had asked how the redecorations were going on at a 'certain address'—the current scandal concerned the Bishop's mistress, not his having one but her installation in ecclesiastical property. The priest rolled up his eyes, shrugged his shoulders and took his place at the ponderous committee table.

Whilst the debate proceeded in Portuguese, Robert, for whom each oration was cleverly summed up in a few translated words by Luiz Figueiredo, had time to reflect on the fantastic nature of Lung Yeung's success in Canton. It had, so he'd learned from Diana, been due to the Chairman of the Central and South China Military and Administrative Committee, sensing a subtle change in the millionaire's attitude; the old man had been seemingly unperturbed by the calculated delays to which the Communists had subjected him, gently conveying to them that he was no longer particularly interested in his empire's preservation. His remarks about death (though he had felt much better of late), must have worried the Reds so much that, "Would you believe it," Diana exclaimed, "in the end they were persuading him to look after his own business interests." In fact, as Lung Yeung had calculated, Peking's need for war materials had made a mild settlement certain and overshadowed Canton's greed for a larger indemnity. "Do you know," Lung Yeung told Diana. "Before we left, Ming Yuk and I were moved into a mansion that once belonged to Chan-Tek, the sugar king. You've never heard of him? He's in Taiwan now. Though I didn't see those beautiful carpets of his."

A self-satisfied expression extended over Robert's face as he gazed through the window at the lengthening shadows. What an odd, yet what a pleasant place in which to find himself in the forty-fifth year, the midpoint, he liked to think, of his life. He had the distinct, though he at once recognised it as illusory, feeling that this hour was pivotal in his existence without, however, the arms of time stretching before and after either ascending or descending; nor should they be, for it was not time that moved but the pivot—a thought more typical of Peter, he chided himself with a mental chuckle that manifested itself in a smirk for anyone to see. He pulled himself together, hoping his expression had coincided with something amusing said by one of the committee members. And this marvellous equilibrium he was experiencing had come about as a result of his doing nothing. No, not 'doing nothing'; that was too active, but 'not doing anything', action in inaction, he corrected himself, becoming Taoist Peter again. As proof of this: Diana's affair with Carlos, started of its own volition, had made his liaison with Soolan equally possible. Diana would never have stood it otherwise and his old screwing different cabaret girls act would have run on (not that it was going to stop completely). But equally, just because he was sure Diana would never leave him for Carlos, Soolan would have to accept the self locking device on her own ambitions. Yes, everything was exquisitely balanced and entirely to his advantage; he felt like a pilot cruising serenely at twenty thousand feet with the controls on automatic.

A voice in English, Lobato's, asked Signor Sheraton for his comments on something or other; he had none and as Luiz began to speak, Robert's attention returned to the window. Through it was a scene of the sort that might be termed, 'vue générale' on eighteenth century prints: to the left, artfully placed, the Chapel whose foundation was attributed to St. Francis Xavier—from its roof a figure like an Aleijadhinho prophet gesticulated with baroque abandon along an imaginary line of perspective over zig-zag ramparts towards the façade of St. Paul's, always the last building to catch the light of the setting sun. Looming majestically to the right was the elegant domed Rotunda, a structure whose purpose was lost in obscurity; now it stood empty, save for bats and those tattered banners so dear to Lobato and his ilk, an eerie chamber of martial silence. But after all, was it so strange that the Colonel took pride in these sumptuous buildings whose foundations seemed laid down by giants, whose roofs were manifestly of timbers left over from the Ark—solid testimony to the endurance of Portugal? Between the Rotunda and the Senate House was the little horse shoe theatre where, soon after Robert and Diana had arrived, they were transported back to a courtly age when the Colony's elegant society rose to greet its new Governor in the vice-regal box. How avidly the speakers of this sibilant Latin tongue had followed the performance: haunting poetry—from Camões to Pessoa, colourful dances, rending fados. No wonder he and Diana had stayed.

Luiz concluded with a passionate peroration—surely some proposition for the regeneration of mankind, then he leaned over towards Robert's ear. "I've proposed a compromise; the Chamber of Commerce to pay for the banquet, the Government to redecorate the Club—the Committee's tried to raise money to do that for years." Permanent Secretary Robert, backing his Minister, pursed his lips sagely. Father Antonio nodded his support of the proposal and Luiz sat back, arms folded, his expression serene. World peace was saved; perhaps they could all go home now.

But no, Father Antonio had proceeded to speak in a low, urgent voice. Robert's small knowledge of Portuguese told him it was about the ancient Chapel from which, centuries ago, an heroic effort had been mounted to convert the Ming emperors. "I can show you documents," Father Antonio had once told him, "listing Peking notabilities who were baptised—they took names like Orosius and Theodora. The last Ming Empress' child was christened Constantine. How near we came. How near." In the archives below the Chapel the records of the Padroado, the patronage granted by Rome to the Portuguese crown over all its eastern evangelic work, now mouldered and the Church itself had been driven from China. "But it will go back." To Father Antonio it was a matter of faith that from the Chapel, the still living heart of the City, the tide would turn and sweep back to success. The occasional religious ceremonies held there were like magical lustrations to ensure that ultimate victory.

"The Father's suggesting," Luiz whispered, "that on the night of the Banquet, the Chapel and the Rotunda should be locked and the keys held by the Bishop and the Garrison Commander." Robert wondered at this weird formula to preserve the honour of the shrines from the heathen. But it was no dream: a Chinese gentleman rose and gravely welcomed the proposal, adding, almost as an afterthought and amidst murmurs of thanks, that the Chinese Chamber of Commerce would distribute charity to the poor on the occasion—a pataca to invalids and fifty avos to anyone else who queued up for it. A vague suspicion crossed Robert's mind—hadn't the general idea been to limit the celebration to the favoured few? But as no one questioned the generosity he held his tongue even when, to his irritation, Lobato switched to English yet again to ask him if he wished to say anything. Was he expected to announce that the Anglo Saxon community would put on a Morris dance or perform Twelfth Night? The arrangements for Lung Yeung's Triumph complete, the meeting broke up with the Chairman's formula of dismissal unaccountably delivered in English.

The great victor Lung Yeung was at that moment in the Idly Viewing the Plum Blossom Pavilion, holding a dish up to the light and studying the fine web of crackling spread over its lavender tinted smoothness. "It's certainly beautiful, Mrs. Sheraton. I compliment you. Soon you'll be quite an expert." The word 'soon' hinted at her error and Diana spared herself further convoluted politeness by remarking how skillfully later potters were at reproducing early wares; that would give an excuse for him to show off his knowledge and for her to soak it up.

She was privileged, she knew, to be allowed these visits, all on her own, to the Pearl River Mansion and never did she set foot amidst its bizarre luxury, a combination of eastern and western extravagance, without dressing as elegantly as her modest wardrobe and jewelry allowed. Listening to Lung Yeung talk of the skill of the ancient potters had the same effect on her as her solitary walks about the City—both were productive of calm. "They learned to copy the Ju vessels perfectly—too perfectly for they could control their kilns better than the Sung masters. See the evenness of this crackle; it lacks the spontaneity of an original." The precise English paused, and then resumed with, "Perhaps they did succeed sometimes—when they weren't trying too hard. But in that case we'd never know, would we Mrs. Sheraton?"

The words 'tried too hard' echoed in her mind. That was exactly what she'd been doing with Robert and when you try too hard you can't keep up with yourself. Now, she wasn't trying at all and things were going better. The process of her confession to Robert had been simplicity itself, little more than, "Everyone knows you're having an affair with Soolan. Well, I'm having an affair too. I've got a lover—a policeman; his name's Carlos." And how had he reacted? With a little silence, by emptying his pipe with a few hard taps on his shoe and then saying something quite inconsequential. What was it? The words of a Zen master: "Have a cup of tea." Suddenly they'd burst out laughing and she had said he should study Zen some more and she would too. When he saw her suitcases had been at the ready for packing they both became hysterical and threw cushions at each other. But she hadn't told him about the triune love making with Peter; probably he'd have asked her to draw a diagram and his glee would have led to apoplexy. In any case the night in the golden room had been a flash in the pan though she would never forget it. No, never. A wave of sadness was rising and her calm mood began to disintegrate. Lung Yeung's words failed to reach her; if only the love making à trois could have continued, perhaps she could have drawn Peter closer to her. But now it was impossible; he blamed himself both for Ah Tung's crime and for his subsequent arrest. Though she still saw him as much as ever, he'd drawn away from her. Holding her thoughts in check she forced herself to listen again to Lung Yeung's words—something complicated about firing temperatures. To give an impression of concentration she held the fake bowl against her cheek and then cupped it in her hands. Looking at it she felt pleased; just because it wasn't what it claimed to be, she'd not be tempted to get rid of it.

Little did she realise, as her thoughts roamed on, that in her presence Lung Yeung felt that his valuable dishes had acquired a miraculous newness and that he was the potter taking each piece from the kiln for the first time. As she poured out two cups of tea, English style, he translated a poem for her, something he remembered by Chou Pang-Yen:

How lucky I am
Some one lovely as a moon fairy
Is raising her sunset sleeves
And filling my wine cup.

...and she gave him a radiant smile as though he had written the poem himself.

Could it be, Diana wondered, that we're both flattered to be with one another? Yet hardly so, for when later they looked at other Sung pieces—dove grey Kuan ware from Phoenix Hill, jade green celadons of Lung Chuan and multi-coloured flower bowls of Chun Chou, their dappled glazes richly suffused with purple—they both felt drawn together in the face of a mysterious problem to which neither could fathom an answer; why, during a particular moment of time, were the delicate and the strong so taut in their relationship but without either overbalancing the other, that what the potters had produced then remained forever unsurpassed.

Yet this exquisite pleasure couldn't entirely banish Peter and his difficulties from her mind; the fear he'd lose himself in endless opium smoking was oppressing her, which was why she found herself directing the conversation away from porcelain and blurting out that she'd recently tried opium. "Some people think religious experiences are possible under its influence," she added quickly, trying hard to conceal the embarrassment she felt for having alluded to the commodity on which Lung Yeung's deplorable business activities were based by making a show of her own tolerance. "That would be an excellent justification for some people I know," he chuckled. "But don't believe it. They're deluded by the morphine in their blood." Diana wasn't going to be put off so easily; her ignorance of the subject only heightened its fascination for her. "In ancient times people got into a state of ecstasy by chewing ivy and in Mexico…" She got no further, for Lung Yeung interjected harshly, "Entirely different drugs, Mrs. Sheraton. Yes, some of them do make you lose yourself in a kind of ecstasy. But others do something else. They widen perception. They give rise to images of terrible clarity, exquisite clarity. Perhaps artists see the world like that. You go beyond your normal self into—into a crystalline awareness; yes, that's how it might seem—crystalline. Or,"—there was a disturbing pause—"into a nightmare." He shook his head rapidly before going on, but to himself now, "No. No. That was never the Light of the Masters." Then he recalled her presence and his mild speech resumed. "The Taoist adepts say drugs can take you up to the Jade Pass but never through it." His bony fingers gestured in self deprecation. "Who am I to speak of these matters? The Taoist methods aren't easy. To master the mind is like taming a dragon and only those who have done it can ride through the heavens. It's too late for me to try and probably too soon for you."

His shrill, not exactly pleasant laugh went unnoticed by Diana who was now the brash student at a tutorial, keener to blurt out her own views than listen to others. "Maybe the awareness induced by Taoist methods is no more valid than that caused by drugs. There's no way of judging. Maybe all of them are worth trying only to learn that they lead nowhere."

The sage nodded his all-knowing head at her with an indulgent smile. How inexperienced she was but how curious about everything and how delightful to listen to her enthusiastic nonsense; and how beautiful she was in that pink dress and how he would love her if he was young—or even not so young."

"Peter's idea is…"

"Ah, Mr. Morgan, the poet; they say that flowers spring up under his pen. But a wild young man too, so I've heard—with odd friendships." Lung Yeung noticed a shadow pass over her eyes. "I'm sorry to interrupt. Yes. What does he say?" His interest was not entirely affected. He knew that her friend was not just another of those young westerners who were rejecting causality for chance, dabbling amidst the hexagrams of the *I Ching* and prattling of Lao Tzu. There were those excellent translations he'd seen somewhere or other. Nor had the best Chinese poets always been so disciplined in their ways.

Diana was off again. "He seems to think all the esoteric doctrines are superfluous." Under that amused gaze a blush began to rise to her cheeks but she went on, "He says the true experience comes unexpectedly—in some insignificant action; stumbling, listening to the wind, any little event. It doesn't depend on techniques or drugs. They neither help nor hinder. It can come at work or play, amidst nature or in love." She hesitated; it was an act of betrayal to be putting over someone else's ideas, probably badly, to a man who'd deride them. Yet she looked at Lung Yeung challengingly. "It can come to anyone, good or bad, rich or poor, educated or simple. You just have to be ready. Yes, that's it. It can come to a murderer even, provided he's ready."

The old man rose to his feet; the wisdom of the young could be extremely tedious. An irritated face with piercing eyes stared at her. "Ready? Ready? What does he mean by ready?" His hand reached out to her arm; its grip seemed strong for so frail a body. She said, "Lung *Shin Saang*, I really must go. I'm tiring you with my chatter. Talking above my head." She hesitated, reflecting how little good Peter's notions seemed to be doing him now. "You should speak with Peter Morgan yourself. You could discuss all this better with him." Lung Yeung recovered his composure and they talked of lighter things. Before she left she took the bowl she'd found and gave it to him. "This really is a 'humble' present," she said. But I'd be happy if you'd accept it."

Soon after that, making her way towards Peter's house, she came to the coastal road. It had started to rain so she stood under a tree, trying her best to think of nothing as she watched the scurrying yachts, the brawling of the ravenous sea birds and the waves pounding the grey rocks before churning up the shingle and sweeping along the spumy shore. But to think of nothing after wrestling with matters deeper than she could manage was easier said than done so she let her thoughts drift back to another time, another broad expanse of water, let the plangent waves beguile her into Tasmanian memories she had not wished to arouse. For even though the admonitions of Lung Yeung had been infinitely gentler than those of her father yet coming down to the coast had reminded her of those brief periods of liberation when, to escape the tyrant and his gloomy ménage, she had clambered down the cliffs to her favourite cove facing the vast ocean. What if she had remained at St. Mawes instead of running after Robert, instead of coming here where, sad to say, so many things had turned out unsatisfactorily? But then, would she ever have got away at all to the mainland, well away, to support herself in Perth, in Darwin even? Something made her doubt it. Her father had subtly instilled in her mind the fear that she would never be good at anything but running his house. What was more she had always thought him capable of tracking her down and forcing her back home. Nevertheless, but for two things, she reflected grudgingly, she might have been able to accept his compulsion. She had not rebelled against the household rules, the methodical planning of domestic duties, the hours of serious reading (neither a radio nor a gramophone had been allowed, though there was an old rosewood piano, essentially for religious use) or even the Bible study for there had been a certain rationale to them; in any case reading and thinking had provided the gateway to a freedom more expansive than mere physical liberty. No, the first cause of her revolt had been the absurd fact that her young brother James, though otherwise subject to the same regimen as herself, was exempt from virtually all household chores, as these, in the gospel according to the Rev. Stanley Trevorrow, were not the duties of the male, and especially of a male destined to follow his father into the Church. It was almost as though the old devil had devised a system to prevent his children, already divided in their younger days by attendance at different schools in Hobart, from becoming friendly, which would have meant united instead of being forever at loggerheads. Far worse than that, however, followed her discovery, through the malice of a former classmate, that her father, when in Hobart, was in the habit of slipping into a certain backstreet bar where he could pick up a woman. Diana never begrudged him his pleasure but his hypocrisy stuck in her craw over what he had done to James, then in his sixteenth year, after (deliberately snooping, of that she had no doubt) he had discovered his son 'behaving like a filthy ape', as he put it, in an outhouse. For his solitary act of imagined love the slim adolescent had received three dreadful thrashings on successive nights to 'purify him,' so the Rev. Trevorrow said with his customary sardonic humour, before the Father, the Son and the Holy Spirit. A crazy reign of terror had then been instituted against the lad (she refused even to think of its sordid details), making him more difficult towards her than ever. It was still running strong three months later when she decided to flit. Staring up at the turbulent sky she wondered whether it was going on now. Then she looked down and saw her hands trembling. She clasped them but, just then, the wild screeching of birds rent the air. "No daddy, no," she cried as though she had heard James' screams again. She began to sob but knew she was weeping not so much for her brother as, strangely enough, her own lost childhood, even though she had hated it. The anger of those days surged up afresh but it quickly changed to guilt as she accused herself of deserting a poor tortured boy who, to survive, must now have become more deceitful, and more of a wreck, than ever. "I'll put them both out of my head," she told herself desperately but even as she mouthed the words the sombre figure of her father reared itself so hugely in her mind that she felt the creeping shadow of the clouds blackening the wind-swept sea was being cast by him. No longer could she admit to the slightest affection for him but why couldn't she fill the place in her mind that he had once occupied with anyone else? Neither with Robert, nor Peter, nor old Lung Yeung, and certainly not with her newest male acquisition, radiant Carlos. "Surely, surely," she heard herself saying, "he could have replied to me or said he was trying to forgive me." For she had long ago written to him, without a hint of accusation, to explain that she had had to leave home to make her own life. All there had been, and all, she was sure now, there ever would be, was silence, the muteness of one of those ruined Tasmanian penitentiaries standing fast against the pleading wind.

In the Intramuros the wind was disturbing the silence of the ancient courtyards, rustling the wild flowers and bushes and rippling the water on fish ponds and tanks intended to sustain a garrison under siege. The sound of Robert's footsteps on the smooth granite blocks created echoes as though other more mysterious walkers were a little ahead or slightly behind—the ghosts of proud fidalgos who ever observed but were not themselves seen. Such footsteps seemed to be following now. He turned and Lobato caught up with him saying, "I believe—I believe you often come here Senhor." He was quite out of breath. Robert was surprised that the Head of Security should know such details about him. "Yes I do. It's so peaceful."

"These buildings used to be magnificently furnished. I could show you and Senhora Sheraton some old lithographs—oh so magnificent." Robert detected in those melancholy eyes that longing—that Portuguese *saudade*—for the wonder that never was. "Then you must find it very depressing as it is, Senhor Colonel."

"The eye of the historian can be as imaginative as that of the artist." If Lobato's manner of delivery was didactic, his feeling seemed genuine. "For me the halls are far from empty. Come. Let's go down together."

As they went on beneath colonnades that gave some unity to the rambling complex, Robert observed that the tinted plaster silhouetting ornate lintels and sometimes breaking out into florid scrolls, though made too well to crumble for a long time yet, was discoloured by green and purple mould which, now the dusk was gathering, produced impossible shadows; that in crevices where dust had collected, delicate flowered creepers had put down their roots while fragments of stone staircases that led into the empty air and other untrod surfaces, were carpeted with grass and dwarf ferns.

He wondered if the Colonel's historic eye banished all this evidence of decay. In a wild garden they passed two ancient stones supporting a third monolith; it was difficult to say whether it was man-made or a natural structure but the Portuguese claimed it as their own, naming it the Grotto of Camões. Here, according to a plaque, the poet had sat in the shade composing *Os Lusiadas* in praise of his countrymen who'd opened up the world. A relief showed Venus leading the mariners on in face of the monstrous Adamastor. For a moment Robert felt less critical of Lobato's chauvinism. Perhaps guessing his thoughts the Colonel said, "You must think we were making a fuss at the meeting. But Dr. Salazar is right. We must never compromise."

"You have to compromise when the monster is Chairman Mao. You have to tolerate the Communists here. Where else does that happen in your empire? Venus can't help you in the least."

"We compromise unofficially—not otherwise. And we survive. Look about you. Here everything is Portuguese."

"Even the monoliths?"

"Made Portuguese by our national poet."

"If ever he came here."

"If we say he came, he came. But what would you do? Hand everything over to the Communists?"

"Haven't you virtually handed over to Lung Yeung?"

"We use him—as he uses us. That way we conserve something."

"I don't like the word 'conserve'. When things are finished, they'll die whatever you do."

"You'd let go so easily—without a struggle? Don't you believe in fighting for anything—or for anyone?" It was on the tip of his tongue to say, 'Not even for the beautiful Senhora Sheraton,' but he held himself in check.

"No. I don't believe in possessing colonies—or people." He gave Lobato a smug stare.

"Ah, I begin to understand your country's national policy."

"I didn't know we had one."

Lobato didn't reply. Talking to such a man disconcerted him. What would become of a state without rules, without pride. A gust struck them and he thrust his hands deep in his pockets shuddering.

"Wrap yourself up Colonel. We can't afford a sick Head of Security—not with so many undesirable elements about."

They'd reached the gate leading into the brightly lit town. Lobato seemed to recover his poise. "Exactly so Mr. Sheraton; I'm rather concerned about your friend Mr. Morgan. Ah, there's my car. We'll talk again. *Boa noite*, Senhor. My regards to your charming wife." Robert felt a bit colder than the temperature justified but decided not to go home for a couple of hours. Diana had inadvertently left Carlos' duty roster lying around; she wouldn't be back for some time. He walked on into the noisy Chinese street to distract himself with its bustle.

At the less frequented end of the same street, where it led down to the shore, Diana saw Peter sitting on the sea wall hunched up and dejected. Forgetting her assignation with Carlos she ran across to him and put her arm around his shoulders. For a while they sat together in silence; she sensed his remoteness from her as he gazed across the surging waves that must mirror his heart's unease. "Ah Tung always wanted to get across that water out of this place," Peter said quietly. "And I never took him. Now he'll never leave." Diana turned towards him, her tears starting as she saw his pallid face and his eyes unnaturally large and bright. "Don't despair, love," she said. "Don't despair. You've not been sleeping properly have you? I can see it. Let me be close to you. Things may turn out alright. You must be well when Ah Tung gets out of prison. Then you can take him away to some other place." She tried to speak as though it was a foregone conclusion that Ah Tung would be freed. "Why, you could even take him to England. Start a new life there completely." She kissed him. "Oh, but I'd miss you so much. I wouldn't like it here without you." Peter's expression brightened up just slightly. "Carlos is waiting for you at my place. You've got him, haven't you. You'll be happy from now on." Though her eyes were downcast he insisted, "He's just what you wanted, isn't he Diana? He lives for you. Did you know?" The drawn look returned to his face and he added half derisively, "In his fleshy way."

"Don't talk like that. You mean more to me than Carlos. Much, much more. If you knew how miserable it makes me to see you like this, you'd understand. I'd give up Carlos if it could bring Ah Tung back to you." Once more she embraced him, trying to find some way through the barrier. "Come on Peter. Come home with me. No, we won't do that at all. Why don't we go to the cinema? There's a Gene Kelly musical at the Victoria; I'm sure you'd enjoy it." The memory of happier days when they did such things brought more tears to her eyes.

"No. No. I'd only spoil it for you." Peter wasn't to be cured so easily. "Carlos is waiting. It's best for me to be on my own." Again he looked towards the sea and Diana got the feeling she wasn't even there. "They won't let me visit him in the prison. He'll think I've forgotten him—let him down."

"Never. He'd never think that." Even though she still had the strongest doubts about Ah Tung, she forced conviction into her voice. "Think about it rationally. No one knows exactly what happened, do they? All they've got is Old Chong's word that Lim was making a bolt for Hong Kong and he asked Ah Tung to help him get there. There's no body. Just a boat reported stolen that night. I bet Ah Tung told the police he changed his mind about going and said Lim went off on his own. The boat could have sailed into Chinese waters—and then been seized. Lim might be alive— in China." Neither believed the story was likely, nor would the police. But how could she say, 'Forget Ah Tung; he's a murderer.' And even if he was a murderer, Diana thought, how could Peter forget him?

"He'll be in a terrible state without opium. He'll confess to anything, just to get it." Peter closed his eyes. His head seemed to quiver for an instant as though he was doing his best to control some more violent movement. Then the self accusation burst forth. "I should never have got mad with him that night. It's my fault. I should have gone home with him. He asked me. He asked me."

Drawn into his desperation Diana tried to assess her own guilt. Had she, in that golden room, in trying to get Peter's love, done some violence to his nature? She squeezed his hands. "What can I do? I'll do anything. Anything at all." But he pulled away and stood up. "Go to Carlos. Enjoy yourself while you can." Then he turned abruptly and went off. As she watched him walking away the sight of his body, thinner than before and with a hint of a stoop, moved her so much she started to cry. She longed to run after him just to comfort him, and the knowledge that it was pointless to follow added to her dejection.

Reluctantly she went up the hill to Peter's house which stood white and green tiled, in a garden of luxuriant bamboo and flowers, but there was no sign of Carlos. How immaculate the place was; Ping must be making a real effort to preserve normality. The top of Peter's desk was neatly laid out for him to work, with open note books and pens at the ready. Then Ping's head popped round the kitchen door; she gestured towards the verandah. "*Shin saang*'s not in; your friend's out there." Diana felt embarrassed. Ping must disapprove of her infidelity to Robert and she probably didn't like anyone enjoying themselves in this house when its master was so sad.

Diana saw her policeman sitting sullen faced at the end of the verandah and said "I've just been speaking to Peter. He looks very…" Carlos waved his arm irritably. "I know. I've seen him." His hostile voice went on, "Why don't you do something to help him? He's the one you love, not me. I don't know why you bother with me." She didn't want him to see her face and went upstairs to the bedroom to lie down.

"What are you going up there for?" His angry shout followed her. "I'm not going to make love." His mood was even angrier than his voice but he didn't really want to antagonize her. The suspicion lurked in his mind that he was being made use of for one purpose. And because he couldn't resist that purpose, he was sure he'd be treated with contempt. Who was she to be late just now, for instance? And ultimately, when he was no longer of use, he'd be hurt—perhaps as badly as Peter. He tiptoed up the stairs and skulked around on the landing unable to bring himself to go into the bedroom.

"Shall I make you something to eat," she called in a concerned voice, knowing the importance to him of food, but he was silent. She lay on the bed and looked at the books, the flowers, the simple furniture and the brightly coloured rugs and curtains so effective against the white walls; everything was conducive to happiness and indeed the room did have the effect of making her feel that one day Peter's way of life, which surely posed no threat to the world, would be serene again. It had to be. This attractive little house, this pleasant bedroom demanded that it should be so. At the same time, she wondered whether her own serenity with Carlos had not become too smug? Why was it that, though she was quite happy with him, whenever he was being difficult, as now, it didn't bother her at all? She was afraid he'd sense her attitude and interpret it as indifference though it wasn't so. Yet what was wrong with wanting things to be on an even keel? She refused to become obsessed like Peter. Nor would she let Carlos get that way either. After a while he came into the bedroom and lay beside her. She was very gentle to him and stroked him as though to say, 'Now you're a good boy, you'll get your reward.' The compassion Peter had rejected flowed out to him and when he started to make love to her, her tenderness turned into desire. But in the midst of her pleasure, Peter's face, sad and lonely, kept returning to her mind, and also Lung Yeung's words about him: 'A wild young man with odd friendships.' Was she included in that category?

After Diana had left him, Lung Yeung lay on a couch watching the ragged clouds racing across the sky and listening to the wind in the eaves of the Mansion. The clouds are ever changing and free, he thought, but the sound of the wind has an emptiness as though it comes from my soul. I should like to be free yet without having to choose—the freedom of the cloud to be blown by the empty wind, the freedom of the boat to drift where the current takes it. His thoughts became confused; now his own family came to mind and now that quick young woman in pink. Sometimes he opened his eyes to look about him and then he closed them trying to think of nothing. It seemed the Mansion was growing larger about the room in which he lay; courtyard after courtyard stretched northward up to the inner precinct of the Imperial Presence. The room was becoming a crimson pillared audience chamber filled with courtiers in gorgeous robes. He stared at them impassively from the eminence of his Dragon Throne. Everywhere the character 'Lung,' the dragon name of his dynasty, was emblazoned in gold, and dragons writhed on his imperial robes. Behind a screen, fretted with Yin and Yang symbols, a lavender dragon danced lightly on the gown of the Imperial Concubine with sunset sleeves. About his head kingfisher banners floated up to the sky and before him, ascending the vermilion steps, he saw Ming Yuk in the magnificent robes of a Grand Eunuch paying homage and addressing him as Lord of Ten Thousand Years. Gravely he nodded his head beneath the twelve-tasselled headdress, appreciative of fidelity, without danger to his dynasty, and affixed a seal to a scroll proclaiming to his loyal servant that the Imperial Favour would never be withdrawn. He waved his hand and an official bestowed a jade symbol on Ming Yuk who went through the prescribed prostrations and begged leave to present the new Imperial Eunuchs. Lung Yeung raised his eyes towards the Southern Nine Fold Gates and saw several figures clad as Eunuchs of the Pepper Room approaching with mincing steps. He arose full of fear, pearl and jade ornaments clattering on swaying tassels, for he saw that they were his own sons. Then he awoke and trembling, peered into the courtyard. A light in an opposite window told him Ming Yuk was still hard at work. Looking up he saw the wind had blown the clouds away and the moon was naked in a black sky. He lay back murmuring, "If only I could let go; just once let go. Then I might be ready."

From the wooded slopes of the Observatory Hill, Peter stared down at the ochre walls of Sao Francisco prison. Which of those cells each marked by small barred windows was occupied by Ah Tung? A corner of the exercise yard was visible; occasionally convicts moved into it and then disappeared from view. The possibility of glimpsing him was remote; but Peter's blind hopes now fed on scraps.

Under the high canopy of trees a few men, some young and muscular, others old and skinny, were shadow boxing— how graceful those slow controlled movements of the art of tai chi—all of them wearing the wrapt expressions of people whose actions only had an inner significance. The sight filled Peter with nostalgia; in the early days, he and Ah Tung had come here to exercise.

He felt he was no longer living in the present, or not fully so. In his desolation memories preoccupied him; wherever he looked sights, sounds and people triggered them off. But there was one that was always on the threshold of his awareness, full of white light: a deserted cove on one of the nearby islands, sand which some geological freak had made to look like snow. They had lived there for a week, until their bodies, brown and sinewy from exercise in the sun and the sea, had grown as much a part of the place as the green water, the grained rocks and the echoing sea shells. It was then, he liked to think, that their love had changed from the gross into something else, perhaps most fully on that last night when they had seemed to lose themselves in each other's eyes and when Ah Tung had cut their palms for them to drink each other's blood. Before they left he had watched the incoming waves washing away the bloodstains on the sand. How quickly it was white again. Who would know that the two of them had ever been there? Had it all been a fantasy? He longed to know how Ah Tung had viewed it; did he even remember it and if he did, had it meant anything to him at all? Closing his eyes to banish the sight of the prison, he recalled the blade cutting his flesh, the blood oozing out and the peculiar excitement as he lowered his head to drink. No. It had not been a fantasy. He must keep faith. From that communion he could still derive strength.

Yet strength was not to be bought so easily for the next minute the certainty flooded into his mind that Ah Tung's execution was inevitable. At the last hour would the authorities let him into the prison for a brief meeting before the time of death? And could he bear to go? With a weird sense of remorse in anticipation he wondered whether, once Ah Tung was dead, it would be as though they had never loved, the sand as white as snow again. Away from here would he be happy with someone else whilst Ah Tung's lips, his eyes, the fight scars on his body, rotted? Surely, he himself was the betrayer; selfishly he'd wanted those days of naked perfection to last, whilst Ah Tung had seen them merely as a prelude to a better life—which had never come. No wonder that in his despair Ah Tung had resumed his interest in opium and led him into the vice.

Bitterly he remembered the weeks when opium had become their sustainer and how, during those reiterated days of petty quarrels, a subtler addiction had developed. Bit by bit as Ah Tung's interest in making love had waned, he himself had started to see each act of love as a victory, while Ah Tung had deliberately made it as brief and violent as possible. Forcing Ah Tung to want him had become as necessary to him as opium. He remembered too his own possessive jealousy and how Ah Tung had tantalised him, hinting at an affair with a mysterious woman. One day he'd even followed Ah Tung along a dismal street and at length up some stairs inside a shop house. In the upper room what a strange sight: walls hung with red and green crepe paper, an altar, a cockerel in a basket, other paraphernalia whose meaning escaped him. But stranger still Ah Tung's expression—angry yet full of concern when he turned. "Get out. Get out of here. Quickly. Quickly." He'd had the wit to run. The place was ready for some Triad ritual which outsiders were forbidden to see.

Now the conflict was over he saw the illusion of existence it had given him for what it was. The centre of his life had been planted in Ah Tung and with its displacement the circumference had gone awry. He cursed himself for not listening to those reproaches: "If I had your education," or, "If I was as clever as you, I wouldn't rot in this hole." Time couldn't be rolled back, the chance of happiness would never come again. Grief burned in his mind and from it hatred arose for the City and those who ran it. Then he noticed that the wood was silent as death, the graceful athletes no longer there to assuage his rage with reminders of past joy. Wrapt in his own misery he started slowly back home.

Along the coast road, he caught sight of Diana in black Chinese clothes, crossing the swaying cat-walk to a hut on a fish trap. They both knew its owners, the Kams, an elderly couple with two sons, who gave their entire time and skill to the trap, collecting just enough food to go on living in poverty. At least he could see that their lives, in the grip of the rise and fall of that great net, were held more terribly in thrall by the moody water swirling below than his own life was held by Ah Tung.

Inside the hut, Diana was squatting in front of a cooking pot into which she was popping some live fishes. Peter quite amazed himself by greeting her gaily with, "I'm an inspector from the R.S.P.C. Fish." She looked up open mouthed, equally taken aback by his facetious manner. Then, glad to see him in better spirits, she smiled so inviting a let down. It came. "I'm leaving soon Di (he hardly ever called her that and she hated it). Ah Tung has had it. There's no point in hanging around for an execution." He laughed loudly. "Hanging around for an execution, funny eh?" Then he screwed up his mouth as though he'd forgotten something. "Oh yes. I'd better leave you some money—you can send a wreath for him. I suggest white poppies if you can get them." Diana told herself not to smile, not to cry, just to feign indifference. "Darling, don't hold that fish in the steam so long. Drop it in. Waiting's the worst form of torture." She put the fish into the pot and began to stir the soup silently with a large wooden spoon. Peter squatted opposite her, lit a cigarette and put on the air of a man with a lot to plan. "Yes. I'm going back to my old job in Hong Kong. Just for a while of course. I've been in touch with Drake in Tokyo; he's told me I can get a teaching job at Waseda University." Diana looked at him stonily. He took her expression as one of doubt. "I can. I can. You've no idea how much we members of Intersod help each other in this part of the world."

"I believe you can get a job at Waseda. Everyone knows Peter Morgan the brilliant linguist." She gave all her attention to the soup as she spoke. "But I don't believe you'd go off and leave Ah Tung like that."

"You don't. You'll see my dear. You've a lot to learn, Di. I'll tell you a secret: men never really love men. Never. It's just sex with people like me. Surely you've read the British papers. We're just depraved. Only 'normal' men and women know how to love. People like you, people like Robert. You see I like tasting men, just as you're going to taste those fish— without any feeling for them. By Jove, that smells good. Can I have some?" He gave her a sudden intense stare. "You're a funny girl. Fancy thinking you and me and Carlos could have a romantic threesome. You've no idea of the difficulties. It would've ended up in murder, jealous murder. Of course a threesome's good just for sex, but keep out the emotion. Though if you really want that sort of thing I'm sure Carlos will help. Why don't you ask him to bring along his cousin Orlando. Orlando the Organ I call him—and for good reason you'll see." He picked up a spoon and stirred it next to hers in the pot.

Just then the two Kam boys came in and Peter, after a final barb in English—"These two are smashers—and I should know. You should try them too," went off in a stream of richly idiomatic Cantonese about fishing and boats, which Diana couldn't follow for her life. Then Mr. and Mrs. Kam arrived and asked everyone to eat. Peter looked at his watch and put on a flustered air. "Oh no. Excuse me. I've got to go." He went off singing, "Bye bye Di. Bye bye di o do do Di," like some idiotic nineteen twenties popular song.

As she ate with the Kams, Diana did her best to contain her fury. She ordered herself to feel sorry for Peter. He'd never been obliged to discipline himself—like the Kams for instance. Compared with him, this family was a beacon of sanity; if only they knew what that kind Moh *Shin Saang*, with his glib manner, was really like what would they say? And she too could learn from them. They couldn't afford the sort of estrangement she and Robert had gone through. She remembered Mrs. Kam telling her how, in the fishing village she came from, when a married couple quarreled, on a night when it was very cold they would be left alone in the open on a rocky islet. When they were taken off the next day, everyone would laugh because the cold night air had always brought them together again. But the idea of that happening to herself and Robert made her smile. He'd probably spend the night trying to make her discuss Kierkegaard.

The hut started to shudder as a series of waves struck its supporting stakes. "The wake from the ferry boat," Mr. Kam said to Diana who'd looked up in alarm. At once she remembered her promise to meet Robert, bid the Kams goodbye and left for the harbour, getting there just in time to see the first of the passengers from Hong Kong coming down the gangway. Robert stood out hugely among them, encumbered with boxes of painting materials and canvasses.

She could tell he was in a mellow mood after his few days away, pawing and affectionate, asking with the sincerest expression, all gazes and contracted eyebrows, how she'd been, and travelling with his arm round her as they drove home in a taxi. What a charade and how it disgusted her. Occasionally he looked at the passing buildings with the interest of a newcomer; driving by the elegant old villas along the coast road, set in well tended gardens whose pergolas and painted tubs of flowers kept an army of gardeners busy, he said, "How this place grows on one. I really feel it's home now." adding warmly, "I think we should stay for a long time." Diana had mixed feelings. It struck her that the longer they stayed, the deeper the roots would go; it might become very difficult to detach themselves from anything or anyone before long.

His remark gave her a natural opening. "Well Peter's leaving." And she went on to give him a censored version of her conversation in the Kam's hut. It was easier to do this now; her anger with Peter had gone to be replaced by a longing to know why he had to dissimulate, with her of all people. As they passed the fishtrap she sat forward, away from Robert's arm which was too hot anyway, and stared at the hut. She wished Peter was still there so she could go in and shout, 'Why Peter? Why? Why? Why? Can't you see how much I love you? You don't have to protect yourself from me.'

"Dear trusting Diana. So you actually believed what he said?"

Here we go, Mr. Wordly Wisdom now, she thought as she replied, "He seemed all set as far as I could see. I think he's made the arrangements to go. How could he treat poor Ah Tung like that."

"Poor Ah Tung!" Robert's voice was incredulous. "Poor Ah Tung! Whenever you met the lad at Peter's you were cool to him. You used to say he was a thug—and you were right.

But now he's become poor Ah Tung." He gave one of the high haw hawing laughs he affected at any manifestation of the follies of mankind. "If it's true you should be glad Peter's seen the light. It may seem hard but if he doesn't steel himself and get away, he'll be bloody miserable. Thank God he's got some instinct for survival. I was beginning to doubt it." Diana was glad when they reached the apartment where Robert's flow of good solid common sense, of which he had such a superfluity when it came to other people's behaviour, had to come to an end.

As he unpacked the materials in the studio, Robert continued to enjoy his mood of self congratulation. The things he'd bought seemed a visible proof that a period of productivity lay ahead; the sunlight drenching the room's surfaces was already reflecting colours onto the waiting canvasses, hinting at the shapes of future masterpieces. As for his personal relationships, the counters were satisfactorily placed on the board. Peter's departure, if true, would even improve the pattern. He'd no longer be there to disturb Diana's calm content with his baneful influence for, as a result of what he'd learned in Hong Hong, he had no doubt now that it could only be baneful.

He'd stayed there with his old friend Adrian Hills in a Tudor mansion overlooking Repulse Bay. The place was the scene of a perpetual house party, full of people determinedly English. Even if he wasn't keen on everyone who was there, he did enjoy Adrian Hills' company, for A.H. had a sensitive and kindly nature, understanding towards human frailty— within limits. Robert had enjoyed talking to him about their schooldays at Stowe, mutual friends and, above all, cricket, a subject Diana quickly tired of but which for him was one of those few topics that stood like stout bollards in a world of quicksand. It so happened that A.H. knew a lot about Peter. "Oh, young Morgan. Born here you know. Used to work for Baker and Sweetman, the investment company. Took him on because of his old man. Very influential in the Colony his father, very influential. In any case they reckoned Peter'd be useful to them with his perfect Chinese. And the fact is, he was good. Could do the work with a fraction of his brain. So he must have lost interest earlier than they suspected. Mastered things far too quickly. Well, before long he started making mistakes—things to embarrass his bosses." A.H.'s blue eyes twinkled as he drawled on, "Deliberately of course. Obviously wanted to make a break. The father may be one of their biggest clients but Baker and Sweetman will never let the son through their doors again."

Yet even Robert had found himself laughing at the story of Peter's last day at work. "He came dressed up as a coolie—pulling a rickshaw, with some drunken Aussie sailor in it. He wouldn't speak anything but Cantonese in the office, except over the 'phone. And then he used 'Australian' to insult some of the firm's best clients. Later he was heard calling up the Colonial Secretary and telling him the Company was turning all its assets over to a workers' cooperative; he said all British companies would be asked to follow the lead. That's when they chucked him out. He ended up in some run-down Chinese hotel in Kowloon. That's where he was living when his book of Chinese poems came out." There was an awkward pause, then "He has talent," was added sincerely. But there was something else that even fair minded A.H. found a bit embarrassing to talk about, so he told it bluffly. "You know Bob, someone in the police told me that Morgan was down at the docks most nights. Well, no reason for you not to know why. He'd become a male whore. Picking up sailors, dammit. No self discipline of course. None at all. Talent or not, he'll ruin his life." Robert had been impressed by A.H.'s confident prediction and left Hong Kong determined Peter shouldn't ruin Diana's as well.

When unpacking Robert's case in his dressing room, Diana came across three little boxes marked 'Diana', 'Soolan', and 'Carlos'. In a flash she saw how his mind was working. It annoyed her far more than Peter's bad behaviour. After putting back the shirts she'd already taken out, she called into the studio, "Robert dear, I'll ask Group to unpack your case. I'm not feeling too well." An insistent, "No. Don't you bother to do it," came back. Then he shouted, "You seemed alright in the taxi." She called, "Yes. But I've started to feel sick. I'll be on the balcony."

After a while he came out with her present, a mutton fat jade pendant, intricately carved, and she admired it. "It'll go beautifully on that long silver chain you got me." Then, rather shyly he produced a little black box from his pocket, opened it and showed her a pair of gold cuff links, each stud bearing an almost indecipherable Gothic letter. "Oh Robert. They're very elegant. Real gold?" He nodded. "I'm so glad you've got yourself a present for once. And look they're engraved. What's on them. R for Robert?" He looked shamefaced and replied, "We'll, actually it's a C." She waited. "C. for Carlos."

"For Carlos?" Her face was replete with tenderness. "Oh, you're so understanding." He knelt beside the settee and showed her the cuff links more closely. "Will he like them?" he asked.

"Everybody likes gold." She gave him a kiss and a long loving look and repeated, "Robert, you're so understanding."

"Are you feeling better?" he asked, brimming over with solicitude.

"No. Not really. It's been like this a few days now. I…"

"Yes dear?"

She sat up and took his hands. "Robert." She hesitated as if on the brink of a momentous decision. "Robert, I'm going to have a baby."

His hand clasp became limp and he stared at her, all manner of thoughts charging like the Light Brigade across his mind. No. Someone had blundered. It couldn't be true. "A baby. You're going to have a baby. Then it must be…?"

"Yes dear. I'm so glad you got the cuff links for him. He'll know you accept things for what they are."

"A baby," he repeated. "Are you sure?"

"Oh absolutely. There's no doubt. You're not angry are you?"

"Oh no. No. These things happen." He did his best to be phlegmatic.

"Robert." Had the word been in Chinese, it might have been described as being in a falling tone, whilst the "Yes?" of his reply was most distinctly a rising one.

"Thank you for taking it so marvellously. You're wonderful." For her adulation she received a wan smile.

He went off to the studio and returned with a large volume Soolan had recommended to him on the *Shanghai Impressionists*. With an air of intense concentration he buried his nose in it but as page followed page his interest waned, though not through any lack of merit in the artists. The reality was dawning that the counters on the board were not made of wood. They were flesh and blood; and so was he. The truth forced itself out; he'd been obscurely jealous of the sultry Apollo the first time Diana pointed him out on duty in front of the Leal Senado. 'The young in one another's arms,' he'd thought at the time. The depression, whose cause he'd refused to recognise then, now flooded back several times stronger.

Diana lay back on the settee and from time to time let out sighs as though to relieve her suffering but keeping him under surveillance out of the corner of her eyes. The act prompted the emergence of a little fantasy about what she'd do if the story was true; she'd have the baby—it would be an act of desecration to destroy the offspring of the sun god. But she wouldn't stay with Robert. She'd get a job in Hong Kong, or like Peter, in Tokyo and find some one else to make her life with. The fantasy expanded; perhaps if she were in Tokyo, Peter wouldn't mind being a surrogate father, provided there were no strings attached. The whole idea seemed so pleasant, she began to wish she was going to have the baby. But the thought of living with Carlos, still less of marrying him, never entered her head. She couldn't settle down in the stifling society of the local

Portuguese. But this thought in turn produced misgivings over her own condescending attitude towards Carlos. She was like a spoiled child with a luxury toy. I don't deserve to have his baby, she chided herself and then remembered she wasn't having one anyway. The fantasy ended with the sad conviction that she should end the affair with him before he was hurt.

Robert closed the *Shanghai Impressionists* with a snap. 'A Portrait of the Artist's son' had been the last straw. "Have you seen a doctor?" There was a slight tremor in his voice. "You haven't thought of..."

"Robert. You don't want me to get rid—no I don't believe you'd want that."

"I was only thinking how difficult it might be for you. The way we travel around and so forth."

"But you said we were going to stay here." She put on the most ingenuous expression she could manage but the laughter was welling up.

"Damn it all Diana." His temper burst out at last. "Everyone in town will know. The child might be... Well, Carlos isn't exactly the Nordic type, is he?"

"But Robert. You're an artist, an intellectual, a left wing intellectual. What do bourgeois values matter? Look dear, if it's a girl we'll call it Roberta, and if it's a boy, even a sweet little black boy, it can..." What started as a snort turned into uncontrollable peals of laughter. She rolled and twisted on the settee. "Oh you bastard, you liar," he shouted. The *Shanghai Impressionists* flew through the air in a high arc, landing face upward before her. The sight of the title increased her mirth. "*Shanghai Impressionists.* Is Soolan a Shanghai Impressionist?" she screamed. "What a lark. *Shanghai Impressionists.*" Only gradually was calm restored. "Yes Robert I was lying. But I'm glad you can admit the truth about yourself—even if it does take a long time."

Carlos couldn't believe the cuff links were from Robert when she gave them to him the next night. He sat gazing at them, fascinated by the complexities of the gothic

C. "Honestly?" he asked several times. "They're from Mr. Sheraton?" He was only convinced when she told him to 'phone Robert if he wanted to say 'Thank you'. But he was too shy to do that and instead wrote a courteous little note in Portuguese (he didn't trust himself to writing in English).

For the first time their tryst didn't take place in Peter's house, for which Diana was thankful. Carlos' parents had gone off for a year's holiday to Lisbon—their first visit to Portugal. They'd been promising themselves the trip for twenty years. As his numerous brothers and sisters were either married or had found jobs in Hong Kong, Carlos now had the family house with its sombre wallpaper and heavy furniture to himself. He looked forward to spending many a cosy romantic evening there with Diana. But she'd not forgotten her resolution. "I wish you liked Peter and not me," she remarked when they'd finished the food he'd taken all day to prepare: crab soup, roast pork with lots of peppery sauce and a jelly which was too stiff and sweet, served on rarely used best family porcelain with candlelight and wine. His efforts didn't stop her going on to say, "You've more in common than we have. You told me you could be excited by men as well as women."

Carlos' eyes stared straight at her, his eyes unblinking and solemn. He reminded her of an owlet. What the hell if I am being cruel, she thought; let's see if he can take it. So, forgetting that pleasure runs shallow but sorrow deep, she said, "Why don't you make love to him together with your cousin Orlando. Take him out of himself; make him forget Ah Tung. You'd be very happy together."

He replied in a thoughtful voice as if to show he recognized the sense of her suggestion. "I did. But he wasn't very keen. He wants to suffer I guess. Yes maybe you're right. Pity he didn't meet me before Ah Tung." It was Diana's turn to feel slighted; nor did she enjoy an unexpected pang of jealousy. Perhaps Carlos wasn't so satisfied with her after all. Her manner became blasé and her voice harder than she intended. "Oh really. So you're not so faithful to me then.

Only on Monday, Wednesday and Friday. Peter on Saturday. Who else on the other days?"

Carlos jumped to his feet. A rush of blood to his head made his olive skin darker where others would have gone red. "Oh, I see it now," the tirade began. "You want me to become like Peter, do you? You want me to love you so much I'll go crazy like him when you decide to throw me over. When you decide, you decide—oh not me. My feelings won't matter." His anger was the greater because, though he often went to talk to Mei Ling now and knew he'd go to her for comfort if ever this affair ended, he'd deliberately kept his actions in check. In his way, he had been faithful to Diana.

She pulled him down to her and kissed away his passionate tears, her resolution dissipated. "My poor sweet boy. I'm sorry. You were good, very good, to try that with Peter. (Carlos gave her a doe eyed look and decided to take the credit.) Don't think so badly of me, Carlos; whatever happens." Naturally their reconciliation ended in sharing the unutterable bliss of the bursting cloud on the elder Nolasco's four poster bed.

She returned home in the early hours of the morning to find Robert still up. He greeted her with "Carlos 'phoned."

"Oh, he said he wouldn't 'phone you. He wrote you this note."

"Yes, I know about that. No it's something else. Apparently the boat Lim went off in has been returned by the Chinese authorities. Even Lim's suitcase was in it. The boat drifted into their waters. They're very correct about these things, it seems. Carlos has already told Peter."

Diana tried to work out the implications of it all. "But did Ah Tung say anything in gaol? Peter was afraid he'd talk—deprived of opium."

"No. Carlos' friend in the prison said Ah Tung admitted to nothing despite some rough treatment. So, as far as the Portuguese are concerned there are no charges. No body, no charge. Lim could be held in China. No one knows. Ah Tung can't even be accused of robbery. There was nothing on him when he was arrested." Since Diana was looking very pleased, Robert continued, "Remember, Lim's clansmen won't need any proof. Do you think Ah Tung will be safe when he's out?"

"Surely we can help him to get away with Peter," she insisted. "We can't stand by and do nothing. Now's your chance to get rid of Peter's bad influence on me too," she added wryly, "So you must do something. You must."

As Robert didn't want an argument at this time of night the best thing to do was to promise he'd think about it—positively. Since Diana was tired she accepted this meekly and after a smile and a kiss on his cheek, she was off to bed.

For Robert it was a restless night. After trying to sleep he pottered round the studio but the new canvasses didn't stimulate him at all. Flat and grey in the artificial light, the most they seemed to say was, 'Even if we're covered with the genius of Botticelli, one day we'll rot away. It was pointless to buy us.' What disturbed him most was not the problem of Ah Tung but the memory of Carlos' voice, warm yet soft as oiled silk on the 'phone; it suggested sensuality, subtle movements, youth. Whenever he tried to sleep the thought of Diana giving herself to Carlos made it impossible to relax. Something told him that she must despise his age, his corpulence, his..., the list was endless. He managed to lull himself off at last by telling himself that he was a fool to worry so. What did it matter if Diana thought nothing of him physically when he, for so long, had failed to respond to her? But after merely half an hour's sleep, he awoke in the black hours of the early morning with the conviction that she'd despise him even more if he sat back and did nothing to help Ah Tung.

It struck him that the only person who knew enough about the ins and outs of things in the Colony, to advise him properly, was Soolan. When he went to her unproletarian apartment in the evening he asked what was likely to happen next.

"With the likes of Ah Tung," she answered casually, her hands poised in the air as she made sure the dining table had everything needed on it, "they'll do as they see fit. They can go on holding him till Kingdom come. Oh, I forgot the chili sauce."

"What do you mean, 'with the likes of...'?"

"Well, if he was a member of one of our unions, we'd have him out tomorrow—and he'd be safe."

"And you're not interested in 'the likes of Ah Tung'?" His frown accused her of hardness.

She looked embarrassed. "Oh, I didn't mean that. Our party stands for justice." She paused. "You know Robert, we have to face up to realities. Ah Tung broke the Triad rule. Lim was an important man in the drug world. There's bound to be revenge. Lung Yeung's setup will demand punishment. That devil Ming Yuk will see to it. Wherever he goes, Ah Tung won't escape the Triad net."

Robert sighed. "I knew there'd be complications but I had to ask you. I think you know why its important to me." He changed the conversation but wasn't his usual self. She was disappointed when he left earlier than she'd expected.

The incident, small though it was, jolted Soolan. She'd been reminded of the side of Robert's life which they now tried not to talk about. She always did her best to be casual and amusing with him; she wanted to become a pleasant habit he couldn't do without. And just because things had been going well between them, she mustn't take success for granted. But when the plum tree and the snow were fighting for the spring, as the Chinese saying went, nothing should be taken for granted (she preferred not to speculate on which of the two contestants she and Diana should be identified with). Without thinking, she'd given a casual answer to a question that wasn't casual at all. She should have remembered that westerners tended to forget the misery of millions and concentrate on individual sorrows. No, that was wrong, she told herself. What about her own personal preoccupations. Generalities about easterners and westerners were all rubbish.

The next time she met Robert, they went to the theatre. It was a modern western style play, Tsao Yu's *Thunder and Rain* and in Mandarin. No one seemed to mind Soolan's buzz of translation and commentary on the story of a feudal family cracking under modern pressures, though Robert hardly listened, for he was busy sketching. Afterwards they went to the green room where his drawings were a great success. She was glad to see him so happy, fitting in naturally with the progressive actors. On the way home she talked sympathetically about Ah Tung. "No one could say Lim's disappearance was a bad thing," and, "What a pity a clever young man like that couldn't serve society," was her general theme. Quite suddenly she announced, "By the way, the Chamber of Commerce wants to commission a portrait of Lung Yeung—to give him at the Banquet. They want a modern style picture. You don't think you could do it, do you?" The fee she then mentioned was so handsome that Robert had no hesitation in accepting. Soolan clapped her hands in surprised delight and said she'd let the Chamber know. Robert showed his appreciation in the bedroom and even promised to come round the following day. "Dahling," she said, as he straightened his tie in the mirror, "I wish you could come here every day. But," she added, all woman of the world, "We're both busy people." Then she became casual again. "I'll see what I can find out about Ah Tung." That was the secret, she decided, tidying her hair, casual but full of concern. She also decided, simultaneously, that the plum tree was more in accordance with her nature. Snow might be beautiful but it was quickly dispelled by warmth—and it became slushy before it vanished.

To Robert's surprise, Lung Yeung didn't insist on the sittings taking place at the Pearl River Mansion. He was willing to come to the Sheraton's apartment. When he arrived—it was his first visit—he admired the simple pottery, fabrics and carvings Robert and Diana had picked up on their travels. They grinned at each other behind him; what insincerity. But he'd a large eye in the back of his head. "Oh, I know you think I'm a hypocrite, praising your things when they're not very valuable. But they show your taste. One day they'll sell, for a lot, as no doubt, Mr. Sheraton, will your paintings." Famed-in-the-future Mr. Sheraton whispered to the artist's wife, "Ah the deep spiritual perceptions of the east," and got on with his work.

Since Diana felt Robert and his new subject should get to know one another, she went out when Lung Yeung came, but little contact was made initially. Lung Yeung didn't have much understanding of western art and Robert was bemused by the thought that this frail old man, who to Diana was the epitome of venerable Chinese culture—a sort of superannuated Confucius—controlled wealth and vice beyond imagination. But one afternoon Lung Yeung said in his quiet way, "What made you come here Mr. Sheraton?"

"Let's say I like the calm, the innocence of the place."

Lung Yeung's eyes twinkled. "And you think it's good for your wife?"

"She likes it very much. She's always telling me what a lot she learns from you, for instance."

"Then she must be bored indeed if she finds an old man like me interesting. I think she looks sad these days."

A thought struck Robert and he abandoned his reserve to tell Lung Yeung enough about Peter's troubles to give him a basis for action if he wanted. The old man said nothing during the rest of the sitting. Well here's a chance for him to show if he's got any humanity in his desiccated heart, Robert thought. It was worthwhile telling Diana what he'd done; light the blue touch paper and retire, he said to himself.

She made a point of being around the next time there was a sitting. The conversation such as it was, dwelt on the Korean war and whether 'the bomb' might be used. As Lung Yeung was leaving and they were alone at the doorway, he said quietly to Diana, "I'm sorry, I can do nothing. My power is limited. Advise Mr. Morgan to leave."

The same evening, the only light in Peter's house when she went there came from the kitchen. Sitting in the darkness on the verandah, Peter didn't notice her until she was nearly up to him. He was lost in reverie. But as so often, his behaviour made another of those unexpected turns she never quite got used to. With the most charming smile he was on his feet, embracing her warmly and saying, "I'm so sorry Diana—about that day at the Kam's. I couldn't face you after that. I really feel ashamed." Though anyone less ashamed looking she couldn't imagine.

"I know you didn't mean a word you said."

"Come. Sit beside. It's old times again. You've not turned against me then?"

"No one will ever turn me against you."

"Ah, so someone's been trying?" He was as quick on the uptake as ever. "Well I was rude to you. I can understand Robert's attitude."

"I didn't tell him about that, only what you said about leaving."

There was a little silence and then Peter said, "Good Lord, you must have something to eat. I'm being rude again." He returned with some madeira cake and a box of Huntley and Palmer's Assorted Biscuits.

Diana asked, "Have you made any more enquiries—at the prison I mean?"

"They'll still tell me nothing. Maybe they're going on with the pressure—trying for a confession; or maybe they're afraid of another murder, Ah Tung's murder by Lim's cronies. Don't ask me have I seen a lawyer. I have. But he can't take action until there are charges. The police are a law to themselves here. They'll hold him as long as they want." He looked at her sharply. "You see, I've thought of everything—including the fact that sensible people would tell me I really should leave. That's Robert's view isn't it?"

"Ah Tung's in great danger. There's nothing you can do. It's Robert's view, Lung Yeung's view, Carlos' view. Yes everybody's. They think you should go."

"And your view too?" he asked airily before digging in to the biscuits.

"I love you because you're Peter. If you deserted Ah Tung you wouldn't be Peter would you? Anyway, whatever anyone says you won't leave." Though Diana spoke lightly, as if they were talking of trivialities, she was convinced that beneath his seeming nonchalance something wild was stirring; if Ah Tung was killed Peter might easily court death from his killers. "Just be careful Peter." she begged. "I don't want anything to happen to you. I don't want to lose you."

He stroked her long hair and said, "Have another bicky. No, these are smashing. I don't want to lose you either dear. You see I love you too." He gave her a wink, "…almost as much as Ah Tung. No. Take one of those with the red stuff in the middle. They're the best."

"Funny so many of them are left then," Diana replied, pushing one into his mouth.

Later that night when Robert had filled every room in the apartment with the, for Diana, turgid strains of a Brahms symphony, she sought out the calm sympathy of the Kam's hut from which came the tune of a flute, plaintive, simple and very pure. Mr. Kam, who was watching the net, saw her and shouted, "The old woman's out but the boys are in." Diana went inside, squatted beside them and watched the elder boy gutting a fish; its innards were ripped open and its dying eyes took in God knew what. The younger boy put down his flute and offered her a bowl of tea which she took with both hands bowing her thanks. No one said a word and in the silence she gazed at their lean bodies flattered by the lamp light. The elder boy reached over to pull another victim from the basket and brushed up against her; she smelt his skin fresh and tangy like the sea. His hand groped in the basket and his shoulder pressed against her cheeks and mouth; she didn't draw back but instead closed her lips, as it were accidentally, against him. The fish he finally drew out was only a little one and wriggled vainly in his hand; he bit the head off, spat it out and grinned. Diana smiled and lit a cigarette and then two more which she handed to the brothers. Vague thoughts began to advance from the back of her mind; she knew that if she'd just been wrecked on some deserted island with this family, she would become one of them and before long her old life would seem like an unnatural dream. She would possess nothing, just the clothes she stood up in like old Mrs. Kam. All day long they'd work and eat and sleep and talk of simple things and when one of the brothers wanted her, it would be no more complex than when he gutted fish. And always she and they and everything they touched would be washed clean by the eternal sea. The dream seemed infinitely preferable to her life with Robert and all its falsehood. She glanced up; the elder boy was watching her curiously though pretending to deal with the fish; his brother smiled, said something which Diana couldn't catch, and received a playful blow in return. She looked at the boys openly as though she understood and they all laughed aloud together. Mr. Kam appeared at the door and joined in but he'd no idea what it was all about.

Since the negotiations in Canton, Ming Yuk's appearance had changed. Ever somber it reflected the increased authority Lung Yeung had given him, the burden of work and hours spent poring over reports. But it was also the result of his own efforts. Where once he had affected long hair, a film star moustache and western clothes, now he cultivated a severe style; clean shaven and close cropped, clad in restrained Peking style jackets and trousers of grey or blue, even the expensive cuff links in which he once took pride were discarded. Modelling himself on his master, he went through the reports from the organisation's trading agencies with care, the accounts receiving particular attention since he was aware of the rackets that could creep into the activities Lung Yeung controlled. A number of offenders were brought to book and the discipline of the organisation was rigidly tightened. He had grown superbly aloof to all who approached him; even people who once imagined he was their friend now came before him in fear. The aura of isolation needed for power was complete.

Observing all this, Lung Yeung added to Ming Yuk's responsibilities so that gradually a barrier grew between the emperor and his organisation. Agents who once had access to the master now found that if they were to see him at all, it was only after consultation with Ming Yuk. For the most part they were content to deal with the vizier who, they realised, was empowered to make decisions formerly taken on high.

Ming Yuk was now allowed access to secret records that gave him an insight into the system; he was surprised at the number of highly placed people in the most varied organisations, even in foreign governments, over whom Lung Yeung had established influence. Yet he knew there were still some parts of the system, particularly those concerning relations with Peking, that Lung Yeung kept to himself; he also suspected that there were channels of information, parallel to those he manipulated, kept from him. The strength of the organisation lay in the separation of its parts; the lines of communication radiated to them only from the centre. Ming Yuk felt he was near the middle of the hub but not quite at its pivot. Despite his increased power he refused to give up his personal duties and remained Lung Yeung's companion at the end of each day, adamantly refusing to allow anyone else access to the private apartments at such times.

The members of Lung Yeung's inner family had no complaints. When his number one wife and her favourite youngest son, who now spent most of their time on the Riviera, paid a visit to the Colony shortly after the negotiations in Canton, they found him more at ease than when they'd last come; true he seemed slightly remote but it was a remoteness that contrived to be benign. For one thing, without being asked (little did they know that Ming Yuk had suggested it) he doubled their already huge allowances; of course, they left feeling that everything was ordered for the best. And since the organisation's power had to be wielded with a criminal ruthlessness of which they wished to know as little as possible, Ming Yuk was welcome to inherit command as far as they were concerned.

Lung Yeung found the arrangements conducive to his ease for, like many an emperor, he had found it easier to rule a kingdom than his family, but sometimes he would complain that Ming Yuk no longer sent girls to visit him, though his desire for such casual pleasures had almost gone. "No doubt," he said, "when I'm asleep, you're off to enjoy them yourself." Ming Yuk looked hurt. "You know I give up everything for you. I've no time for people that don't matter." Among the people who did matter was Ah Tung; in him was a means of breaking his master's friendship with that Sheraton woman. Late one afternoon, when his routine work was done, he decided that the time had come to catch a fish in muddy water. The private exchange put him through to the Portuguese Security Headquarters where Colonel Lobato, having learned of Ming Yuk's rising influence and therefore acquainted himself with the new man's K.M.T. background, took the call. "Ah," he said sardonically, "the *éminence grise*."

"I beg your pardon Colonel?"

"Forgive me. It's just one of our expressions for a very important man. We haven't met but I've heard a lot about you. We must get together sometime."

Ming Yuk felt unsure of himself talking to the Colonel but he put on a confident tone which struck Lobato by its curious resemblance to the voice of Lung Yeung. "Colonel, I'd like to talk to you about the Lim murder."

"So, the report's in front of you."

Ming Yuk was taken aback. The Colonel must know his police reports were passed on but he didn't expect the fact to be referred to so openly.

"Don't worry dear sir," Lobato continued. "As we're going to deal with each other in future, it's best if we accept the fact that each of us gets a good look at the other's documents." This was bluff on Lobato's part for he was certain that any espionage balance sheet would stand in favour of Lung Yeung's organisation.

"Well Colonel, people are saying that Lim's murderer, this man Kai Tung (he used Ah Tung's full name) shouldn't be released."

"Be that as it may; but we can't produce evidence to convict. Everything's circumstantial. He'd probably get off with a poor lawyer and Morgan's bound to engage a good one. The Government can't afford to get beaten in its own courts. No, I'm afraid there's nothing for it. We'll have to wash our hands of the matter."

Ming Yuk now came to the point. "Perhaps you could let me know when he'll be released then."

Lobato glanced at a memo on his desk, one evidently not in Ming Yuk's possession. "Let me see. Ah yes, Sunday, tomorrow. Yes, it'll be at noon tomorrow." His words were a death sentence, but cooperation in minor matters could facilitate the resolution of issues of greater moment.

"Thank you Colonel. It's all I wish to know."

"Most obliged. My regards to your master."

Ming Yuk made a few more phone calls, contacting members of the wharfside cell to which Lim had belonged, as well as certain warders in the Prison. It was arranged that the next day at ten o'clock in the morning a trishaw would go up the alley next to the prison and Kai Tung would be bundled into it by the warders. He'd then be taken before the cell committee and done to death in whatever way they decided; Ming Yuk emphasised the organisation wanted an example to be made.

The men who were to arrange the pick-up were in Old Chong's hotel playing mahjong when they received instructions. They talked about the plan over their game which went on all night. Big ears Siu Ching, going in and out of the room serving drinks, took everything in and passed the news on to Mei Ling.

"Ah Tung's a gonner," she whispered in the kitchen, "but I don't think he should be killed for doing in that rotten egg Lim. What are you going to do about it?"

Mei Ling couldn't see what she could do. No one could oppose the Triads and get away with it. She thought too of Ah Tung's family in the Little Bird Garden and the poverty that would now face them. She had to repay his kindness, but how? One thing for sure, she wouldn't call Carlos; she'd promised to keep his involvement a secret. Nothing was going to spoil the understanding that grew between them with each of his visits. She thought too of Mr. Morgan—though what a foreigner could do she couldn't imagine. When the hall was empty she 'phoned his house but Ping said he was out.

She went to bed but couldn't sleep with the thought of Ah Tung's death on her mind. She got out her *English for Beginners* but that didn't help her to relax either. The clicking of mahjong pieces went on punctuated by raucous voices. A loathing for the things men did when they got into groups, seized her. Why did they like uniforms and secret societies. Why did they get pleasure out of persecuting people. The men below had killed people as cruelly as the Communists killed her parents, just to show their power. How could they sit down there gambling, drinking and annoying Siu Ching or the other girls when tomorrow they were going to kill again. Wild ideas of how she'd poison the lot of them went through her mind. To calm herself she thought about Carlos and as she was imagining a little house in the country where they'd be happy together, she fell asleep.

When she awoke in the early morning the mahjong game was still going on. She went to work, her panic rising. Several times she 'phoned Morgan but he was still out. The gamblers occasionally glanced at their watches and talked less than before. She thought of begging their mercy, but remembering the People's Trials, knew it was useless. There was nothing in the world she could do to save Ah Tung as the hour of his death drew near.

She wasn't alone in her desire to help him. Determined not to fail Peter as she believed she had failed her own brother, Diana had taken action, without a word to Robert. Colonel Lobato was surprised on returning from Mass to learn that Mrs. Sheraton was in his sitting room. He knew in his bones that the call was connected with the young thug who'd got Morgan in his grip. However, that was no reason to enjoy it any the less. He slipped into his bedroom, put on a freshly pressed suit with tasteful wine coloured tie and matching pocket handkerchief and, as a final touch, opened a new bottle of gentleman's eau de toilette and liberally doused his bewhiskered face. "Lord, make me chaste—but not yet," he quipped aloud as he surveyed his handiwork with satisfaction.

To Diana's apology for calling at such short notice he gushed, "Ah Senhora, a visit from a lovely woman can never be inconvenient. How do you manage to dress so well in this place? You're as much an artist as your husband. What an honour this is."

"What a fine house this is Senhor Colonel." Gazing around like a tourist in a stately home Diana felt gloomily certain of the futility of her mission.

"I don't deny it. It was built for a great family in the seventeenth century. A pity it had to be divided into apartments. But where are my manners? Come sit with me here. Let's have a nice talk together." Like characters in a drawing room comedy they took up their positions at either end of a huge settee.

"I suppose if you'd lived then, you'd have been a fidalgo." It was worth responding to his pride in the place and Diana decided to play on him as best she could, though she already felt outclassed in whatever game it was.

"A son of someone." Lobato translated the Portuguese word. "Well, I suppose I could claim to be a fidalgo. My family has a creditable record in our history—though on occasion some of its members were black sheep." He stroked his moustache—almost saucily, quite the ludicrous old lecher with a glittering eye.

"Are you a black sheep?"

"Maybe; it depends on the mood I'm in."

"You don't strike me as a moody person at all; Luiz Figueiredo says you're a very kind man—behind that military exterior." But she suspected Lobato's opinion of himself might be nearer the truth than that of Luiz.

A servant brought coffee; Lobato dismissed him curtly. "Well, Figueiredo's judgement and mine don't always coincide. But I thought you didn't see him much nowadays." Did he know about her affair with Carlos, Diana wondered. As she poured out the coffee she said casually, "Oh, we see him from time to time. But he's always so busy. He asked me out one day last week and then cancelled it at the last minute because of some emergency in the hospital."

"Ah your Anglo-Saxon ways! Asked you out! On your own! You have such freedom. It isn't like that in Portugal. We expect our women to be..." Lobato hesitated, looking a little alarmed at whatever reactionary thing he was about to say, for so he knew it would be taken, but ended up with, "more circumspect."

"I can believe it. But Portuguese men do pretty well don't they. I've seen them night after night at the Casino with those girls—whilst their wives sit at home." The feminist in Diana showed up in the note of anger and the suddenly flashing eyes.

Lobato laughed heartily. "Perhaps their wives get up to more than you imagine—discreetly of course."

"I doubt it. You keep your women under lock and key. But don't think Robert and I are completely free—though I don't believe that abstinence is better than moderation; surely a bit of freedom makes a marriage tolerable."

Lobato raised his eyebrows by way of reply and a silence more embarrassing to Diana than himself ensued. She glanced about the room playing nervously with a large-stoned ring on her little finger and the horrid thought struck her that if she took a wrong step, tomorrow this scene could be all over town. Noticing the lithographs of the Intramuros she said, "Are those the pictures you mentioned to Robert? I must look at them."

"Do you think you should—just now? I'm more interested to hear your views on marriage. I think your motto's 'Love and do what you will.'"

The hardness, or was it the note of impertinence in his voice, acted as a challenge. What the hell? If the whole of this flea-blown dump found out that she had come here and why, what did she care? "You wouldn't agree with my views any more than you agree with Luiz." She threw back her head impulsively—a gesture the Colonel found most attractive. "Or perhaps I'd shock you."

"Me. The Head of Security. I know everything—it's my job. And that means I know a great deal since this place tends to bring out the worst in everyone."

"Never the best?"

"I've not noticed it so far." He paused before continuing nonchalantly, "Your friend Peter Morgan for instance. Look what it's doing to him. Intelligent, quite a scholar, a poet. Mother of God, who'd have imagined such a thing. Three generations of Morgans pillars of the Hong Kong establishment and the fourth? Going to ruin." The last phrase was uttered with an air of finality that chilled Diana, yet since the conversation was taking the direction she wanted she let him go on. "But does it matter?" His brow puckered. "What we do with out bodies seems to me to be of little consequence; the important thing is our emotional, our spiritual attitudes. Physical actions are the overflowing of processes in the soul; to be prejudiced over them betrays ignorance of the human mind." Deeply concerned with the state of her soul, Torquemada-like, he leaned forward and said in an insistent voice, "Frankly I'm only concerned with Senhor Morgan's problems insofar as they affect you my dear. I know you're very close to him. Very close."

At any other time her reaction would have been to laugh in his face; as it was, she felt sure that all her fears would be realised; he'd do nothing. No doubt he considered Peter a degenerate and as for Ah Tung, to the likes of Lobato, a trishaw boy must be less than dirt. She got up and walked about the room looking at the lithographs, uttering such things as, "Oh, that's the Theatre; Is this the ballroom? Was the Chapel like that?" and so forth, whilst Lobato watched her with amused detachment.

"My dear Mrs. Sheraton, sit down. Sit down and tell me the purpose of this visit? It's Morgan's friend isn't it?"

Diana did as she was told but no longer at the end of the settee. "Yes. Yes. Peter and I are very close. But not as lovers, if that's what you think—though if I could help him like that I would." She paused and looked intently into Lobato's eyes." Yes. I would do that to help him."

Lobato took her hand gently. "And you're saying that if you could help him by 'doing that' with me, you would, aren't you?" At first Diana felt that dramatically speaking, he should have spoken these words softly, with the greatest delicacy, and certainly after a pregnant pause. In fact he had said them so casually and without a hint of delay, that what might have been a few moments of embarrassment for both of them had tripped by easily. He had been like a skillful dentist whipping out a child's tooth so swiftly that pain, and worse still, the anticipation of pain, had been totally avoided. She felt grateful to him. Just as matter-of-factly she replied, "I'm not ashamed of wanting to help Peter. I don't want his life ruined. Yes. I'd do that if it's the price to help him. I'll do it without holding back. Do you understand? I want him to be with the person who makes him happy."

"I feel quite jealous of Senhor Morgan." Lobato lowered his head in a courtly gesture and raised Diana's hand to his lips. "You'd do so much for him?"

"No need for anyone to be jealous of Peter." She regretted her impetuosity. How crude she must seem to Lobato. "So there's nothing you can do?"

"On the contrary. I've news for you. I hope you'll forgive me for not telling you earlier. There's no case against the boy, though I'm sure he did it. We interrogated him of course but he didn't crack. Since then I've held on to him—deliberately, because of Morgan—I hoped he'd leave. But we've reached the limit. The boy's to be released today. I'm afraid there's only one chance for him and that's for Morgan to spirit him away." Lobato paused as if considering the implications. Then he said, "For your sake Senhora, I'll delay the release and order the prison Commandant to deliver him to Morgan personally. Perhaps you know where he is?"

Diana's anxiety for action left little room for embarrassment over her misjudgement of Lobato. That would come later. "I've no idea where he is but never mind, Senhor Lobato. I'll find him. I'll see they get away tonight."

Whilst Lobato went out to make a call to the prison, Diana paced up and down hardly able to control her excitement. Peter would be in danger but she knew the arrangement was what he would want. At the same time she was appalled by her own action. She was playing with death. When she sat down to steady herself the reality of it all became fiercer. Oh God, she thought, if Peter's killed too, it'll be my fault. She started as the door opened and turned to see Lobato looking at her with a grave expression.

"Is it arranged?" she asked but at once knew from his gesture to sit down that something was wrong.

"I'm afraid it's too late; the Commandant tells me the prisoner Kai Tung has already been released." He paused. "He's probably dead already."

Tears welled up in Diana's eyes. Lobato tried to comfort her. "I'm sorry. But perhaps it's for the best where Morgan's concerned. Make him leave. If he stays on he'll go to pieces here." He looked sternly at her. "Don't you see that?"

Diana walked across to the window and stared into the road, too numb to say more than, "Thank you for trying Colonel Lobato."

As she left, Lobato leaned towards her and kissed her cheek. Then he looked into her strained face and said, "As for this place always bringing out the worst in people—well, perhaps I'm wrong. I wonder if Senhor Sheraton appreciates what sort of woman you are." And what sort of man are you, he asked himself, once the door had closed on her. To get credit for what he had all the time known to be impossible hardly accorded with a fidalgo's concept of honour.

But the information Lobato had been given was wrong; the warders in Ming Yuk's pay had lied to the Commandant for they daren't change the arrangement that had been made. Ah Tung was still in his cell, lying on his narrow pallet, savouring the breeze playing on his face. It came from over the wooded Observatory Hill bringing with it the smell of the sea, the scent of trees and flowers and the dry odour of burning charcoal; each of them, sometimes singly, sometimes mingled, had such intensity that if he closed his eyes it was easy to imagine he was on the shore walking against the wind or in the woods with a high canopy of trees above him and the charcoal burners stacking their piles of burned wood ready for the market. From nearby the breeze bore the noises of the street; the roar of cars, the tinkling of bells and the cries of hawkers; these too amazed him with their sharpness as if they were new noises never heard on earth before.

The horror of the early days in the cell had gone. When first deprived of opium, the agony had been complete; he'd longed for death to release him from his craving. He'd begged for just a bit of heroin and raved at the warders for denying it. But when detectives promised him drugs if he confessed he never did.

During the first weeks in prison he slept little and then lightly, his rest disturbed by nightmares in which his craving was mixed with memories of being tortured. Awake the warders appeared to him as monsters intent on his destruction, leering at each other, joking about him and plotting ways of increasing his misery. Everything was hostile and in the blue-green light through which his eyes saw everything, the objects around him grimaced and threatened in league with the human persecutors.

Then occasionally, amidst the pain, he experienced moments in which his sensations were speeded up and he felt on the edge of recalling some strange joy; he never made it out for pain still ruled his life; not surface pain but a sharp force that probed outward into all parts of him from some deep core. Yet in course of time the pain did give way to amazing moments of pleasure. Gradually, these moments became more frequent and when they happened he felt he'd become a child again. But often they were so extreme that all at once the joy changed to pain leaving him angry and sick. At last the radiant moments began to link up and when they did the simple objects in the cell became intensely beautiful and he would stare and stare at the roundness of the light bulb, the slenderness of the flex or the whiteness of the ceiling, sure that everything he saw was more alive than he was; yet the beauty could still become menacing so that the bulb burned his eyes, the flex writhed like a snake and the whiteness of the ceiling became an empty waste.

One morning he awoke very early without passing through his usual nightmare and heard the sound of birds chirping. Hardly any light entered the cell but the bird song was like flecks of silver ransoming his heart so that nothing mattered more than that sound. Later he yawned and sneezed, his eyes watered and he became more conscious of the world outside. The month of agony was a dark night that had gone on for centuries, separating the present from the old days when he was free. From the past an image kept returning; a picture in a Portuguese church Carlos had once shown him, of the Christian God rising from the dead and coming through the black doorway of a tomb into the light. Carlos' words 'risen from the dead' echoed in his mind. His own flesh was still weak but its strength was coming back; he was sure his eyes must possess the light of that risen God. For an instant his mind was beset by some question about Carlos. Yes, he was glad; he had said nothing about Carlos to the police.

A warder brought the food. He ate it hungrily and banged on the bars for more. Later he was taken out and told to wash and shave. By the time he returned to the cell he was worn out and had to be supported; once more everything looked threatening. He dozed off and it seemed he was walking with Peter along brightly lit streets in some big town. They were outside a building. A door was opening. He awoke to see two warders standing above him. One of them held the clothes he was wearing when arrested; his wallet was on top. "Get dressed. You're being released." He obeyed but as he changed his clothes he only thought of the danger outside the prison. If there'd been a few more days in which to recover he could have bribed a warder to get Peter. "I can't leave. I feel ill." The warders grinned at each other. "Don't worry. You won't have to walk far. Your friends are waiting."

As soon as he was ready, they held him up and took him down long corridors to a door at the side of the prison. One of them unlocked it quietly and glancing at his watch, peered out. Ah Tung could see the cobblestones wet in the drizzle; no one was about, no one he could ask for help. "There's a trishaw at the corner," the first warder whispered. "It must be it. The driver's looking down here. Yes, he's moving. Quick, get ready."

Ah Tung saw the trishaw boy, his head hidden beneath a rattan hat, his body draped in a long cape, pedalling up furiously. He knew the man belonged to the Triads and trembled with fear. The trishaw was moving so quickly that it passed by and came to a stop with a loud screech of brakes a little way down the lane. Ah Tung expected someone to jump out of the passenger seat from behind the rain sheet but there was no movement. The driver just said gruffly, "What are you waiting for? Put him in and go. I don't want to hang around." The warders dragged Ah Tung along and pushed him behind the canvas sheet onto the seat. Then they ran back; the prison door was slammed and all was silent. Surprised to find himself alone inside Ah Tung tried to get out but he was too weak; he could easily be overpowered by the driver who had now begun to pedal down the lane. If he was going to escape, best to wait until they reached a place where people were about. But before he could do anything he heard a girl's voice. "Keep inside Ah Tung. Don't get out. It's me, Mei Ling." He sank back in the seat and sobbed uncontrollably. Just as he started to pull himself together, he saw they were careering dangerously out of the lane onto the Praia Grande. Fortunately there were no cars coming and since the drizzling rain had driven people from the streets there were no witnesses to Mei Ling's reckless progress. Gradually she lost speed and got control again, turning away from the town onto a half made-up road running across the reclaimed land.

"Are you alright?" she shouted breathlessly. "I thought I was going to crash." Without waiting for a reply she began to pedal again, forcing the trishaw on over bumps and through puddles until they reached the surfaced drive behind the sea wall. It was raining heavily now and the raindrops were mixed with spray bursting over the sea wall. The wind flapped the canvas but still Mei Ling pushed on, making for the Vasco da Gama monument—a huge group of bronze statues on a quoin. When she reached it she went to its seaward side so they were hidden from view. "Come on," she cried. "This is a good place to hide. I used to sleep here when I got out of the refugee camp." She helped him up the steps into the shelter of a cloaked figure whose arms gestured upward at the great navigator. Then she brought up the canvas sheet and some rice and fish. "Eat this." She looked down at him with pity, and then knelt beside him. "How did you do it, Mei Ling?" he asked, but she made him start on the food before answering. "The gang was in the hotel. I tried to phone Mr. Morgan but I couldn't get him. Then came our good luck; Mrs. Chong told me to do some shopping. One of the men ordered me to get a trishaw. There were a couple behind the hotel but I could only see one boy—eating rice. 'Where's your friend?' I asked, and he pointed to the lavatory. I said he was wanted at the front door. I put on the other boy's cape and hat and took his trishaw. That's his food you're eating. On the way people tried to hire me but I rode on."

"What a risk. Just for me. The warders might have suspected with no one in the trishaw."

"We were just both lucky. Luck's a funny thing. Sometimes it's with you, the next moment it's gone."

"The other trishaw can't have been much behind."

"Oh I know that trishaw boy. I'm a girl but I can ride quicker than that old fool. He'd arrive at the prison at least five minutes after me."

"Five minutes." Ah Tung drew in his breath. "Are you sure no one saw you?"

"I hope not. Anyway I'll dump the trishaw somewhere quiet when I leave you, do the shopping, and go back to the hotel. I'll contact Mr. Morgan and tell him you're safe. We'll come back for you tonight. You just stay here and keep warm." Ah Tung was shivering with cold so she wrapped the cape around him cradling him in her arms and feeling protective. Ah, she thought, if only he'd been interested in me when they'd first met; it would have been as easy to fall for him as for Carlos. She bent over him and kissed him like a child.

For a while he clung to her in silence, fearing to be left alone. Then he said, "Tell Peter I want you to come to Hong Kong with us. You'll be in danger after this. We're all in it together now." Mei Ling was half attracted by the idea but again she thought of Carlos. "Oh there's no danger. I must be off now. I'll say I had to shelter from the rain."

Before, she had hardly noticed what a strain it was riding a trishaw; now every pedal required a huge effort. By the time she was on the Praia Grande she was exhausted; all the same she pushed on to a deserted alley where she abandoned the trishaw. Then she went to the market, did Mrs. Chong's shopping and returned to the hotel, slipping in the back way.

No sooner had she closed the door behind her when some one seized her by the arm and dragged her into the kitchen where Old Chong, his wife and the servants were standing terrified before the mahjong players of last night; but there was a newcomer—a powerfully built young man clearly held in awe by the others. Two trishaw boys were also there and in the corner Siu Ching, whose face was tear stained.

"That's her," one of the trishaw boys said. "She's the one who sent me off."

"So you like shopping in the rain," Ming Yuk said, barely controlling his rage at being thwarted by a slip of a girl. "Come. We know everything. But you can still save yourself. Tell us where Kai Tung is." She knew it was useless to deny what she'd done. "You're wearing red slippers," Ming Yuk lied astutely. "Just like the trishaw boy who picked up Kai Tung. You see—the warders told us." The memory of the People's Trials flashed across Mei Ling's mind; better to give a good excuse than plead not guilty. "When I was a refugee, the only job anyone offered me was in a brothel; but Ah Tung helped me," she stated boldly. "He gave me food and money; yes, he saved me. And he helped me get a job here. I owe him something. I had to help him." She hoped Old Chong would support her but it was Mrs. Chong who sprang to her help. "It's true. Ah Tung brought her here. He asked us to give her a job. She'd a terrible time over there." The words were addressed more to the other men than Ming Yuk; they glanced at each other uneasily.

"Shut up you old crow," Ming Yuk shouted. He was boiling over; Kai Tung must be caught or else his own reputation would suffer. He repeated his promise that Mei Ling could save herself if she helped him find Ah Tung.

"In my village I saw people protect their families when it was useless. I saw my father and mother die. Ah Tung was a brother when I'd lost my family. I won't betray him."

"Where did you take him?" Ming Yuk screamed furiously striking her across the face. "I suppose you're hand in glove with that sod Morgan. "Tell us or you'll be sorry."

Before she could say a word, Mrs. Chong threw herself on her knees before him and set up the most fearful caterwauling. The men were taken aback by the noise and perhaps a bit amused by Mei Ling's defiance. One tried to persuade her in wheedling tones. "Tell us where you've taken him. Alright you had to give him a chance. But now you've got to help us." Mei Ling glanced over Ming Yuk's shoulder and saw Old Chong give her a nod. She joined Mrs. Chong on the floor and began to add to her wails. "I didn't know how important it was. I'll tell you where I left him." The room fell silent. "I wanted to take him to Morgan's house. It was alright riding along the sea road but I couldn't get up that steep hill so I dropped him at the bottom—he went the rest of the way on foot. I left the trishaw in an alley." She threw an appealing glance around the room.

Everyone began to talk of going to Morgan's house to trap Kai Tung; one of the men beckoned furtively to Old Chong to get the women out of the way. But Ming Yuk turned on them all. "Very convincing. One minute she says nothing would make her give him away; the next she decides to tell everything. Do you think I'm a fool? Do you think I'm going to let her off? I want to be sure I can get my hands on her. Kai Tung saved her from being a prostitute did he. Well we'll change all that. Take her to the Barrier Gate brothel. That'll break her spirits."

Mrs. Chong put her arms around Mei Ling. Everyone knew the brothel near the Barrier Gate was under contract to the Portuguese Army for the Angolese soldiers. "If you must make her a whore," Mrs. Chong yelled as if she were suffering a personal loss, "keep her for a rich man. She's still a virgin." Even Old Chong plucked up courage to speak out. "You must show mercy. She didn't know what she was doing."

"She's a traitor. Take her," Ming Yuk ordered his henchmen. Siu Ching ran up to him to plead but he struck her savagely. She spat at him shouting, "Stinking devil.

Filthy turd. *Tiu nei lo mo kei fa hai*—fuck your mother's cunt."
Old Chong pushed her from the room still struggling and
cursing. Within a few moments Mei Ling was in Ming Yuk's
car and forced on the floor beneath his feet. Yet even in her
terror she felt triumphant; whatever might happen she'd
won Ah Tung time to escape.

Thunder woke Soolan up from a troubled sleep. She had vague
recollections of an unpleasant dream—some row with Diana
while Robert stood by, arms folded, laughing like a drain,
until his noise filled the huge building in which they were
gathered. She sat up and looked through the window at the
doleful day. Who were the others jeering at her discomfiture.
She didn't have to ask again. It was the throng that tomorrow
would be at the Banquet in the Intramuros. She shuddered.
"I can't stand this bloody hole much longer," she said in
English thinking of last night when she'd lectured the wives
of Chinese businessmen on the need to, 'wear simple clothes
for the Banquet and resolutely oppose bourgeois fashions.'
All agreed and applauded but she knew they'd turn up in
expensive *cheong sams* and their usual clonking jewellery.
Though not superstitious she had a foreboding that the
Banquet would be unpleasant. The thought of seeing Robert
and Diana together was enough to mar the event already.

Her counterpart in the quadrangle, Carlos, was
experiencing similar gloom in another part of town. With a
little wire pulling he generally kept Mondays free, usually
for Diana. But tomorrow he was on crowd control at the
Intramuros, marshalling the poor who'd turn up to get the
Chamber of Commerce's charity. "Why can't it be handed
out in town," people complained. Others pointed out, "Not
many of them will climb up there; the rich bastards won't
have to give so much away." That didn't worry Carlos; nor did
the possibility of glimpsing Robert and Diana together—the
'old man' couldn't rival his erotic powers. But he didn't like

the idea of Diana being admired in the glittering ballroom by young officers from Lisbon from whom he feared more deadly rivalry. "Carlos has had a rough night," a fellow policeman whispered and everyone kept their distance.

An idea was developing in his mind. Here his future was limited but in Hong Kong prospects might be brighter. Mightn't it be possible to persuade Diana to leave Robert and live with him there. If she loved him as she said she did, he'd show her how hard he could work to support her. He wasn't the playboy everyone imagined; he longed to have children by her and show what sort of a father he could be. And if she wouldn't go with him, better to end the affair. The fear of that happening turned his thoughts to Mei Ling. If Diana wouldn't be his wife, there was someone else who would. An officer barked an order at him. "Nolasco. You'll be in charge of B section at the east gate." He replied, "Yes sir," but immediately found himself resenting having to take orders from anyone. He was fed up with being in the police, fed up with being here, fed up with playing second fiddle. No, Mei Ling wasn't an alternative. It had to be Diana; he wouldn't imagine it otherwise.

Soolan's imagination was also hard at work as she rubbed skin restoring unguents on her face and gazed in the mirror; she looked like a geisha, her cheeks all white, her eyes like piss holes in the snow. The effect made her chuckle. Holding her head stiffly, arching her eyebrows and making a rose bud mouth she chanted, "*Ashita Kabuki-wa yatte imasu-ka?*"—Is there a kabuki performance tomorrow?" in a Japanese theatre voice. "There sure is baby. Shit honey there sure is," she replied à l'Al Capone. Then looking toffee-nosed she drawled, "And I wouldn't miss it for all the tea in China old chap," in a hoity-toity English accent. She glided into the kitchen to make coffee, fluttering her dressing gown sleeves like a dancer in a Ginza stage show. Christ, she thought, starting to giggle, if those dreary buggers on the Committee could see me now. She'd as many roles as any actress.

Since it hadn't been possible to conceal her affair with Robert from the Party altogether, she'd always stressed to her colleagues that he wasn't a typical Englishman. "He may be a bourgeois intellectual," she maintained, "but he's a progressive. He could be useful to us in the future." But as of now she couldn't think of any way in which he might be used. Party members nodded sagely when she continued, "I believe he accepts the inevitable victory of the proletariat," and reserved judgement. She knew her file at Headquarters in Canton must contain details of the affair. But how many? What was the point of worrying? In any case no-one else was available to report as well as her on the Colony's activities. The Party naturally accepted her need to live a cosmopolitan life; it was conducive to success. But she wondered whether Robert would have found her so interesting had she been less sophisticated. And how much was her way of life a veneer? If Robert asked her to go to Europe with him what would she say? But that was most unlikely. She'd done everything possible to draw him towards her but the nearer he came, the more she was conscious of that final unbridgeable gap; Diana was the rival over whom she could never triumph. In a way she was relieved, for there was another part of her which so loved China that to abandon it would be like ripping a tree from the earth. If she enjoyed the symphonies of the west, she was more enamoured of the harsh tunes of Kwang Tung or the shrill melodies of Shantung. Yes, that's where I belong, she thought, that's what I must work for. She took out her notes to write up the weekly intelligence summary and prepared brushes and ink—she prided herself on her calligraphy. As she did so little tears at the corners of her eyes began to make patches on the skin cream. Plaintively she sang a snatch from the 'Lamentation Over the Lo River':

> *My grief has no end*
> *My love no limit*
> *They are longer than the Yellow River*
> *Deeper than the green sea.*

Then she got on with the report. As usual she drafted it meticulously. This week she analysed trends in the Trades Union and student movements, made pertinent observations on the motivations of certain businessmen, ostensibly supporters of the Party but slyly keeping up connections with KMT remnants and finally detailed the movements of two agents, probably working for the Americans, checking the passage of war materials through the harbour. The last section was important at the moment; the People's Republic was short of ball bearings and a consignment was due to be smuggled in via Hong Kong. Although her observations were cloaked in the Marxist jargon that helped Canton comprehend an unfamiliar situation, she was objective, even forthright, in her judgements.

The report signed she finished dressing and returned to the kitchen. Now she'd show Robert she was as good as Diana at preparing English food. She chose recipes '937—Toad-in-the-hole (A homely but savoury dish),' and '2000—Lemon Cream,' in the tattered old Mrs. Beeton he'd given her. They would be fine. Her servant was despatched for the rump steak and sheep's kidneys apparently required.

But the meal was destined to be wasted. Carlos had just received a guarded 'phone call from a warder friend in the Sao Francisco prison to tell him how a certain prisoner had been whisked away by some unknown person and that Ming Yuk was in a fury. Carlos' immediate feeling was of relief; Ah Tung must have held his tongue. However, best not to tell Peter lest he did something foolish. Diana was the person to keep informed; she'd know what to do. But at that moment since she was just leaving her unhappy interview with Lobato, it was Robert who received the hurried information.

Damn and blast it. She would be out when she's wanted, Robert thought as he put down the receiver. His irritation wasn't caused solely by the thought of having to deal with Peter, nor by the prospect of delaying his visit to Soolan. What really needled him was the finished portrait of

Lung Yeung glaring at him from the other side of the studio. He wasn't exactly dissatisfied with the picture; in some way, as Diana kept telling him, it was the best portrait he'd done. But there was something he didn't like in the face. The head and shoulders were not placed centrally but were in the lower right hand area of the canvas, the greater part of which consisted of a sheet of glowing yellow suffused with bronzed red, saffron and gold, creating opulence. In contrast with the life of this background, the face was not so much delineated as built up of blocks of icy greens, greys and blues whose total effect, whilst giving a vivid impression of Lung Yeung, contrived to be a representation of death itself or of a shade lost forever in a fiery hell. What disconcerted Robert were the eyes; in a head otherwise suggesting weariness and decay they stared with Byzantine intensity, proclaiming that all was known, all understood and all found wanting. From what part of himself, Robert wondered, had he found the expression in those eyes; they told something more about Lung Yeung than he himself had consciously recognised. It was as though the old man, sitting there passively all those hours, had won a victory over him. He could almost hear the gentle voice saying, 'You see Mr. Sheraton, you didn't know everything about me did you?' though what Lung Yeung had actually said was, "I congratulate you Mr. Sheraton. You're an artist who sees the truth and sets it down fearlessly. I'll keep this picture near me to dispel the distorted image I sometimes have of myself." Of course Diana would grasp the essence of it straight away. "You've caught him Robert," she'd said. "Or he's caught you. Those eyes. Those eyes." He walked up to the picture and stared back at it awhile, then said, "I hope you rot in hell." But the eyes showed no hint of resentment. Then a thought struck him and he smiled remembering the news about Ah Tung. "Well your lot haven't crushed him at least; he's escaped you."

It was no use speaking to Peter over the phone. It was essential to see him, if necessary control him. All the same Robert tried to get through to say he was on his way. There was no reply but that meant nothing. Leaving a note for Diana, "At Peter's. Good news," he set off.

The sound of the phone aroused Peter to a vague consciousness. His dream was still with him; he had died, found out that Christianity was true and pressed an alarm bell to warn everyone that the Universe was in the hands of a raving lunatic. The bell went on for an age, piercing his ear drums and starting up fancies of different people calling him—Diana, Robert, Carlos, the Archangel Gabriel. Let them ring; he refused to face judgement. He was staying put in this crude cell, this body that ached in a half way, as though some part of it was already dead and a burden to what remained. Awake at last he felt feverish, his mouth was dry, his head throbbed. The he noticed that his blanket was damp; the wind had blown the rain in through the open shutters whilst he slept. It still did so and sometimes the cold drizzle moistened his face when a gust of wind beat roughly against the house. Pulling the blanket around him he turned on one side and looked between the window balusters towards the town and harbour. His eyes rested on the blue tower of the Old Pawnshop—a model building in a miniature world. If its roof and the roof of the monastery further up the road were to be lifted off, surely the gaunt abbot would look no different from a skeletal opium addict; nor would there be any difference between kneeling penitents receiving absolution and sensual youth afire for pleasure. What difference was there between the visions of a religious reaching up to some imagined deity and his own heroin dreams roaming about in a timeless void? Both experiences were equally illusory; whether one or the other was preferred depended on psychosomatic make up, environment, chance. The deeper reality lay behind the façade of tissues and events; it lay behind the consciousness of man, the unconsciousness of the trees, the inanimation of the rocks; its experience had nothing to do with ordinary mental processes. He turned away from the town and closed his eyes. An abyss yawned; if there was neither evil nor good and suffering was a random matter depending on the vagaries of the nervous system, why not accept whatever transitory pleasure came his way? Or if he couldn't find a comfortable resting place at the centre of his being, why not push on to the extremities of experience? Perhaps the world was but a room enclosing him from the outer light which could only be reached if the walls were battered until they fell and he escaped to freedom.

During the past few weeks he'd smoked opium more and more, and moved on to heroin. He knew Ah Tung wouldn't have let him go so far. Indeed with Ah Tung he wouldn't have wanted to. But there was more; his guilt had made him invent ways of combining the pain he felt to be his due with his craving for morphine. To a back room in the Red Pleasure Pavilion he called the masseur Pai Chai and paid him to see that under the influence of the drug, he was tied up for the leprous practitioner to inflict the whip upon him. Under drugs, the torment flashed on and off like a lighthouse and he alternately felt pain and pleasure. Like a reckless driver he was pressing the accelerator further and further down, although the road was getting narrower. Whenever he thought about Ah Tung, despair filled him completely; despair which he could hardly endure; which made him long to escape to the future or to the past.

The wind blustered, the rain swept through the window and he heard the bougainvillea rustling against the wall. Then, most strangely, he seemed to be on one of his yearly six-month long visits to his mother's home (but never truly his) in Cheshire, the domain she had fled to when his father had gone off for good with another woman. He was sitting on the terrace, snuggling for warmth up to Ah Yi, the amah who cared for him on his ping pong-like journeys to and from the east, wishing she could look after him without ever moving from her own noisy little house, full of children and fun, in the New Territories. All around were his mother's fields and woods and far away, over the sandy Dee estuary, the brooding hills of Wales where, he'd been told, Arthur and his knights still rode. But soon, his brain began to fish out a later memory, an incident painful as a blade twisting in a muscle: a wintry Saturday night at a boisterous London pub, three years after the war when he was in the Navy. Fondly, he remembered the smoky, noisy Fitzroy so heady with the boozy comradeship, underscored by sexuality, of servicemen: the reputedly dangerous Horse Guardsmen, the sharp faced RAF lads, the wily sailors with their knowing winks and chummy embraces, the marines in unbelievably healthy condition but too high priced, and quite often a clutch of black Americans whose smooth, better cut, army trousers suggested the most profuse delights. On that night, he recalled, such a crew was present and correct for inspection by the usual complement of actors, artists, academics, businessmen, civil servants, a Liberal MP and a vainly incognito Anglican Canon. Both groups, hunters and prey, if one could decide which was which, though being many, were also of one bread and one body through their participation, however much some of the members of H.M. forces present might like to disguise it, in the ineffable mysteries of upstanding Priapus.

Agreeably, not to mention surprisingly, for one so marinated in opium, stimulated by this conceit Peter experienced a quite physical sensation of actually being back in the bar; he was sure he could hear the nostalgic music of the out of tune piano, the occasional drunken refrain, the rich welter of regional tongues lathered by raucous laughter and feel the warm breath on his ear from a Scots Guardsman's whiskey moistened lips while some bloke behind him slyly groped his bell-bottoms. And what had become, he wondered, with a twinge of regret, of the two sailors who'd come up with him from Chatham that freezing day in January? Their names? He could remember: Kevin Rooney and Trevor Waite, jolly tars both and beautiful down to their toe nails. Although, ostensibly like them, he was keeping a weather eye open for some generous brown hatters who'd give them a whale of a time, mainly in liquid form, and lodging in exchange for a nice friendly fuck, he'd figured on getting Kevin Rooney, with his coal black hair and ever blushing cheeks, for himself at some point during the night under the guise of being drunk, the oldest trick in the game when 'real men' get together.

They'd been in the pub not an hour when, in the midst of a posse of bright eyed, firm limbed, lustful, desirable soldiery, his guard had, not unnaturally, slipped; some unmanly gesture, some hint of femininity in his limbs or his face, some movement that was so much a part of him that he couldn't think what it might have been, had caused the languid bean pole of a poet with thick lensed glasses and a mop of unkempt hair, who'd been pestering him since he'd come in, to squint at him quizzically like someone afraid of food poisoning, give a contemptuous smile and sneer, loudly enough for the men around to hear, "God, how you're going to suffer in your life, darling," having uttered which he turned away to pay court to an Adonis-headed Royal Marine built like a gorilla.

The humiliation was appalling but as far as he himself was concerned it had been far worse that his fate should be revealed not by an ecstatic crone cursed with the gift of prophecy but by a supercilious don whose anaemic neo-classical verses were devoid of even a shred of magic; that had enraged him. Like a massive hammer blow on one of those try-your-own-strength machines at a fair ground, the malicious words had struck home; the bell had resounded, telling him that never could he be what nature had made him and at the same time move easily in the world. Nothing, he had thought at the time, lay ahead but falsehood to himself or wastage of his talents. Could it have been then that he had secretly resolved on the course which, after his industrious university days and that drudgery in Hong Kong, had brought him to this place where, with Ah Tung, he had for the first time openly expressed his nature? The question made the memory of the Fitzroy fade away. He opened his eyes and saw the jumbled roof tops of the City before him and, somehow or other, knew that this was his last destination. Well then, neither had he failed to suffer nor had he failed to waste his talents but no one could deny that for once he had been fully himself. This thought so consoled him that he started, very confidently, to get up to face what was left of the day only at once to feel giddy. After sitting still for a few minutes he draped the blanket around him then made his way hesitatingly into the sitting room where Ping brought him some coffee and toast with a disapproving look. The sight of the food made him feel sick; he opened up a cigarette, put some heroin in it and started to smoke. Bit by bit his composure returned, then he went to the bathroom. The vague recollection of an invitation to the Banquet came to his mind; was it tonight or tomorrow? He'd promised Diana and Robert to go with them; he must keep his word. It would be easy to take some heroin cigarettes to help him through and afterwards he'd make for the Red Pleasure Pavilion. After shaving he took a shower. Through the swish of water he heard Robert's voice outside. "Come in," he shouted. "I'm not shy." He watched Robert's eyes widen at the sight of his body crisscrossed with the marks left by Pai Chai's whip the night before. "What the hell..." Abruptly Robert turned and went out. Putting on some dark blue pyjamas and an orange kimono, Peter joined him in the sitting room and spread himself comfortably on a chaise lounge opposite his guest. Despite the sallowness of his complexion and his heavy eyes, something of his former smartness had returned; Robert was relieved at the transformation and amazed at such resilience.

"So what brings you here Bobbie? It must be something madly important. I know; Diana's dead and you're demented. I never see you nowadays."

"Your fault, not mine."

Peter ignored Robert's untruth. "The portrait's finished?"

"Yes."

"Is it good?"

"I loathe it."

"Then it's good. Lung Yeung outrages you. You must have caught him."

"It shows him where I wish him—in hell."

"So you believe in life after death?"

"Don't you?"

"I believe in sex after death. Priapus is my god; I'm destined for his heaven."

Robert's contempt showed in his face but he said lightly, "Aren't you going to offer me something before you go there—which doesn't look too far off?"

"Opium or heroin?" Peter smiled and poured Robert a large straight whiskey. "Come to the point. You've some news about Ah Tung. I'm sure that's why you're here. But I'll only listen if it's good. Diana must have told you; I live in a world of make-believe."

Robert drank the whiskey and held out his glass for another. "You see I'm as uncontrollable in vice as you."

"Drink up then." Peter leant forward and pushed the almost full decanter across the table. For an instant their eyes met intently, then he watched Robert fill up his glass and down the drink in silence before saying, "You don't like me much do you. No, I've put it wrong. You don't like me being too cozy with Diana. I'm bad for her. Terribly bad!"

Robert looked at him thoughtfully. Some part of himself wanted to tell Peter that he found him a totally unsympathetic character, the sort of person who gave homosexuals a bad name, but another part of his mind told him that this pathetic creature, who always found the strength from somewhere to comfort Diana in the misery caused by himself, and who was generally liked among the poor and the destitute of the town, must have learned something by suffering in ways of which he himself had no inkling. In the end he said, "To tell the truth I don't really know. Sometimes I think you're an idiot, a clever idiot of course; other times—now for instance—you just amaze me. God knows what you've been up to, yet here you sit looking like an oriental Noel Coward."

"Such flattery. Would you like another sort of drink? Champagne if you want."

Robert put down his glass firmly. "Ah Tung's out. No, he's not been harmed. It seems someone helped him get away. I don't know where."

Peter sat up. For a brief moment a wild look came into his eyes but he said quite coolly, "I knew it. I knew it. I knew he'd get away."

"You felt it in what's left of your heart, I suppose."

"At least I started off with one." Brittle Peter re-emerged determined that this self satisfied man before him should know nothing of his inner turmoil. He sank back and waited for such details as Robert had.

"Take my advice then. Don't do anything. Don't look for him. Don't ask anyone about him. Remember that law of Azimov or someone; if two space ships lose each other, one must stay still. Let him contact you. Then we'll work out what to do."

"You're really terrific Bobbie. Way out in space now. By the way how do they know which ship isn't to move?"

Robert felt bored. He was fed up with responding to Peter's play acting. If he doesn't care what happens to himself why should I, he thought. But when he got up to leave, Peter insisted, "No. Don't go. Sit down. Please. I am grateful to you for coming. I'll do everything you say." Yet as soon as Robert sat down again there was a reversion in Peter's manner. "You mustn't worry about Diana and me. I'll not lead her astray. I couldn't harm her if I tried. You're the expert on that."

"And what does that mean?" Robert asked loudly, thinking, alright then, if you want a bit of nastiness let's have it. But Peter was evasive. "I don't know really. Probably I'm just sounding you out. I can be a real bitch."

"I know that and I can see through you as well. You've nothing but contempt for me. You think I'm the one who's bad for Diana, don't you?"

"Who am I to judge you? Or you me? Or anyone anyone? I'll tell you though: I can get close to Diana because she's so spontaneous. You I find much too cautious."

"There's nothing wrong with caution. You could do with a bit of it yourself from what I can see. I put my spontaneity into my paintings."

"Where it's still safely yours. Anyway Diana lives with you—not with a canvas. Tell me: how do you make her feel unwanted yet still under your thumb?" As he indulged in his effrontery Peter turned the gentlest of smiles on Robert's sagging features.

"Nonsense. Look at the freedom I give her." But Robert became embarrassed under Peter's amused scrutiny. "I mean the freedom we give each other."

"You give her money and comfort. But why did you recoil from her so soon after your marriage, Robert? Maybe you should let me teach you a thing or two."

"Like what? How to finish myself off in three easy moves?"

"Oh no. More difficult than that. How to appreciate Diana and how to give her what really matters. After all, you must admit it; she does see something in me. And as you don't, you must be averse to something she likes—and needs."

"You're too facile. And I don't think you of all people can teach me about love. What you love, Peter, is being different, negating the natural order of things. Does it never strike you that maybe the problems Diana and I have spring from nothing more complex than the difference in our ages? You've an advantage there.

"How clever of you to find the simple answer. But I'm not surprised; Diana told me you're fond of philosophy."

Robert tried to control his mounting anger. Who was this cocksure interfering whipper-snapper to speak to him so derisively? He'd no idea of the complexities of married life—or even of the relationship between a man and a woman. He decided to take the offensive. "And what about yourself. Try to explain those lashes for instance. The answer can be simple or complex as far as I'm concerned. But I'd like to hear it."

Peter was silent as though giving serious consideration to his reply. Then he asked naively, "Why do you paint Bobbie?"

"Because I want to. Because I have to."

"Does that answer your own question then? No it doesn't. It doesn't answer your question or mine. No one knows why they want to, or why they have to, when it comes down to it. Maybe we want to, or we have to, just to find out what's inside us." He grinned. "In my case I guess there's a cesspit, but I'd like to take the lid off and look at the shit. But let's get back to you and your paintings. Don't they ever tell you anything about yourself? The one you've just finished for instance. Ah, I've touched a nerve. What's Lung Yeung's old face just told you?"

The memory of those piercing eyes rose up sharp in Robert's mind. He was sure that if Peter had done the picture, he'd stand in front of those eyes until some horrid vision sped into his brain from them; yet instead of resisting whatever came over, he'd let himself be devoured by it. But he, Robert Sheraton, rational being as well as acute delineator of fact, would hold the madness at bay. If necessary he'd make his own eyes into mirrors and the Gorgon would turn itself to stone. He stood up feeling very sure of himself, adopted a jocular manner and replied, "Lung Yeung told me to put a ball and chain on you and keep you prisoner till you learn to use that clever head of yours properly." He leant down and stroked Peter's shoulder almost tenderly. "And get yourself fit again, eh." He felt a slight tremor, a distinctly sensual reflex, go through Peter's body and was surprised that it evoked a little echo somewhere in himself. No, this young man couldn't do Diana any harm at all. She was much stronger than him. He was only an object of pity. "Come on, my friend," he said gently, "Come on. The rain has stopped. We'll go for a walk together. It'll do us both good."

Peter immediately adopted the pose of Madame Récamier on her chaise lounge and extended his hand languidly. "Bye-bye, Bobbie." The avuncular role was reversed. "Have a nice walkies."

Robert left with his tail between his legs but before he went through the door to piddle on the first lamp post, he tried to reassert himself, calling sternly. "We'll pick you up at seven thirty tomorrow night. Formal dress; remember where you're going." The bored voice of the clever child called too many times to tea from something more interesting, floated into the garden. "Don't worry Bobbie. I'll be ready."

Wrathfully he strode down the wet street towards the Intramuros muttering, "Bloody well serves you right." But gradually his irritation with Peter dissolved into amusement—once he had convinced himself that anything such a deviant said wasn't worth taking seriously.

Some lorries crammed with police were coming; he pressed into a doorway as they sped by. In the last lorry, rows of olive skinned young men sat up stiffly holding rifles, their heads covered with huge helmets turning them into mushrooms. Their immature faces and acceptance of uniformity seemed repulsive. He wondered if Carlos was amongst them; again that stab of jealousy. What was Carlos really like? A crony of Peter; that alone was disturbing. The sight of those lacerations returned to his mind. Did Peter realise he'd passed the danger point already? How could anyone obsessed by sensation judge such a question? That sensual-looking Carlos, what did he get up to with Diana and where could he lead her? "You're a fool to let it go on like this," he said aloud as he walked on. Some children playing in the street mocked the red haired devil talking to himself. Ahead of him loomed the immutable outlines of the Intramuros, setting limits to the rambling streets all about. That's how it should be, he thought, with Peter again in mind, with certain people—limits set to their ways. And as for the masses, most decidedly there had to be rules, Soolan's, Lobato's, the Bishop's, whose hardly mattered provided they stood there firmly to prevent indiscipline and the easy descent into the pit; people needed to be saved not from sin but from themselves. Amidst his certainty, not exactly expressed but imminent in his mind, was the notion that only for a few, the philosopher and, above all, the artist was total freedom from controls desirable, for how else could they express the truth. Permitting himself such freedom, as was his wont when his own desires were at issue, he then bent the rules of behaviour sufficiently to give Soolan's lunch a miss. He was in no mood for love; tomorrow he'd invent some specious excuse.

As soon as he was within the Intramuros, the labyrinthine nature of his problems seemed to be mirrored in the endless corridors, passages and courtyards of the buildings around him; he felt he'd strayed into some manifestation of mind in which each doorway posed a mystery and each unturned corner a challenge. Walking the silent streets he was alone save for the erratic wind that swirled dead leaves about his feet. It started to rain once more, at first a drizzle but then more heavily and he made for the Club.

Apart from the bent-up porter who mumbled, "*Boas dias Senhor,*" and then hobbled away, there was no one around. He was impressed by the transformation brought about for the Banquet by the new paint but in the muted splendour of the unlit ballroom with its three chandeliers casting dim reflections on the floor smooth with scented polish, he experienced an eerie sensation that some ancient long dead monster was starting to breathe again. Somehow the wind had found ways of penetrating the building and the crimson curtains billowed out like huge sails; occasionally crystals on the chandeliers tinkled like derisive laughter. The whiteness of the walls was engaged in a struggle with the shadows of the late afternoon and the sombre light seemed to resent the temporary set-back to ruin caused by armies of departed workmen. Despite the restored glory he was oppressed by the certainty that decay would win. As he gazed around a gust of wind blew the rain against the long windows overlooking a cloistered courtyard, around which mossy walls suggested the triumph of vegetation over the work of men. Then the wind sighed through the hall and made its way through other doors and down corridors to distant chambers so that the building uttered a drawn-out moan. But there was more in the wind than the sound of rain; he was certain he could hear the distant murmur of voices—were they saying, 'we are returning'—and the noise of shuffling footsteps on the pavements outside; more than that there was the sound of an unseen choir chanting exquisite music from afar. The wind blew again and the leaves scraping at the panes were voices demanding entrance for the admission of people returned from deepest time. He felt a chill creeping down his backbone and a prickling across his scalp. Walking over to the windows, his footsteps on the floor like thumps from a seneschal's mace, he looked into the courtyard. A slight cry escaped his lips—for on the opposite side beneath the shadow of the Chapel, he saw a procession of chanting cowled figures. How could they disappear into the wall to which they were walking? Before his reason could re-assert itself and let him discern that they were going into the Chapel through a doorway which caused each of them to stoop, a cold hand touched him and made him start. A quiet voice said, "Senhor Sheraton I saw you in the ballroom. Would you like to hear Mass? You'd enjoy the music; it's by Cardoso."

Father Antonio rambled on about Evora and its school of polyphonic music. In a dream and hardly listening, Robert let himself be led around the draughty cloister in time to see the last monk disappearing into the Chapel; ah well, it might be interesting to hear ancient music in such a setting. As they went in, it was obvious the place was a reservoir of cold air. He shivered. Father Antonio beckoned him up the spiral stairway to a gallery which faced the altar from behind a fretted screen with narrow apertures carved in the shape of wind blown flames.

"Sit here Senhor." Father Antonio thrust an open missal into his hands. "This is the gallery of the Captains-General;

you're the only member of the congregation. You can follow the service." He pointed to the page. "Excuse me; the Bishop will be here shortly." He went downstairs.

The gallery was dark and the complicated screen in front of the throne on which he sat impeded a full view of the interior. Below him were restrained movements and occasional coughs; candles flickered against wood-panelled walls. Sometimes a robed figure crossed the floor genuflecting perfunctorily before the altar which glittered in the obscurity. Through the high windows at which the wind and the rain beat fitfully, hardly any light entered but enough for him to distinguish heavy beams at whose intersections bosses bulged darkly, adding to the oppressive heaviness.

He felt depressed, regretting he'd been so easily persuaded to come inside. How many Captains-General had caught pneumonia up here; or had they received spiritual strength to help them in the tasks of government? He quite envied the monks their certainty of belief and their willingness, if the opportunity ever arose again, to impose their faith on mankind. Presently a short procession led by Father Antonio entered the Chapel, brought up by the tall figure of the Bishop resplendent in gold vestments. Robert knelt on a footstool so his eyes at an aperture could see the east end. His gaze was riveted on the life-sized crucifixion slightly higher than the gallery so that the eyes of the emaciated Christ of painted wood stared down at him. The Bishop approached the altar and the service began. As the music went on Robert abandoned himself to Cardoso's opulent counterpoint; its sustained rhythm was like a long breath without pause or alternation. Again his eyes were drawn towards the distant icon which hung gem-like in the flickering light and to the words below it: *"Eu sou o pão vivo que desceu do céu*—I am the living bread which came down from heaven." The same sight had been seen over centuries by a succession of Captains-General sitting in this very seat; he imagined himself one of them. Outside, the City was full of life; soldiers wearing polished casques awaited his command; in the harbour galleons were berthing or casting off. Jesuits had come with new learning intent on capturing the Emperor of Cathay for Rome; and all the while he, the Captain-General, master of it all, controlled the gateway between two worlds. To live in such an age, serving Mammon, the Crown and the Faith with no misgivings, to be Governor of such a City, how necessary to have a hidden place like this in which to commune with God.

The Mass went on with its unfamiliar ritual; he was no longer conscious of the gallery's discomfort amidst the music, the incense and the colour; he was advancing through the windblown flames nearer and nearer the suspended figure which stared ever more intensely at him, its eyes challenging him to refute the implications of all they saw and heard. Yet strange to relate, the music seemed to fade away and he was disgusted by the carved beads of sweat and blood about the thorn-crowned head and the square tipped nails splitting the waxen flesh asunder. The memory of Peter's whip-lashed body crossed his mind and he sat back gripping the carved armrests. The screen obscured the upper part of the figure but he could see the limbs below with that flat and dismal cloth veiling its manhood. Compared with this obscenity, Peter's nakedness was beautiful. He leaned forward again and was sickened by the realistic gash in the side of the tortured Christ, re-enacting his ancient drama. Saddened by this worship of death, he longed for an emphasis on rebirth, for despite the words of gladness and the promise of life, something told him there was no message of joy in this ceremony. Why listen further to the music or watch a measured ritual become a charade. He stood up and the wind blown flames rushed downward before his eyes across the crucifixion; the candle light played tricks on the vestments. Momentarily tongues of fire licked around the base of the reredos, intent on consuming the hanging figure; then they vanished— illusory as any other vision. As he left, the words of the Credo continued in exultant chant—"*et iterum venturus est cum gloria iudicare vivos et mortuos, cuius regni non erit finis*—and he will come again in glory to judge the quick and the dead and his kingdom will have no end..." He closed the door behind him and walked briskly away in the rain, rejoicing that he had no faith to shackle him, rejoicing that he, Robert Sheraton, artist, was free to do exactly as he chose.

The Angolan soldier was powerfully built; all the same Mei Ling, cowering in the corner of the bed, thought of fighting him but that would please Ming Yuk who was outside the door. It would also add to her ill-treatment. Staring at the ceiling she kept her face expressionless as the soldier got on the bed. Instead of resisting, she looked into his eyes and put her arms around him pleading, "Help me. Help me to escape." He said something in Portuguese which she didn't understand. Shrugging his shoulders he got up and took off his uniform, grinning at her as he did so; soon he was beside her again making her touch his body. He undressed her and she went stiff with fear as his fingers began to roam over her. There was laughter outside; the soldier jumped up and struck the wall shouting loudly. She covered herself with a sheet and saw him hang his coat over a peep-hole; silence was followed by more laughter and retreating footsteps. His action relieved her tension; ever practical, she wanted to get it over with quickly but it seemed he'd decided not to hurry, pulling the sheet over the two of them, fondling her, trying to arouse her. She told herself he wasn't a black devil, she was not in a whore house, she was giving herself to Carlos. She saw no point in fighting, no point in anything but making the best of it. He pressed into her slowly but forcefully; in pain she called out Carlos' name as he drew her to him tightly, muffling her cries by pressing his lips over her mouth so she could hardly breathe. Her body burned around his cock but in the pain she became conscious of an excitement which was unfulfilled when he came. For a while they lay together but he didn't withdraw. He touched her hair and kissed her and she couldn't help feeling he was a child, helpless and weak now his lust was satisfied. She opened her eyes and looked at him. His face was broad and generous; his eyes kind and lively. She didn't mind holding him; it made her feel protective and she remembered how she'd put her arms around Ah Tung that afternoon pitying his weakness. After a while he got hard again but this time he was less violent and when the hint of pleasure she experienced returned, it grew with his movements, finally equalling and mingling with her pain. Later she listened to his voice which was deep and soft. Although ashamed to have given herself so easily, she didn't want him to go. He dressed slowly, chatting away, obviously reluctant to leave her. She made him understand her name and he told her his was Xavier.

When he'd gone an old servant woman led Mei Ling to a bathroom and stood by as she washed herself, asking what she thought of the black devil. "He's a real man. All the girls like him. You were lucky to get him to break you in." She cackled at Mei Ling's embarrassment. "He's got a lot hasn't he, eh?"

The old woman brought some fish and rice to the room and the brothel keeper came in whilst she ate. He told her Ming Yuk had received a message to go back to his office just after the soldier had come into the room. "If he'd not gone, he'd have sent some more of them in. Ah that man, he's a fiend with the eyes of a wasp and the howl of a jackal. He's a madman. And he knows nothing about women." Despite their dislike of Ming Yuk, she was repelled by the talk of what to do and what not to do to keep men happy. Once or twice the keeper touched her but she drew back. "Never mind; I can wait. You'll want me soon." When he'd gone the old woman spat. "The fool; the girls only want him for what they get out of him. Who wants the likes of him when they've got used to the black devils."

She learned the girls weren't badly treated if they did as they were told. "But don't run off or you'll end up with your face slashed—or worse," the woman warned. Then her voice became milder. "Anyway most of them like it after a time when they take this." She took out a couple of mouldy looking cigars which she said contained hemp. Mei Ling refused to smoke and the old woman put them back in her pocket. "No, it's not for me either. I like the white powder." From another voluminous pocket she took some heroin, heated it on a bit of foil over a candle and began to 'chase the dragon'. Mei Ling looked at her wide eyed, fearful that in a few years time she too would be such an old hag. The woman noticed and said, "Oh yes, I was as pretty as you once," then exhaled with a long "Aah," adding, "Prettier maybe. But you'll be worn out before long. Wait till you see the place on payday. They never let up." A long whinny of a laugh followed. "You'll see something. A queue right down the corridor and three or four in the room." Mei Ling saw no reason to doubt the woman's words. Xavier had been as gentle as he could with her but others would be rough and coarse.

The hag leaned towards her. "Cheer up. Things needn't be so bad—if you and I are friends. If you get extra money don't give it to the keeper. I need a bit of cash to buy white powder. Listen. Let's eat the bitter and the sweet fruit together. I'll get good food for you and the pick of the boys. There is the odd raspberry among the nettles. You know the ones I mean." She grinned and spread her fingers in a vulgar gesture. "And I'll keep the rough ones out." Mei Ling promised to follow her advice; it was better to have her as a friend. The keeper's voice bellowed outside and the woman hurriedly picked up the tray. "Still here?" he shouted at the doorway. "Get on with your work." He glared at Mei Ling. "Don't listen to her shit. She'd talk her way out of hell. Anything you get, you hand over to me." Mei Ling quailed under his eyes and he laughed. "Don't worry, I'll not touch you—yet. You've made a conquest; that black devil's coming back to spend the night with you. Now get this; in the day you work 'short time' only.

At night some of the men want to spend more. So have a rest. You won't get much sleep tonight."

Mei Ling was glad to be alone; Xavier didn't frighten her as much as the keeper or the other men she'd have to face. Despite her fears she fell into a heavy sleep. When she woke up Xavier was sitting on the bed reading a book. For a time they tried to talk but conversation was impossible; there was a limit to signs and his friendly grins. Her English wasn't much use either; he only knew a few words. She submitted to his love making but to her own bewilderment she was drawn to him. This time she no longer kidded herself he was Carlos. Without any doubt she knew she wanted him. She was attracted by his smooth black skin and massive limbs, more exciting, to her, than those of Chinese men. His unfamiliar odour made her think of fallen leaves; his lips were soft and full. She forgot the squalor of her surroundings. A twinge of shame crossed her mind. Perhaps I was meant to be a whore, she thought. Then his presence made her say aloud, although he couldn't understand her, "Come on beautiful black man. Take me. Do what you want. Make me happy. I need to be made happy."

Xavier did make Mei Ling happy. He explored her body with his lips; how strange it was, she thought, that after so brief a time she could let him do so without being frightened. The electric light made his blackness gleam. She didn't want it switched off so she could look at every bit of him. The sight filled her with tenderness. As her fingers, growing bolder, went over him from head to foot, he closed his eyes, moving his head slowly from side to side; it made her think of the trances Taoist priests went into. He put her hand on his balls; she squeezed them a little until he moaned. They were heavy like autumn fruits. How good it would be to be filled with life from a man like him. When he sucked her tits and rubbed and twisted his fingers in her cunt, it was not possible to hold back the sobs and gasps she used to hear and deride at Old Chong's place. She didn't care who was listening and throwing aside all modesty let him see she wanted him to play every trick in his book. How sweet his tongue was, now in her mouth or her ears, or, which she liked better, probing and teasing between her legs. So much did it unleash her that she had to show that she could do as much to please him, nuzzling her face in the cleft between his buttocks, licking and kissing him where his skin was smooth as satin. He groaned and writhed under her touch. Then she caressed his groin where he smelt musky and nibbled all the length of his stiff cock; its head filled her mouth and she drew on it until he shouted with pleasure. At last he raised her legs over his shoulders and pumped it in her in different ways, twisting and turning her to his own delight, making her greedy for every clever thrust. She'd never imagined being screwed could make her forget everything but the moment of screwing. Her troubles were nothing; she was nothing but a song of joy around his dancing prick. The tears were pouring down her cheeks and, "Xavier, Xavier," she shouted as they came together and she felt his spunk shooting into her. For a while they rested but it was far into the night before they fell asleep with him still inside her.

Some time later she was awakened and they made love again but when it was over, instead of wanting to hold her, he got up. In gestures he told her to put on her clothes. Standing on the bed, he tested the strength of the iron bar over the window. With all his might he pressed until it bent to one side, enough to let some one not too big climb through. Heavy rain was falling outside in the darkness; occasionally cold drops were blown into the room. Xavier picked up his army cape and gave it to her. It seemed he'd already thought of helping her for he handed over some money bound with an elastic band and a piece of paper with words on it in Portuguese. Mei Ling read his name and address.

She must seize the opportunity of escape. Clinging to him she whispered, "Thank you, Xavier. Thank you." in English. "OK, OK," he said and hastened her up to the window which she managed to wriggle through. Outside, her feet touched a ledge; the drop to the ground was not great and she jumped onto the wet cobblestones. Looking up she saw his smile broadly white in the darkness. Throwing the cape around her she ran down the deserted alley. Soon it was easier to walk, for yellow lights lit up a road full of the noise of water—the swishing of rain in the blustering wind, its fast coursing in gutters, its gurgling down drains. She liked the sound for now she was moving as freely as the water through the windy night. As she went along, half running, half walking across the town towards the monument where Ah Tung was waiting, she thought how easily her affections had altered with necessity; perhaps there was something wrong with her being able to change so quickly. At one moment she thought of Carlos, feeling she'd betrayed him; the next instant, resolving to tell no one about Xavier, it seemed she was betraying him too. Why be ashamed of someone who'd saved her. One thing was sure; she couldn't go back to her old life; nor could she face Carlos again. But why have regrets about that? She'd never get him as long as Mrs. Sheraton lived here. These thoughts, mingled with anxiety over Ah Tung so occupied her mind she hardly noticed crossing the town.

Near the Praia Grande she turned into a poor quarter where destitutes slept under arcades and food stalls were lively under the warm glow of kerosene lamps. There she bought some dumplings and noodles; Ah Tung was bound to be famished. No one paid any attention to her and before long she was approaching the bronzes of Vasco da Gama and his comrades. The wind was blowing more strongly than ever from the sea and from time to time there was a long rumble of distant thunder, but it was no longer raining and the drifting clouds had begun to reveal the deep blackness of the sky in which the stars gleamed brilliantly upon an earth cleansed by the passing storm. She wasn't surprised to find Ah Tung gone from under the folds of the statues but was confident he'd only just left. As she nestled in the shelter, something of his presence was still there. She was sure he was safe, but safe or not, there was nothing else she could do; soon she fell asleep.

Yet her mind was unable to give up its quest for Ah Tung. Outside the wind increased in force, howling around the rigid figures, even finding ways of penetrating their hollowness so that their eyes, mouths and nostrils began to let out weird whistles and groans and trumpet blasts of warning towards the heedless town. Beyond the quoin, waves surged landward making the shore shudder when they broke. The clouds had gone from the sky deep into the mountains of China and the naked town lay open to the will of Heaven. Like a whiplash, a sudden blast bore down on the monument and the statues let out despairing shrieks that burst their lips and eye sockets asunder and left them faceless; the earth trembled as arms snatched her into the air and she was whirled around as powerless as a leaf; the sky above the houses with their sleeping thousands was wild in the fury of the wind but instead of awakening, the multitudes went on slumbering except for Xavier who, from the brothel, was caught up and borne towards her. She saw him approaching through the sky and felt him embracing her. Their bodies of ivory and jet joined together as they were carried towards the ancient City which neither of them had ever visited. The strength of his love was mightier than the wind and she felt him possessing her so completely she became herself and him.

The splendid buildings of the City were spread below them. Clearly arrayed around the central Rotunda were the Club and the Theatre, the tall Chapel and a cloistered courtyard with a shining pool at its centre. From afar and yet as close as though they could touch him, with mercuric vision they saw Ah Tung making his way through roads and archways. For a while he kept close to the walls, peering round corners before he advanced but gradually he grew bolder as he saw the City was empty and walked more quickly towards its centre until at last he entered the courtyard that lay on one side of the Rotunda. The eeriness of the buildings and the wind around the cloisters frightened him and he thought he heard voices of the dead. Then all at once he threw off fear and ran into the centre of the courtyard where he could hear the water playing in the deep basin and shouted, "I'm not afraid. I'm afraid of no-one, alive or dead." No living voice answered him and the shades declined his challenge. Stripping off his clothes he lowered himself into the cold water. It was deeper than he expected and he sank down and down; then he emerged with a splutter and began to swim about—splashing, laughing and shouting until the whole courtyard echoed noisily. Sometimes he climbed out and ran through the wild garden whose shrubs and trees were swaying to and fro in the wind; then he returned to the pool and dived in, swimming to the bottom and bringing up rocks and pebbles and throwing them into the air; some hit the curved tiles and clattered to the gutters with a musical echo. Why should he ever again need the dreams of opium when his body as it was now, could give him such joy? Squatting on the edge of the pool, he trailed a fallen branch in the water thinking of Peter. For the first time in many months he wanted to hold and possess him completely as in the first days of their love together. His desire grew stronger and he jumped to his feet and began to dance circling the bubbling water, jumping, laughing, waving his arms, sometimes singing and sometimes pressing himself on the ground as though he wanted to make love to the world. Then he jumped into the water again and felt it surging around him; the sensation produced a rapture even greater than the mysterious pleasure he'd experienced when he revenged his father. It lifted him out of the water and into the air above the City and the roaring wind, beyond the friendly eyes of mysterious observers watching him from an endlessly turning sphere of darkness and light—and out into the heavens. At last he was reborn and the whole world had become new.

By the water's edge, his body glowing with warmth, he lay wondering how long he'd been there and how long he'd lived before he was reborn. Some crimson flowers growing by the pool caught his attention and he plucked them, pressing them against his face and enjoying their sweetness. A few he threw in the water where they eddied about in tiny currents but one he put in his hair, laughing at his foolishness. As long fingered dawn was reddening the sky, he ate the food he'd bought on his way from the monument and dressed slowly as though reluctant to spoil his nakedness with such drab garments. Then he skirted around the Rotunda and came to the Chapel. Below it he noticed a room that was half carved into the rock. Breaking a pane in a small window he released the catch to open it and climbed through to find himself in a long chamber whose walls were lined with deep shelves crammed with books and papers. Here he'd hide. The wind died away and the guardian eyes that had watched over him were closed in sleep.

When Mei Ling awoke, the vision was still vivid in her mind. She lay for a while thinking about it. The air was still, the day balmy. Peering out she saw a fleet of brown sailed junks hardly moving over the green sea; voices and the cackling of boat chickens reached her across the calm water and she wished she too was sailing away. Wondering what to do next she rolled up Xavier's cape and saw two characters scratched on the stone. They said, 'Old City.' There was no doubt about it; Ah Tung had made them before he left. Now she knew what to do, but she mustn't be seen. Climbing down to the shore she made her way along the water's edge below the sea wall and struck up the hill to Peter's house.

Light had invaded the ancient Palace; it blazed from chandeliers and flickered from slender candles; it bathed the white plaster of walls heavy with acanthus leaves, grapes and heraldic motifs, kindled gilded scrolls of wood to glow like embers and turned folds of damask curtains into tongues of fire. From elaborate frames antique yellowing glass distorted visions of the brilliance of other mirrors. The Palace was a Chinese puzzle of endless halls of light, filled with a dressy crowd made more splendid by musical comedy uniforms. At any other time Diana would have been at the centre of one of those noisy little groups of gossiping people, doing her best to enjoy herself, but as she threaded her way between them with Robert and Peter towards the banqueting hall, she whispered to Robert, "Let's take our seats straightaway," without letting Peter hear her, for he was full of inconsequential gaiety, cracking idiotic jokes which she found nerve racking. Fortunately he went off to join the Portuguese officers who were already at his table. He must have said something to amuse them straight off for Diana and Robert heard a burst of raucous male laughter as they took their own places.

Other guests, no less than four hundred of them, were coming in. The ones at the Sheratons' table were mainly punctilious Portuguese functionaries but naturally Luiz Figueiredo happened to be right next to Diana. The moment he appeared she felt like saying, I wished you'd pulled the strings to get Peter next to me instead of yourself. But that was unfair; Luiz didn't know how anxious she was. Soon the lofty hall was filled with a monstrous burble of voices while a string orchestra, situated in the gallery, played unheard Portuguese music. Each of the dishes, borne in by a host of scarlet coated waiters, was greeted by the guests, Chinese style, with roars of delight like a long lost friend, before it was torn apart by an armoury of silver knives and forks and ivory chopsticks. It wasn't every night that the dragon was cooked and the phoenix killed. As the vast meal went on Diana could hardly bring herself to respond to Luiz' chatter, for her attention, however much she might try to disguise it, was constantly wandering off towards that table where Peter seemed to be the life and soul of the party. If noise was the measure, it must be the most hilarious group there. She could see that he wasn't eating much; a glass of champagne was constantly in his hand or raised to his lips; and incessantly he smoked those cigarettes. His fellow guests must be very discreet or ignorant about the odour. At one point there was a loud clatter—he'd accidentally knocked over an empty tureen, then a flurry of waiters clearing the mess up amidst more roars of laughter. She wished she could make herself say to Robert the moment they left the hall, 'I want to go straight home. Let's leave him to it,' but she knew she never would. She was trapped.

Toasts were proposed and fulsome speeches made which at least gave her the opportunity of closing her eyes, listening to no-one and hoping that nothing else untoward would happen on Peter's table. After the longest speech, by the President of the Chamber of Commerce, Lung Yeung's portrait was carried in (Why didn't someone mention Robert's name?) and His Excellency was asked to present it. Lung Yeung merely bowed to the entire company and very soon the proceedings drew to a close. The crowd then began to drift into the ballroom.

Diana sensed a change in Peter. His gaiety had dissipated, his voice was loud, his mannerisms exaggerated, he was inclined to rudeness. "Tell me when you're going to look for Ah Tung," she whispered. Then feeling she must show solicitude she added, "Peter dear. You mustn't bank on that dream of Mei Ling. It was a dream, Peter. Only a dream. I don't want you to be disappointed." He looked at her as if she'd just slithered from under a stone. "Oh do go and talk to El Fig. Ah Tung and I need no one's advice. Stop holding on to me. Look. Here comes the pillar of law and order." A beaming Lobato complimented Diana on her appearance. He was not the first to do so that evening; a white lace dress and a golden coil holding her hair, Greek style, so that it fell in a glossy black wave down her back, made her an outstanding figure in the crowd. Confidentially he leaned forward and whispered, "I'm glad he got away. I've heard the news." He even gave a friendly smile to Peter who immediately waved his arm towards the handsome Angolese guards at the doorway and asked, "Did you pick them yourself Colonel? You've got hidden taste." Lobato stiffened and turned away. Before Diana could utter a word, Peter said in a voice heard by all around, including the retreating Colonel, "I've had enough of these fascist clowns." Diana looked for support from Robert but he was talking to someone further down the room. Again Peter changed; this time his voice was low. "He's in the City. I know it's true. It's got to be. I have to find him." He gripped Diana's arm so hard it hurt. She replied in a threatening whisper, "Then for God's sake behave yourself if you want to help him." At which point the Seneschal announced the entry of the Governor and his party. The double doors were thrown open and the Angolese soldiers went through an obsolete salute ending with a stamp of halberds, the signal for the national anthem.

The Governor and his wife, nodding to guests, advanced slowly. Behind them Lung Yeung in a purple robe leaned on a similarly clad, though in black, Ming Yuk who not once reminded the triumpher that he was only a man. Then came the Bishop in cassock and sash, the Colonial Secretary and the Governor's two pretty daughters accompanied by officers twice their age. The simple dignity of the procession was not inappropriate to the grandeur and the beauty of the room which it had entered. Hardly a word was spoken and both men and women, Chinese and Europeans, Communists and capitalists bowed their respects as the Governor passed by so that the atmosphere was indeed regal.

As Lung Yeung approached, Peter thought how easy to strike him and shout words of denunciation. How monstrous that this room full of frivolous Eloi should be host to Ah Tung's destroyer. For an instant their eyes met and he felt he was gazing into the pupils of a reptile; then his mind performed another trick and he pitied the withered features and frail body. Ming Yuk noticed him and he glared back but when he took in that hard physique he found himself imagining what it would be like to be in such a monster's power, riven by his own lust and fear. His thoughts were cut short however once the dignitaries were seated on the canopied dais in gold and crimson chairs around the Governor who, with a gracious smile, gestured towards the conductor of the orchestra which immediately struck up. At that point, Diana led Peter firmly onto the floor. They liked dancing together and there were many glances both admiring and envious in their direction.

Robert found himself next to Lobato who was gazing thoughtfully after Diana. "Senhor Lobato, as our expert in law and order do you think this place brings out the worst or the best in people?" All unwittingly he had used words much the same as those the Colonel had spoken to Diana.

"Ah. So your wife told you what I said yesterday. In that man Morgan's case the worst, most certainly."

"Yesterday?"

Lobato was halfway through his reply, "Why yes, when she called on me to..." when he realised that Diana must have told no one, least of all Robert, of the visit. The narrowing of Robert's eyes made him speak too quickly. "Come Senhor. Her motives were exceptional. She asked me, beseeched me to protect Morgan." But if Robert's speech was slow his thoughts, especially his suspicions, were swift. Beseeching had no need of secrecy. Lobato continued, "If you don't believe me just look at her now. How strange she should like such an unsympathetic creature. But it's true; she's like a keeper. She's terrified he'll come to no good. She's thinking of no one but him."

"It looks as if you and I won't come to much good either if we don't watch our tongues," Robert commented testily. "I think, Colonel, that it's time Diana and I got away from this town. It's destructive."

"On the contrary. Everyone admires your portrait—it's so frank. This place is conducive to your work."

The attempt to mollify went in vain. Robert felt he'd been made a fool of and Lobato became his butt. "So you admire frankness. Then don't mind me saying I hope you won't entertain my wife again—without me." Yet even as he spoke he had started to wonder at his own anger. Maybe it wasn't jealousy but nothing more than possessiveness that motivated him. He felt that he might just as well have said, 'Don't use my car again without my permission.' The thought disconcerted him.

Lobato ran his hand over his greying hair. "You misunderstand what happened." Then his irritation got the better of him. He gestured towards the dancers. "You expect too much. Even Morgan finds her attractive. What hope have mere mortals like me." He used the barb as an exit line and moved off with a punctilious bow. Robert drifted dejectedly through the splendidly garbed gossiping crowds, reluctant to talk to anyone. So inward looking had he become that he didn't notice Soolan until he heard her cold, "Good evening," uttered with the falsest of smiles. "Shall we dance?" he asked automatically like someone in a musical. She went with him onto the floor where they moved slowly along ignoring the fast rhythm.

"Why didn't you turn up yesterday, Robert? Don't you need me now?" Temporarily ill-disposed towards the opposite sex as well as his own, he answered coldly, "If you want to know the truth I don't need anyone."

"But I have my uses sometimes—like a sing song girl."

"Are we going over the same old ground again? You know what I'm like."

She pressed her cheek close to his, her mouth next to his ear. "Yes, you're a blasted hypocrite. I suggest you do a self-portrait—with the same accuracy as you depicted Lung Yeung." Then she left him alone in the crowd of dancers who, however, hardly gave him a glance. A whole world of gossip and intrigue was circulating about him of which he knew little and which cared even less for him; such is generally the position of the expatriate. So he made no pretence of accompanying her and went off in the opposite direction, glad at least not to be dancing; it was an art in which he did not excel. Soolan almost at once regretted her impetuosity; thinking he must be following she turned anxiously but he was nowhere to be seen. The wife of a Chinese businessman came up with some problem faced by a cultural troupe. "We've been told we can only sing one song; what about 'Red Flags Inspire Production.' Soolan looked at her in cold fury and said, "Tell them to sing what you damned well like," in English and went off.

"I can't ask you to dance Mr. Sheraton," said Lung Yeung who had descended from his seat on the Governor's dais towards which Robert had inadvertently wandered. "But we'll take a walk together. Let me lean on you." Bony fingers rested on Robert's arm with the lightness of a formal gesture. "I tire easily. I hope I'm not weighing too heavily. We'll go to the library and have a drink." As they began their progress, slow as a pavane through the crowd, Robert asked him whether he was enjoying the evening. "Ah Mr. Sheraton," he said, "I can't help thinking of the words of Chuang Tzu, 'Men who dream of a great banquet, may find themselves weeping the next morning.'" Since Robert couldn't imagine Lung Yeung even possessing tear-ducts, he led him on in silence.

The chairs and ottomans of gilded rosewood and patterned silk along the side of the grand ballroom were largely occupied by elderly guests who were having a wonderful time just watching and gossiping, and there was much for them to see and hear since the entire society of the colony, except for those at death's door, was there. As Lung Yeung approached them, once after another they stood up and greeted him with the respect that might be paid to a visiting prince. He presented them to Robert as though this itinerant painter were the guest of honour, perhaps maliciously amused to be seen bestowing favour on an outsider and one whose portrait of him contained elements far from flattering. Whether or not it was so, his action would certainly be taken as an expression of contempt for critics; as an emperor he was above reproach

The formidable figure of Dona Justina, doyenne of the oldest Portuguese family in the Colony, rose before them.

"It's just like the old days Senhor Lung," she gushed as if speaking to some notability with whom half a century ago she'd shared the pleasure of brilliant seasons. He replied curtly, "I don't think my young days were ever as gay as yours, Dona Justina." She ignored the observation and spoke about a Manchu prince who'd told her so much about the Ch'ing court, reeling off names of vanished aristocrats to persuade him to share her nostalgia for days and places neither of them had ever known. "But returning to the present," he said. "I believe you know Mr. Sheraton. You couldn't have met a better artist even in those days." Don Justina glanced at Robert condescendingly and said, "At home we have a number of paintings by Chinnery," as though the Irish artist who once lived in the City had been the equal of Goya. "You must come to see them." She didn't quite add, 'They could teach you a thing or two,' but the implication hovered in the air. Robert murmured his thanks as the gentle arm moved him on. Dona Justina lowered her enormous bum onto the thick pouf of a bergère and his acceptance of her invitation went unheard. "She comes of a very aristocratic family," Lung Yeung observed and Robert replied curtly, "So I see from her manners."

The Governor's ADC came up and asked Lung Yeung to return to the dais; some folk songs were about to begin. He fluttered his hand irritably at the interruption and said, "I was going to ask you Mr. Sheraton. Do you think you caught my character in the portrait?" How the old devil's eaten up with himself, Robert thought. "I tried to say what I feel," he replied casually. Then, as if his voice was no longer under his own control, he heard it saying impertinently, "But to tell the truth, *Shin Saang* I don't think there's anything very interesting about you—except money. That enables you to delude yourself more than most people can afford to do. It's a common failing of the rich." He was aghast at himself but the unreality of the place was to blame; the room was a dream room, Lung Yeung an apparition and his own words those of a somnambulist. The eyes of the portrait glared back at him; the phantom turned and walked briskly away, quashed with the flinging of a little dust.

"Did you enjoy your progress?" Luiz' voice brought him back to earth. "You've had a tonic effect on the old man. He's back on the dais already. Quite a cure. Tell me how you did it." In fact a number of people had remarked on Lung Yeung's quick passage and curious eyes were turned towards Robert from all sides. "Some other time Luiz," he replied gaily. The incident had quite restored his good spirits. "Look. There's Diana—and Peter. Let's give her a hand with him. It looks as if she needs it."

Diana was glad to see them approaching, exceedingly so. It wasn't just the strain of watching over Peter that was now depressing her. She sensed that in some way or other he'd slipped way beyond her reach and indubitably out of her control. In any case she needed a rest. "Why don't you go out now and look for you-know-who," she whispered to him urgently. "Walk about in the courtyard. Give him a chance to see you. But be careful. I'll be here if you want me." That said she stretched out her arm to take Robert's hand. It was the first time she'd ever been glad to see the back of Peter, who pushed off quite rudely through a circle of sombrely dressed Portuguese matrons who stared at him in disgust, They would have been even more disgusted if they had known he was in search of such a person as Ah Tung. As he left the room he noticed some officers talking acrimoniously around Lobato. The Colonel was angry. "The main road must be kept clear," he shouted. "Make the crowds queue up in the side lanes." The voices went on disputing trifles. Peter looked at them with contempt. What fools people in military uniforms were, when they were officers.

Before going outside he went downstairs to the cloakroom where, presumably by chance, he encountered Ming Yuk just standing there, motionless as an angler. He paused, conscious of obsidian eyes questioning him and felt particularly elated when he noticed that they were alone. "The Portuguese singers are on," he heard himself saying conspiratorially, though he'd never spoken to Ming Yuk before. "You don't want to watch that stuff do you?" Ming Yuk shut the door and stood still close behind him, no longer questioning but, it seemed, anticipating something, keenly. Peter found himself justifying his incipient treachery by telling himself that with this man's friendship he could help Ah Tung. Then he had to admit to himself that he wasn't envisaging Ah Tung's welfare at all. He walked off abruptly, stood in one of the huge Victorian urinals and peed against the bull's eye target thoughtfully provided by the Invicta Vitreous Enamel Co. Ltd., Stoke, 1895. Ming Yuk's departure was as noiseless as a snake's.

When he emerged from the dank stone walled basement, voices in the ballroom were singing, *"Vestidos lindos para nossa penha..."* in gay accord. Everyone was turned towards the singers so no one noticed him slip through a french window onto the verandah. The night was cold and he shivered; his head ached, his body wanted more morphine. Leaning against a pillar he smoked a heroin cigarette. When it was finished he walked away from the light into the gardens and by-ways that lay amidst and about the labyrinthine buildings.

Sometimes he approached the outer boundaries of the Old City. Over the walls he heard the staccato voices of police giving orders or blowing whistles, no doubt carrying out Lobato's instructions to keep the waiting crowd of destitutes under control; at other times he drew near the ballroom and heard the beat of drums, the lilt of peasant dances or the wail of fados, interspersed with gay applause or bursts of excited laughter. Poverty and privilege were both within earshot but he belonged to neither. This was what he'd been doing all his life—wandering in the half light of a nether world of his own creation, seeking for the ideal love life had hidden from him. "Ah Tung," he sighed, "Where are you hiding? Ah Tung where have you gone to? Say where you are." The cold wind in the crenellated rooftops repeated, "Ah, ah, ah," but never completed his lover's name. Sometimes he crossed an over-grown garden and branches caught on his clothes, tugging for a moment like hidden fingers grasping but their tendrils always released him when he stopped to see who was there. He heard footsteps, coughs, sounds of hidden breathing but whenever he paused the sounds died away. The corridors and porticos that led on and on from within darkened buildings into the sinister blackness of night were dismal caverns of the underworld; always he was followed and always when he turned, like Orpheus, the dim shades murmured, "Eheu, Eheu" and fled into the twittering darkness.

He felt it was possible to wander on amongst these buildings for ever, for always when an end was at hand another doorway opened, another vista beckoned. Stairways led downward into courtyards whose existence he'd not suspected; in them he saw massive walls resting on boulders fused together in dampness by lichens and mosses as though the Intramuros was rooted in the earth. Cavern entrances yawned in rocks and he paused at their openings listening to the plangent sounds of water but fearing to enter lest once inside he could never return. Yet not far away bright rooms were filled with laughing people fondly deluding themselves that the City was sustained by an aged dragon who could protect it from the fury of the changing world beyond its walls.

He drew close to the ballroom again; the Portuguese music had finished and he heard the insistent drumming of a Chinese lion dance—thump, thump, thump, tat-tat, tat-tat-tat in reiterated pattern whilst the nodding head of the lion followed the grinning mask and tantalising gestures of a little man with a fan. Peter imagined the strong thighs of the young men bearing the lion head, each vying in acrobatic leaps. The drums were louder than he'd ever heard before, reverberating through the buildings and echoing around. To escape them he went towards the Chapel and sheltered in a doorway. As he leant against its panels, someone inside raised a latch and the door opened a little. This time it wasn't his imagination; he pushed open the gloomy portal of the realm of Dis and went along a passage filled with unfathomable night. The way was narrow, the walls moist; he felt low steps leading up toward another door which stood open. Through it he found himself in a gallery. Below, someone was walking up the nave towards the altar; someone who wanted him to follow. There could be no doubt; it was Ah Tung. He went downstairs and ran over the pavement towards the chancel steps. "Ah Tung," he cried. "Is it you? Speak to me." All was silent. Again, "Ah Tung," he cried and straightaway the dark hall echoed in reply but, horrible to relate, the tones he heard were deeper than his voice; it must be a trick of his imagination. Once more he called, "Ah Tung" and the responding voice—was it from the altar or a gallery—changed into a long hiss, "East, East, East," instead of "Tung, Tung, Tung." Peter stood still, his scalp tingling, his eyes staring. How could an echo translate a word. "Who is it?" he shouted. "Who's calling East?" The voice replied in solemn moan, "Tung, Tung." Outside the distant thump, thump, thump, tat-tat, tat-tat-tat of the lion dancers was getting closer—the troupe must be leaving the ballroom—the membranes in his ears seemed struck by violent hands "Who are you?" he groaned. "What are you?" The voice replied amidst peals of laughter, "Ah Tung, Morgan, Ah Tung." In his fear, Peter found time to think, 'It's the heroin, the heroin'. Seizing the cigarettes from his pocket he scattered them over the floor. Then he backed away from the altar to flee from the Chapel. He must get to the passage and rush up it, nor would he ever make that fatal turn around. The voice continued to call and mock but now it came distinctly from the white figure above the altar—yes, that was where it came from, from the mutilated monarch of death. This was madness, delusion. "Ah Tung, are you here?" he screamed but his cry was lost amidst the thunder of the lion drums outside. A shape emerged from behind the altar and as it approached, he made out a man in a black Chinese robe. "Ah Tung, Pai Chai, Ming Yuk, who do you want, lonely Mr. Morgan? Do you want me now, here, before I get Ah Tung?"

The drums stopped and in the silence Peter heard Ming Yuk chuckling. He felt no resentment against his persecutor and when Ming Yuk struck a light to pick up the cigarettes he stared in fascination at the broad shoulders bent before him. The cigarettes were thrust into his hand. "You'll need these—and more." Peter put one of them between his lips. His hands trembled so much that Ming Yuk had to light it for him. Then he heard a strangely insinuating whisper, "Goodnight my dear Mr. Morgan," and for an instant saw that cruel face smiling at him before the match went out. There was no more. Peter stood trembling in the dark. Abruptly Ming Yuk left him alone in the chapel to rejoin the festivities in the ballroom. Intoxicated by the power he had just exercised he knew that his victim was trapped and squirming. If only, he thought, as his narrowing eyes took in the frivolous hateful crowd before him, if only he could do as much to all these people around him. Ah, to see them writhe under his lash. One day, perhaps... But since serving an emperor was like sleeping with a tiger, he ran like a footman when a Portuguese officer told him crisply that he was required at once in the entrance hall where the Governor and Lung Yeung were about to leave. The Governor, apparently, didn't think it appropriate that he should listen to strains of praise for Chairman Mao from a Chinese choir; as for Lung Yeung, he'd had quite enough for one evening.

The road from the Club to the City gate had been cleared for their cars but at all the crossways queues of silent poverty-stricken people were controlled by policemen equipped with wicker shields and bamboo staffs. The Governor behaved as if they weren't there but his wife had to be called back from the porte cochère where she'd been looking at the sight. "Adriano, it's terrible, quite terrible. Can't something be done?" she cried but her husband averted his eyes. She turned to Lung Yeung, clasping her hands together. "Senhor Lung..." he saw her eyes full of tears. Before she could say any more the ADC took her by the arm and led her to the car.

Glancing at the dejected crowd, Lung Yeung was contemptuous of the woman's compassion. Did any of them, old or young, whole or maimed, suffer any more than he did; they still wanted to possess something—even the pittance they were getting tonight; they could still hope. To judge by the number of children they could still make love. He could hope for nothing. Why should that presumptuous woman look appealingly at him; if he gave, what would he gain, or if they were to receive, what true significance would enter their lives; all of them, rich or poor, would soon be borne away like dust. No doubt the Governor's wife would inaugurate some charity to assuage her guilt; it was a foible of such women with their misplaced humanitarianism. If only they would consider, as suggested in their Christian scriptures, that the wealthy had more need of help than the poor.

His sharp eyes suddenly noticed some marks, bits of tobacco, ash, on Ming Yuk's robe. "Brush your arm Ming Yuk. And your collar—it isn't very neat. What have you been up to?" The two of them drove off in the Rolls Royce looking neither to the left nor to the right at the mute crowds.

With the Governor and his principal guest out of the way, the atmosphere in the ballroom became less restrained. The band abandoned the waltzes, foxtrots and paso dobles they'd been playing earlier and switched to more modern rhythms. In the alcove below the musician's gallery, Lobato joined some senior officers who were enjoying a champagne party which was periodically punctuated by explosions of the braying laughter so typical of military men the world over. "He needs to relax," the ever charitable Luiz said to Soolan as they danced by. "If the crowd hadn't been cleared the Governor would have been stuck. Then Lobato would really have got it in the neck." Soolan looked surprised. "But I thought the money had already been handed out." Luiz shrugged his shoulders. "They've not even started. It'll go on all night. I hope they don't run out of change." He added,

"There are thousands of them. Far more than expected. And they must be famished. There's a cold wind blowing."

Oblivious of the chilly world outside the great party was hotting up, ever more stimulated by an apparently endless stream of alcohol, but especially champagne. The music was louder, the voices and laughter more strident and couples were dancing wildly. Amidst it all, Luiz stopped in his tracks, filled with horrid misgivings at the unexpected sight of Dona Justina dancing with Peter. Her feet stamped and her fingers snapped in a weird attempt to relate Iberian gestures to a boogie woogie roll whilst her broad hips gyrated provocatively like a belly dancer's. Still worse, Peter, his clothes dishevelled, was inventing lewdly pelvic movements as he pranced about her like a ballet dancer gone insane. But Dona Justina seemed delighted and kept calling, "Jump higher Peter. Jump higher. Come on. Dance. Everyone. You young people. Enjoy yourselves. Dance."

"My God. What a sight," Soolan said. "I thought she was a pillar of convention." To which Luiz, now thoroughly alarmed, replied, "In some moods she is; at other times she breaks out. As now it seems, as now. Her family does its best to straight-jacket her. They'll be furious with Peter. Quite furious. We must stop it at once." His feelings were shared by Robert and Diana who were nearby, uncertain what to do. For once Luiz became the man of action, telling Diana to grab Peter whilst he himself cut in with Dona Justina. The operation took some doing, but succeeded. Meanwhile Robert put out his arms to dance with Soolan but she turned away from him and was lost in the crowd. He shrugged his shoulders and, glad to escape the babel, went outside.

The crush on the floor was now growing intense so that it became more difficult for Peter to dance so demonically. Diana felt drained. She tried appealing to him. "Calm down Peter, calm down." But he was possessed, shaking his head and shouting, "Bom, bom, bom," in time to the music and laughing hysterically. "What about Ah Tung?" she protested. "I thought you were looking for him." His feverish eyes lit up and he all but yelled, "Don't worry. I'll find him later. Everything's fine, fine, fine."

They were moving towards the officers in the alcove. "Let's see what those fascist fuckers are doing," Peter yelled, propelling Diana through the mêlée. "Oh, they're with that clown Lobato. I wonder if he's beaten any one up today." With an intuition of doom Diana tried to hold him back but the dancing bore them forward. As they reached the alcove an officer called out, "To Colonel Lobato," and champagne glasses were raised all round, one within Peter's reach; he seized it and shouting, "To Portugal's one and only Colonel Cunt," poured the sparkling liquid over Lobato's head.

In the terrible instant when the Colonel rose spluttering and furious, before any officer could reach towards the assailant, Diana pushed Peter with all her might through the crowd. "Get out. Get out at once," she screamed. The shock of what he had done made him obey. The dancing stopped, the music died away, people demanded to know what was happening, stood on chairs to get a better view. In short confusion reigned in the ballroom.

Outside Peter ran into the darkness until he found a deserted place where he lay down panting breathlessly. Above him the crescent Moon was brilliant in a black sky and as he looked up at her the unpremeditated incident in the ballroom slowly grew less important. All that mattered was to find Ah Tung, to find him wherever he was hidden and together they'd begin to ascend hand in hand from this abyss. Together they'd erase self and learn to give. At some time in the future he himself would make amends for his foolish act but when he did so it would only be part of the enormous amendment he'd make to the world for his life. The whole of his being would become an act of giving; he'd keep nothing for himself and Ah Tung would follow him in a life devoted to love. Yes, he could see it clearly now. He got up and began to make his way down an alley that seemed strangely familiar. It would lead him to what he had to do. Yet all was so dark he had to finger the rough walls in search of the way. And then it was that he was touched by the insidious music of the Moon and began to sing, "Love. Giving. Love. Giving," his song an exaltation of the vision she had, so suddenly, given to him.

The music in the ballroom seemed to have resumed but it became less and less distinct as he went on, still delighting in the words of his new life until at length, approaching a high wall, he became aware of the murmuring of the waiting crowd on the other side and amidst it the voice, as of a boy or a girl, repeating, "*Hoi, hoi,* open, open," or was it just the meaningless sound of its wailing. Never before could he remember hearing such an insistent cry; it seemed to be commanding him alone. Again it came thinly through the night air, "*Hoi, Hoi,*" and its plaintiveness filled his eyes with tears. Before him there was an ancient barred door—unconsciously he'd stopped before it. The moment had come; he'd open the barrier and go from the City into the world, proclaiming that the distinctions between them had vanished. The rusty iron bolts slid back with difficulty, but at last they were withdrawn and the wooden door yawned open on heavy hinges. Outside in the half darkness appeared the ghastly vision of the hell it was his mission to harrow; the gloomy lane was full of miserable shades, patient despite their rags and hunger, their subdued voices sometimes broken by the whimpering of children. He knew they were waiting for him and yearning for the air above. They need wait no longer; the rule of Saturn was restored and justice returned to earth. He ought to free them. He could free them. The pure must be free. Climbing onto a stone he called out, "Come in. Come into the Palace. Come and follow me. Eat and drink with me. Come in." For an instant they gazed at him. Then their patience gave way and they began, first in a trickle but soon in a torrent to pour through the door, making their way to the brightness and warmth in the distance. "Come in," Peter went on shouting, half laughing and half crying as he saw their wretchedness and heard their voices. As they came in, a serene light filled his heart and all the darkness of his doubts vanished. He threw his money to them, then his ring and then his watch. An old man caught his attention; he took off his shoes and threw them to him. To one he gave his coat, to another his shirt, until at last he stood, a naked figure of vengeance, gesturing them onwards to take whatever they liked. There was no end to the pale procession as it swarmed along; he wanted to be amidst it, moving like a fish in a river. Jumping down he fell among the people and was borne into the Palace still calling, "Love. Giving. Love. Giving." Because of him the world was freed from its night of horror. Time could start again.

Inside the ballroom the gaiety prevented the tumult from being noticed—but soon people who'd been cooling off on the terraces heard the noise and rushed inside shouting that the mob had broken in. The music trailed away and everyone stood still. A chilling roar was heard outside. "It's a revolution," screamed a female voice. "The Revolution," boomed Dona Justina. "At last. At last." Pandemonium broke out on all sides. People struggled to get out; officers gave orders but the only soldiers were the Angolese halberdiers, the weight of whose helmets had made them unfit for further duties that evening. Lobato found himself at the centre of a crowd blaming him for everything and asking him what to do. In desperation he shouted, "Barricade the windows," an ominous order which made a few women get hysterics as the men rushed to do as Lobato said. "To the barricades. To the barricades," shouted Dona Justina jogging about near the Colonel. "Oh, this is marvellous. I haven't had a night like this for years."

"Get her out of the way. She's a fool," Lobato shouted. He never wanted another night like this as long as he lived.

"Oh am I," the great dame replied. "You're the fool who didn't do his duty." Lobato's humiliation was complete. From the back of his mind surged an infuriating tide of suspicion. "Morgan. Kai Tung," he fumed. "It's something to do with those sodomites."

Amidst the mob one of the self-same sodomites was pushing from window to window peering inside the Palace. The celebration had prevented Ah Tung from emerging any earlier but the mounting confusion gave him the opportunity to move unobserved. He realised it was impossible to find Peter. He must get away altogether. But it was unsafe to venture too far. If only the confusion could be increased. He went back to think in his hideout below the Chapel. Striking a match he looked round the old room. At the further end he noticed for the first time two ornate oil lamps on a long table. A fire, he decided, would help. Without more ado he toppled four bookcases holding rows and rows of old volumes to the floor and for good measure piled up some chairs and tables against the walls which were panelled to the wooden ceiling. The lamps were full of oil and he poured it over his handiwork. Then he threw a match.

The room sprang alight as though it had always awaited this moment of destruction. Ah Tung piled on more furniture, laughing as the flames roared upward. They were already licking the ceiling before the ecstatic incendiarist made his getaway.

It was a little while before the fire was noticed, what with so many people milling around. Thinking it was the work of the mob, the police began to strike out with their staffs. Screams could be heard and here and there fighting broke out; even a few shots were fired. Of course, none of this was in the least bit helpful. Lobato tried to organise fire fighting but no equipment could be found. Very soon, since everyone had poured into the open, the streets and courtyards were too crowded for anyone to do anything effective even if they had known what to do. Confusion turned into chaos and the fire went on burning. From somewhere or other the bishop turned up, furious that the Chapel hadn't been locked as had been agreed and shouting that it was the Committee members' duty to save the documents and relics. Neither was this at all helpful; it was too late for such a rescue. In less than half an hour the flames had thrust upward into the Chapel which became a beautiful lantern with long crimson apertures down its sides. Most of the Portuguese just stood staring as if hypnotised by the fate of the building. Men crossed themselves, women fell to their knees, faces streamed with tears. Even the Chinese were subdued by the destruction of such a venerable place. The Blessed Virgin and St. Francis were invoked but they took no discernible action; at length flames were even seen flickering through the roof. Nothing could be done to save the Chapel now; it was too late.

Diana dug her fingers into Robert's arm as they watched. The suspicion that had lurked in Lobato's mind was a certainty in hers. "They did it. They did it," she whispered. Her words echoed Robert's fears but he hushed her. She heard Carlos' voice somewhere nearby. "Mother of God," he was repeating. Though not devout he was superstitious and took the destruction of the Chapel as a dreadful omen. He wanted to cling to Diana but daren't.

It was out of the question to go home—the crush was too great; and there was no way of helping. There was nothing to do but watch. Diana couldn't help thinking how beautiful the burning Chapel was, a marvel to behold. When Robert asked her to return indoors, she refused adamantly. "No. I must watch. I want to watch." What was happening was the inevitable conclusion to the evening—and to much more besides. It would be wrong not to see it out. Anything that happened to Peter and Ah Tung was now beyond her power and so great was her relief before this fact that she began to experience an extraordinary lightness of heart. The fire seemed to be cleansing her mind of all the rubbish piled up there. She wanted to sing, to shout, to cry. If it was a funeral pyre, so much more reason to do so. Peter wouldn't mind; he'd probably expect her to celebrate him that way.

Of such an histrionic nature were the thoughts that for a little while blustered around her mind, bringing tears to her eyes and producing the kind of artificial emotion people experience in the theatre and which is quickly dissipated once they get out into the everyday life of the streets again. And so gradually, as she observed the general disarray instead of that romantic magic lantern up above, the feeling of exhilaration passed away and she recognized that what had just been going on in her head was all but meaningless, no more real than the ruddy glow on the base of the low clouds above the conflagration. It had been brought about by a combination of nervous excitement and physical exhaustion. All feelings, it now seemed to her, were the result of something like that, the by-product of a concatenation of circumstances over which no one had much control but which produced frames of mind which people vehemently maintained to be themselves. How obvious that was with Peter and Ah Tung; unwittingly they had been turned into the demonic forces which had caused the destruction in front of her. Nothing about it said what the two of them really were. Everything about them would seem to be an insane aberration; their feelings, the good in them as well as the bad, their suffering would be judged utterly invalid by the narrow-minded society of the town. Nevertheless, if they were deranged, wasn't that society itself just as mad? But that wouldn't matter. The madness of the majority always won and tyrannized over the rest. And now it became quite impossible for her to contain the disquiet seeping through her mind so she abandoned herself to it until all she felt was the strongest of cravings to escape from even the memory of the entanglements that had tyrannized over her entire life since her youth—oh so far off now, it seemed—in Australia. She longed to begin anew. Yet how to do so when she had no idea where she stood in the world's confusion or whether she herself was nothing but an illusion created by passing circumstance. She stared uncomprehendingly at the chaos around her and raised her eyes again towards the fiery beacon standing over the City, but could find no answer at all.

At long last the fire brigade managed to force its engines through the congested streets and before long the ballroom roof was swarming with firemen. Water from the courtyard pools was used first to check then to kill the flames. Slowly the crowd was pushed back by the police until it thinned out and the situation was brought fully under control. Only then was it considered safe for the guests at the banquet, now dishevelled and woebegone, to leave for their homes. The remaining poor were just chased away.

"Let's go," Robert said taking Diana protectively by the hand. "We can get away now." She got up slowly scrutinizing the people in the courtyard and noticed Carlos watching her anxiously with mournful cow eyes. She called him and he came over, smiling shyly at Robert. "Carlos," she asked. "Please look for Peter. You're in uniform. You could go in search of him. We'll wait at his place. Then all at once she lost control and cried out desperately, "Oh Carlos, find him. Bring him safely to me. Please." Carlos promised to do his best even though he could not help wondering how she could still care about such a madman.

In the early hours of the morning he made his way alone to Peter's house where Diana and Robert were standing with Mei Ling on the verandah, watching the last agonies of the Chapel. The roof had fallen in and showers of sparks were driven heavenwards by the hot air like a gigantic firework, illuminating the ancient City with glorious light. When she had been told of Carlos' fruitless search Diana grieved silently and deeply for Peter and a little for herself as well. And Robert was silent too for he could not help thinking, with the self satisfaction of the successful if unintentional prophet, of the service in the Chapel—the gold vestments, the screen fretted with wind-blown flames and the optical illusion of fire that was, after all, a vision.

PART III

The Imperial Edict

PART III

The Imperial Edict

Somewhere in the room a clock was ticking persistently. It perplexed her; it shouldn't be there. Was it one of Robert's silly jokes? Her hand reached out to the table where cigarettes were always at the ready, but waved in the empty air. Diana opened her eyes; she was in Peter's bedroom. From the garden came the sound of Robert's voice; she couldn't hear the words but the cadences were familiar. The lighter tones of Carlos and Mei Ling followed. Laughter suggested they were all getting on well together. But there was no hint of Peter. She sighed at the memory of the Banquet; all too clearly now she saw how terribly his mind had been bent by the loss of Ah Tung and excessive drug taking. She had failed him. She should have anticipated disaster.

Across the room she saw her white dress thrown over a chair, looking very sorry for itself. She decided never to wear it again, indeed to get rid of it as soon as possible. Then she noticed she had on a pair of flowery pyjamas belonging to Peter. Her anxiety returned; they must move heaven and earth to help him. At this very moment he might be in serious danger. He might even be dead. Benumbed by the latter possibility, she closed her eyes and just lay there, reluctant to get up, reluctant to face another day of the tawdry existence which she had drifted into and which, in the absence of Peter, would become yet more tawdry. But the world was not to be so easily kept at bay; Robert's voice was no longer audible but Mei Ling and Carlos, now alone it seemed, were talking in quick harsh exchanges and their laughter had dried up. After a while their voices grew louder with angry outbursts jabbing the air. She heard Carlos shouting something about prostitutes and brothels and Mei Ling yelling back ever louder as her voice receded. The metal garden gate was slammed and all was silent. In a while Carlos came into the room wearing a gloomy face. "Where's Robert?" Diana demanded warily.

Carlos prowled around the bed, unwilling to catch her eye and taking his time before he mumbled, "Somewhere or other."

"I think you should go. He may come in." As she warned him, she couldn't help thinking how comical his face looked. It made her think of the party game Peter had invented in which one had to put on a 'Confucian' face with contradictory elements. Just now Carlos' face was a mixture of lust and anger. No wonder he answered "I don't care," so furiously.

"I do." She did her best to make her voice firm without revealing her irritation or her amusement. Either might upset her lover boy's male pride.

"Oh yes. You would."

"Well, if you must stay, don't talk so loud. What was all that about with Mei Ling?"

"She was cross because I didn't find Peter. Always Peter. Peter. Who is this Peter? An idiot. Yet everyone thinks of him first." A new ingredient had come into his expression, puzzlement; surely some immense mystery must be involved in the greater popularity of a person like Peter over a paragon such as himself.

"Why shout at Mei Ling about it? I heard you both mentioning something else."

"None of your business." He sat down so heavily on the bed that the mattress sagged mightily, took her hand, stroked it, rubbed it against his cheek and then leaned over her. Less than godlike this morning his breath was unpleasantly stale.

"Please Carlos. Robert..." She turned her head away but he took her chin in his hand and turned it towards him roughly. His words exploded into her face. "He doesn't care for you like me. Hah. You think he's different because he's an artist, when he's just like every other man; his own prick comes first. He's a hypocrite I can tell you. I know. In the police we watch where foreigners go. I tell you, I know."

"You don't know. Oh for goodness' sake dear, do let go of me. And stop telling lies. You know nothing about him." That, of course, was the best way of making Carlos talk.

"I do. I do. Brothels in the Rua da Felicidade. Ever since you've been living here. Anyway, it's easy to see it in his eyes. And you don't love him. You think you do. You're just stuck together. I've seen married people like you two before. Afraid to make a break. They go on for years grinding each other down, until they're rotten as old shit."

"It isn't like that at all. But I don't want to listen to all this nonsense so early in the morning. After last night I'm worn out Carlos, absolutely drained."

Carlos laughed bitterly. "Oh yes, I only talk nonsense don't I? You'd never admit it; you think it's just a bit of fun with me. I'm nothing to you. Ah, Diana, why can't you see what's in front of your nose? We're really happy together."

"In bed, yes." She'd better say something to humour him, she told herself, but oh God, the tawdriness of it all. Why wouldn't this silly boy just get out.

"That's important. Yes, we're happy in bed. Give me a chance. We'd be happy out of bed too." Carlos suddenly addressed an invisible audience. "God, what a woman: She thinks I'm just a machine with no feelings; just a contraption designed for fucking." Then he stroked her cheek tenderly and pleaded once more, "Give me a chance, Diana." Tears glistened in the corners of his eyes, flowed onto his long eyelashes. Diana's manner became gentler even though her words remained determined. "How Carlos? How? It's too difficult. Please go. I must get up. Please dear."

"No. Stay where you are. Listen to me. You've split yourself into three people. With Robert it's a fake marriage. Then another part of you wants Peter; and I get what's left."

"It's an important part. In any case I don't want Peter. I'm sorry for him."

"You love him."

"Then if I love him, how can I give you a chance." But what was the point, she asked herself, of trying to confound him with logic.

"Forget him. He's finished. Leave Robert. Live with me. Give me a chance, Diana." He leant down trapping her under the bedclothes. This was most uncomfortable but she did her best to be patient, ran her fingers through his glossy wavy hair and tried, not easily, to see it as he did. "We could leave here." He looked intently at her as he spoke. "I can get a job in Hong Kong as a—as a translator. In an office maybe. We could live cheaply. You'd try it if you loved me."

"Carlos. You'd regret it. You like your police work. It suits you down to the ground." And that's certainly true, she thought, though it wasn't very flattering to him. At this reflection she almost at once began to feel guilty over her condescending attitude towards his distress.

He got up and walked around the room thumping his fist into his hand. "It doesn't matter if I do regret it. But I only want to regret it when I've tried. I don't want to regret something that's never happened. Oh Jesus. What sort of a woman are you? How can you like someone just for sex? How can you do it to me?" He flopped down in a chair and began to sob dabbing his eyes with a large yellow handkerchief. Diana got out of bed and went to him; if she didn't there'd be another of his explosions. He pressed her hand against his wet face to make sure she was aware of his intense emotion. "Carlos," she began, unsure how to continue.

"Yes? Please say you will."

"I've heard you're interested in Mei Ling. Are you sure I'm the right person for you?"

"Mei Ling and I are quite finished." He was loud and vehement. The sobbing and the tears seemed quite finished too.

"I see."

"What do you see?" His eyes were still shiny but now with a dangerous glint.

"The quarrel this morning. You're on the rebound." Oh God, she thought the moment the words were out, mistake, mistake, mistake, for his answer was to sweep everything on the dressing table to the floor. She stared at the scattered toiletries, a broken vase and the water soaking into the magazines—not a very good advertisement for life with Carlos. But it was her fault; she'd been too direct. "I'm only trying to get at the truth," she said gently. "Perhaps Mei Ling would be better for you."

"You mean I'm too poor," he shouted, his voice full of passion as he stamped around the room, arms flailing.

"Don't break anything else Carlos."

"I will." A lamp went flying. "See. I will."

"Then break everything. Go on. Break everything. They're not yours so it doesn't matter, does it?" At once she realized she'd made another error. He couldn't take the sort of gibe that Australians so easily make at one another and was clearly deciding which of the larger objects in the room to strike when the door opened and Robert appeared. "What's going on?" he asked blandly, surveying the wreckage.

Diana became offhand. "Carlos quarrelled with Mei Ling. He's worked up." She did a quick putting everything in order job as she spoke. "He's very worked up indeed. And tired too after last night. Aren't you Carlos?" She turned her back on him and addressed Robert, "Where's Mei Ling?"

"I don't know."

"Perhaps you should go and find her Carlos." She swung round and stared at him very coolly. Awed by this as well as by Robert's large presence and puckering his mouth like a bad boy, Carlos went off. Diana put the broken vase into a waste paper basket. "Do sit down Robert. Did you have a good sleep? There's no news then?"

Robert took a chair, shook his head in reply and looked at her curiously. Then he said, "It seems a morning for high spirits. We should have a disaster every night."

"Carlos wants me to leave you." She said as she sat at Peter's dressing table on which the most noteworthy remaining objects were a solid silver hairbrush and mirror and a silver and ivory comb, all of which had belonged to his long dead mother and which were always left there for Diana to use, as she did now.

"Not unnaturally." Robert was affecting to be interested in one of Peter's male physique magazines.

"And live with him in Hong Kong."

"Really." His reply had a dry ring to it, as dry as she was endeavouring to make her manner.

"He says you don't love me. He can see it in your eyes." Diana glanced into Mrs. Morgan's antique mirror to see how Robert was taking it, but she might have saved herself the effort.

"I haven't noticed him looking in my eyes. Jesus, don't men look grotesque when they build themselves up like this?" It was on the tip of Diana's occasionally vitriolic tongue to say, 'You've certainly built yourself up in certain directions—with booze,' but she confined herself to replying, "He's quite observant, is my muscular Carlos."

"What are you going to do then? Live with him?" The physique magazine was tossed untidily to the floor and Robert looked up as if Diana's reply might merit at least a modicum of his interest.

"Do you want me to?"

'It's up to you,' he nearly replied but instead he looked philosophic, did his pipe filling act at a snail's pace and then heaved a sigh as a prelude to his forthcoming profundities. "Poor young man. When people like us have affairs with the likes of Carlos we forget they have feelings. Don't interrupt me. (Diana had wheeled round toward him.) I'm not condemning you. In the east this sort of thing's common. Europeans get boiled up over some beautiful young creature who's just a love object. A romantic symbol. It's really a variation on the theme of masturbation. Then one day the genie pops out of the bottle. The object is a human being. It has feelings. The young man's really fallen in love with the beautiful white woman. And what does he have to do then, poor thing? Hide his head under his wing, poor thing." He shook his head and curled his lower lip to indicate his general contempt for human behaviour.

Diana surveyed him with rising gall. The thought of those brothels Carlos had mentioned hovered darkly in her mind, even though she had known about them long enough. "If this wasn't Peter's room I'd throw everything in it at your pompous head. Thank you for not condemning me Mr. Know-all. I've seen this before, I've seen that before. Yes, you have seen it all, from personal experience haven't you? My God, you're a shifty devil. Right then, if you know so much, why didn't you prevent it? If you're so clever, you're the one to be condemned." Her fit of peak ebbed. "Do you know, when you speak like that you're just an opinionated bore. You and your observations on life—they're nearly always wrong. I've never seen Carlos as an object. I knew the risk. There's always a risk when you do what I'm doing—and what you're doing too Robert. Remember? In fact I'd never live with Carlos because…"

"I'm glad to hear it." Robert was still condescending; it was a good way of admitting to nothing.

"Because I'd rather live by myself for a while. I'm fed up with this hole, and everyone in it. Do you hear? Everyone. I think I'll go to Hong Kong."

"And how pray will you live?" His condescension had become almost unbearable but she replied to him in the coldest voice she could muster. "If necessary I'll be a high class tart." At this he burst into guffaws of laughter so she got up, imitated him with three heftily sardonic 'Hah, hah, hah's' and went downstairs.

In the dining room there was no sign of Carlos but Mei Ling, now back and looking agitated, was speaking rapidly on the phone. "What is it?" Diana asked. Mei Ling beckoned her to silence; at last she put the receiver down. "It was Siu Ching—I phoned her. She heard Ah Tung's gone to his mother's place in the Little Bird Garden. The gunmen are after him." Where others might have wept Mei Ling shouted angrily, "Sheraton *Taai Taai*. This time there's really nothing we can do. Nothing at all. Nothing. Where can Mr. Morgan have got to?" She clung to Diana for support.

Peter too was on his way to the Little Bird Garden. When the sun was already high he had come to, in an alley full of destitutes who had been at the Intramuros the night before. How he had got there he didn't know, nor where the ill fitting Chinese trousers he was wearing had come from. Confused memories filled his mind: the brilliance of the ballroom, the cruelty of Ming Yuk, an insult to Lobato and the sound of endless multitudes coursing through corridors. He knew he had been near Ah Tung last night. But where was Ah Tung now? Perhaps he had gone to his family; they might try to protect him. Peter decided to go to them himself and made his way across town to the single roomed shack which he had visited only twice before. The door was open and Ah Tung's mother, her face deeply lined, her head covered with wisps of white hair, was sitting on a stool near the entrance. She raised her hands deferentially towards him. Behind him someone closed the door quietly. He glanced round and saw Ah Tung's younger brother.

"Where's Ah Tung?"

"Gone, *Shin Saang*." The old woman's voice was scarcely audible.

"When?"

"Not long ago."

Peter felt his heart beating violently. If only he had woken up earlier.

"We heard the gunmen coming. He ran off the back way."

"Where to? Where to?"

"We don't know." It seemed to Peter they didn't care either. For a moment he was unable to move; then he said, "Thank you," and turned towards the door. As he did so the old lady stood up. "I've something for you," she said and limped to a corner of the room from which she brought out a rolled up quilt which had once been in his own flat; Peter remembered Ah Tung taking it home when it was getting threadbare. "This is for you," she said offering him the bundle. He looked at the poverty of the room; obviously the quilt would be useful to the family. "No, it's alright. You keep it," he replied but she thrust it into his hands. "He always used it when he spent the night here. He wouldn't let anyone else touch it. He said you must have it." Peter remembered how the quilt had been the first covering of their love together and understood Ah Tung's last message. Stunned he left the house. As he walked down the lane Ah Tung's brother ran after him and whispered, "I think he's gone to the new harbour; perhaps he'll get away in a boat."

To steal a boat and sail off was the last remote chance. Like a madman Peter ran along the crooked streets, pushing aside anyone who blocked his way towards the long breakwater behind which small craft were moored in the new harbour. Yet there was little hope; the quilt was a farewell gift but it was also a sign that nothing had changed between them.

The volley of shots that struck Ah Tung was heard by many people along the wide sweep of the south facing bay; passers by on the Praia Grande, in the cool shade of the banyan trees, stopped to look enquiringly out to sea where, at the end of the breakwater, some figures could be seen running and pointing at an empty boat with an idly flapping sail; solitary fishermen sitting on rocks raised their broad-brimmed hats, forgetting their reveries as they tried to make out the distant commotion. Peter knew at once what had happened even though he was some distance from the scene. He paused because it seemed he was looking at something that had taken place long ago; its meaning had already been accepted and assimilated by him as a mere instant in a sequence of events whose end he knew. The story had been there all the time, complete like a book; it could be taken up then, now or in days to come and read and read again and because of that this instant of death on a sunny promontory seemed totally unimportant. If by chance the book had fallen open at this moment of final separation, equally well it might have opened, perhaps at the moment of time—it didn't matter whether the words in the past or in the future were used—when they were lying together on the warm sands of that deserted cove, watching sea birds dive for fishes, hearing the waves gurgling and surging around the ancient rocks, neither of them afflicted with a craving for drugs and ever returning to each other for love. But Peter knew he too was trapped between the covers of the narrow volume and that if he was the reader, he was also what was read; there was no possibility of putting the volume down, the story known, and saying, 'very interesting' or 'very sad' or 'now we'll read something else'. The sequence of events was moving to its end, but equally it seemed that the end was responsible for what had happened in the beginning. The only assurance lay in the volume's indestructibility; it was engraved inalienably in time, beside whose power all human effort was as a frail tendril clinging to a granite pillar. Therefore to want to resist or escape from a course of events that was inevitable was nothing but folly, a refusal to escape the artistry of his own being in which death was a mere flourish to a signature. If there was separation and ending, so also there was loving and beginning; the joining and the parting were identical and agony of the heart the corollary of its delight. He'd sensed the uncertainty of happiness in his relationship with Ah Tung when their love had started but in the time of its dissolution he also remembered more vividly than ever the radiance of its beginning. There was no need to look round, to go out to the boat or mourn by the sea; he turned his back on the sun and went away.

Far off in the rolling waves Ah Tung felt the water entering his lungs and the tide carrying him out and away to the darkness. The brilliant sun flashed for an instant in his eyes; there had been shots and a dull pain, three gunmen in black and a figure at the other end of the breakwater, the wide sweep of the bay and the water closing around him, an icy pool and crimson flowers swirled down by a current. At last he was leaving the City.

But the very next day the name, if not the body, of Ah Tung was the subject of a marvellous resurrection. Colonel Lobato read the news in disbelief when the report of a broadcast from Canton Radio was put before him. "The toiling masses in the Portuguese imperialist territory on Monday night rose in righteous fury against their colonial masters and vigorously protested against recent oppressive acts of the so-called Government. Led by heroic worker, Kai Tung, they set fire to certain imperialist symbols of Portuguese rule. Subsequently heroic worker Kai Tung was murdered by the running dogs of the fascist oppressors. The workers and students of the occupied territory intend to intensify their freedom struggle and will strenuously resist any attempt to obliterate the name of the dead hero." Lobato groaned. Would there never be an end to the trouble caused by that young man. The memory of his own loss of face was green in everybody's mind. With this new turn the blame heaped on himself was likely to grow. God! Why hadn't he been posted to Angola where the natives knew their place?

He speculated on the source of the information. If he knew who was responsible, he could guess at the motives involved and the turn that coming events were likely to take. It couldn't be Lung Yeung; his organisation had nothing to gain from workers 'intensifying their freedom struggle.' Could it be Soolan? He doubted it; he didn't like her but at least her reports to Canton were factually accurate. He then thought of Morgan. Was it possible he'd some other connections in the Colony, perhaps among the unionised workers and students who were constantly demanding the withdrawal of the Portuguese presence? Again he dismissed the thought. In any case he was safe in that direction. The Colonial Secretary had already signed the order for Morgan's expulsion as an undesirable alien. There was only one problem however; Morgan couldn't be found. Lobato made some phone calls but all the replies were negative. Searches had been made of places the Britisher was likely to visit but there was no trace. Nor did the immigration authorities have any record of his departure. Lobato's mind returned to the night of the fire. Could Morgan have been in the Chapel? Perhaps he was dead. Lobato put on his hat and coat. He'd promised the civil and church authorities to take a look at the damage anyway.

When he got to the Club courtyard he saw Father Antonio and a group of clerics laying out charred wooden figures recovered from the smouldering interior of the Chapel. Four priests were carrying the remains of the crucified Christ that had hung above the altar towards the pool; it was still hot and had to be borne on two bars beneath the body. The figure might easily have been mistaken for any piece of burned wood. The proof of what it had been was attested by the metal crown of thorns encircling the mutilated head. Lobato was moved not so much by the ruination of the statue as by the doleful faces of its bearers. He was almost inclined to help as they laid down their burden at the edge of the pool. Smoke still escaped from cracks in its blackened surface. The priests, after exchanging glances with each other and with Father Antonio, launched it into the water where it hissed violently in a cloud of steam which, on disappearing, revealed a torso, black and shiny as the body of an African, floating languorously in the darkened waters. Lobato noticed the expressions of surprise on the faces of the priests. It was as though the baptism of the figure with the unexpected revelation of its sensuous qualities had fanned into fleeting life some better hidden thoughts—but as the sum of religion lay in imitating what was worshipped, he thought sarcastically, why should they feel uneasy?

He got the impression that the priests would prefer to work on their own and turned away, but Father Antonio called almost gaily after him, "Colonel. Things could have been worse. The fire might have spread." He didn't seem to care that it was the Chapel that had been burned. "Is there anything I can do?" Lobato asked but the priest waved his hands deprecatingly. "Not in the least senhor. We're wasting our time digging out these things." He gestured at the floating figure. "But the Bishop's asked us to do it. He's taking it badly. What does it matter if the Chapel is destroyed. The Church is cluttered up with too much from the past. Why keep that statue. A new image can be made easily enough."

"Symbols are important." Lobato insisted. His religion had no place for progressive priests.

"If faith is alive, people will find symbols for it; if it's dead, symbols are nothing but idols." The Father had an answer for everything; perhaps he even held salvation existed outside the church.

Lobato stared at the long limbed negro in the pool. "When idols are cast down they can take root and grow into unexpected shapes. Never underestimate the power of idolatry, Father." But he had no intention of discussing theology and his voice became official again. "You've not found anything else in there?"

"Anything else. What for instance?" Father Antonio looked baffled.

"No—no human remains?"

"Oh, I see. No. Of course not. No one was in the Chapel, thanks be to God. The Fire Chief searched thoroughly. Didn't he inform you?"

"Yes. Yes. But your colleagues seem to be going over the place meticulously."

"There was nothing like that at all Colonel." Father Antonio bowed courteously and returned to the salvage operations.

Lobato decided to have a drink in the Club. When he got there he found the old place enjoying a new lease of life.

Quite a number of people were in the dining room, one of them Luiz Figueiredo who was polishing off a dish of spiced chicken and a bottle of Moncao. He insisted that Lobato should join him and called for another glass, then launched into a request that the order for Morgan's expulsion be cancelled. "An undesirable alien indeed! If we deported everyone who's undesirable there'd be a real exodus. It's against all the traditions of the Colony as a refuge."

Lobato was unresponsive. "Morgan isn't a refugee."

"He's a man without a country."

"You speak metaphorically."

"But truly."

"No Luiz. I can't accept your argument. His behaviour was disgraceful. You forget I was personally insulted."

"Colonel. You're too big for that sort of talk. And remember the fellow was drunk."

"But there's the political side. Didn't you hear him calling our country fascist?"

"Well, isn't it?"

"Yes. But it isn't done to say so in that tone of voice." Lobato started to laugh as he spoke. "Come on Luiz. What's the real reason behind this."

"It's the Sheratons. If Peter… Mr. Morgan goes, Diana will go too. I'm sure of it."

Lobato savoured the bouquet of the wine and shook his glass to remove a touch of sulphur. Then he said, "Ah. So that's it. It's not Morgan you're interested in. It's Senhora Sheraton."

"I like the Sheratons. They're different. Come Manuel. Admit it. Neither of us wants them to go."

Lobato's left thumb began to itch. He scratched it thoughtfully. I'm afraid there's not much love lost between me and Senhor Sheraton." He paused. "No, I don't want them to go. On the other hand, Luiz, this is all very academic. Morgan's disappeared."

"But I thought—the Sheratons think he's in custody."

"How did they get that impression?"

"They rang up the immigration department and were told that no information would be given about him at present. We just assumed…"

"You assumed wrongly. Obviously a verbal error. Could, not would." Lobato paused before going on, "And have you heard how Canton Radio described Monday night?"

"Yes. Soolan told me."

"How did she tell you? I mean what was her manner like?"

Luiz thought back. As he perceived Lobato's drift, he recognised that Soolan had a similar reason to himself for not wanting Morgan's deportation. He replied, "Oh, in her usual brisk manner. She said the Canton interpretation was true in a sense."

"In what sense?"

Luiz drummed his fingers on the table, then shrugged his shoulders. "You're the intelligence expert Colonel. Don't ask me. I must go." Of course Luiz didn't have to go anywhere and both of them knew it. But once motivated to find something out, the Colony's number one purveyor of gossip would have journeyed to the middle of Tibet to lay the truth about any shred of rumour. Lobato therefore smiled benignly, shook his hand and joined a party of Portuguese ladies at another table. As for Luiz, his next port of call was the Chinese Chamber of Commerce, which he slipped into unobserved by a back door conveniently adjacent to the rear of his own clinic. Soolan, clad in a lumpy Chinese jacket, was surprised to see him; Portuguese officials were not regular visitors. She was also very busy at her desk. Whilst she finished dealing with some document, he glanced through the window into the drab courtyard and saw blue uniformed students and workers talking loudly in groups. Some speakers with clenched fists were exhorting listeners resolutely to oppose this, that or the other. "There doesn't seem to be much commerce going on," he commented wryly. "What's up?"

"There's going to be a demonstration," Soolan replied offhandedly. He thought she looked evasive. "Nothing for you to bother about—provided you keep off the streets when it's on." She poured him some tea from one of those huge, hideously painted thermos flasks that always seemed to be standing about in Chinese communist offices. He took a little sip and bowed his false gratitude. "You know the Sheratons are leaving," he said boldly, reckoning he could justify the lie later.

Soolan's business like manner wilted. She was clearly thrown by the news. So much for the inscrutable Chinese, he thought. "Leaving? Who said so? When? Why?" She gave the document she'd being dealing with to her secretary, who left the room.

"It's really Diana," said Luiz putting on a thoughtful, though distinctly despondent mien, "Now Peter's being slung out, she doesn't want to stay. I think Robert's had enough too." To show the depth of his own feelings about the matter he emitted a deep sigh.

The phrase 'had enough' reverberated in Soolan's head. Had enough of what? Of whom? Unpleasant words such as bastard, shit, treacherous sod came to her mind in several languages. Before she could recover, Luiz' dart-like words hit her again. "So why do you want to embarrass us Portuguese with your weird reports?"

"It certainly wasn't me. I..." She halted in her tracks. "You're a sly devil Luiz. You're in the wrong profession." She had swiftly resumed her suave manner.

"Perhaps both of us are. Then if it wasn't you and it couldn't be Lung Yeung's set up, who's responsible?"

The secretary came in with some more papers. Soolan said loudly, "Thank you for your invitation Doctor. The Chamber will be delighted..." The secretary disappeared. Sotto voce she continued, "Certain radical elements, both here and in Canton do have ideas of their own you know. They want to cause turmoil. It won't be so easy to control things, but I...we will."

Luiz looked at Soolan with some amazement. What a subtle, devious woman she was. He shook his head—she knew it was a gesture of sympathy—and said, "Well I can see you're more than a little busy." Then he rose to leave. He'd found out what he wanted; perhaps, in return, he should give her a ray of hope. "By the way there's something a bit odd going on."

"Yes?" Soolan's voice was edgy.

"But I don't suppose you'd know."

"Oh, for God's sake Luiz. Come on."

He wondered why Communists liked to refer to God. Wouldn't it be more appropriate to say 'For Marx' sake' or 'For Mao's sake.' "Well, no one knows where Morgan is. So I don't suppose Robert and Diana will leave until that little matter's cleared up." He shook her hand and said, "Don't worry," as he left by the same back entrance. Soolan pondered for a while, going over every detail of the conversation with Luiz, and then decided to phone Ming Yuk, a thing she seldom did for she loathed the man instinctively.

A male secretary enquired who was calling and took an age to put her through, which was unusual. Again she had the feeling she was being played with. Ming Yuk airily but not convincingly dismissed any idea he might know where Morgan was and then launched into a staccato attack. "That broadcast from Canton. Most irresponsible. It's not going to help any of us. Not in the least. I'd like to know who's behind it. The military command in Peking will be highly annoyed. The Korean war's going badly. This place must be kept open for supplies to get through. Yet some party members seem intent on fomenting trouble here. Whoever's responsible will have to give a good explanation." He was clearly giving the impression he thought she was the culprit.

"I must commend you for your patriotic enthusiasm for the war against the American imperialists, Comrade Ming Yuk, but I suggest you ask Canton. They must have many sources of information here."

"Don't worry. We've already done so. Perhaps you'll let me know what the students are up to." This intention to 'resist any attempt to obliterate the name of the dead hero.' What does that mean?"

It was now Soolan's turn to take the offensive. "Well you know dear friend, there are certain criminal elements here who take the law into their own hands. If it's in our country's interests to let the Portuguese remain for a time we have to respect their laws. I'm sure you'll agree that Kai Tung's murderers should be brought to justice. Personally I feel some sympathy for him. Lim was a drug trafficker. You know the attitude of the People's Republic towards drugs."

"I know its attitude towards many things." Ming Yuk's tone was threatening.

"Good. I'm glad we're on the same side." Soolan's reply was just nicely derisive.

There was no point in continuing the conversation and they rang off without any of the usual courtesies. When he had put down the receiver Ming Yuk sat back and chuckled. He was confident he could ride out the murder of Kai Tung and because of this, without consulting Lung Yeung, had arranged with certain people on the extreme left of the unions to give Canton a distorted impression of events on the night of the Banquet. It was his deliberate intention to foment trouble in the Colony, confident that at the end of the day, it would be the likes of Soolan with her doctrinaire contempt for Lung Yeung and the other business men, who'd be swept aside in the period of recrimination. She'd make a fatal mistake; he wasn't quite sure what it would be but knew it would involve her lover Sheraton.

For the next hour and a half he was obliged to deal with matters which a western style company might term 'Personnel—Training and Promotions' but which, in Lung Yeung's organization, were known as 'climbing the tapering celestial ladder'. With that done he put a call through to Lobato to enquire whether Morgan had been deported and affected irritation to hear there was still no trace of him.

"I shouldn't think it's a matter of interest to you," Lobato stated blankly. Ming Yuk was not as subtle as he thought himself to be. The Colonel's police mind had experienced a twinge of suspicion that such an enquiry should be made at all.

"We're interested in everything that goes on here Colonel."

"I can believe that entirely, most excellent Senhor Ming Yuk," replied Lobato. "Most truly I can believe you entirely—for once."

An hour later the most excellent Senhor Ming Yuk was in an apartment not far from the Red Pleasure Pavilion, which he had prepared with Pai Chai's fearful complicity, for Peter's confinement. Not that it made much difference to Peter where he was, for Ming Yuk had arranged for him to be heavily injected with heroin. His capture had been easy; Kai Tung's murderers had recognised Peter on the breakwater and picked him up as Ming Yuk had ordered.

Peter's eyes focused uncertainly; Ming Yuk seemed to be looking at him from the end of a narrow corridor. He wanted to advance along it, to get close to him, to kneel at his feet, to give thanks for being in his custody. He raised his arm weakly, a gesture of supplication, towards the source of all his happiness. Yet the figure stayed as distant as ever. Then he closed his eyes but the corridor was still before him, growing ever longer. How could he see it stretching away so distantly when the figure was suddenly close to him, staring down at him sternly, enormous in size and height, rigid as an ancient deity, a Moloch or a Baal? It was squatting right by him; power flowed in visible streaks from its limbs and from its head down on him, bathing him in comfort. Its eyes were opening ever wider, burning like coals, twin fires of retribution and rage. Now he could see the features clearly. Filled with impossible joy he murmured, "Ah Tung. You've come back. Take me with you now."

Ming Yuk experienced a glow of pleasure as he heard the words. Here his power was absolute. Not only was he the complete master, he was the adored master, godlike and above judgement. He could experiment, torture and in the end destroy. No one could stop him; it was the one secret he would keep from Lung Yeung. He bent down and put his lips near Peter's ear. "Are you sure you don't want to go home?" he asked.

The answer was deliberate and in a voice so faint that Ming Yuk could scarcely hear it. "I am home. In you I live and have my being." Again archaic images shimmered in his brain, mirages in the heat of summer. He saw himself lying there as an unresisting sacrifice to whatever god wanted to be worshipped. But the eyes he saw with were no longer his own; they were also the eyes of Ah Tung. The mind in which his own image shimmered was also the mind of Ah Tung. He had been so penetrated by Ah Tung that a composite being had arisen from both their sorrows. He repeated his words to Ming Yuk, but with a change. "In you—we have our being."

For an instant Ming Yuk was baffled; then he decided Morgan wasn't in proper control of his tongue. "Are you getting everything you want here?" he asked loudly.

Peter made an effort to keep his eyes wide open; now he could see Ming Yuk and the whole room very clearly. But where had Ah Tung gone? He began to breathe rapidly, conscious of a rising pain he couldn't place in any particular part of his body. There was no one to protect him any more. A vague terror roved in his mind. He called out Diana's name, tried to raise himself up and looked anxiously at the door, hoping she'd come in to help him. A second time he called her name. Ming Yuk pushed him down roughly shouting, "That whore won't see you again. Never. Do you understand? Never."

Unable to focus his sight anymore, Peter felt that everything around him was flying apart. Nothing was left to hold onto, to give him succour. Why had he been deserted? How could he endure without the anchor of his life? There was nothing left to believe in. He raised his hand and touched

Ming Yuk's face. "You're so far away." he sighed, "Come nearer. Help me. I'm weak. I want to feel your strength."

"You will Moh *Shin Saang*. You will, Peter. You're going to feel my strength alright. I'm going to punish you for everything you've done." Suddenly he slapped Peter's face with all his might. "Don't you know you betrayed Ah Tung? Don't you know it was you who murdered him? That's why I'm going to punish you. You must beg me to punish you."

The pain in Peter's body intensified. He wanted to be punished for he was indeed the cause of Ah Tung's death, but not like this. Ah Tung wouldn't want this of him. It was right that Ming Yuk should punish him, in any way he wanted, but not like this. Right now there was only one thing he needed to end this agony. He had to get it, even if he had to murder again. He wanted the heroin that would take this agony away. "Give it me." His cry became a moan. "O God. Give it me."

Screwing his hand over Peter's mouth to silence him Ming Yuk said, "I'll give it to you when I come back. When you feel my whip you'll know what pain is." Then he realised that Peter had cried out for something different. He moved his hand and the cries came again. "Give it me Ming Yuk. I can't stand it anymore. Give it me."

Ming Yuk called Pai Chai, who took a hypodermic syringe from a cupboard to prepare the injection. As he stood by and watched Peter's anguish, Ming Yuk's pleasure grew. Nothing could be more beautiful than this. It was a glimpse of the power he wielded over addicts throughout the world; in the most distant cities the operations he controlled resulted in this delectable wastage. The things he'd done in China in the old days, to Communist supporters, were child's play. Even burying people alive ended in silence when the soil finally muted their screams. But this went on and on, here and everywhere. It was as though he'd been given a vision of his power. His eyes took on a maniacal stare. He was filled with exaltation. But as soon as Pai Chai tied a rubber tube around Peter's arm and flexed the elbow to pump the veins up, he left. The sight of a hypodermic needle piercing flesh always made him queasy.

When he had returned to his office in the Pearl River Mansion he felt indisposed to work and from to time glanced towards the Cinnabar Hill Pavilion, the new building in which Lung Yeung was now spending most of his time. Set on a steep headland it commanded views of the islands and mountains opposite the western bay. From the landward side its one approach was a path that threaded its way between trees and boulders to an artificial pool crossed by a demon-defying bridge that could be raised by a control inside his study by Lung Yeung, who was thus able to cut himself off from care and spend hours in peaceful retirement. Or that was the theory; in fact the master was, to his chagrin, finding it less easy to achieve tranquillity in doing nothing than in working. It was precisely because he himself had foreseen this that Ming Yuk had ensured that the appearance of the exquisite new abode should be belied by numerous more functional features. Thus, though the Pavilion looked as though it had come out of a painting from some early dynasty, tradition was tempered by such refinements as an air-conditioning system whose ducts breathed discreetly behind lattices of carved wood and various push button devices that would ensure the comfort or diversion of the sage in his elegant hermitage. Moreover, whereas the scrolls on the walls illustrated the well worn topic of the poet communing with nature or expressed the emotion felt at some single theme—water surging between rocks, the transitory beauty of a white hibiscus or the submission of wind blown peonies—lest these exquisite images should pall and Lung Yeung might wish to break his isolation, a closed circuit television link concealed behind a sliding panel enabled contact to be made with Ming Yuk, as for instance, having just observed the vizier's new American limousine sweeping up the distant drive, he did now.

When the distorted image had composed itself, Ming Yuk's face peered with a curious expression into the

Pavilion named after the fairyland where immortals dwelt in everlasting day. Lung Yeung realised he wasn't in front of the camera and moved a little. "Can you see me now?"

"Yes sir. Is there anything you want?"

"I'd like to know the reactions to Monday's events." Lung Yeung demanded and Ming Yuk began to quote from newspapers, occasionally holding up a photograph for Lung Yeung to see. Whilst one part of his mind absorbed the information, Lung Yeung was taken by the idea that each of them, instead of looking into a television screen, might be peering at his own reflection in some miraculous way transposed in time. He saw his face still smooth and fleshy with only about the eyes a slight expression of that weariness which time would gradually extend to ravage the ultimate image which Ming Yuk could see himself yet to be. Time was all that lay between them. Yet time, he had read, was an illusion.

Ming Yuk gave an account of the broadcast from Canton and suggested it could have political repercussions locally. Lung Yeung interrupted him sharply. "And that girl who was put in a brothel—on your orders. What of her?"

Ming Yuk was embarrassed. He had to report that Mei Ling had escaped. Lung Yeung glared at him, said he wanted to know what had happened to her and switched off, his ancient features dissolving into a persistent pin-prick of light that gave his vizier the feeling that the gaze was still on him though the face had disappeared. He clenched his hands, momentarily filled with loathing for the ancient body that battened on him and longed for freedom to run the organisation on his own. Yet even as he entertained the thought, he knew he would rather be a great demon in a glorious temple than a little god in a wayside shrine. Without Lung Yeung he'd be nothing; Lung Yeung could suck him dry before he'd forgo the patronage of such a master.

His own vulnerability, or rather his own lack of sufficient foresight, came to light again later in the day when a report came in of a meeting in the Chamber of Commerce at which the Trade Unions and Students organisations, long jealous of Lung Yeung's power, had unanimously decided to stage a demonstration to protest against the murderous political assassination of Kai Tung. In something of a panic Ming Yuk recognised that his own trouble making might rebound on him; if the students and workers got to know of the Mei Ling affair, they might make it a more intractable issue, a righteous attack on colonialist military brothels maybe. Under such circumstances his own position would be much endangered. Lung Yeung might even decide to restore his own prestige by sacrificing his servant. The more Ming Yuk thought of this, the more dangerous the possibilities seemed. Orders were therefore swiftly passed to his henchmen that Mei Ling must be found at all cost. There was only one way out: he must compensate the girl and pay off the policeman Nolasco, who was interested in her, to make sure that she was not made use of by his own or Lung Yeung's enemies.

Relieved to have made this decision Ming Yuk went to perform his last duty of the day for the tired old dragon who, somewhat unusually but very cautiously, was already performing a decorous breast stroke in his new underwater-illuminated swimming pool. Ming Yuk stripped off his clothes and, in fascination, gazed down on a creature that looked for all the world like some misshapen translucent tropical fish nosing its way around the edge of the circular marble tank that circumscribed its existence. Then, a willing victim, he dived into the sacrificial water.

"Tonight," Lung Yeung said when they had finished swimming, "we'll sit for a while and talk for the last time here." Ming Yuk at once misinterpreted the words and a wild thought formed in his mind: if he was to be cast down, he'd take Lung Yeung with him. He couldn't live without power; he'd rather kill himself and Lung Yeung as well. But before such unbalanced notions could change into action, the gentle voice continued, "I'm handing the general control of business over to you from now on. You have the ability to work things out. Naturally I shall require reports of your stewardship from time to time. And I'll always be ready to help if there are difficulties."

Although Ming Yuk didn't believe that things would be in the slightest degree different he went through the motions of protesting his insufficiency but Lung Yeung waved his arm imperiously. "You want me to set everything in order and then hand over. No, the best way to assert authority is to make decisions when times are difficult. Don't think I built up our present position without mistakes. You must understand Ming Yuk; I need rest and peace. I'm too old except for one further effort: how to find content in solitude; how truly to return to youth from old age—though not as you think I mean it."

Quite aghast, Ming Yuk fell to his knees, touched his forehead on the floor three times and begged that they might spend the end of each day together as before, but Lung Yeung replied, "No need for that any more, nor to kow-tow; to bend the body is easy, to bend the mind hard. Only keep your power and be self sufficient; the main danger in your work lies in giving way to personal feelings. Loneliness may tempt you there. And if the time comes when you're satiated with power, abandon it. Follow whatever impulse stirs. I have not done so. Now I may never achieve the freedom you can find if you heed my words."

For some reason, which he could scarcely understand, save that this old man was, except for one person, the only being on earth for whom he had the least feeling of affection, Ming Yuk sat beside the canopied bed until Lung Yeung seemed to be asleep, then he returned to his own private rooms where he had the policeman Nolasco brought to him. Carlos, already wise in the ways of the powerful, impassively accepted the regret expressed over Mei Ling's misfortunes and nodded understandingly at the hint that they were the result of superior errors of judgement. Ming Yuk, relieved to observe that Carlos was the sort of person who could be bought, said he wanted Mei Ling told she was out of danger, for with Kai Tung's death the matter of Lim's murder could be considered closed. Carlos' nose took the scent as he continued, "There's a small-holding on one of the islands; I could make it available for the girl. But it might be best for her to be married when she settles there. It's a good place." Carlos realised Ming Yuk had deeper worries than he admitted and said the proposal was most generous, adding, "I know where to find her. I'll fix things to suit you." His tone suggested there was no need for further anxiety where Mei Ling was concerned.

"Naturally we'll show our appreciation of your services," Ming Yuk added as a further incentive. Both men were pleased over their discussion; Carlos left, already working out to his own advantage the details of a marriage with a wife conveniently tucked away on one of the islands (his parents would accept it when they knew of the dowry) while Ming Yuk went back almost at once to the captive of his distorted desire, taking with him some whips and other implements. He had a sense of liberation. The danger was passed. He was secure in office. The memory of Lung Yeung's warning about personal feelings came into his mind but he decided it was nonsense. His pleasures with Peter would purge him and make him free to carry out his new responsibilities.

Alone in the Cinnabar Hill Pavilion and very far from sleep, Lung Yeung took a volume from the scattered pile of Buddhist and Taoist writings that lay on his bed and read a while; then he walked about the room uneasily. The destruction of the Chapel worried him; it seemed to portend the ruin of his own endeavours. How long could the mightiest dynasty last; even the Han, the T'ang, the Ming empires had disintegrated. All that remained of them was history, some precious scrolls and poetry, the exquisite silence of porcelain; nor in these was there any sure promise of immortality—they'd rot, break and dissolve in time.

He took up a treatise that told how the life of man was like a vast wheel, ever revolving around the central light.

The generality of mankind was on the outside of the circle looking towards the darkness and only knew the light when it was reflected on objects that lay deeper in the void. As men moved along and saw the reflection of the light, they had the illusion of passage of time and movement in physical dimension. But there were a few people who could turn and see the fire at the hub and when they witnessed it and let it circulate within them, there was no motion either in time or in space; the only true movement lay in the life of the inner brilliance. If he had been one of those illuminated beings, his fear of the future and of the dissolution of what he'd created would be at an end. He'd comprehend that whatever was created could never cease to be and that to have created at all or remained still, were the same thing, for only the central flame was significant.

I understand the meaning and I believe but where is the experience, he repeated to himself; I'm fastened to the wheel with the fire behind me; sometimes I can almost feel its heat but I can never turn to see it. Why can't I turn? He pressed a button and a record of chanting began to play. Gongs boomed and the voices of monks droned like the buzzing of an immense beehive in the heavy days of summer. He increased the volume and the whole room was filled with sound, deluging his fear with hope; again he adjusted the control, now to maximum, as if such strength of prayer would help him to see. The gongs reverberated in his brain, filling him with a concept of holiness, or was it just his dying emotions responding to sound waves imprisoned on a record and released by a mechanical device onto his senses? Again and again he felt he was approaching the edge of the experience. Sometimes he joined in the chanted prayers, for repetition had made them familiar to him; now, now the moment was at hand—but again it eluded him. Still chanting, he stood at one of the windows and pushed back the sliding glass panels; the music flowed out over the ornamental garden hidden in the darkness away to the sea and the distant mountains. Could it be that in their remote heights, hanging in the night above banks of mist, he might turn towards the light like the sages who understood the meaning of the Way. The record player clicked and the waves of sound vanished into an emptiness in which only his thin voice quavered alone for a moment on the phrase of a sutra, then trailed away. The breeze stirred the pages of books on the bed and in the distance he could hear waves breaking on the deserted shore. Cold and lonely, he retreated from the window, remembering his words to Ming Yuk that there was no longer any need for a relationship between them. No, there was no going back to that. Ming Yuk could serve him at a distance and keep from him the harsh details he wanted put out of his mind. Now was the time for a milder friendship. In his occasional meetings with the lovely Mrs. Sheraton, he could still savour the freshness of youth and the kindness he'd kept at bay in his own nature. "Hah. You're going into your second childhood," he said aloud. It was pointless to delude himself; he no longer cared for anyone. The breeze blew again and he indifferently heard the papers on his desk rustling and falling. There are only states of mind, he thought, and all of them are illusions. There's no truth, no falsehood, no light and no darkness; the nearest we can get to the truth is the consciousness that there's nothing, the nothingness that showed in his own eyes and which Robert Sheraton had revealed so clearly. And yet? There was that Hidden City. He took a brush, picked up one of the scattered pages and wrote:

Above the mist golden roofs float up to Heaven
On porcelain tiles white hoar frost greets the sun
Courtiers in the Palace of Unending Bliss
Gaze at the tribute borne from barbarous lands.

A wild bird soars in the autumn sky
Scared by the sound of flutes and trumpets.

The mace-bearer beckons us rank by rank
Through the courtyards of the Purple Forbidden City

Entering by the southern nine-fold gates
Dutifully we await the morning levée.

The hibiscus curtains are withdrawn
On swirling dragons jewels flash with light.
Above the vermilion steps
Sweet perfumed incense rises to the throne
Bowing before the many tasselled headdress
I await the Imperial Edict.

"This is what I said about last Monday." Soolan proceeded to read the briefest and most factual report of the events leading up to the fire. "You'll see that I haven't referred to the mob as 'toiling masses.' Why not Comrades? Because you know as well as I that the majority of them were K.M.T. scum, refugees from the People's justice." That at least was true; the poorest people in the Colony were virulently anti-communist. Kai Tung's murder, she pointed out, merely appeared as a single line entry under the section dealing with 'other activities.' The word 'other' was, as everyone knew, a euphemism for Lung Yeung.

"You seem to be accusing someone Comrade," an earnest student member commented from behind the thickest of horn rimmed spectacles. Like everyone else at the meeting he was far more impressed by Soolan's irritability than by her words.

"I'm saying that Canton must always receive factual information first," she snapped back. "Then it can make valid policy decisions. As it happens I think the demonstration's an excellent idea." But was it, she wondered? Canton had instructed that the demonstration should embarrass the Portuguese and cause concern to Lung Yeung without producing a change in the status quo. Why should responsible people have to pander all the time to the radicals? "My main contention is that comrades here must not try to manipulate the Party by submitting inaccurate information." Her case was incontrovertible and a resolution to that effect was recorded before the meeting broke up.

There were several lines in her report, under the section headed 'Western Personalities', which she didn't bring to the Committee's attention. These suggested that among the European population there were a few who were well disposed towards the People's Republic. There was for instance a Mr. Robert Sheraton, described as a progressive artist, whose work could probably be made use of. As an example of his output she enclosed half a dozen realistic sketches he'd once given her. They showed peasants and fishermen engaged in honest toil. She selected the ones showing smiling, upward-looking faces. With the right sort of titles such felicity could easily be ascribed to the wisdom of the Party's teachings.

When she'd sealed up the report, the thought 'what the hell are you thinking about', came into her head. 'I must be crazy', another part of her brain replied. But the paper knife she picked up to rip open the envelope remained poised in the air and the document went into the 'Out' tray again. All sorts of justifications for her action lined up: Robert was well disposed to them, he was a progressive, she wasn't lying. True she was having an affair with him—or was she since the Banquet?—but she would never have associated with a man whose ideology was basically opposed to her own. Behind them all loomed the hope that moved her: some few westerners had thrown in their lot with the People's Republic and lived there. One or two had Chinese wives. Why couldn't that happen to Robert? She'd try, even if the odds were stacked against her.

Over the next couple of days she succeeded in persuading a few close associates on the Committee that it might be a good idea if non-Chinese sympathisers, code word in her mind for R. Sheraton, were invited to the demonstration. She remembered how much Robert had enjoyed a concert she'd taken him to a few weeks ago; his applause for a choir of teenage girls which had sung "Heroes of the Korean People's Struggle," was much more vigorous than her own. Perhaps some hidden part of himself wanted a life of purpose. The demonstration was something that might fan that desire and help him to see the possibilities she had in mind.

It wasn't long before Ming Yuk knew of Soolan's suggestion from his spies among the radicals. At last, he thought, she was beginning to create the situation which would eliminate herself and the Sheratons from the scene.

Fate now decided to advance Soolan's plans. A few days after the Banquet, Robert unexpectedly called on her at home. She wasn't prepared for him and looked rather dowdy in blue jacket and trousers and without her usual precise make up. A little gasp gave away her misgivings over her appearance the moment she opened the door. "Robert. It's you. I never expected you. And so early. Come in. But give me a few minutes to change."

As soon as he got in the hall, he stopped her from going off. He was moved by her little exhibition of vanity and the fact that she looked her age. People could be more attractive when their defences were down. She was surprised when he took her in his arms, almost lifting her off her feet, and holding her so tightly that it stopped her breathing properly. When he reduced the pressure she said, "So, it isn't all over between us. I've been so afraid." Then she clasped him as hard as she could. "It's nearly a week since I've seen you. I've missed you so much."

"I didn't think you'd want to see me after that night at the Banquet. I behaved so badly. I'm deeply sorry." It was true he had missed her, but he was sure she had missed him more. He wondered why it was that when he was away from someone he liked, he wanted them, but the moment he was with them the reverse process set in; he hadn't missed her in a passionate way, he'd missed her sexually and he'd wanted her company. For an instant he doubted the wisdom of coming here; it could all have been ended quite easily, so it seemed. Then the compassionate feeling he'd experienced when he'd seen her unprepared for his visit returned and the pendulum swung back. "It was lousy of me not to come around earlier. I owed you an explanation. All that business about Peter got me down. I…"

She silenced him by putting her fingers to his lips. "I understand. I really do understand." Even as she spoke, she was conscious of understanding very little about this wily man. Exactly why had he suddenly turned up like this? Was it because she hadn't pestered him. Certainly she'd never expected him to apologise. The best she'd hoped for was a 'phone call to see if the coast was clear, followed by a visit during which they'd both behave as though nothing had happened. She'd even been prepared to accept it as the only way of resuming the old pattern between them.

"And Diana," she asked, "How is she? Poor thing; she must be upset about Peter." Her words weren't false; she did feel sorry for Diana—at the moment; perhaps because she herself had just gone through a little period of separation from Robert. Her real concern must have shown in her voice for Robert, though stating that Diana was worried and upset, almost immediately gave her a kindly smile which said, 'Now that's how I'd like it to be all the time, the two of you accepting each other, so that everything in the garden can be lovely for me, me, me.'

On an impulse he led her into the bedroom and made love with hardly any preliminaries. When it was over she put on a red silk dressing gown and sat on the bed looking at his naked body. There was such a lot of him. She nearly laughed as she thought, you're greedy wanting him all to yourself. The words, "You can't have had it for ages," popped out of her mouth, quite unaccompanied by any devious intent of finding out about his relations with Diana. She just felt close to him again. Her eyes sparkled. Life, she decided, had its moments after all, even if they seemed to be getting fewer.

"Not since I last came here." But his expression said, 'I know you don't believe me though.' And after all why should she? Experience had taught him that practically no one was to be trusted when it came to talk about sex. Certainly that stricture applied to himself.

"Tell that to the Royal Marines," she said, her manner simultaneously so arch and so kittenish that he was conscious of a little frisson of pleasure in some nerve obscurely hidden in his crutch. Why didn't Diana's gestures ever affect him like that, he wondered, as he replied like a language master correcting a foreign student's English idiom, "You mean to the marines."

"I know the saying. After your performance I want you to tell it to the Royal Marines." Then very softly she added, "God knows why I love you so much Robert."

"It was so good eh, you red-blooded Royal Marxist?" He replied but also quietly tailed his remark with, "Loneliness, Soolan. You long for something more human that communism. Anything. Even me."

"Do you think so? Is it all as simple as that? What rubbish you talk sometimes. No, it's your complexity that I find fascinating." She kissed him and whispered, "As well as your love making, and the way you indulge yourself first and foremost, and the way you won't do anything that isn't for number one. It appeals to me. It makes me realize that we really still are in the jungle."

He gave a little laugh, a bit uncertain maybe but quite surely self satisfied as he stretched himself like a big strong lion. They lapsed into silence listening to an approaching street-cry of a hawker selling, "*Aap keuk paau*—duck's foot dumplings," each call falling in a high, sad cadence, followed by the clapping of two pieces of metal just in case no-one had heard. Soolan suddenly asked, "Do you want some?" And he replied, "Why not? Why not?" She got her purse and went downstairs.

As he lay there, Robert felt extraordinarily content. It wasn't just the relaxation resulting from good sex. It was as though he was at home. Apart from the sound of Soolan talking and laughing with the hawker, everything was so tranquil and, if it came to that, the chatter below was part of the tranquillity. There was a pleasant ordinariness about everything. The sun was shining; birds were hopping about on the window sill enjoying the social round, quite indifferent to the presence of the large ginger cat from next door who sat upright on a ledge blinking lazily at their antics. Robert had the pleasant feeling that nothing out of the way was ever going to happen again, which was exactly how he would like things to be. What a pity his studio wasn't in the next room so he could get up and do a few hours work before indulging himself again with this marvellously complaisant woman who, it seemed, accepted him for exactly what he was.

When they were eating the dumplings he remarked, "This is the life eh."

"What. Eating dumplings?"

"No. Not the dumplings, though nothing could be more important really. No, just living without anticipation. Like bushmen in the Kalahari, collecting just enough food, eating when you want, screwing when you want, sleeping when you want. Not being anxious about anything. No stresses and strains. Above all, no decisions."

"What romantic rubbish. I bet bushmen have a lousy time, especially their women. Anyway how do you know they're never anxious?" Soolan replied between sucking noisily on a morsel of duck.

"They don't seem to be." Robert rather resented his idyll being questioned.

"Anxiety's what drives us on."

"Now you're talking like a westerner. Drives us on to what? More anxiety? Bushmen don't bother about being driven on. They just follow their food around. They drift."

"Like you do." She found it impossible to resist saying that.

"Like I'd like to. They don't conceive of distant past and future. Just yesterday and tomorrow, if that. Look how we live. Always planning and scheming. Making demands on each other that can't be satisfied. Always getting our knickers in a twist."

She leaned over and fondled him between his legs. "You're not wearing any knickers, dah-ling." He put his arms behind his head and, with a silly grin on his face, watched the mounting success brought about by her tongue as it flickered around the tip of his cock. Then he too became playful, though still only verbally, with her. "Your breasts are bigger. You've been having injections like those cabaret girls."

"You're just saying that because the thing you think with has grown." She let her dressing gown slip off and lay down beside him. "You've been to a quack doctor."

"If he was a quack it wouldn't work."

"What did he give you for it?"

"I have to recite a spell and rub it every day after meals with the rarified blood of a long randy sea snake."

"I suppose you enjoy that more than making love to me?"

"Naturally, my real name's Onan. Onan, wisest of men. Onan the self sufficient. That's me."

"Ah, so the great male secret is out, I've been using the wrong technique." She reversed herself on the bed and teased him with long finger nails, straddling his head with her thighs so that he could go to work on her most conveniently with his tongue until, rousing himself, he applied delicious little bites to her flesh and used his fingers so tantalisingly that she grew wild. Then, with yang firm and yin flowing they did all sorts of uninhibited things around the room and in front of the mirror, finishing off in the 'old fellow pushing a wheelbarrow position,' Soolan lying legs akimbo on a table and Robert standing so that her jade portal could conveniently receive his noble yak whisk. At length, exhausted by the play of clouds and rain, they collapsed on the bed.

At about the same time in the Nolasco family home Diana was in a love position in which only her legs were on the bed and her body was arched backward so her head touched the floor. Carlos' body rested backward on the bed while his legs, looped over hers, held her in a vice. He'd got the position from Li Yu's *Prayer Mat of Flesh*. Encircling the base of his jade stem was a brass ring inscribed with magical Chinese characters while its head, held in the tight grasp of a goat's eye ring from which little hairs protruded (purchasable from all reputable Chinese apothecaries) and lovingly anointed with Eight Immortals desensitising unguent, probed more cunningly, or so it seemed, into her crimson cave than ever before. The pleasure went on and on. "Can you feel it. Can you feel it, Diana?" he gasped as he thrust or withheld or churned, determined to achieve the highest degree of erotic satisfaction. But even the most superlative physical pleasure, unless the protagonists know how sexual bliss may be translated into divine bliss, has its limit, marked in this case by Diana, crying, "Carlos. My Carlos," and the object of her ardour emitting both the usual flood of his pearly seed and an almost tuneful yelp. Downstairs the servants, who had been listening to the creaking of the bed, the wanton laughter and the groans and the sighs from above grinned with vicarious delight then resumed their noisy chatter; their favourite naughty boy Carlos certainly had a good time when his parents were away.

Soon, Carlos' regular breathing told Diana that he was asleep. How easily he could always drop off. Not in the least like herself—or Robert. She lit a cigarette, turned on one side and looked at him. He was extraordinarily beautiful. She reflected that in Australia the narcissistic beefcake, the beer bellies and the acres of freckled flesh on the beaches had put her off the male body. In any case, women were the ones who were supposed to be beautiful; men's looks started from the neck upward. But in the east she'd grown accustomed to men's bodies revealed in an unselfconscious way. She thought of brown-skinned Malays, dappled by sunlight through forest trees, bathing in rivers; they'd been the first to open her eyes. And those old Chinese men in striped underpants, relaxing in front of their shop houses, made one conscious of the vulnerability of the male body. Ah, the male body; perhaps that would constitute her future if Peter really had gone away. Just drifting on with Robert, drifting with him from one eastern so-called paradise to another, drifting into old age and becoming but another of those tedious expatriate 'great characters' one encounters in oriental cities and never noticing the rotting and the shrivelling because she'd be buoyed up or maybe she should say 'boyed up' by an endless chain of beautiful young lovers, living a life filled with fucking, and ending up as an antique oriental cock fancier. It had happened to other women. Why not her? She knew it was in her and shuddered at the thought. And it then struck her that she'd been unfair to Carlos; because he made love to her so easily, she'd taken him for granted, ignored his real qualities, especially the sincerity of his love for her. Suppose she did as he asked and 'gave it a try.' She'd miss him and their love making very much if she was on her own. She leaned over to inspect the brass ring and recognised the characters for love, everlasting and heaven. The others she didn't know. As she turned it, he stirred and awoke.

"Don't take it off. It's magic," he said with one of his insinuating smiles.

"Do you really believe it's magic?"

"Maybe. No." He curled himself around her so that she felt she was merging into him, and he tried to stop her unnecessary questions with tickles and kisses. However, she persisted. "Why do you wear it?"

"It makes me feel more sexy."

"Nothing could make you more sexy, Carlos."

He uncurled, lay back, smiled and closed his eyes; she kissed his lips, his nipples and tickled his armpit with her tongue—he always liked that, then rested her head beside his.

"Diana," he said a bit shyly.

"Yes Carlos."

There was a long, long pause after which he said very rapidly, "I'm getting married." But his voice was so soft she wasn't quite sure if she'd heard aright and asked, "You're what?"

He sat up and looked down on her. "I'm getting married. I've got to get married. I didn't want you to hear it from anyone else."

It wasn't the announcement that made her angry. It was the memory, if one could apply memory to something that was barely over, of their love making. He'd behaved as though his passion was moving onto new heights yet all it had been was some sort of ecstatic envoi. "You've no right...," she began.

"What d'you mean I've no right. You're married. Everyone gets married."

"I'm not talking about getting married."

"Then what?"

"Making love."

He looked baffled. He really didn't see what he'd done wrong. "I don't understand," he replied with a frown.

"Making love to me like that. Making love so I'll never want anyone but you. Doing your best to make me love you and then calmly saying, 'I'm getting married.' Why didn't you just tell me the news and then go away." She got up and started to put on her clothes.

Carlos watched her as though she'd gone berserk. Unconcerned he played with his cock and made it stand. Diana stared at him incredulously and said, "Are you mad? Haven't you any sensitivity at all? I don't want to see that damned thing again. I don't want to see you at all now you're getting married." A look of alarm crossed his eyes; he jumped up and tried to embrace her. She pushed him away violently.

"But I'll still see you, Diana. Let me explain. It's Ming Yuk. He's compensating Mei Ling. She's been given a small holding on one of the islands. He wants me to—to arrange things, so there'll be no trouble for him."

Diana grew calmer. This was China not Australia. She remembered how annoyed her servant Group had been when her supposedly dying mother, whose clothes had all been disposed of, effected an unexpected recovery. "Now we'll have to buy her some new clothes," had been the main reaction. Another chance of getting his hands on a nice bit of land wouldn't come Carlos' way until his parents died; anyway, they'd certainly approve of his step.

Diana sat down disconsolately; of course, land always came first—the world over. And now that Carlos could see that the danger was passed he went to her and pressed her face down on him. "Hold it. Kiss it. Suck it. It belongs to you, only you," he ordered. She did so. Why not? That was how he saw it. He should really possess a harem. Things were just different here. Then she felt his body shaking uncontrollably and looked up. His cheeks bore rivulets of tears. Surely there must be some sort of lake inside Carlos. "I won't marry her if you'll go away with me," he begged. "Please Diana. I'm not married yet. Let's leave together."

She had to say "No." It wasn't just a question of being generous to Mei Ling, or even the thought that in the long run he'd be better off and happier on the little farm. It wasn't that at all. If she'd wanted him, generosity would have gone by the board. Nor was it anything to do with Robert. She had to face the fact that her feelings for Carlos were pretty much the same as his must be for her, whatever his protests, but unlike him, she didn't think that those feelings, however named, were a basis for marriage. When the physical passion had gone, what compensation would there be? He'd go off with other women and expect her to be faithful—probably minding a brood of children, the Asian pattern, the southern European pattern. No. Not on your Nelly, she said to herself. But aloud she told him, "I'll go on seeing you. As long as I'm here—if that's what you want." Even as she reassured him she wondered if, after all, he was to be but the first of that long string of young lovers at the idea of which her feelings had just recoiled. But what the hell? Why should they recoil? There could be worse fates: no lover at all, for instance. Total loneliness.

Carlos remained silent, his face woebegone. Then he opened her handbag, took out her handkerchief, dabbed his eyes, blew his nose thoroughly and inspected the result. Everything had turned out as he had expected but at least he could console himself that she wouldn't be leaving for a long time. "I'll see you as often as ever," he declared. "More often." Naturally he wanted to make love again and she had to let him, even though the gilt on the gingerbread had, by now, worn somewhat thin.

Soolan's tryst with Robert ended on a more satisfactory note. When their amorous activities were over she started to talk about life in Shanghai during her youth which led on to her political involvement there and in the remote fastnesses of Shensi in the days when a Communist victory was far from sure. For the first time she felt confident enough to give him an insight into the lives and characters of some of the leaders she knew. She wanted him to see them in a light different from the one given in those formalized pictures when they lined the ramparts of the Gate of Heavenly Peace. In a world in which such persons were shrouded in mystery he'd be more than human, she reckoned, not to be intrigued by her information and flattered he should be told it. She also gave him a glowing report on the experimental work being done in the Peking Central Institute of Arts, hinting the place was receptive to outside influences—provided they were for the people. "You know Bob," she said at one point in their session, "I'm western enough to understand how you see my country—and me. You think we're like ants and hostile to the individual. But it isn't like that at all. We're in the midst of a great transformation of society. China's being reborn. You think I'm hard; you think the Chinese leaders are hard. Do you think anyone wants to be like that? No." She shook her head vehemently to suggest intense personal struggle. "We believe in the right of everyone to a full life. That's why we're prepared to be as we are." She leaned forward and the confidentiality of her manner grew. "I think I've told you enough for you to realise there has to be an elite—though we don't use the word—whose lives are more open to the world. Otherwise how could the country be led effectively?" She looked thoughtful. "I'd love you to have an opportunity of seeing things at first hand. You could make a record of it yourself."

"But that's impossible Soo." He paused, highly intrigued. "Isn't it?" She looked Delphic. "Arrangements can be made." The ensuing silence between them was ended by Robert saying firmly, "I'd like to. Yes I'd like to." At his words Soolan, for no apparent reason, stood up and changed chairs, the movement betraying an inner excitement which she found difficult to control. In the lowest regions of Robert's mind, just on the threshold of consciousness, the thought stirred that she might be taking his words as an expression of more than just a desire to visit China. At the same time and much more forcefully, he remembered Diana's words that she'd go off to Hong Kong and be a tart. Good God, he thought sensing danger with the instinct of a quarry. I'd better not mention that to Soolan. She'd think Diana really meant it. Satisfied he'd avoided a trap, he forgot the first thought in the sequence that had warned him he was already in it.

As though preparing an apologia applying for a visa he began, in measured tones, to outline his own political views, the gist of which was that he was virtually as far to the left as Soolan was but that the different situations in their countries made the fulfilment of his notions unlikely. During his ponderous exposition, Soolan did for a moment allow the uncharitable thought to cross her mind that anyone who could go on and on like this would fit in quite well into a Communist society, but unlike Diana, on such occasions, she preserved an expression of intense interest. When he had concluded, with some unmemorable quip, she nodded her head in vigorous affirmation but saw to it that they soon returned to trivialities and then to tenderness. The hours they spent together must be happy in every way. On his way home, Robert felt that new vistas were opening all around him. Of course, he had accepted Soolan's invitation to come to the great Kai Tung demonstration as if it were of no more significance than going to a village jamboree.

His bubbling happiness was sensed that evening by Diana even before he came into the apartment. His footsteps on the stairs had been sprightly, two or three treads at a time, and deliberately intended, she well knew, to suggest virility. Immediately he started chatting about this or that and in the face of such friendliness she experienced a pang of regret for the days when she'd first known him. But whereas only a few weeks ago she'd have retreated to her room to get over a bout of jealousy, now she put off going to bed for a while and responded to his talk, which was largely about things Chinese, not enthusiastically perhaps, but as a good natured friend. The next morning he was in much the same form and over breakfast blurted out, "Next month let's have a little holiday. What about the Philippines again? We could afford it with the money from Lung Yeung's portrait."

Diana marvelled that he should feel so sure of her; it was almost an affront considering everything that had happened. She could only put it down as yet another example of the immensity of male conceit. Nevertheless she replied casually, "What a nice idea. You really like the Philippines don't you. The people are so good-natured—and so easy." She could see he hadn't taken her point. But then, she reflected, why should he? Hadn't she now accepted the pattern, his pattern, he to have his women, she to have her young men. Didn't that imply, against a background of gracious social living for all the world to see, a doctrine of non-interference in each other's emotions. Therefore, my dear, she told herself, no more snide remarks, no more jealous quips, no more vitriol. He would be the artist, she the artist's wife and the portrait she must comport to must be what he felt should be depicted.

"Where are you off to?" he asked, suddenly noticing that she was dressed to go out.

"To Peter's house." He looked puzzled. "I want to see if everything's alright. We might have to give Ping some money, until Peter comes…" She fell silent and looked depressed, deeply and perhaps obsessively depressed. Obscurely she realized that nowadays the principal concern of her life was what had happened to her dearest friend. The sense of loss was almost unbearable. Could she perhaps, she wondered, only be tolerating her life here because she was waiting for Peter to turn up.

Robert went to her and gave her a kiss. "Soolan said how sorry she is about Peter. She knows how you feel. She really is sorry. She wishes she could help." Yet though he wanted to express the extent of his own concern for Diana, nothing warmer came from his mouth than, "You know you have my deepest sympathy." It sounded like a royal message to a mining village after a pit disaster.

"Tell her thank you," Diana said as she went to the door. She turned and looked back at him. He'd seemed to have forgotten about Peter already and was striding up and down the room, occasionally bowling an imaginary cricket ball and obviously thinking about something else. She smiled to see him so much his old self and realised she didn't envy his contentment. She even experienced a transient moment of tenderness for him, but it was nothing more than an undischarged reflex from days gone by. "Robert, " she said. He stared at her vaguely. "I do love you." Then she left wondering why she couldn't have said what she had really meant, 'I did love you.' But how could she use such words and expect him to understand that they represented something precious to her.

Peter's house, at the top of its little hill, tree-girt and shielded by bushes and creepers, looked as attractive as ever. Approaching it up the narrow cobbled street she indulged in a fantasy that he was up there waiting for her; soon they'd be laughing together and talking about all the things that interested them, as in times past. Unhappily this daydream was shattered the moment she went in. Furniture was piled up in the dining room and wooden crates stood on the verandah. Upstairs there was the sound of hammering. Ping came from the kitchen, her face drawn. "Oh, Sheraton *Taai Taai*. Men are upstairs packing *Shin Saang*'s things. They're taking the furniture away. What am I to do?"

Diana rushed up the stairs angrily and found three men dismantling Peter's bed. "Who's in charge here?" she cried; one of them said he was the foreman. "Who told you to do this? Who told you?" Her voice had become slightly hysterical.

The man took two letters from an inside pocket and put them in her hand without a word. They were addressed to his firm, a packing agency, and had Hong Kong stamps and post-marks on them. She scanned them rapidly; both were typed, both bore Peter's signature. One was a request that his personal effects should be sent to a certain depository in Hong Kong; the other was a direction to dispose of the furniture at the best possible price. The letters were copied to the manager of the Banco Ultramarino with a note asking him to pay the packing charges and saying that the proceeds of the sale of furniture would be credited to his account. Ping came up to her and produced another envelope; this contained a letter in Chinese which, she said, thanked her for her services; three month's salary was enclosed. The men went on with their work as noisily as ever.

Diana led Ping downstairs and they sat together in the kitchen. She was stunned. The letters were clear; Peter's signature was incontrovertible even to that huge flourish. She looked up and saw tears flowing down Ping's cheeks. "Oh Ping. Don't cry. I'll help you to get a new job. You can stay with Group till I fix something up."

"No. No. I'm alright. I can go home. It's Moh *Shin Saang* going away like that. I knew something would happen to him the day Ah Tung first came. He put a spell on him, I'm sure. *Shin Saang* was so kind to me. He was the best man I've ever worked for. I was so fond of him."

Ping's grief communicated itself to Diana as she put her arm around the sad little woman. The two of them sat there and cried until their tears had all come out. At last they pulled themselves together. "There's nothing we can do Ping," Diana said. "I'll check up with the Bank Manager about the letters. But there's nothing he can do either. Come and see Group and me as soon as you can."

Strangely enough, as she walked down the Rua do Padre Antonio towards the town centre she felt quite serene. Was it because, in the mid afternoon sun, everything was so peaceful, drenched with light that sharpened the varied colour washed walls and obscured the shady nooks where people were taking siestas, or was it because she had cried so much. But more than that, was it because she had at last accepted Peter's absence and, therefore, had become suddenly free? Whatever it was the few minutes of grief she'd shared with Ping had been a turning point. Before and after the outburst had already become like B.C. and A.D.; she could only go on. The situation with Carlos had been resolved even if it still had to wither away. Peter would never come back; she didn't try to think of his motives apart from a quick guess that with Ah Tung's death he couldn't face the place or anything to do with it anymore. But that was it, that was it entirely; neither could she. So it was that, as she rested for a little while on the terrace that lay in the shadow of the twin towers of St. Lorenzo's Church, she knew that a third break must now be made. Naturally, being Celtic, she had to do things in threes; it was inexorable. The time to leave Robert had come. What was more, the moment was opportune, considering his present happiness. That pleased her, for it would make everything so much easier.

The bank was closed but Diana knew the manager, Senhor Morais, well enough to call on him. She hailed a taxi and went in it to his sumptuous house in the recently constructed Avenida Conselheiro Horta e Costa. Fortunately his siesta was over and he invited her into his library where he told her that he'd received his copies of Senhor Morgan's instructions and was satisfied that the signatures were genuine. He'd also kept Colonel Lobato informed.

Like everyone in town he knew of Peter's involvement with Ah Tung, but unlike most people, Senhor Morais who was a cripple, showed sympathy. "I think, Senhora, your friend's done the right thing going away. He must be full of bitterness. Give him time to forget everything. I'm sure he'll write to you after a while." An angelic faced house-boy, crippled more badly than his master, insisted on conducting Diana slowly out to the taxi. She started for home but on the way was seized by an impulse: Soolan must know the decision she'd come to.

She found the apartment, which was in a maze of narrow old streets quite unfamiliar to her, with difficulty, for small though the Colony was there were still many places which she had never visited. Soolan was taken aback to see her; it was the first time she'd received such a call. "Come in," she said in an overfriendly voice that revealed her apprehension. "Come in and sit down. I'll make some tea."

Diana looked about the room. It was modern and comfortable; the home of a middle class intellectual. Robert must enjoy sitting here with Soolan discussing left wing politics, rather like Lenin in Switzerland. Come to that, there was a connection; what was that ornate cuckoo clock doing in this otherwise tastefully furnished room? The place certainly looked lived in; there were plenty of books, pictures, a couple by Robert, games, including Monopoly, plants and records. Only the man of the house was missing. No, there he was; she noticed a photograph of Robert taken by herself in Singapore over a year ago. She wasn't quite cool enough to repress a little feeling of irritation. He might have had a new photograph taken. But he probably had clothes she'd given him in the place as well. Jackets and shoes were always appearing and disappearing mysteriously in his wardrobe.

She tried to put Soolan at ease the moment she reappeared with tea and a large cake by saying she was on her way back from looking all over Senhor Morais' showpiece of a home, which wasn't quite true. This soon led to the conversation with him about Peter. It turned out that Soolan's opinion was pretty much the same as the Bank Manager's but she went on to insist, rather too fulsomely for Diana's liking, how very, very sorry she was about it all because she knew how close Diana had been to Peter and what a clever young man he was and how amusing and what a pity etcetera, etcetera, etcetera. Diana answered calmly, indeed almost indifferently, for she was a good actress, "Oh, it's all in the past now, Soo. I've got over it. Let's hope he'll be more happy wherever he is."

When she had finished off two pieces of cake, Diana sat back feeling very composed and looked Soolan straight in the eye. "I've not come to talk about Peter," she said. "I've come to tell you I'm leaving."

"You're leaving." Soolan's voice was edgy. "You—and Robert?"

Diana waited a few seconds, though letting an expression of surprise pass over her face, before saying lightly, "No. Just me." She gave more time for the message to sink in.

"For home?" A hint of incredulity had crept into Soolan's voice. It intensified as she added, "For Australia?"

Oh yes, Diana thought; Robert's been giving her his personal low-down on Australia. But I wonder if he told her of the money he'd made there, smoothly cashing in on his reputation at the Slade and as an established British artist. She felt riled but said airily, "But where else darling?"

Soolan looked ill at ease. She said. "What does Robert think about all this?"

"He doesn't know."

All Soolan could say was "Oh." She tried to pour herself another cup of tea but there was none left. Used as she was to intrigue, the possibility, no, the probability crossed her mind that Diana was up to something. She stared back, not intentionally rudely, but because she didn't know what to make of it all. As she looked at Diana, she realised that there before her was someone who'd changed. Apart from a brief 'hello' at the Banquet, neither of them had spoken to each other for long enough, avoiding one another with tacit agreement. This young woman, Soolan saw, was no longer the impetuous creature who used to irritate her. She was self-controlled and dignified. Her words seemed to be weighed; unlike before, she gave the impression of holding many things back. But she herself was sensible enough to weigh her words too. It was no good starting to rejoice when matters could still rebound to her disadvantage. "Diana, why like this? I think you ought to discuss things with Robert first. He should have a say you know."

"He does have the say in what he wants to do—as we both know so well, but I have the say in my own life, at least I intend to from now on. I've made up my mind. There's nothing to discuss. I'm not even going to give anyone my reasons. But I am glad he's content with you Soo. I'm really glad of it. It makes my leaving less difficult. I wouldn't like him to be lonely. As a matter of fact dear, I've come to tell you I bear you no ill will. None at all." She gave Soolan a friendly smile. "Do you mind?" she said and cut herself another piece of cake.

In the face of such equanimity Soolan decided to become the sophisticated, sensible woman of the world, like someone in an eighteenth century novel calmly regulating the disorderly trivialities of emotion with the dictates of pure reason, and asked what Diana's future plans and intentions were—if, of course, she felt like revealing them. But she was still perplexed; the capitulation had been unexpected—like the final collapse of the K.M.T. in China—and so her cool questions didn't quite conceal her anxiety.

"I'll borrow the money from Robert to go back. Yes, borrow Soo. I'll pay back every cent. But I'll stop on the way in Hong Kong and Tokyo. I might even get a job somewhere for a while. Peter used to talk of working at Waseda University. Maybe I'll find him there. I'll be alright. I once told Robert if I left him I'd never be on the streets." She gave a little laugh and Soolan began to look more at ease. Then she ran her fingers round the plate picking up the crumbs. "Lovely fruit cake Soo. Did you make it?"

"It's from Lane Crawford. I should have got you one."

"Do you think you'll be off to Peking one of these days? Robert would love that, I'm sure. Is it possible?"

"Yes. Maybe. Yes. I don't know." Soolan was thrown by the thought that her innermost desire was transparently obvious to Diana.

"Well I must be off. I won't call again, Soo. I'm glad I've come here to tell you though. Robert will know all about it when next you see him." Noticing the dubious look on Soolan's face, she lent forward and kissed her. "Honestly Soo. Everything's fine. There's nothing to worry about."

"Diana." Soolan suddenly became all consideration. "If you really want a job in Hong Kong, I can help. I know people there." She gave the name of a well known Chinese millionaire as an example. "I'll contact him. Go to him. He'll help—after I've spoken to him." Diana looked hesitant. "Please," Soolan insisted. Diana gave her a smile. "Alright Soo. I promise I will. Thanks a lot. " A warm sisterly hug followed and she was gone.

As soon as she was alone, Soolan changed out of her silk house coat into a baggy Mao jacket, trousers and cap. "God, what a frump," she told her face in the mirror as she wiped off her lipstick. Then she asked herself, "How does she keep that figure when she loves to stuff herself with cakes and sweets?" But it was no time for jealousy; frump or not the eyes facing her were bright, elated even. No doubt the Party members at the meeting she was going to would think it sprang from enthusiasm about the demonstration. "And bully for them," she said, remembering the slang at her English girls' school in Shanghai. Then she left the house for the so-called Chamber of Commerce.

The proceedings at the meeting were uneventful up to the moment when the Chairman, recently arrived from Hong Kong and named Mr. Winston Lu Hua Nan, though he only used his Churchillian name amongst his English speaking friends, gestured to a middle-school representative to take the floor. The student, a fiery mouthed girl with radical views and gap teeth, always in the forefront with her high, strident voice when it came to demands for action, launched into a vehement diatribe on the iniquities of prostitution and opium that seemed irrelevant to the matters in hand until out it came, a highly dramatic version of Mei Ling's experience in the brothel. The student organisation had gone far with its investigations and Mei Ling's attempt to help Kai Tung, now fully revealed as the justifiable executioner of an opium trafficker, was reported. The whole tale was told with such passion that before long there were shouts for revenge against the K.M.T. stooges who were behind such iniquities.

Soolan noticed that the men who represented Ming Yuk's interests, probably merely to ensure that the demonstration would go off just forcefully enough for Lung Yeung to be able to pose as the people's protector when, as would certainly happen, some of the demonstrators were arrested, looked disconcerted at these revelations. However, she was more concerned about Winston Lu; his background, like hers, was obviously that of a middle-class English-educated family but he seemed, behind his high-domed forehead and small gold-rimmed spectacles, to suggest a doctrinaire coldness. One part of her welcomed the new development. It was a way of striking at Ming Yuk. Certainly he'd think she was behind it. On the other hand her sense of discipline made her fear that things could really get out of hand. She looked directly at Winston Lu; he glanced away. Were his loyalties to the calculators or to the radicals in the Party?

The facts revealed seemed incontrovertible; another student announced that the identity of the African soldier who'd raped Mei Ling was known and demanded the Portuguese government should execute him. Although the room resounded with cries for action, an older trades union representative made an appeal for moderation. Observing a slightly perplexed look on Winston Lu's face at this intervention, Soolan seized the opportunity to rise and denounce the unionist's proposals as bourgeois compromise, her words obviously delighting the younger workers and students who stamped their feet and loudly reiterated their view that demands for redress should be sent at once to the Portuguese Governor. "I'd willingly go myself to the Governor's office," Soolan shouted fiercely, firmly identifying herself with the extremists. "But we mustn't play into the hands of the American imperialists by giving their Portuguese lackeys an excuse for holding up vital war supplies. Let us correctly and fearlessly proceed with an orderly demonstration. But let the persecuted girl be present at the rally so the working masses of the town may all learn how she supported People's Hero Kai Tung." She finished up passionately to the plaudits of the meeting. "In this way the toiling masses will be prepared to show solidarity with her struggle when we raise the case later. Finally, comrades, I congratulate you for ensuring that we shall have a massive turnout tomorrow. Let the fascist imperialists learn how the people feel."

She was relieved when Winston Lu supported her from the chair, apparently approving her orthodoxy, which contrived to keep everyone's temper at boiling point without precipitating any real action. But she still feared that the enthusiasm so many representatives had shown at the meeting would be transmitted to their followers. Maybe that was what Winston Lu was bargaining for.

As soon as the meeting was over, Ming Yuk's spies at the meeting gave him the danger signal. The new situation required immediate action. Without delay he contacted Lobato to tell him of the risks posed by popular resentment over Mei Ling's treatment and his plans, involving Carlos, to deal with it. Lobato's voice over the phone at first sounded as if he couldn't care less. It rather amused him that Ming Yuk should find himself in difficulties on account of sending a mere girl to a brothel but his tone changed as Ming Yuk elaborated his fears that it might be difficult to hold the radicals in check. "Are you willing to order your police to open fire if a mob goes on the rampage?" Ming Yuk demanded coldly. Lobato saw the point. He agreed that

Carlos should be posted within the hour to the island where the small holding lay. There, Mei Ling would be married off to him, equally without delay; special arrangements would have to be made with the marriage registry. Communists wouldn't demonstrate on behalf of a Portuguese policemen's wife. "And I should get that black devil out of town as well—back to Africa if you can," Ming Yuk suggested, adding as a final touch, "If you can't arrange to have him shot."

The call concluded he sat back and ran his hand over his forehead. He didn't really feel at ease at all. A report had been given to him that the letters he'd forced Peter to sign had been accepted as genuine but he was still anxious to get the Sheratons away. And were his arrangements for the imprisonment of Peter secret enough? He banished his doubts on that score. Pai Chai was too terrified of him to do anything and the guards were picked men. No, the Sheratons were the only danger. But if Robert Sheraton really did attend the demonstration, his expulsion by the Portuguese could be manipulated.

He need have had no doubts about that attendance for Robert had already received a phone call from Soolan who, taking it for granted that he would be going to the demonstration, told him that a car would call for him at three p.m. the next day; she herself would be in it. Still in an enthusiastic mood about going to China and quite careless what the Portuguese might think, he at once replied. "Yes, I'll be ready," then went on casually to ask whether he'd left his fountain pen at her house. It was a present from his mother. He hoped he hadn't lost it. "Bob", Soolan said firmly, "Don't go into town tomorrow. Things are tense. Very tense. There could be clashes between our people and K.M.T. supporters."

However, the next morning, overcome by curiosity, Robert just had to go out to look around for surely it couldn't be so dangerous. He had only walked a little way along the sea front towards the Avenida Carlos de Silva when he realised that Soolan was right. There was marked tension in the air. All the shops were shuttered and their doors secured by thick slotted staves, except for his tobacco shop which had left a gap in the doorway for customers to go in and out. He bought his favourite brand and stood in the empty street filling his pipe. Some lorry loads of students went by banging gongs and drums, waving banners and shouting slogans. From a side street a stone was slung. It hit a student and Robert saw blood pouring from a gash in his forehead. Perhaps it was better to get out of the way.

Confident that the Hotel Lisboa would be safe he went inside. But in the verandah cafe, which was quite crowded with people who mattered, there out of solidarity and also because no business could be done with things as they were, he was surprised by the obvious aloofness towards him of various Portuguese acquaintances. No-one invited him to join a table. Disconsolately he sat alone with a glass of anisette, idly observing the delicate crystals on the twig inside the half consumed bottle which had been set beside him—an act of deliberate friendliness, it seemed, on the part of a Chinese waiter. Then he watched the clutch of Portuguese liberals that was always at the end table of the verandah— exiles banished to an eastern sea by Dictator Salazar. Would they never finish perusing those antique copies of home newspapers or cease their conversations about returning to Lisbon, once more to philosophize in the Chiado or, better still, to enjoy the sweet life in the Bairro Alto? There was one who was everlastingly engaged in writing letters; it made Robert think of those sad ex-pontine poems he'd once struggled to translate. He hoped these exiles would enjoy a better fate than poor old Ovid.

As there was nothing to see through the window onto the street, he wound up the clockwork fly catcher on his table, a Heath Robinson device that vainly sought, with the rotation of a sticky drum, to exercise a degree of population control over the insects that invaded the hotel from the reclaimed land. Suddenly he was conscious of someone standing over him.

"Not yet lunch time and half a bottle gone." Luiz smiled down at him. "Can I join you—if you still feel friendly to us Portuguese." Luiz glanced around. "I hope you haven't met with any rudeness."

"Why of course not. You Portuguese are too courteous ever to be rude. Yes, do join me. But I think your reserve can be more wounding," he added.

Luiz snapped his fingers; a foki appeared like a genie—even now this stimulus and reaction still bothered egalitarian Robert—and Luiz ordered a vermouth. "I'd like to see an end to all this nonsense." His eyes gazed seriously at Robert as he spoke. "The main trouble's Lobato."

"I don't get you." Robert realised something else was going on of which he was unaware. Luiz looked surprised. "Haven't you seen this?" He fished out of his pocket a crumpled pamphlet headed in Chinese and English, 'Demonstration in memory of People's Hero Kai Tung and against Portuguese Imperialism.'

"I know about that, " Robert said sharply. "I'm going to it."

Although to himself Luiz thought, 'Idiot', by way of answer he straightened out the pamphlet and Robert saw one of his own academically excellent sketches, actually of Mr. and Mrs. Kam's two beautiful sons, done one day when it wasn't worth their while using the fish trap. Though they were smiling and looking into the sun-filled future confidently, Robert had imbued them with something of the perfection of Greek ephebes rather than of the subject matter suggested in the caption: "Young workers resolutely oppose K.M.T. rotten eggs," by artist R. Sheraton. Robert's immediate reaction was to laugh at the words 'rotten eggs'. It made him think of some schoolgirl magazine: 'Rotten egg', hissed Hilda Chetwynd-Smythe tossing her pigtails over her shoulder. Luiz was irritated. "It's not so funny. My people think you're on the side of the Reds. There was hostility towards you even before this."

"Why Luiz? Why? It really is stupid."

"Robert you're ingenuous. You're Peter's friend. Think what he did to Lobato. It's well known he let the mob into the Club. He's blamed for the fire. Besides that some people are jealous over the attention Lung Yeung paid you. Can't you foresee anything? This pamphlet's the last straw."

"I didn't know anything about it." Robert looked perplexed. Luiz folded up the embarrassing piece of paper and said, "I keep a folder for things like this. More interesting than snapshots." He added, "I'd give Soolan a dressing down about it if I were you."

But Robert didn't feel annoyed with Soolan for what she'd done. In a way he even admired the tenacity with which she tried to involve him. "Why should I?" he replied. "I wish I was as determined about things myself." Even these liberal intellectuals still sitting here discussing their country's future had more guts than he did. "Adeus Luiz," he said coolly as he got up. "I'm glad you're not against me at any rate." He walked out, head held high, even with a slight look of contempt on his face, so Luiz thought, no doubt to show these colonials around him that he was not to be so easily intimated.

Diana said nothing but, "Oh yes," when he got home and told her he'd be back late because of the demonstration. If she'd not made up her mind to end things, no doubt she would have found herself advising him how foolish it was to go. It was a relief not to be involved. She felt that Robert had already fully committed himself to Soolan, even before she herself had told him of her own decision. But of course it wasn't like that at all; words like commitment and decision, were written in invisible ink in Robert's vocabulary. She had intended to tell him she was leaving him for good some time during the evening, over dinner perhaps, but as he was going to the demonstration and was coming back the Lord knew when, why not let him go fully aware that in his fantastic new life, she wouldn't be around. "Robert, let's have a drink together before you leave," she said. "A cognac will keep you going in that mob."

"You don't want to come?" he asked as he took up a semi-recumbent position, rather like an Etruscan sarcophagus figure, Diana thought, on the settee at the end of the balcony.

"Wild horses wouldn't get me there," she replied, pouring the drinks, a large brandy with a dash of dry ginger for Robert and a small neat gin for herself, after which she sat down opposite him, a minor figure, she suspected, a mere female, a slave no doubt, to one side of the tomb.

As soon as the glass was in his hand, he began wondering aloud what he should wear at the demonstration. She listened to him in bemused silence while he came to the conclusion it was best to go as he was, in white slacks and a shirt flapping coolly around his waist. "No one cares about clothes in China," he finished up.

"That'll suit you dear, won't it." Her words, uttered in frosty tones, seemed to strike home. He looked at her slightly surprised. Perhaps he suspected she'd asked him to have drink as a prelude to a confrontation—she had once been guilty of such behaviour—so she gave him a pleasant smile to put him at ease. All the same she must take the bull by the horns. "Robert," she said, "I've something to tell you. Can I ask you in advance to take it seriously?"

"Oh there's no harm in my going to the demonstration," he said, sure it was bound to be about that. "I'll be under the aegis of Soolan."

"I'm sure there isn't. In fact, as things are, it's probably a good idea, especially as you're going under the aegis of…" In her more hostile days she would indubitably have said, 'the goddess' or, 'Pallas Athene,' but she ended the sentence simply enough with, "Soolan."

"As things are?"

"Yes. Because of my decision. I'm leaving here. No, that's not the way to put it. I'm leaving you. I want to leave you. And I want to tell you of my decision to your face. No disappearing and leaving notes behind. Things must be right between us. I want to keep in contact. Stay your friend—if you want me to be."

Something in her face warned him not to brush her statement off, even if he didn't really believe things would turn out that way. He decided to be adroit. "But what about Carlos. You like him, don't you? You're happy with him?" Nevertheless his face sagged a bit; he really meant, 'What about our modus vivendi. I though we'd worked everything out. Why are you upsetting the apple cart?'

"Carlos is getting married," she said, though it wasn't the answer to his objections.

"Married?"

"Yes. To Mei Ling."

He was disinclined to ask for details. "Then if you're upset, let's go away. I said we should have a holiday." She still looked determined so he changed tack. "Or is it because of Peter? Do you want to go to Tokyo?" The Etruscan Lars now sat up, both hands cupping the brandy glass. The bushy eyebrows seemed, as they were raised, to be complaining, 'How can you be doing this to me? It's not fair. Take it all back.'

"Please try to understand. It's nothing to do with Carlos or Peter. It's to do with you and me. Or rather just me. You look after me. You're good to me. But you don't need me. So I must make a life of my own. Find a role for myself. I can't say much else than that because it's as simple as that and as complex as that. Please understand me, Robert."

"I don't understand. I think the whole Peter business has knocked you off balance." A look of consternation was on his face but Diana felt sure it was merely at the thought of having to rearrange his pattern of living. Once he'd fallen into a new routine, he'd be perfectly alright. She got up. "It's nearly three," she said, looking at her watch.

"I'm not going."

"You are," she said. "You promised Soo. Don't worry. I'll be here when you get back. If I'm awake we'll talk if you want. And if I'm asleep you can wake me up for a talk. But you won't change my mind. All I want you to do is lend me enough money to go home."

"Diana…" His voice was appealing. She went up to him and held his hands. "Listen. The car's arrived to take you to the demonstration, Robert. Don't worry. I'll be fine. I'm glad for you and Soolan. She smiled at him and brushed his hair back lightly with her hand. "It's what I have to do; don't you see? "I'm not blaming you. And I don't regret a single moment with you. I only wish I'd been more…" She was too upset to say anything else and went quickly to her bedroom. There she looked over the balcony to watch him go pensively down the garden steps to the ancient vehicle in which Soolan had come for him. I'm afraid, she thought, that life in China won't be so conducive to your creature comforts, Robert, as living here with me.

On the reclaimed land, the demonstrating workers and students were several thousand strong. As soon as the car stopped, Soolan and Robert were met by a group of men and women, some of whom Robert remembered from the days when Soolan used to take him about town. Together they formed a little procession and made their way between the applauding demonstrators towards the speakers platform which, though it was not dark, was festooned with strings of electric light bulbs like a stage prepared for a side show at a circus: see the two-headed fat lady or some human freak. Certainly, among so many slightly built people, Robert felt elephantine and abnormal. He noticed everyone was wearing a red rosette except himself but this defect was remedied at the platform steps where a pretty girl came up and pinned on his shirt a large red favour with a plastic button bearing a photograph of Mao Tse Tung. Soolan and the other party officials turned towards him and applauded and he responded by clapping as he'd seen people do on Communist newsreels.

Once on the platform he was torn between nervousness at the situation in which he'd landed and an unfamiliar emotion, which he wasn't able to identify as pleasurable or otherwise, at the sight of the vast throng moved by emotions that were foreign to him. As the speeches and the drum-accompanied songs, all in Mandarin which he couldn't understand, went on, he felt the enthusiasm of the crowd tugging at him, insistent on transporting him outside himself into a world hypnotized by flags and chanted slogans. How easy it would be to follow those strident tunes towards a radiance that must surely lie somewhere beyond the fluttering red bunting; he kept thinking of the words Soolan once used to him about living in a country where everything was being reborn. The desire for youth, when he was already floundering in the dismal reaches of middle age, made her suggestion that he could become identified with a young country more seductive than ever.

Towards the end of the ceremony, Soolan made a speech in Cantonese in praise of the heroic Kai Tung who, despite being merely a trishaw boy, had diligently studied the words of Mao Tse Tung and joined in the struggle against imperialism. Though corrupted by opium he'd overcome the vice with the strength he'd derived from Marxist-Leninist teaching; when the masses struggled against the colonial oppressors in the Old City, he heroically led them. Later the colonial imperialists had hired Kuomintang running dogs to do their dirty work and assassinated him because they realised the danger to their system of such a brave man, inspired as he was with the teachings of the Communist Party. It was the duty of all Party members to see that his memory didn't die. No reference was made to the affair of Mei Ling. Robert's command of Cantonese was insufficient for him to understand all the speech, otherwise amazement would have destroyed the euphoria he was now experiencing. When Soolan finished, she turned towards him amidst the thunderous applause and shouted, "Please say something," and the other people on the platform turned towards him with their inane applause. "I can't," he replied, horrified at the suggestion and then, desperately seeking an excuse, protested that everyone would laugh at his accent. She was not to be put off so easily. "Just say, 'Long live Chairman Mao'." she insisted, repeating in Chinese "Chairman Mao. Ten thousand years." He knew the hackneyed phrase well enough; it would look ridiculous to refuse. He let Soolan lead him towards the microphone. A sea of faces lay before him and there was an expectant hush as though the crowd was awaiting a sign from heaven. The whole ceremony had acquired a nightmarish quality in which he was being pushed on by the crazy mood that the drums, the music and the many voices had engendered in him. He was aware of raising his right arm, clenching his fist and thrice shouting the phrase Soolan had prompted him to, "*Mao chu hsi—wan sui.*" As he did so, protean Winston Lu Hua Nan pulled a trailing cord and a red flag with the one large and four smaller five pointed yellow stars of the People's Republic unfurled impertinently from near Vasco da Gama's unprotesting head. "*Wan Sui. Wan Sui.* Ten thousand years. Ten thousand years," the happy crowd roared back and Soolan drew Robert's attention to the flag for whose release his words had been the unwitting signal. Newspaper cameramen were taking their customary unnecessarily large number of photographs recording Robert's bewildered features for posterity against da Gama's backside, next to grinning, inevitably applauding, Party members, or with the People's Flag floating deepest red high above him. As the crowd began to sing the Chinese National Anthem, the March of the Volunteers, he felt trapped. "*Chi lai! Pu yuang tsou nu li ti jen men,*" he heard Soolan's voice ardently singing nearby. "Arise all you who refuse to be slaves. From each," people were chanting, "comes forth his loudest call: Arise! Arise! Arise!" After this insult to the Portuguese national hero there was no staying here now. "Millions with but one heart; braving the enemy's fire; march on," the anthem was concluding and Robert joined in the final line because it was easy, "*Ch'ien chin!* March on! *Ch'ien chin!*"

A few hours later Colonel Lobato looked at the photograph a police agent had taken of Soolan and Robert at the demonstration. He chuckled; what an odd position

Sheraton had been tricked into—unfurled flags and clenched fists indeed. Really, why didn't the man stick to his art—and Diana.

The room Diana was shown into when she paid her farewell visit to Lung Yeung was an ornate salon designed in an eighteenth century French style. It was one of the whims of his wife in those pre-war days when she still spent a lot of time at home. Those parts which were reproduction looked slightly wrong, as though the craftsmen hadn't quite grasped the style, but there were some valuable antiques there too, collected by someone of taste it seemed. Sitting on the delicate watered silk, Diana felt she was breaking a museum regulation.

The door opened; a frock coated elegant in a wig should have come in but it was Ming Yuk in a black *cheong sam*. He looked sinister, like someone out of a Fu Manchu film—'in exactly twenty four hours, Missy Shelaton I shall give order to hold enti planet at lansom,' she said staccato to herself. He also looked more careworn than usual. She persuaded herself he had a shifty look about his eyes.

"Ah Mrs. Sheraton. Most honoured to see you." He is from Fu Manchu, she thought. "You wish to see Lung *Shin Saang*. I'm glad. He's spending too much time on his own." His manner was solicitous, more like a family doctor than the ambitious heir to the throne. "He's been sleeping. Perhaps you'd care to wait a little. He'll see you soon."

She expected him to leave and was going to inspect a genuine looking escritoire with curious inset panels of Japanese lacquer just to while the time away when he came across the room, sat stiffly upon an oval backed chair and looked at her with unblinking eyes. Holding her back bolt upright, like someone undergoing a lesson in deportment, she stared back at him full in the eye, wondering why on earth he was sitting there at all. She knew he resented her.

No doubt he'd be pleased to learn that this was her last visit but she'd no intention of letting him know.

"Your husband was loudly applauded at the demonstration Mrs. Sheraton. We Chinese appreciate his support in our struggle."

Diana's eyebrows shot up. Our struggle. What part did he play in any struggle except for his own advantage. "Did you yourself make a revolutionary speech?" She asked icily.

"No. Unfortunately my work prevented me from going," he said without batting an eyelid. He leaned over to offer her a cigarette. She refused it. If she hadn't been in Lung Yeung's house she'd have asked him to clear off. She felt like striking him for what he'd done to Mei Ling. Taking out one of her own cigarettes, she lit it and blew the smoke defiantly in his direction.

His next question angered her further. "Have you heard from Mr. Morgan since he left? I'm told he's gone to Hong Kong."

"Really. Who told you that?"

"It seems to be common knowledge in town."

"And is it common knowledge who the murderers of Ah Tung are?"

Suavely he replied, "I'm sure they'll be brought to justice." He looked down shyly. "Mrs. Sheraton, may I make a request?" As she said nothing he went on, "If you hear from Mr. Morgan, could you give him my regards when you reply?"

"Your regards?" Diana was enraged by the question. Quite directly she asked, "Why on earth should I do that? Let's not beat about the bush, Ming Yuk. You were responsible for the rape of Mei Ling." She stood up angrily. "You were responsible for Ah Tung's murder. That's common knowledge too isn't it? Isn't it? I wouldn't have lost Peter if it hadn't been for you." As she looked at him it suddenly struck her that behind that still face, Ming Yuk's eyes were dancing with some sort of joy. Or was it her imagination? No. He was happy over her misery. She got up and stared down at him. "It's funny to watch people suffer, isn't it Ming Yuk? I'm sure you're glad to know Peter's suffering right now." As she said the words the slightest of gasps escaped his lips; he seemed to quail a little. "You…," he began and quickly stopped.

She walked across the room and then turned to face him. "*Zao gao*—running dog," she commanded loudly, "Go and tell your master Mrs. Sheraton is here. Go. Go at once." She threw him a glance as imperious as any empress. He left quickly.

All at once the room struck her for what it was, a vulgar imitation, a hideous mockery. She was glad this was her last visit to the place. It was no good shouting 'running dog' at Ming Yuk when he was carrying out the will, however much on his own initiative, of the master she was friendly with. Here was an instance in which Robert had been much quicker than her to see the truth. If she was friendly with Lung Yeung, didn't she concur in his activities; and if his organisation had injured Peter, wasn't she an accessory? How could the degree of guilt that passed from each link in this chain be measured? Perhaps Lung Yeung didn't know the full extent of Ming Yuk's activities. Perhaps he didn't think about it, as she hadn't thought. But it was too late to speculate about it now. She was leaving. Lung Yeung was an old man and whatever he'd done she could still pity his age. Their final meeting would be tranquil.

Outside the room a bell sounded; somewhere someone was being summoned to do something in this house of orders. The bell rang again and it summoned to her mind the memory of Ming Yuk's face when she'd shouted at him. That little gasp when she'd mentioned Peter's suffering. Why was it needling her? Why had he asked her to send his regards to Peter? There was something she couldn't fathom. Yet how could anyone fathom the likes of Ming Yuk? A young man came into the room, said the master would receive her in the Cinnabar Hill Pavilion and asked her, with much ceremony, to follow him through the gardens to the island fane.

Lung Yeung bowed to her politely. Almost at once he pointed to Robert's portrait of him which was opposite an opened wall-high sliding screen. "You see. I've placed it where the light's good. I like it more and more. Do you think it's my vanity or my love of art? Perhaps I'm falling for my own inestimable features—like your story of Narcissus." He tittered at the thought of an old man behaving like that intemperate youth, nor could Diana repress a smile.

She humoured him by asking about the new building; there was plenty to admire in it. Many rich Chinese tended to put up houses in an ornate style; Lung Yeung's taste had at last become simple, almost Japanese in its purity. He made the customary self disparaging replies about his humble abode, but added, "My good Ming Yuk has seen to it that the refinements of modern science are incorporated." He slid back a panel and the good Ming Yuk's head swam into view on a television screen, apparently engrossed in a document.

"You require something Lung *Shin Saang*?"

"No. No. Just showing Mrs. Sheraton how advanced we are. Thank you." He smiled and decapitated Ming Yuk with his fingertip. As he did so he gave Diana an odd look, a slight knitting of the eyebrows, something like a frown and she had the feeling that he was passing her a message. Before long she also sensed that for some reason or other he was doing his best to prevent her seizing any openings for more serious conversation. On and on went his conducted tour of the Pavilion. Perhaps he suspected she'd come for some important reason and was determined to keep her at bay. "Now," he announced when they'd seen the entire building, "I'll show you the rock garden and the pools." She followed him outside, listening to the names of plants, trees and creepers. As usual, it was difficult not to fall under his spell as he amused her with translations of the Chinese names. Here he pointed out the purple wei, sometimes he said, referred to as 'the hundred days red,' or 'afraid of being tickled'; there the red bean, effective in love potions with flowers like butterflies and leaves like bird's wings, nicknamed 'mutually lovesick.' At one point in their circuitous perambulation he came out with his inevitable quotation (did he prepare them in advance? she wondered) when they came across a pair of not too healthy looking Wu Tung trees, symbolic of conjugal happiness. This time it was the T'ang poet, Meng Chiao:

> Together the Wu Tung trees grow older
> The Mandarin duck pairs for life with the drake
> A chaste woman is proud of following her husband in death
> And sacrifices her own life.

Unfortunately Mrs. Sheraton, my wife and I have not tended these trees, which we planted many years ago, very successfully, as you can see. They require careful nurturing."

Was he making this cynical reference to his own marriage as a means of telling her how she should not behave? Did he perhaps know why she'd come? No, that wasn't possible. But it was amusing to think of Robert and herself as Wu Tung trees; she must tell him when she got back. Still no opportunity of getting a word in presented itself. They went on through the garden designed in unnatural imitation of nature until they came to a pool into which water trickled over mossy rocks, delighting somnolent carp with trails of bubbles. Here he stooped down with remarkable alacrity for a man so old, lifted a tiny hydrant and turned a tap. The water gushed from the rocks somewhere above them filling the air with spray as it splashed over a waterfall into the pool where the fish took to darting about swiftly, forgetting their reveries. "I seem to remember," he said as he straightened up, "that in Byzantium your Emperors (she was amused at his use today of 'your' when referring to western things) had a room in their palace with water always playing around it—so they could speak without fearing eavesdroppers." He gave her a sidelong glance. "I don't think even Ming Yuk's little gadgets can pick us up now."

She looked incredulously from the water to his face; what a clever old devil he was. He fluttered his hands as if dismissing it as unimportant. "He does it for my benefit, I'm sure. He wants to find out everything to serve me better. Above all he longs to know how my mind works. But that's a problem; what he doesn't grasp is that my control over him—over everything I rule—rests on retaining a little mystery. If people knew everything about their rulers, they'd lose respect for them. What's more it would be dangerous, wouldn't it? If he became me, I'd no longer be indispensable, would I?" He motioned her to sit beside the pool with him and dabbled his hand in the water. "What a pleasant life fishes have. Now tell me why you've come. Well, I suppose I know: the husband sings, the wife accompanies. It is about your husband, isn't it? But I'm afraid I can't do anything about it. He should never have gone to that demonstration. The heart can trick us into doing foolish things. The Portuguese don't like it at all. That flag at da Gama's head. They feel insulted." Then he added, "You know there was a terrible fuss about that statue. The Peking Government didn't want it at all. The great discoverer indeed. For a long time after it was put up, it was under hoardings." He gave a little chuckle. "And quite rightly so. After all, we Chinese did exist before Europe 'discovered' us."

Diana laughed. "Well *Shin Saang*, I've not come to see you about Robert. Or not exactly. I suppose the Portuguese will ask him to leave. But it doesn't matter. He'll be leaving anyway."

"I don't quite understand you."

"He'll be off to China sooner or later with Soolan. I'm going away myself."

Lung Yeung was silent. The corners of his mouth drooped a little. In a younger person it might have been interpreted as a sign of sadness. "So the purpose of this visit is to say goodbye, isn't it. I'm truly sorry you're leaving. I..."

"Yes Lung *Shin Saang*."

"I must confess to being surprised. Surprised that Robert should want such a thing. Or perhaps you yourself are lowering the curtain and asking to leave. Ah, your pardon: an old way of saying that a woman wants a divorce."

"I like that, *Shin Saang*. Such a delicate way of handling unpleasantness. Yes. I am lowering the curtain. It's my decision. I have my reasons. They're very personal."

"Then I shan't question you about them." He paused before going on. "What makes you so sure that Robert can go with Soolan to China?"

"I'm not sure. I assume she has influence."

"Come let's take a turn together."

Diana led him slowly around the pool thinking how sad it was that he should be sharing this lovely place with no-one who meant anything to him for the rest of his life. By what slow process had his autocratic power deprived him of his first wife and sons, not to mention his concubines and their offspring? All of his children, even his daughters, worked in professions outside his loathsome organisation. Perhaps he had encouraged them to escape from the hive. If so, he must have decided long ago that his power was of too corrupt a nature to be passed on to anyone for whom he cared. In a sense then, this terminal loneliness was a self-imposed punishment for his crimes. It was a loneliness most unusual in a rich, or indeed, in any Chinese.

He halted. For a moment Diana thought he was tired. Then she saw he was looking at her very deliberately. He said, "You don't know much about the political situation here, or in China, do you? So if you wanted help, you wouldn't know how to go about it, would you?"

"But I don't want help. I'm not asking for help at all. What help should I want?" His question had baffled her; surely he couldn't think she wanted pressure turned on Soolan. Yes, he must do; how little he understood her if so. Then that other nagging thought returned to her mind, or rather reared itself higher, for it hadn't entirely left her since her encounter with Ming Yuk. They had returned to sit by the cascade where the water music was at its loudest. "Lung *Shin Saang*. There is one thing that does worry me."

"Yes, what is it?"

"You don't think Ming Yuk knows anything about Peter do you? Ah Tung was killed by—by his men. Could they have…"

"No one knows where Mr. Morgan is. Certainly not Ming Yuk. I was curious myself. I questioned him. Ming Yuk would never dare to lie to me."

"He showed an odd interest in Peter when I spoke to him just now." Diana gave a quick account of Ming Yuk's reactions to her hostility.

"The explanation's simple I believe," Lung Yeung replied without a moment's hesitation. "Mr. Morgan and Kai Tung weren't just 'friends' as we know. I suspect Ming Yuk also likes to share the peach. I'm sure that accounts for his interest." He shrugged his shoulders to dismiss the matter and Diana accepted the explanation; after all, it seemed the only one.

The time had now come to say goodbye. But quite abruptly Lung Yeung said, "Soolan has enemies. She knows it of course but I don't think she realises how far things have gone. She's loyal to her cause; no doubt of that. But her way of life and her élitism don't endear her to the radicals. She's played into their hands. Does Robert know that, do you think?"

"I couldn't say at all, *Shin Saang*. I haven't followed political matters as closely as I should. I thought Marxists were just Marxists. I didn't know there were different parties inside the Party. In any case I always thought you were the kingpin here—even though you could never be a Communist. Surely you're the one who deals with Peking though."

Lung Yeung smiled. "How simple for me if it were just like that. What you say is true—and not true. It's like a shadow play." He paused. "Strange that I should speak to you like this. You know, even China isn't what it seems to be. From outside it looks monolithic but behind the façade there are many different voices. For instance there are people in Canton who want to support their friends here in taking the place over at once. They won't succeed—not yet I assure you."

"So what effect will the demonstration…"

"Oh that was nothing—what's your English expression—a typhoon in a teapot."

She laughed gaily. "You know perfectly well what it is, Lung *Shin Saang*. But I think your saying is better. I'll use it in future." She noticed that he had suddenly and quite unaccountably become downcast. A silence had arisen between them, a silence which she tried to bridge with her eyes, searching his face for something which might help her to make contact, but in vain. "In future," he said at last turning away and looking into the air at nothing in particular. "There is no future." She felt an urge to put her arms around him but felt it would be thoroughly inappropriate. At least she must stay a little while to give him what comfort was possible for old age. The words 'in future' seemed to have thrown him into an abstracted mood in which she had no part. She observed the direction in which he was gazing, across the garden and beyond the curling rooftops of the Pearl River Mansion towards the dark mass of the Intramuros and the golden dome that hung over the Rotunda. Then, very softly he said, "The Golden Castle, the City of Jade. A Hidden City. Look Diana. See how perfect it is." She stared and yes, she thought she saw, but was she seeing what he was seeing? The seconds passed and then the minutes before he murmured, "How mysterious is the Hidden City. It lies sleeping, waiting to be entered, in the deepest part of all of us, dreaming of the day when the golden flower returns to life, when we return to youth from old age. But not in me. Never in me. Ah, but in you Diana. In you…"

It seemed to Diana as she bent forward to listen, that Lung Yeung was riven by a deep personal grief; was he mourning his failure to be something which he knew he might have been? And was the City really something more than the wall-encompassed space towards which they were now looking? Yet surmise as she might, Diana sensed that, as ever, his words must be interpreted at different levels. Sometimes they were intended in a personal way, other times in an esoteric sense, or in the terms of politics to which he now reverted. "If the Colony is taken over maybe the City will be lost but if I can preserve it for a while, when they finally take over, their regime will have softened and they too will appreciate the City." His eyes closed; he seemed no longer aware of Diana's presence and he took to mumbling so indistinctly that the most she could make out were a few disjointed phrases: "The wild bird soars... taste the elixir... the Golden Flower... the Purple Hall... Not in me. Never in me." After which another much more profound silence arose between them, a silence in which only the water in the pool could be heard, gurgling mightily but saying nothing in particular.

They returned slowly to the Cinnabar Hill Pavilion still without exchanging a word, Lung Yeung leaning heavily on Diana's arm. Before they bid each other goodbye in a formal Chinese way, Lung Yeung took a rolled up scroll from a cupboard, where it seemed to have been awaiting this occasion, and presented it to her. "As a simple present for use on a long journey," was how he put it, "though I didn't think I would be giving it to you so soon." At the Pavilion door he gestured towards a table on which the bowl she'd discovered, now rested. She felt curiously gratified that the inexpensive gift should give him pleasure, and surprised too, for the only other object near it was a large photograph of Lung Yeung and his wife standing in front of an Hispano-Suiza motorcar, wearing smart 1920s clothes, both of them, it seemed, full of the joy of an affluent youth.

By the time she got down to the waterfront the late afternoon had grown dismal but she hardly noticed it for her head was still full of thoughts about Lung Yeung. Suddenly, however, she became aware that, quite unconsciously, she had started to untie the cord that bound his present. She sat on a bench and partly unrolled it: a picture maybe, no, calligraphy and in Lung Yeung's own swift flowing style; that at least she recognized, though not the meaning of the difficult characters. Protruding from the unrolled part she then glimpsed the curled up end of another, smaller scroll with English written on it, again in Lung Yeung's hand. She drew it out gently. Of course, he would want her to know what the Chinese characters meant; this must be the translation. The gift had been carefully prepared by Lung Yeung for her alone, the lines written for her alone. As there was no one about she read them aloud.

Lady with sunset sleeves
Who replenished my wine cup
Do not cling
Do not hold
Make no effort.
Break the yoke
And wander through the sky,
Avoid the opposites
And gain freedom.

The sun is eclipsed
By the pure light of the void,
Therefore be still
And conquer distraction.
Let your mind become
As a hollow bamboo,
Your thoughts
Rise and fall
Like ocean waves.

In your life to come
Neither pain nor sin
Shall cause you sorrow.
Knowing only
Goodness and joy

As a wild torrent
Flow on swiftly,
As clear water
Reach the boundless sea.

She read the lines a second time, recognizing
something of the esoteric teaching without really grasping
its meaning. Only a few of the terse phrases stuck in her
mind to begin with: 'Do not cling', 'Do not grasp', 'Break the
yoke', and 'Reach the boundless sea'. Yes, she had always
thought of the sea, the boundless sea, whatever its mood,
as the ultimate comforter, the concealer of a hidden truth;
that was what it had been to her as a child in Tasmania
where its vastness, spread around the peninsula where
her home stood, had so dwarfed herself and her problems
with her father and her brother that merely to look at it
acted like a balm. That same sea stretched before her now,
to assuage and to heal. Though the tide was high, the water
was smooth, extending outward until it vanished beneath
a white curtain of rising mist. Gazing at the insubstantial
barrier she realized how little she had suspected the extent
of Lung Yeung's affection for her but how could she ever
have hoped to get into his old mind; she read his lines once
more and wondered if she would ever be able to master
such transcendental teaching, or indeed would ever want
to. Then, all at once, after glancing around to see that no
one was watching, she collected a few flat stones and
skimmed them over the water, listening with rapt attention
to their interrupted trajectory into the mist. She had made
no effort; her school girl prowess was undimmed in glory—
one, two, three, four, five—six, no, that last one, not in time
and too splashy must be something else—a fish jumping
perhaps; a good skim anyway. A car was coming down the
road and she hid behind a tree; it passed and she sat on the
parapet looking over the water. Perhaps that sea out there
created half the problems in this place. It was an isolating,
not a connecting sea, an ambiguous comforter. She threw

another stone, this time angrily, and the now questionable mystery before her responded with a single, and the same to you, plop. Here, everyone was cut off from the world at large; she discounted that narrow isthmus into China and journeys on those glittering ferry boats to Hong Kong were like flights in space ships from a forgotten planet. Or to put it in another way, they were like nuns in a convent, a walled-in world where tiny incidents became momentous issues and everyone lost sense of proportion; where the wisest might forget that the sun is eclipsed by the pure light of the void. If the world beyond that encompassing wall of mist were to vanish, what would it matter? In this oriental Ruritania, the explosion of an atomic bomb in the Korean war would probably receive less attention in the daily Noticias than a ball at the Governor's Palace. Looking at the sea, smooth as polished slate, she was struck by its eerie tranquillity; how could such an enormous mass of water come up and retreat so stealthily and how could her own thoughts ever rise and fall like these ocean waves? She leaned over the parapet to wash her hands but suddenly the dark water rose up to her elbows and she drew her arms back quickly; despite its smoothness the sea was forcefully rising and falling, yet only with a hollow sobbing at once mournful and deceptive. At least her own calm was not so false, she flattered herself, now trying to analyse its origins. Could it be connected with her lessening self reproach over Peter, or was she just getting used to his absence, for now she saw that no-one could have moderated his excesses. But no, that too was only an effect; the root cause must lie in her new found feeling of acceptance that expressed itself in a growing conviction of why bother to oppose the inevitable. She must indeed let her mind become as a hollow bamboo. From now on, that being the case, she would no longer waste time regretting things: her stifling childhood, the chance encounter in Hobart with Robert that had led to her foolish marriage, the transience of her love with Carlos and so forth, or imagining that with a modified version of Peter, life could have been any better. There were limits, Canute-like by the sea she admitted, to the possibilities in the world around her; there were limits to what she could expect from other people. Do not cling, do not hold, Lung Yeung had told her. He was right; the truth was that until she had learned to live on her own she would never understand how to live with another person for the right reasons. Yet old clothes were reluctant to be so easily shed and when she tried to deride her youthful foolishness with forced laughter, the noise sounded more like a little cry. She admonished herself sternly; for God's sake, now you're leaving Robert, work out some way of life without all this emotional twaddle. The moment of regret and weakness was banished; no longer would she try to make herself bigger by sponging up other people's ideas—like the little fish that tried to understand the ocean by swallowing it. There was nothing, nothing in the entire universe to hold on to; from this time on she would depend on herself alone, she would break the yoke and gain freedom, as Lung Yeung must have long foreseen. Just then, the insistent crack of bamboo sticks made by a *meehoon* seller disturbed her reverie and she called him over to buy some, eating it hungrily on the sea wall, dangling her bare feet in the water, not very clear water but of the same boundless sea of beauty. The boy watched her, asking the usual questions: "Are you married? How much does your husband earn? How many children have you?" and so on. "Six" she replied. "Five boys and one girl—but she's adopted." The boy exclaimed, "*Sap fan ho*—ten measures good," after which she went her way leaving him to marvel at her youthful fecundity.

As she walked home she recalled Lung Yeung's warning about the danger Soolan was in. She had no wish to see Robert suffer, but her thoughts didn't dwell on him for long. Unexpectedly she found herself imagining the unhappiness of Soolan whose gamble had been enormous in the face of such risks; what love she had shown for Robert.

Diana reproached herself for dawdling by the sea when she should have been steeling Robert to do something quickly for once, if he wanted to keep Soolan. She hurried on, hoping there was still time to help but knowing quite surely that her actions didn't really matter in the least one way or the other. Either this or that were, in essence, the same.

And as it happened her haste was in vain; party officials were already on their way to the rambling old house in which Soolan's apartment was situated. Soolan heard the car stopping outside and peeped through the window to recognise Winston Lu's scholarly forehead emerging from one of those black vehicles the Party used when journeys were to be made to Canton. Her heart pounded. She knew he was the bearer of important news, unpleasant news. Before they could ring the bell she opened the door and invited Mr. Lu and the two men with him to come in.

Winston Lu apologised for disturbing her and looked embarrassed; he'd come to admire her ability and wondered whether one day her fate, to be sent back to China, would happen to him. He told her she was being recalled and that he must take over her files. Knowing it was useless to argue, she started to pack a few possessions. Since the other men were hardly known to her—she'd always thought of them, apparently wrongly, as unimportant trades union officials—she didn't ask any questions. But now she knew the reason why Mr. Lu had come to the Colony. At least her work would be in good hands.

She wanted to pass a message to Robert but daren't ask if she might phone him. On top of a bookcase stood a bowl decorated with a seascape. The characters on it said 'western sea mountains and water'. The character for 'west' had the sound 'sai', the first syllable in the Cantonese way of saying 'Sheraton'. It also meant 'foreign'. As she moved about the room gathering up her things and putting a few ornaments in her cases, she picked the bowl up and said, "Comrade Lu, I'd like to give you this bowl." He got up to take it and as she stood before him, her back to his two companions, she handed it over so that her index finger pointed towards the character 'west'; at the same time her eyebrows arched in interrogation. Mr. Lu bowed slightly and took the bowl saying, "You've such excellent judgement in art, Comrade Kwok. I'll certainly see the bowl is put somewhere it can be appreciated."

Her two suitcases were packed and placed by the door. She hesitated before a still unfinished portrait Robert was painting of her and then, announcing her readiness to leave, gave the key of the flat to Winston Lu. Unconvincingly he insisted she'd need it back from him before long.

Mr. Lu and his companions got out at the Barrier Gate and politely said goodbye. Before long Soolan was being driven through Chung San County, a fertile land where it was low lying but rough and little used where it rose ever more hilly to become a mountainous landscape of crags and ravines. Near the road peasants were threading their way along narrow paths from their work and the lush fields seemed serene and beautiful. In the distance, streams cascaded down the mountains catching the last rays of the setting sun but on the plain they flowed more placidly through well kept channels or fed canals and duck ponds. Occasionally, a mellow old mansion or a temple, now used as an office or a school, would catch her eye, or she'd glimpse a turreted village wall standing sternly beside a lotus-filled moat, a distant pagoda, or a ruined look-out tower. She had seen it all many times of course but now she seemed to be viewing it differently. Before, something about it would often repel her: maybe the poverty of the people, the decrepit machinery, or the antiquated methods. This time there was no brake on her, no weight to hold her back from being a part of what she saw. So it was that, as the car journeyed on, she was able to accept the truth that the world she'd just left had become infinitely remote and love for Robert an impossibility. Amidst the beauty of this countryside she knew that she was returning to her natural way so that, despite China's imperfections and despite the abruptness with which she'd been forced to leave the City, she felt unexpectedly at peace. The car turned on a hillside and for a moment gave the illusion of heading back to the distant City, silhouetted on its gently rising hills by the placid sea; then the road twisted again and Robert and the unreal City were lost to her forever.

Later in the day, Soolan's bowl was delivered to Robert accompanied by a note. "Dear Mr. Sheraton. I regret to inform you that Mrs. Kwok Soolan has been unexpectedly called back to China. She asked me to see that you received this present. Perhaps she will write to you. I do not know. Sincerely, Winston Lu." Diana had told him what Lung Yeung had said about Soolan's vulnerability but he hadn't tried to pass the information on. Rather vaguely he'd thought of letting her know later in the evening. Remorselessly, he told himself, the decision's been taken for you now. But was that true? Wasn't his own failure to rush round and plan getting away with her, if that was what she wanted, a form of decision. Yet even though he tried to persuade himself that whatever he might have done would have been much too late, he could not help reflecting on the dullness of his own reactions. How was it that he could so coolly decide that he would no more complain about Soolan's loss than he would about Diana's decision to leave him? He recalled Job's "The Lord gave and the Lord hath taken away; blessed be the name of the Lord." But no, that wasn't his attitude in the least; he hadn't been unable to decide, he had been unwilling; there was a positive pleasure to be derived from being so easily divested of attachments and responsibilities. Perhaps he wanted to be no more than the male that hunted and, being sated, passed on.

Diana studied him quietly. She couldn't say, 'I'm sorry Robert' because she wasn't sure whether she was or not. In any case she'd never believed he'd be happy with Soolan in China. The whole idea had struck her as preposterous. But Soolan's departure wasn't going to change her own decision. Robert's choice of women was fortunately wider than between herself and Soolan. Then the thought struck her that after all, Robert had never chosen Soolan. Events had merely occurred, as a result of Soolan's and her own activities. It was as though Robert had been driving along a road until he came to a fork; the two of them had blocked off the road marked Diana and kept the other one open. Robert had merely swerved to avoid trouble. Sitting there with the bowl before him like that, made her think of Eeyore with his shattered balloon and pot. Was he thinking he'd lost a chance of happiness, or was he relieved? Perhaps all of this so-called love was nothing but a glorified attachment to some object, just like animals in biology experiments becoming attached to the feeding machine in their cage.

There and then she couldn't help admitting that she had fallen into a cage herself by accepting Robert as her feeding machine. And so as, somewhat furtively, she observed him reading, or perhaps pretending to read, a book on Aztec art (maybe he had it in mind to go to Mexico next) the depressing conviction invaded her brain that she was the one from whom most of the misery in their relationship had stemmed. She had sought him out, not he her. She had trespassed on his settled ways, his hallowed ground, and then expected him, whatever she might have prated about not intending to disturb his life, to accord with the ways and sentiments of youth, which he had long discarded, and of marriage, which he had always sought to avoid. By what right then, had she accused him of being shifty? Under her pressure, not to mention the machinations of Soolan, what alternative had been open to him, if he wanted to preserve what he had found conducive to his happiness, but to resort to shifts? She felt that she had been a tyrant. How much better for him to live as he had lived before their marriage. With feelings of shame and remorse she could only rejoice that in two days time she would be leaving, that her things were already sorted out and a lot of clothes and ornaments given to Group and her sisters. Indeed she had intended going on with her packing during the evening, expecting Robert to be with Soolan. Now her plans must be changed;

the least she could do was to make an effort to please him. She told Group to send out for something very special for dinner. Group decided on eight precious duck, one of Robert's favourites.

But as they ate she began to wonder whether her efforts to be friendly were worth it. For a while all the topics of conversation she raised came to nought. When she told him of her encounter with Ming Yuk he just grumbled, "Letting your imagination run riot as usual. Do you think Ming Yuk's had Peter walled up or something?" When she reported on Lung Yeung's mystical outburst, (though she didn't show him her precious new scroll) he became positively contemptuous. "Golden domes. Elixirs. What nonsense. It's mist not mysticism," he said angrily. "Or thick fog most likely. I wish you'd stop being impressed by all that crap. You should have had enough of it from Peter. Look where it's got him." Yet where had it got him, Diana wondered as, forcing herself, not entirely successfully she suspected, to sound meek, she enquired, "Then how should I see things, Robert? I should love to know. Truly."

"In real terms. In practical terms."

"Like your Communist friends?" It wasn't possible to stop that touch of sarcasm, or was it also boredom, from entering her voice?

"They're not realists. They're romantics. Their heaven on earth is only another version of the rubbish you got at the feet of Lung Yeung or Peter, not to mention your father." His voice got louder as he went on. "There's nothing but what we can get at through our senses or through the machinery we invent to extend our senses. There are no heavens—on earth or anywhere else. There's nothing but the harsh reality of nature of which we are part. All we can do is to accept that reality and try to understand it on its terms."

"As you are doing now?" But despite her derisive air it perplexed her that she couldn't just let him be. Naughty children had made a mess of his neat garden, rooted up the trim shrubs and flowers. He was bound to be angry.

"As I'm doing now. As I'm going to go on doing through my art." His voice had grown stentorian and was shot through with fury, a fury that seemed directed not outward but inward at some flaw in himself.

"So I mustn't ask questions about things beyond nature?" Ostensibly she was submissive again.

"Only ask questions which have a hope of being answered. Questions which can't be answered don't exist as far as I'm concerned," he stated curtly.

The meal ended in silence; she excused herself and went to her bedroom. A little later Robert called her to the phone. An unknown voice gave her a message that Sergeant Nolasco was sorry he hadn't told her he was already posted to the police station on the island but maybe would come over and see her the next day. She put the phone down and sat quietly for a while. Of course she had known that Carlos would be going off. But everything had happened so quickly. In her loneliness she felt like a candle being burnt down and down. What will be left of me by tomorrow she thought despairingly?

As Robert had gone to work in the studio, late though it was, she decided to visit the Kam family just for the sake of company, though for a while, being so despondent, she found it difficult to join in their talk. Occasionally, she looked across the water towards the dark, almost lampless, island where Carlos was living and wished that she could be with him over there, at least tonight. The Kam brothers noticed her sadness and tried to draw her out. In the end they succeeded with their jokes and silly chatter. One of them, the elder, had broad hands, broad shoulders and broad sensual lips, the younger, who was lithe and winsome, a smile a bit like Carlos'. Well aware that they both wanted her, she asked herself what harm would it do to please them as she had once, an age ago it seemed, pleased Peter and Carlos in that now, in her memory, fabled golden room? What Peter could do, she could do. What Carlos would do, she would do. Why shouldn't she be as defiant? It was men who had taught her to break the yoke and gain freedom. Thus, since there was nothing to hold her back anymore, while everyone in the hut was jabbering away, she gave telling signs with her eyes to the brothers so that, after Mr. and Mrs. Kam had fallen fast asleep, the three of them were at the ready, like athletes, to set off for a secluded wooded dell near the shore. There they made love wordlessly and greedily until they were sated. Had she not once dreamed of being marooned on a distant island with these two young admirers and doing precisely this? It seemed that they were consummating something that all three of them had secretly wanted for a long time; they were unrestrained as prisoners suddenly set free and the pleasure of their love making far exceeded what Diana had expected. Afterwards, she felt entirely happy to have given herself so generously and easily to her salty sea-washed boys and as she made her way home in the small hours of the morning, not caring whether or not Robert was awake, or Carlos came over; she remembered how delectable it had been to be so totally abandoned. Was this the beginning of what Lung Yeung had promised in his poem for her future life? 'Neither pain or sin shall cause you sorrow. Knowing only goodness and joy, as a wild torrent—certainly she would be as a wild torrent—flow on swiftly, as clear water, reach the boundless sea.' She paused for breath half way up to the house and turned to look down on the Kam's hut perched over the water. When they had grown old those two down there would still remember her, as she would remember this renewal of her innocence.

But Carlos' thoughts had been winging irresistibly across the inlet of the sea between his new home and the City. Although the piece of land and the house were delighting Mei Ling, who'd been brought up in the country, Carlos was by nature a city slicker; he couldn't see himself spending quiet evenings at home or tending the pigs and poultry and fruit trees. As often as possible he'd be on the little boat to the bright lights. Whatever mild content lay ahead, he still yearned for the possibility which he'd lost in Diana.

Mei Ling had already cleaned the house and put guardian deities on the door and was talking about growing things and buying animals. He humoured her in this but told her, "I've a lot of things to do in town. And I don't want to lose contact with my friends. You don't mind if I'm not always here do you?"

Mei Ling breathed a secret sigh of relief. She didn't want him moping around when she'd so much to interest her. And so when he announced his intention of going over the water she said, "There's no need to hurry back; I'll be busy and I know you've plenty to do over there."

"Is there anything you want me to get?" he asked feeling both uncertain and elated at her complaisance.

"Why don't you call at Old Chong's and ask Siu Ching if she'd like to come and see us? And if you meet Sheraton *Taai Taai* please give her my best wishes."

Carlos went off feeling content with his good fortune—a pretty wife, a piece of land and a house; he'd fallen on his feet. True, Mei Ling didn't seem to have his kind of interest in love making but that could be an advantage if he still had the freedom he wanted.

As soon as he reached town he went to Old Chong's hotel to ask Siu Ching to visit them. The invitation excited her nor was it less pleasing to Mrs. Chong who was anxious to be shut of her troublesome niece. "She'll be up to no good if she sticks around here much longer—it's too near the Street of Happiness for the likes of her," she said. Siu Ching grinned. "I suppose Mei Ling's very happy now." Her lips pouted. "I wish I had her luck." Carlos replied, "Including the brothel?" Miss Flibbertigibbet tossed her head. "Especially that." He promised to call for her later in the day. "I'll be ready for you," she shouted after him as he went off.

He decided to have a quiet smoke and a nap before calling on Diana. Business in the Old Pawnshop was slack and he found none of his friends. But a little after he had drifted into sleep a hand shook him and he awoke to see the pallid features of the masseur Pai Chai. "Massage?" queried the cracked voiced, but the very idea of being touched by those hands was repellent to Carlos of the satin skin. "No. I've got to leave," he said. Pitying the Lame One he added, "Here's a pataca for you. How's business?" Pai Chai replied, "I've got another job. I'm not doing massage really. I've been here a couple of times looking for you." Carlos could see he was frightened. When next Pai Chai spoke, his voice was low and urgent. "You're a friend of Moh *Shin Saang*. You used to come here with him and Ah Tung."

Carlos felt sad remembering the nights the three of them used to spend together. "Yes. Why?"

Pai Chai looked round furtively. "I thought you'd want to know what's happened to him."

At first Carlos didn't take in the indistinct words but when he did, he sat up and demanded, "What do you mean—happened to him? Tell me—quick."

Pai Chai seemed glad to talk but not before Carlos promised secrecy. "It's that devil Ming Yuk. He's given orders no-one's to find out. Moh *Shin Saang*'s in a place near the Red Pleasure Pavilion." He gave an address. Noticing Carlos' dubious expression, he protested, "You can believe me. Go and look there if you want. Go quickly. He won't last much longer. And he's a bit..." Pai Chai tapped his head. As he spoke Carlos put on his clothes and after slipping Pai Chai a couple more patacas left the opium house for the Sheratons.

The room that Peter's friends found him in was small and dingy and lit by the glow of a small lamp. The air was stale yet curiously sweet like the heavy air on some distant planet inhabited by eternally decaying flowers. On a low table by the bed the opium smoking paraphernalia stood next to a photograph of Ah Tung, a hypodermic syringe and a short handled whip which ended in thin leather thongs. Some bowls of food stood untouched. Peter lay half wrapped in the quilt Ah Tung's mother had given him. It was drawn a little over his shoulder towards his cheek where, if he cared to open his eyes, it could remind him of other days.

His flesh had been so flagellated that, for an instant, it seemed to Diana to be marked with one of those complicated patterns that aborigines paint on themselves for reasons steeped in time. Then she saw it as it was. Even the hardened servants who came in averted their eyes from the sight and whenever they had to clear away the evidence of Ming Yuk's grotesque rituals, in whispers they marvelled that the prisoner had never complained or thought of escaping from an existence whose purpose none of them could comprehend. Yet for some reason Ming Yuk had spared Peter's face; pallid and thin now, its sensitive features seemed more pronounced but perhaps that was only the effect of the lamplight and the shadows.

Carlos produced a mirror which he held to Peter's mouth, felt his pulse and whispered, "At least he's alive. We must get him to a doctor. Figueiredo maybe. I'll go for a taxi. Best not to move him until I'm back." Diana hardly seemed to hear or to notice him leaving. All she could do was to hold Peter, cradling his head gently and murmuring his name over and over again.

Robert sat beside her trying to comfort her but she seemed unaware of his efforts and he gave up. Such a short time ago he remembered watching her dance with Peter; now he was oppressed by the thought that youth, hope and joy could so quickly degenerate into the mask of destruction Peter had deliberately chosen in his defiance of convention. Yet equally this was the ultimate fate of all men, both the misfits and those who knew how to behave, and all human endeavour to alleviate pain and decay, even the Promethean efforts of the Communists, were mere rearguard actions against the black scythe of death.

He saw that Diana's shoulders were shaking convulsively with grief and went to close the door on the faces of the inquisitive servants who'd returned to gape. "We'll do everything we can to help him," he said weakly but he doubted the effectiveness of anything that might be done. In fact he felt strangely remote from this scene. It was like being asked to paint something he didn't want to work on. It appalled him too much. He even felt shut out from Diana's grief which flowed so spontaneously when his own sadness had merely led to dismal inner reflections. "Dearest Peter, don't die, don't die," he heard her whispering. "I won't leave you. I won't leave you my love if only you'll come back to me." Her words produced a fierce pang of jealousy in Robert who wondered whether she would grieve like that for him. Almost angrily he burst out, "You mustn't get so worked up. Luiz will be able to deal with it."

She turned towards him, her eyes perplexed, like someone awakened from a deep sleep. "To deal with it?" she echoed. "It? It? Him. Robert. Him. Peter. Do you think I'll hand him over to someone else now? Do you think I'm going to leave him? No, I'm not leaving; I'll stay with him until he's well. You do what you want. But don't ever condemn him. Don't even try to judge him."

It would have been useless for Robert to say that she had misinterpreted him for in truth she had not. Dejected and abandoned, he became ever more aware of his own fears: of Diana become as Peter was now, of himself alone, lost without hope, of Soolan buffeted by jeering crowds, mocking and deriding her. Everything was in question in the face of his growing terror; nothing distinguished him any more from a savage except his inability to propitiate the demons besetting him, as savages could with immemorial rituals. To stand alone was impossible. How could he have even thought of doing so? He saw how much he needed Diana and, driven by fear to the truth of his own inadequacy, found himself kneeling by the bed, clutching her and begging, "Help me too. I need you as much as he does. Don't abandon me Diana."

The words she had once longed to hear from him had been spoken. Not many weeks ago they would have made her hold fast to him; now she was indifferent. Too late. Too late now. He must find his way without her. It was to Peter that she turned and whispered, "Don't be afraid. You mean more to me than anyone. I shall protect you now."

But ravenous time that erratically clawed Peter to and fro, amidst sleepless dreams and visions, was at last drawing him irrevocably away from the hands of those who would love and those who would torment him. He opened his eyes and saw nothing but the frayed longevity pattern on the well-worn quilt, the longevity of life and love which had cheated himself and Ah Tung; he recalled the beauty of those thighs, the downy seeds of love and the remote gaze that suggested disillusionment with youth. None of these things would trouble him again; he closed his eyes and there was only a wall of darkness. Yet before his mind's eye began to sink into itself, he remembered the feelings of love and hatred, fear and delight that had once raged in him. Now they were slipping away and, as they receded, they became masqued figures prancing around, promising joy, threatening pain but no longer able to accomplish anything. Sinking deeper, he entered an undiscovered realm. Around him black tides ebbed and flowed, driving him, as Ah Tung had been driven, into the darkness. He heard his own voice crying, 'Ah Tung, my heart is restless until it finds its rest in you,' and Ah Tung replying, calling him onwards. Through the darkness a glow began to spread, growing lighter and lighter until at last, beneath him, he discerned the Hidden City rising to the surface from the ocean floor, slowly unfolding itself, disclosing palace after palace of vermilion and gold. Watch towers were soaring upwards, delicate pagodas growing floor upon floor, sending out branches like living trees. Terraces and windows were crowded with courtiers awaiting the Imperial Edict and, as he looked into their faces, each one was remembered as a lover: lonely boys in far off London, long limbed Africans he'd known in Paris, hardy Greek evzones, lustful Berbers and Lebanese, golden limbed Malays, honey tongued Thais, exquisite Khmers, insatiable Australian sailors and Chinese subtle at concealing unusual passions. It was they who had shown him that enlightenment is to be achieved not by eradicating desire but by letting it transport him into the garden of wisdom. Therefore, in long corridors endless rows of Bodhisattvas were smiling benignly down on him, encouraging him onward to that garden which lay at the heart of the City. No obstacle could hold him from it now; it was before him, waiting for him to enter. As he went through its bronze gate fretted with wind-blown flames, he saw Ah Tung coming to meet him but, as they touched, another hand rested on him gently. He knew it was Diana and spoke her name three times. Then soft wings enfolded him and he was borne into the endless dream outside which all is darkness.

The sound of Peter's voice, each faint 'Diana' weaker than the last, stirred up her memories. He was calling to her from a vast ruin that soared in the moonlight, from a fishing trap shuddering in a rough sea, tethered to the shore where she waited, through the babel of dancers in the cabaret when she was lonely; he was repeating her name as something important to be remembered the day they first met in the Portuguese Club; he was about to tell her a funny story, expound an idea, chide her, tease her, make her do something she'd never thought of. Events in their days together flashed on like a string of lights immediate and vivid, here, now and never ending. She longed to believe that nothing was entirely lost, that though they would never be together again yet never again would they be apart.

At this last moment she felt sure that she and Peter were no longer in a sordid room full of decay but in a place of beauty. If she opened her eyes she would see the brightness of a summer sky flecked with wispy clouds, tall hollyhocks and a riot of wild roses, some sort of marvellous overgrown garden resurrected from long ago. It was not true of course, but the mind has many ways of coping with the unaccountable.

When Carlos returned and saw Diana holding Peter he stayed in the doorway remembering that first meeting with her in the golden room. Now, he knew she had gone from him forever. He wanted to cry out, "Come back, come back. Can't you see I'm still here?" But all he could utter was, "I've got a taxi. You can take him to Figueiredo's now."

Unable to control his grief he left the house of death weeping and hailed a trishaw which took him to the wharfside road. There he remembered the scene of chaos he'd witnessed on the night of the bombardment and relived his journey along the water's edge to the place of Lim's murder. It was only a few months ago and yet it seemed so far away. In front of Old Chong's hotel he paused for a while thinking of Diana. Then he wiped away his tears and called for Siu Ching, who was annoyed at being kept waiting and took her to the quay where he hired a fisherman to ferry them home.

Under the attap awning Siu Ching sat between his thighs jabbering on about the small holding. "Do you think Mei Ling would let me work for her?" she asked. Carlos said he thought it might be a good idea.

"I'll be very obedient," she replied. "So don't think you'll always come first."

"Of course not, Siu Ching. Be good and do as she says."

"And don't imagine you can play any of your little games with me." She giggled and pressed against his body. "Mei Ling's your wife you know."

"Don't worry. We'll all be good together."

He felt her mischievous hands between his legs and sighed; if it was going to happen it might as well happen now, he thought, loosening his belt and beginning to put an end to her impatience. Outside, the boatman sang a harsh Cantonese ditty as he wielded his oar:

> Dim gaai ngoh chungyi nei?
> Yan waai nei ho lenga—
> *Why do I love you?*
> *Because you're so pretty.*

"Aiyaah" Siu Ching was soon crying. "Aiyaah. It's too big. It's too much." Who'd have thought she was an unbroken melon? The fisherman laughed at the sport below. "Aiyaah," he shouted into the wind and the little boat cut merrily through the waves.

ABOUT THE AUTHOR

Frederick Lees served in the RAF during the war and afterwards studied at Liverpool and London Universities. He then joined the Colonial Service and served in the Federation of Malaya. Subsequently he entered the British Diplomatic Service which took him back to South East Asia. In the 1970s he became involved in the work of British and European non-governmental agencies concerned with Third World development; this for a while took him to the Sudan and Ethiopia. Later he returned to diplomatic work to train the foreign service of Papua New Guinea. The last part of his career in Asia was spent in the Asian Development Bank in Manila. He is now retired and lives in the United Kingdom. He is married and has two sons.